STING OF LIES
THE LIES MYSTERY SERIES

CAROL POTENZA

Tiny
MAMMOTH

PRESS

This book is a work of fiction, and all names, characters, and locations are derived from the author's imagination. Any resemblance to actual events, places, or people, living or dead, is coincidental.

Copyright © 2023 by Carol Potenza

All rights reserved.

No part of this book may be reproduced in any form or by any electronic or mechanical means, including information storage and retrieval systems, without written permission from the author, except for the use of brief quotations in a book review. No part of this book may be used in any manner for purposes of training artificial intelligence technologies to generate text or audio, or in technologies that are capable of generating works in the same style or genre as this work without the specific and express permission from the author.

PUBLISHED BY TINY MAMMOTH PRESS
website: www.carolpotenza.com

Publisher's Cataloging-in-Publication

(Provided by Cassidy Cataloguing Services, Inc.).

Names: Potenza, Carol, author.

Title: Sting of lies / Carol Potenza.

Description: [Las Cruces, New Mexico] : Tiny Mammoth Press, [2023] | Series: The lies mystery series

Identifiers: ISBN: 979-8-9867690-2-8 (hardback) | 979-8-9867690-4-2 (paperback) | 979-8-9867690-3-5 (ebook)

Subjects: LCSH: Toxicologists--New Mexico--Fiction. | Ranchers--New Mexico--Fiction. | Murder-- Investigation--Fiction. | Treasure troves--New Mexico--Fiction. | Man-woman relationships-- Fiction. | Betrayal--Fiction. | LCGFT: Detective and mystery fiction. | Romance fiction. | Action and adventure fiction. | Thrillers (Fiction) | BISAC: FICTION / Mystery & Detective / Amateur Sleuth. | FICTION / Women. | FICTION / Romance / Suspense.

Classification: LCC: PS3616.O8435 S75 2023 | DDC: 813/.6--dc23

EDITOR: GILLY WRIGHT

PROOFREADER: Rachel Oestreich

COVER ARTIST: Mia Sharp

COVER DESIGN: Brandi Doane McCann

Dedication

For all the dogs who have kindly shared their lives with me and my family: Singsong (Pekinese), Kelly (hound rescued from the dump), Major (Dalmatian), Ziggy (English Springer Spaniel), Ajax (Boston Terrier), Biscuit (Jack Russell Terrier), Zeus (Boston Terrier), Daphne (Boston Terrier), and Hermès (Chihuahua rescued from the front yard).

Thank you for your love, companionship, and sofa time.

STING OF LIES

Can solving a mysterious poisoning save her career? Oh, and lead her to a long-lost buried treasure? Wait. *AND* thrust her into the arms of true love?

Ice Age paleontologist and poisons expert Myrna P. Lee isn't a team player. Not because she doesn't want to be. She's just terrible at it. At least, that's what every one in her lab says. Even her dog, the amazing William Tell, gives her attitude.

Maybe she has a hard time trusting because of past betrayals by people she's loved the most.

So, it's just fine with her when she's dispatched to a remote billionaire's ranch in Northern New Mexico tasked with solving a mysterious environmental poisoning. Besides, there's a secret mammoth kill site on the ranch she desperately hopes will supply enough data so that her megafauna poisons grant won't be rescinded for lack of progress. Myrna is determined to complete her commission, gather her mammoth info, and save her faltering career—all by herself.

Maybe she's used to being alone and doesn't need anything from anyone, no siree.

Until a handsome cowboy, assigned as her minder, moseys up to her side and sets her heart pounding, and a motley bunch of ranch hands embrace her as part of their found family.

Maybe that "alone" part of her life is in the past.

When she and William Tell stumble onto a decades old unsolved murder, the handsome cowboy tells her it's linked to a long-lost treasure *and* the mammoth kill site. And it's hard to stay focused on solving the poisonings when everything she discovers places her in the sights of villains who don't care who they hurt in pursuit of the treasure.

Then betrayal hits Myrna from all sides, and her world shatters into teeny, tiny pieces. She has a choice: retreat back to being alone or fight for her happiness.

But questions remain.
- Will Myrna solve the mysterious poisoning?
- Will she figure out who committed the long-ago murder?
- Will she find the treasure before the bad guys do?
- Will she pick up the pieces of her broken heart and forgive?

And just how will she use those hand grenades she found on her quest for the treasure?

If you like stubborn smart heroines afraid to love, rugged cowboys with slow and sexy smiles who get caught in their own web of seduction, and a small dog who surprises the heck out of people when he's picked up, then you'll love *Sting of Lies*.

Sting Of Lies

The Lies Mystery Series

by

CAROL POTENZA

ONE

Perched high on her lab chair to mitigate her unimpressive size, Dr. Myrna P. Lee's insides quivered like jelly. The scowling faces of her "team" surrounded her in a semi-circle of scientific and personal hostility, trapping her against the lab bench. She suppressed a reflexive instinct to bolt into the supply room and lock the door behind her. But this clean, controlled laboratory environment—so precise, so organized, so *different* from her past—was where she belonged. And these people, their purple nitrile-gloved hands clutching colorful sticky notes of their daily tasks against the wall of their bleach-bright lab coats ... *These* were the people she needed in her life.

If they'd only cooperate.

True, she'd dealt with worse. A tiny smile curved her lips. Like those Siberian permafrost ivory hunters with the rocket launcher. Of course, she'd stolen—*rescued*—something very valuable from them. And they would've followed her up that river and blown her into tiny pieces if she hadn't had the foresight to sink their boat, outboard and all, with that handy grenade. Her smile dissolved into a frown.

Then why did an encounter with homicidal maniacs trying to kill her seem less perilous than the one she faced right now?

That was easy. In Siberia, she'd been alone, relying only on herself. Here in the lab, her boss had appointed her team leader, forcing her to depend on individuals she had no reason to trust. And based on her team's blatant animosity, being who she truly was on the inside wasn't going to convince them to follow orders.

It was also unfortunate that her general description—small, slight, with stupid fluffy blond curls—came with the burden of not being taken as seriously as people who met the height requirements to ride roller coasters *and* made her look much younger than her thirty years.

So she decided to be somebody else today.

Myrna lifted her chin and met their unfriendly faces, attempting to look down her nose.

"Questions about your tasks?" she drawled, remembering to lower her voice for gravitas and add her boss's nasal Bostonian accent.

"You want me to kill the spider in the bathroom?" Kent Sheffield asked incredulously. In his CV, he'd claimed he could successfully analyze minuscule amounts of environmental samples for contaminants. That was a big fat lie. "Dr. Lee, I have a PhD in Paleolithic entomology. I deal with *extinct* bugs."

Myrna swiveled to face him. "That's why I chose you, Kent. I want you to make this bug extinct."

"And I'm supposed to descale the coffee maker?" Noemi Rodriguez was the lab manager—a job she was pretty good at as opposed to her work-a-day bench skills. The woman paused and sneered. "*Mer*-nuh."

Myrna flared her nostrils at the deliberate mispronunciation of her name. If Noemi thought she could out-juvenile her, then she was sadly mistaken. "Don't worry, *Na-o-mee*. I wrote out a detailed protocol on the back of your task list about how to do it *the right way*."

"Dr. Lee? Aren't we supposed to help you with the Khyber project samples?" Rohaan Akbar, first-year grad student. Timid basset hound eyes darted around the group, looking for support. What he needed to look for was a backbone. "We're supposed to make sure you don't ... you know. *Cheat.*"

Ouch. Myrna's cheeks bloomed hot. *Backbone found.*

She'd known sooner or later her checkered past was bound to come up. It wasn't like it was a secret.

With as much dignity as she could muster, Myrna said, "As team leader, I'm making the executive decision that no one is to touch the Khyber samples but me."

If they made one mistake, a lucrative account would swirl down the drain, not something their boss would take lightly. And getting fired from her job *this time* meant the death of a scientific career already on life support. This project was Myrna's last chance to redeem herself.

She swirled around on her stool to face the sleek piece of equipment emitting soothing robotic hums as it analyzed each microscopic preparation. She waved a hand at the screen. "Besides, I've already finished my—our—testing. This is the last run I—*we*—need. There's nothing left for any of you to do."

Dead silence reigned over a palpable anger. Myrna slipped her hand into her pocket, curling it around a tiny flake of stone.

"I thought we were supposed to work together," said Jeannie Darrow, the undergrad dishwasher who always left spots on the glassware. Paper crunched, followed by a crumpled list of tasks bouncing onto the shiny black countertop. "You're a terrible leader, Dr. Lee."

Safety-soled shoes squeaked as her team marched back to their stations.

Myrna was just about to release the pent-up breath she held when Kent whispered from behind her, "You know what I think, Dr. Lee? You finished the Khyber project so fast because you struck out on those Paleolithic spear point samples from the university's museum. *No traces of poison*, am I right?" He leaned in so close, she could feel his breath tickle her neck. "After the wreckage of your scientific career is finally carted away, I call first dibs on your office."

Myrna sat stiff and still until she was sure Kent had gone back to his lab bench. She'd brought the harsh words on herself, but showing weakness would only invite more attack, a hard lesson she'd learned from the time she could toddle.

She released the flake of stone to pull out an envelope and tug the single trifold piece of paper from inside.

Dear Dr. Lee,

The Oxbridge Paleontology Department's Award Committee has reviewed your (second) request for an extension on your grant, #245-662-9C, *Poison and Projectile Points: Possible complicity in the extinction of late Pleistocene Megafauna on the North American Continent.*

While we understand the recent difficulties you have encountered, you have already been granted a one-year extension. Therefore, your request has been denied, and the committee expects your preliminary data to be submitted by the end of the calendar year.

Let us be clear: *If said data is not received by the stated deadline, we will have no choice but to rescind your award.*

Sincerely—

It didn't matter if the award committee was sincere or not. She'd exhausted all known avenues on her megafauna poisons project. Her only choice now was to prove to her boss that she was indispensable in the lab ... at the expense of her team.

She shoved the letter back inside the envelope, ready to repocket it—and stopped. Crimson splotched the page. She opened her hand. Two cuts, the exact distance between them the diameter of the sharp stone flake she'd clutched like a lifeline, oozed sticky scarlet blood.

Myrna sighed. Why did the things she held on to the tightest always end up hurting her?

She hopped off the stool to delve into the first aid kit. No one met her eyes. No one asked if she needed help. No one even acknowledged her existence. Cuts cleaned and bandaged, Myrna returned to the instrument that continued to spool out her perfect Khyber project data.

She'd been proud of herself, getting through that confrontation without letting their hostility overwhelm her.

Except it kinda, sorta had.

What had her mother always said? *"Pride goes before the fall … right off the edge of a cliff."*

And Myrna was on the brink.

Two

Myrna stood in the hallway outside her boss's office, staring at the name plate on the door without seeing it. Slipping her hand into the pocket of her lab coat, she picked up the chip of stone, edges now brown-red with her blood. *Debitage.* A fancy name for something purposefully flaked and discarded by ancient humans when creating stone tools. So small, so trifling, its importance so easily overlooked.

She'd gone home for a quick supper, then back to the lab deserted of personnel, just the way she liked it. Evenings into the small hours had always been the best time for her. She could lose herself in her work. She didn't have to share equipment or a pot of coffee and a package of chocolate snack cakes with anyone, or chat to about small triumphs or tricky techniques or have to hear about someone's most recent vacation or visiting family. No distractions. She hadn't ever needed much sleep anyway. Alone was better.

A text pinged her phone as she was finishing up the Khyber data.

10 minutes, my office.

The summons by her boss hadn't been a total surprise after the face-off with her team that morning. Clutching the stone in her bandaged palm, stomach in a knot, she tapped on the door. Time to make herself indispensable—if she didn't get fired first.

"Come in." Dr. Eleanor Kelly sat poised, fingers hovering over her laptop's keyboard, her silver hair backlit to a coppery hue by the sunset shining through the bank of paned-glass windows. A warm late-summer breeze slipped under an open casement.

"You wanted to see me?" Myrna said, and winced. Along with her lack of height, she'd been gifted with the voice of a prepubescent child that always seemed to rise an octave in stressful situations.

"Take a seat." Eleanor splayed her hand on a sheet of paper next to her computer, the distinctive Oxbridge University seal displayed prominently.

Oh, dear.

Myrna sat on the edge of the chair, balls of her feet just touching the tile floor. She dropped the rock back into her pocket, smoothed hands over her pristine white lab coat, licked her lips. Studies showed a deeper voice made people take women 5.3 times more seriously.

Or was it 3.5?

She took a deep breath and visualized speaking from her sternum. "Sorry, Eleanor. I was in the middle of final data analysis for the Khyber—"

Her boss's lips puckered, and her eyebrows pinched together. "What's wrong with your voice? Are you sick? If you are, get over it immediately. I've already agreed—" She stopped, her eyes widening. "*Final* data analysis? Your instrument modifications?"

"Worked beautifully." Myrna gave up on the voice. She'd readjust and experiment on someone else some other time. "In triplicate, under budget, and ahead of schedule. I already started writing a paper on the results and have a draft of a second manuscript on the software and hardware adjustments needed for pico- to femtomolar sample quantities."

Eleanor's face relaxed into a smile. She was already beautiful, but her pleased expression shed years from her face, making her look closer to Myrna's thirty years of age than the forty-five she'd turned last month.

"Wonderful. Give Dr. Sheffield your data and the protocols. He'll be repeating your experiments."

Myrna blinked. "*Kent?* But he can't— He isn't—" Her cheeks blossomed with angry heat. "*I'm* team leader on the Khyber project for a reason. No one else in your group has the capability, the—the *competence* to— And, Kent, of all people—"

"Careful." Now Eleanor's smile held a warning edge. She sauntered around her desk, picked up a wooden box, a glass insert in its top exposing a stack of old letters tied with a faded ribbon tucked inside, and perched on the front of her desk. "Besides, he needs to be trained to take over for you. Just in case."

The last three words dropped like pebbles in an icy pond. Eleanor swiped her thumb over the box's edge before placing it back on her desk. She exhaled one of her dramatic, long-suffering sighs.

Here we go. Myrna hunched in her chair. *Again.*

"I need to speak to you about your attitude toward your team. *Again.* Why do you think my staff and students dislike working with you?" Eleanor's Boston Brahmin drawl infused every word. She crossed toned arms and an elegant eyebrow rose. "Besides the obvious."

The obvious. Her *disgrace.*

She'd deflected when it was brought up this morning. No chance of that with Eleanor.

"I didn't—" Myrna grimaced.

Actually, she did.

"I tried—"

Probably not as hard as she could have.

Myrna sighed and slipped a hand in her pocket to clutch the flake of stone.

"I admire your loyalty to Tom Hutchinson," Eleanor said, not unkindly. "He placed you in an untenable situation. What he did was unforgivable. But because of your, um, *association* with him, your work is tainted. Your name is poison. You're lucky I hired you. And yes, you are brilliant, but your attitude in the lab alienates your colleagues. Telling everyone a better way to do their work—"

"But I'm always right." Myrna tilted her chin.

"Are you?" Eleanor rotated her laptop, revealing stacks of tabulated numbers on her screen. "Do you know what this is? Your analysis on the Clovis and Folsom stone projectile points in the university's collections. I had your calculations checked. *All* your calculations."

Myrna's stomach curled. "This is my project. You had no right, Eleanor."

"*Your* project? You chose *my* lab because New Mexico was where archaeologists first found evidence humans hunted mammoths. You told me *together* we could solve one of the great mysteries in paleontology, discover actual proof ancient cultures used poisons to kill their prey, natural chemicals with potentially incomprehensible pharmaceutical value. I hired you after you promised me prestige and riches. And you found *nothing*. No data to support your hypothesis. No proof of poison."

"Those museum samples must have been compromised," Myrna said. "Washed, treated, stored improperly. Besides, a bunch of them were fakes. I need untouched field samples. You know that."

"And you won't get those untouched samples if you stay inside, will you?" Eleanor fixed her with a stern look. "Oxbridge has spoken. No more extensions. You have until the end of the year to find a Paleolithic poison so strong it could take down a mammoth with the scratch of a spearpoint. If you don't, you lose your grant, and *this* university won't allow me to keep you on staff, which would drive the final stake into your already tattered career."

Eleanor plucked a folder from her desk, the logo of her environmental consulting company, EcoNano, prominently stamped in the cover's center, and handed it to Myrna. Even though Eleanor had a professorial appointment, the university administrators coveted the fees she paid from EcoNano earnings. Earnings that also paid Myrna's salary.

"Your attitude is only one of the reasons I called you in. You've heard of the Donavans?"

Myrna nodded yes even though she hadn't. Eleanor seemed to expect it.

"I received an urgent phone call this afternoon from their ranch. They have a commission that requires complete secrecy. With Charles Donavan thinking of making a run for president, they're incredibly wary of any adverse publicity. I'm giving you an opportunity to salvage your project." She handed Myrna the folder.

Myrna opened it and read the text of the document—a confidentiality agreement, standard on all EcoNano contracts. She flipped it over. Blank on the back. "I don't understand."

Eleanor straightened and walked to her office windows. Twilight had chased all but the last hint of light from the sky, and the sodium lamps that dotted the campus were flickering on.

"The Donavan Ranch is located northwest of Las Vegas, New Mexico, and southwest of Cimarron. It comprises over one hundred thousand acres of wilderness, which includes four confirmed Clovis Paleoindian archaeological sites and at least three mammoth rubs." The corner of her mouth lifted. "*And* the Donavans have a collection of *uncurated* Clovis and Folsom stone points at their lodge museum."

Myrna's mouth dropped open, eyes widening to the point of watering. Eleanor sauntered over and plucked the folder from her fingers.

"Why haven't I heard about this trove? Why hasn't *anyone* in the field heard about this? There's *nothing* in the literature about these sites, this collection. No research, no gossip ..." Myrna pressed her hands over her knees, gaze becoming unfocused at the potential.

"Why? Because the Donavans have owned this land since the early 1800s, and they hold on tight to their secrets. They rarely let anyone on the ranch they can't control with money"—she tapped the folder—"or threats. But things may be changing now with Charles Donavan's political aspirations. Transparency, inclusiveness, *science*—all the buzz words—are going to be part of the Donavans' reality in the next few years. Charles Donavan's wife, Dame Sylvia, is leading the charge. She's even opening her regenerative farm to the press and public as part of this new openness. She's poached some of the best scientists for her projects and is making tremendous breakthroughs in genetics, robotics, breeding —both crops and livestock."

Myrna sat back, wariness prickling up her neck. "If these people are so secretive, how do *you* know about these sites?"

"Dame Sylvia has hired EcoNano in the past to process water and soil from her farm, as well as samples from their mining reclamation projects, so I've been to the ranch numerous times. And, ah"—Eleanor's smile turned feline—"*developed* a source who works there."

Figures. Some poor sap she'd wrapped around her little finger.

Eleanor sat down and placed the open folder on her desk. "Dame Sylvia Donavan, CBE—"

"CB *what*?"

"C-B-E. Commander of the Most Excellent Order of the British Empire, which comes with the honorific Dame. A fancy British title she earned because of her work on rewilding. She's quite the disciple. Adamantly opposes active resource management and just as adamantly insists on her title being used, even here in the States. In the past, she's personally blocked access to any archaeological exploration on the ranch. If you can convince her to give you access to these sites—in the spirit of transparency and science, of course—and if you can find your hypothetical poison, there's tremendous potential for you to reestablish your scientific credibility. It's what you want, isn't it?"

More than anything.

"What's the job?" Myrna asked.

Eleanor extracted another document and handed it to Myrna. "The Donavan Ranch is experiencing large-animal die-offs, this time elk. The consensus is that these animals are being poisoned, source unknown. The Donavan PR people believe if it gets out, it could be twisted by political rivals. *Bambi murdered under Charles Donavan's watch*, or some such nonsense. You will analyze carcass samples and solve the mystery."

"Alone? No team?"

"Just you."

Excellent. Myrna bounced in her seat. "When do the samples arrive?"

"You weren't listening. I need you to gather supplies tonight and drive up to the ranch tomorrow morning. You'll have two weeks to scout the die-off site, collect tissue, and do the analysis. Field work, Myrna."

"*Outside?*" Myrna shot to her feet, heart thrumming in her chest. "I can't— I *won't*— No."

The lab was the center of her world. Clean, organized, safe. She scooped up the stone flake in her pocket and squeezed it tightly, ignoring the sting of pain through her bandage. "I mean, I can't just leave ... *here* ... tomorrow morning. For two weeks. I—I need time to arrange—"

"They demanded on-site analysis—an issue of control. Don't worry. Their lab facilities are top-notch. They've left the most recent carcasses in situ. Which means by the time you arrive, the animals will have been dead for a day and a half. If samples aren't taken by tomorrow, tissue integrity will be lost."

Myrna straightened to her less than impressive height. "And if I refuse to go?"

"You'll need to find another job—and career—immediately."

"So I have no choice." Panic and bitterness held her in place.

"We all have choices. Like the one you made when you allowed Tom Hutchinson to submit fabricated data."

"I caught every paper he'd falsified before they were published except one."

"Yet you were still punished." Eleanor shook her head, her expression stamped with sympathy even as her eyes glinted. "Let me sweeten the pot. If you find out what's causing these deaths, I'll add you as an author to the Khyber publications. A public endorsement of my trust in you."

And a step toward the restoration of what she once had in the scientific community. The same community that refused to listen. That had shunned her.

But she'd have to be outside. *Outside.* Her gaze slipped to the velvety night framed through Eleanor's windows. A tiny voice taunted her, calling out her cowardice, jeering at her inability to fully control her *need*—

Myrna dropped her gaze, creating and discarding excuses, searching for some way out.

"There's one more thing that might interest you." Eleanor tugged a glossy photo from her desktop and held it out to Myrna. "My source on the ranch says the die-off is within half a mile of recently exposed bones with potential butchering marks."

The picture showed the perpendicular wall of an eroded arroyo, the crumbling earth orange-brown. A huge femur—bigger around than Myrna—protruded out of the dirt next to a long, curved rib.

Shock pinned Myrna's gaze to the picture. "Those are *mammoth* bones."

"*Unexcavated* mammoth bones. Think, Myrna. You'd have two weeks on the ranch to solve these mysterious animal deaths *and* convince the Donavans to give you access to their treasures and those bones." Eleanor strolled to her office door and opened it.

"Either start packing supplies for sample collection and leave tomorrow morning for the Donavan Ranch or gather your belongings and don't come back to the lab. Ever."

Myrna headed to the open doorway, head bent, steps hesitant. She *knew* her hypothesis was correct, knew Paleolithic peoples used poisons to bring down their prey. Knew it with every fiber of her being. But proving it was something altogether more difficult. If she took this commission, she'd have access to untreated artifacts. Even then, it was a crapshoot as to whether these stone tools and points would still hold, after thirteen thousand years, the evidence she needed. If she passed on the commission, she'd be fired. But accepting meant exposing herself to the wild. She shuddered at the thought.

Still, if she could find stone points associated with a mammoth kill, could find poison on them—

She met Eleanor's gaze, chin lifted. "I'll do it."

"You made the right decision, Myrna. It would be such a coup for EcoNano if you prove your hypothesis. You'd change the field forever. Restore your reputation." A long, slow smile crept up her boss's features. "Of course, if you're wrong, it won't hurt me or EcoNano. Only you."

Eleanor closed the door in her face.

So much for being indispensable.

But the opportunity to study a kill site in situ was too significant to pass up.

Myrna hurried to the supply room. As she switched on the light, her mother's wild voice echoed in her head.

"You can't win if you don't play."

She'd play *and* win. Because she had a secret weapon.

Myrna scowled. If he cooperated, the little shit.

THREE

Myrna left her dingy converted-garage apartment, a pile of EcoNano supplies packed in the back of her battered crossover, and headed north from Socorro toward Las Vegas, somehow dodging early morning traffic in Albuquerque. She clutched the steering wheel, pulse thrumming, and pressed down on the accelerator. At this rate, she'd get to the ranch way before lunch. More than enough time to gather samples and do a little unguided exploration.

Except it was after one o'clock when she finally turned down the road to the Donavan Ranch—even with her normally heavy-footed driving.

All thanks to *him*.

Myrna threw a narrow-eyed glance in her rearview at the traveling dog kennel strapped securely in the back seat, but only the snores and smelly farts of William Tell indicated his presence in the car. Until he had to pee. Then he'd announce his demand with a single wheezy bark, and Myrna would be forced to find a convenient place to pull over and accommodate his needs. Over the years she'd learned the hard way that, if she didn't, his retaliatory strike would come when least expected.

To make matters worse, she'd forgotten his favorite dog toy. Every time they'd stopped, eyes like cold black marbles had promised payback.

But that was the least of her worries. Myrna chewed her lip. Since she'd exited the highway, traffic and signs of human occupation had dwindled to almost nothing in the vast grassy expanse of northeastern New Mexico. Now she drove west toward dark forests and towering black mountains, leaving the open plains behind her.

This place certainly was isolated. And extremely *outside*.

Her car trundled past a carved stone tablet embedded in the ground as if it had been for a thousand years: DONAVAN RANCH & LODGE. It might as well have read *Hic Sunt Dracones*—Here Be Dragons. Or maybe, *Here Be Mammoths*. A trickle of exhilaration ran up her spine.

She pulled up to the main security gate of the Donavan Ranch. The guardhouse was staffed by a tanned, athletic woman in a khaki shirt, the Donavan name embroidered in royal blue over her left breast. Myrna lowered her window, wrinkling her nose at the horrible pine-scented air, handed over her driver's license, and held out the signed confidentiality agreement. The woman retreated into the guardhouse to type on her computer.

Curious, Myrna studied the security setup. Two overt deterrence cameras pointed at the entering vehicle. A fob scanner planted in the ground in front of the guardhouse allowed access after-hours. The gate itself was elegant—an embellished wrought iron affair. Except she'd worked at enough high-security facilities to know even a tank couldn't ram through it. A stone wall that ran about a hundred feet in both directions was linked to an eight-foot-high composite fence that extended for as far as she could see, probably sensored to detect intruders.

The guard handed Myrna's license and paperwork back with a smile. "All set, Dr. Lee. They're expecting you up at the staff compound. Here's a temporary placard for your car. You'll be given a permanent one at security."

"Wow. This is some place. Who are you trying to keep out?"

The smile stiffened on the woman's face. Oh, dear. Myrna slacked her expression and opened her eyes wider. A trick, because one of her irises rolled out just the tiniest bit, giving her a sweetly vacant expression that had gotten her out of half a dozen speeding tickets.

The guard relaxed. "Poachers, mostly. The ranch has trophy elk that rival any on the North American continent. Paparazzi, too, but they rarely venture this far into the wilderness."

William Tell let out a rough snort followed by a single *I have to pee* bark.

The guard's gaze sharpened. "You brought a dog?"

"This job came up so fast, I didn't have time to find someone who could take care of him. I hope it's okay. I have his shot records." She dug into her purse and pulled out a little blue booklet. The guard waved it away. "Is there somewhere I can let him out to, uh, go?"

"There's a rest area around that clump of trees. Bathrooms for humans, too. Once you're ready, keep to the main road for ten miles, then follow the painted wooden signs. And FYI"—she pointed to the cardboard french fry box in the console—"make sure you pitch that before you arrive. Dame Sylvia doesn't tolerate junk food. She even fired a staff member because she found hamburger wrappers in his car."

"Sylvia Donavan? Fired?" Myrna blinked in surprise, both at the edge of spite in the woman's voice and because of the large stash of chocolate snack cakes in her backpack. "Why?"

The security guard shot a quick glance at an overhead camera. "Just throw the trash out." She retreated from the car and pressed a button inside the little house. The gate slid open.

Hands clutching the wheel, Myrna drove inside. She crawled

along, watching the gate clank closed behind her in the rearview mirror.

"We're in, William Tell. Let's make this happen."

His wrinkled black face and beady eyes peered at her though the mesh door of his kennel.

She pulled into a parking lot next to the restrooms, turned off her car, and drew in a deep, cleansing breath. After the train wreck of her life and career the last couple of years, there was nowhere to go but up, right? And other than the *outside in the wilderness* part, this commission on the Donavan Ranch was providential. Lucky. Tailored—to her career, her grant, her scientific rehabilitation.

Manipulated, whispered a quiet voice in her head. By Eleanor, the most manipulative person she knew next to her mother or her old boss, Tom Hutchinson.

Myrna firmed her jaw. Success meant her reputation could be salvaged in a few days. And there was no reason to believe her luck would vanish during the two-week window of this assignment.

Especially since she had William Tell to help it along.

Four

The paved road to the Donavan Experimental Farm and Ranch Staff Complex wound through thick fairy-tale forests and wildflower-dusted meadows, and across burbling streams. She should have expected that people as rich as the Donavans—and they were supervillain-with-a-volcano-lair rich according to the internet, ranked twelfth in the country for accumulated wealth—wouldn't have run-of-the-mill blacktop surfaces. Nope. These roads used *exhaust gas-decomposing, permeable, low-heat absorbing, piezoelectric energy harvesting, noise-reducing materials.* So read the sign at the rest area. These people really liked signs.

Mountains loomed in the distance, dark green and gray against towering puffs of clouds so white they dazzled. Topping a rise, a line of man-made structures appeared through the screen of trees. She sailed over another picturesque bridge covering another picturesque stream and followed the picturesque road to an open and unmanned gate. Her car bumped off the piezoelectric pavement and into an expansive yard of hard-packed dirt bounded by rustic single-level buildings with false fronts. Like an old Wild West town, except for the state-of-the-art solar-capture roofs and electric plug-in stations charging dusty utility terrain vehicles in place of hitching posts.

A large man stepped into the street: black jeans and boots, a Donavan-logoed polo stretching across a broad chest, and wearing a black cowboy hat and aviator sunglasses. Myrna stopped and rolled down the window. He strode around to her driver's side and braced a hand against the roof to lean in.

"Dr. Lee? Glad you could make it. Dillon Bard, head of security. If you'll park by the side of that red brick building, I have some paperwork you'll need to sign inside, then we'll get you out to the site."

She pulled out the folder tucked under her computer bag. "But I've already—"

"Yes, ma'am. Just a formality." His sharp-edged jaw relaxed into a reassuring smile. He backed away and waved a guiding arm.

Myrna cranked the wheel and pulled into the spot. It was shaded by a huge cottonwood tree, bright green leaves fluttering in a gentle breeze. She set the brake and powered the driver- and passenger-side windows all the way down, letting the scent of dust and flowers invade her car.

"This will keep you cool for the few minutes I'll be insi—"

William Tell barked his *I have to pee* bark.

She twisted in her seat to glare at him.

"You just went," she hissed. "So I don't even believe you. You're making trouble because I forgot Tan Turtle."

He tilted his head, his arrow-shaped bat ears perked at the mention of his favorite toy.

Dang it, she shouldn't have reminded him. Scowling, Myrna snatched up the folder and her backpack and exited the car—

Right into the hard chest and arms of a handsome brown-haired, green-eyed cowboy. Smile crinkles fanned from the corners of eyes topped by brows lighter than his tanned skin. Young, maybe early twenties.

"I'm Paden, ma'am. If you'll point out what you'll need at the die-off site, I'll get it stowed in the truck."

"Oh. Uh, I'd like to take my car." She remembered to lower her voice.

His smile turned rueful. "Terrain's rough, and it's a long drive. If you'll just show me the gear you'll need."

She chewed her lip as she opened the hatch and pointed to two rectangular chests, both secured by metal latches, and plastic pouches containing disposable white forensic coveralls and purple nitrile gloves. A head covering with a plastic face shield sat on top.

"I'll also need dry ice if you have it. If not, wet ice will do. And I'll need a place to change." Myrna gestured to her pink pedal pushers and knock-off Keds.

"There's a bathroom inside." Paden smiled. "And don't worry, ma'am. I'll watch your little dog."

He hauled out the two chests and stacked them on the wooden slats of the covered porch that ran the length of the red brick building. Leaning into the back of her car, Myrna unzipped her duffle bag, pulled out jeans, socks, and her old, dusty hiking boots that she'd had to dig out of the back of her closet because she'd never wanted to ever wear them again. As she zipped up her bag, she casually adjusted it to hide the edge of the hard case below.

Clothes hugged against her chest, she scuttled across the porch to the screen door. Two more cowboys nodded and smiled as she approached. Neither wore the Donavan polo. Instead, they were dressed in blue chambray work shirts, worn jeans, and laced-up leather work boots. One was tall and lanky and a little stooped, early fifties. He introduced himself as "McJunkin, ma'am, but call me Webb."

The other man was shorter with a whip-cord leanness, midforties, close-cropped blond hair, and a smirky mouth. "Jessup, ma'am."

He caught her eyes in his crystal-blue gaze. Myrna faltered, stomach somersaulting with attraction, her shoes seemingly stuck to the wooden platform for endless seconds before the lanky cowboy stepped between them and politely opened the door. She unstuck herself and hurried through. Both men followed her inside.

The interior walls of the building were pleasantly wainscoted a creamy white, but the mesh-covered windows screamed security. Behind a counter built like it had been plucked from an old-timey Western bank—including lacy ironwork teller cages—plasma video monitors covered a wall. Each screen rotated through multiple views of forests, meadows, ponds—even a manicured golf course and lodge—every few seconds. The displays were manned by a dark-haired woman who didn't turn around. Myrna had seen this type of setup before. Artificial intelligence monitored movement and signaled anomalies across the ranch. It learned to ignore foliage stirred by weather or the wanderings of wildlife.

"This is a standard nondisclosure agreement, like the NDA you signed in Dr. Kelly's office." Dillon Bard handed her a large tablet and stylus. "If you'll scroll through and initial the Xs. Oh, and there's a fingerprint page. Again, standard." He nodded to a scarred wooden rolltop desk and chair against the far wall. Myrna wandered toward it, speed-reading as she walked.

Deep, ugly growling yanked her head up. A huge wolf-dog, shoulders hunched, head down, and lip curled up on one side of a mouth filled with sharp teeth emerged from behind the counter. Myrna froze, pinned by malevolent yellow eyes.

"Briscoe, nein." Dillon Bard spewed a spate of German commands at the animal. Its ears drooped, the ridge of fur along its back flattening. It skulked across the floor and dropped to sit next to a bowl of water by the front door. Fierce eyes remained vigilant.

"Hey, Bard, your damn dog's gonna kill somebody one of these days," the blond cowboy, Jessup, said.

"I can handle him. Besides, he keeps this place free of trespassers."

The exchange between the two men was rote, even practiced. A warning directed at her?

The lanky cowboy, McJunkin, pulled out the chair for Myrna. As she sat, a faint gruff bark sounded through the screen door. Myrna set her teeth, determined to ignore it, but Briscoe's flattened ears flicked. She pressed her thumb on the last page of the agreement when William Tell barked again, this time louder, like he was right outside. But of course, that couldn't be ri—

Paden pulled open the door. William Tell trotted inside the room.

"Dr. Lee, this guy was scratching and— *Oh, shit.*"

With a wild snarl, Briscoe lunged at the smaller dog, teeth barred. Horror stamped every man's expression until they realized Briscoe had stopped mid-attack. His snarl receded into a high squeak.

William Tell swiveled his tan piggy butt with its knotted tail. Bat ears pitched forward, head tipped to one side, he stared down the wolf-dog, who practically folded in half, a puddle forming beneath his shaking back legs. William Tell ambled to Briscoe's water dish, dipped his head, and lapped noisily. Pivoting, he musically broke wind directly into the larger dog's muzzle, then trotted toward the three men—Bard, McJunkin, and Jessup—standing side by side along the counter, blinking in astonishment. Briscoe slunk through the screen door, still clutched open by a slack-jawed Paden. Even the woman at the monitors stood to watch.

But William Tell wasn't finished. He sniffed Bard's foot, lifted his back leg—

Myrna pleaded, "*No, no, no.*"

—and proceeded to hop down the row of boots, arcing a precision stream of pee as he traveled. Myrna hunched her shoulders, cheeks red-hot with embarrassment.

He always made her pay.

Bard and McJunkin danced back, Bard cursing in German as he shook the urine off shiny black leather. William Tell ran out of pee before he hit his final target. He dropped his leg and plunked down to sit on top of the only dry boot.

The owner of that boot—Jessup—shook with silent laughter. "Guess this guy showed us who's boss." His voice was a rich baritone. "Didn't you, boy?"

William Tell tipped his head back, beady eyes staring up at the genesis of sound. The cowboy extended open hands and, as if in slow motion, bent down to wrap his fingers around William Tell's torso. Myrna froze, eyes widening until they burned. Jessup straightened, the dog secure in his grasp, back legs dangling.

And his face changed, his brows contracted—

"*Don't pick him up!*" It came out as a screech, but such was her panic. Myrna launched up, her chair toppling with a *thunk* behind her. She dashed to the man, remembered to close her eyes at the last second, and groped for the dog, her fingers dislodging the cowboy's work-callused hands. Eyes still closed, she placed William Tell on the floor before she cracked open a single lid.

The little dog stood for a moment, shook himself, then trotted past Paden and out the still-open screen door. With a wheezy sigh, he plopped down in a strip of sunshine, one back leg stuck out behind him. Briscoe, tail tucked, skulked off the porch across the sunlit dusty street and into the shadows between buildings.

Jessup stared at her, eyes wide, brows practically pegged in his hairline.

"He's, um ... afraid of heights." Myrna cringed at the high squeakiness of her voice.

She swiveled on the ball of her foot, hurried back to the table, and grabbed the tablet and stylus. Shoving them into Dillon Bard's hands, she babbled brightly, "Let me just put his harness on—and leash—because he can be hard to catch. Ha ha. Then I'll get changed, and we can go. Samples to collect. Right?"

FIVE

Myrna craned her neck to get her bearings from the back seat of the ranch truck driven by Jessup. McJunkin sat in the front passenger seat, William Tell was buckled up beside her. A long, looming cliff face bounded the eastern end of a lush valley she could envision dotted with sweeping herds of elk. The surrounding mosaic of mixed conifer forests were perfect for animals to melt into and disappear during the day or to bed down at night. The truck approached a gently sloping meadow carpeted with native grasses that provided the nutrients needed to grow strong calves, vigorous cows, and the huge racks of antlers that topped enormous bulls.

Except those perfectly healthy animals lay on their sides, eyes open but unseeing, glossy fur riffling in the cool breeze, their death a mystery to be solved.

Jessup stopped the extended-cab pickup next to a parked four-wheeler at the edge of a scraped dirt clearing. A yellow backhoe sat in the shade of the pines, its scoop resting atop dirt piled high next to a large hole—the elks' grave once she completed her sampling. The stench of the dead animals tainted the breeze that swirled through the open truck windows.

His hand splayed on the back of the passenger seat headrest, Jessup twisted his torso toward her. "Ma'am, me and Webb'll go see what Paden's found and make sure it's safe for you to do your work. I'll open the back so you can get your equipment." He nodded to William Tell, a smile deepening the grooves that bracketed his mouth. "Best to keep the little dog inside for now. Don't want him frightening the wildlife." He winked.

Myrna frowned. People always did this to her. Winked or chucked her under her chin or pinched her cheek because of her size and baby face and stupid fluffy hair. Always underestimating her, like she wasn't a serious force to be reckoned with.

Which could be useful under some circumstances.

"How many elk, Mr. Jessup, Mr. McJunkin?" she asked, voice pitched low, a professional scientist who shouldn't be winked at.

McJunkin shifted in the passenger seat. "Only four this time—a small bachelor herd. But they're—were—prime specimens. Each worth about twenty thousand dollars on a guided hunt."

Her breath caught at the price.

"And it's just Webb, ma'am. Mr. McJunkin was my granddaddy." The lanky cowboy's voice was a deep resonant bass.

"And just Jessup," Jessup said.

Myrna hesitated, chewing the inside of her lower lip. If she was to succeed in both of her objectives—gaining access to the collected stone points and mammoth bones—she'd need to develop good working relationships with the Donavans' staff.

"Then please call me Myrna. Not *Mer*-na like *mer*-maid. *Myr*-na like *meer*-kat."

The laugh crinkles that fanned Jessup's eyes became more pronounced. "All right, *Myr*-na like *meer*-kat. I'll come get you when it's safe." He and Webb climbed out of the truck cab.

William Tell's head and ears perked up when Jessup opened the back door on his side, but the man just rubbed a hand over the dog's head. "You stay, boy. We'll watch over your gal."

Myrna bristled. "I'm not his—"

Jessup shut the door.

Webb opened her door and offered his hand, but Myrna shook her head and climbed out by herself. Awkwardly. It was a long way to the ground. Once she'd closed the door, a huge bug dive-bombed her. She ducked, swatting the air wildly, tall grass tangling around her ankles trying to trip her. She hurriedly followed Webb to the back of the truck, arm waving madly at the bug that wouldn't leave her alone. Jessup, a blue salt-stained Donavan ball cap now covering his hair, had the tailgate down and her two equipment chests and a dry ice container on the ground, but his attention was on the long rifle in his hands. Webb grabbed a second gun, checked it, then settled a floppy dark brown cowboy hat over his head. The two walked into the meadow, conferring in low voices.

When the men were out of sight, Myrna sidled to Paden's four-wheeler. The drone box lashed to the back was open and empty. She shaded her eyes and looked skyward but couldn't see any black shapes or hear the buzz. Nothing was watching her. Good, because the four-wheeler's key was still in the ignition, threaded on a flimsy loop of wire that dangled with even more keys. She grabbed the set of keys and splayed them on her palm. One was obviously a spare. She fit it in the ignition—bingo.

Myrna nibbled her lip. This ranch with their restrictions about where she could go and when, and not letting her drive her own car out to the die-off site ... She couldn't—*wouldn't*—allow herself to be caught without transportation. A pocketed key had saved her life once. *Make your own luck.* She squared her jaw and twisted off the spare and one other, dropping it the ground beside a front tire. Since the four-wheeler was the same dark blue as the half a dozen she'd noted at the compound, she scratched a tiny X in the paint before sliding the spare key into her jean pocket. Releasing the pent-up breath she hadn't realized she held, she scurried back to the truck to prepare.

She opened both chests. From the first, she pulled out the

latched plastic toolbox she'd packed with sterile sample tubes. She filled the insulated area at one end with crumbles of dry ice. Since sampling day-and-a-half-dead elk carcasses might get messy, Myrna stepped into the whole-body disposable suit, zipped it closed, raised the hood, and stuffed her pockets with supplies. She slipped off her hiking boots for rubber ones and looped the face shield over her ears, content now that she'd donned a barrier to the outdoors, even if the sterile white suit that separated her from the wild was only a veneer, easily ripped away.

Before she gloved up, Myrna extracted a package hidden at the bottom of the second chest. She unwrapped a small piece of old bone—very, *very* old bone—grabbed her toolbox, and crept to the side of the truck.

She was too short to see into the back seat, so she dangled the bone over the edge of the open window.

"According to the coordinates Eleanor gave me, we're close to the mammoth. Be ready." William Tell snorted at her hand then snatched the bone from her fingers.

"Your suit's too big."

Myrna squeaked and whipped around, pressing a hand to her heart. Jessup stood a few feet behind her, the butt of his rifle propped on a hip, muzzle pointed to the sky. A smile played on his face as his eyes wandered over her puffy white coverall.

"Don't *do* that." She forgot to lower her voice.

"Paden's chased away a bear sow and cubs, but I can't guarantee for how long. They get pretty aggressive when there's this much meat and, uh, smell. You'll need to take your samples quick, Meerkat."

Meerkat. *Great.*

Myrna straightened to her full, completely unimpressive height, and assumed Eleanor's personality again. "Mr. Jessup? I rescind my permission for you to use my first name. You will call me *Doctor* Lee going forward."

His expression sobered. He scratched the back of his neck and sighed. "I apologize, Dr. Lee, if I came across as disrespectful. I, uh, admit to feeling a little bit intimidated by you."

Myrna perked up. No one she'd ever met had *ever* felt intimidated by her.

She nodded regally. "Apology accepted."

Jessup's gaze softened. Myrna's stomach flipped. Jessup held out his hand for the toolbox and smiled. Myrna passed it to him, ignoring the melting warmth permeating her chest. She dug into her coverall pocket for gloves and then scurried to keep up as he waded into the tall grass. Another huge bug buzzed her head. She ducked and shuddered. If only everything wasn't so *outside*.

"This will take longer than just gathering tissue samples from the specimens," she said. "I need to do a thorough walkabout of the area."

"You have about an hour before the sun drops below that line of mountains. We can come back tomorrow, but I want to get those elk carcasses in the ground tonight. Too dangerous once it gets dark."

She smirked at Jessup's back. Not with her skills and William Tell to keep her safe.

Myrna glanced over her shoulder at the truck. Two black paws were set on the edge of the open back window, the tops of William Tell's ears showing. He was intrigued. Excellent. Because she was going to need him after she took her samples.

And later that night when she returned to this spot.

Alone.

Six

“Be careful,” Jessup called just as Myrna’s rubber boot squelched in a pile of fresh bear scat. “Bears aren’t the only thing to worry about. All this meat’s attracted bugs and lots of little creatures—which means snakes are probably thick on the ground.”

“Snakes?” Well, wasn’t this a day of never-ending fun? She’d allowed the bubble of her clean suit to cocoon her artificially from the dangers of *outside*. Myrna stopped and peered around her, but the vegetation hid anything that slithered.

Two scuffed and dusty boots appeared in her sightline. Jessup. His eyes were smiling again. Myrna studied his eyes. They were very fine eyes.

“I didn’t mean to scare you. Only to make sure you were careful where you stepped and reached. Webb’s probably chased most everything off, and it’s been cold up here the last couple of nights. It’s also helped slow decay.” He headed to the first furry brown lump, his steps now matching hers. “You don’t get outside much, do you, Dr. Lee?”

“I prefer my nice sterile lab to ... this.” She flicked a gloved hand at the glorious vista of high mountain meadow and surrounding peaks, her white coveralls brushing the grass with a swooshy sound.

He nodded, but it was obvious he didn't understand. He'd made his own decision to work outside, to *be* outside. She'd never had the choice growing up.

The first elk was mere yards ahead. She held out her arm to stop Jessup.

Careful. Just because everything looks *safe doesn't mean it is*, her mother's voice whispered. *Assess from a distance.*

Flies crawled on the half-opened eye, crept into the mucus membranes of the nose, and buzzed along the tongue protruding from a slack mouth that showed a hint of blocky whitish teeth. Grass shivered behind the carcass as something small and hidden dashed away.

"Tell me what you see," she said to Jessup. "Just this animal."

Jessup put a sleeve across his mouth and nose. The smell was sharper now, literally breathtaking in its pungency, but she'd smelled worse, from rotting tissue samples sent to the lab for analysis to millennia-old carcasses dissolving from the muck of thawing permafrost. Myrna could feel his gaze on her before he spoke.

"Bull elk in his prime, about seven years old. A six-by-six, still in velvet. That fuzzy stuff on his antlers," he added. "They get cagey about this age, harder to find and hunt in the fall and winter, but relatively easy to track in the summer. He's been grazing in this meadow a couple hours in the mornings and evenings with his buddies, disappearing up into the trees to bed down during the high afternoon and at night." He nodded in the direction of the forested mountains that bracketed the valley.

"You've been watching this herd?"

"About a month."

"How do you keep track of them?"

"We scout. On foot, sometimes horseback."

A faint whirring came from overhead. A black drone appeared

against the fading blue sky, zipping through the air until it hovered about fifty feet above them before it zoomed toward a copse of trees.

Jessup nodded toward the drone. "The animals get used to them after a while—the sound, I mean. It doesn't run 'em off anymore."

"You use drones for your hunts? That's not fair."

"Not hunts. It's illegal. But they help us determine the number of hunts we offer on the ranch each year. Clients expect a trophy elk. These bulls fit that bill." Narrowed blue eyes fastened on her. "You've got something against hunting?"

"High-powered rifles? Compound bows? Prey killed from a distance, never alerted, allowed to evade, or fight back? Those antlers are not just used to attract cow elk, but to grapple with rivals, or gore a wolf, or make a bear think twice. You're chipping away at millions of years of evolution and instinct. Raising them for only one thing now—the size of their racks. They might as well be penned up, your customers shooting them through chain-link fence."

"To keep the herd and surrounding land healthy, they have to be culled," Jessup said. "That's why we have the hunts. Man's the apex predator now."

Myrna sniffed and turned her back to him. "Anything odd about his position?" she prompted. The elk lay on its side, limbs extended with only a small amount of bloating.

"No torn-up ground around his legs. He pretty much fell where he stood. A quiet death. Same with the others. During hunting season, they fall like that with a killing shot, but none of these animals were poached, either by a bullet or an arrow."

"We haven't examined the other side of the elk, so how do you know?"

"First shot would have spooked the other three bulls."

Which possibly pointed to poison. But to drop dead at about

the same time? *That* was weird. Myrna chewed her lip, mind racing through and discarding different scenarios.

"Stay there, please." With deliberate steps, she circled the dead elk. All else faded as she mentally cataloged the immediate scene. Rigor complete, neck arched but relaxed. She dug into a pocket and pulled out a magnifying glass, squatted, and stared at the mouth and head. Small animals had nibbled on mucosal tissues, leaving ragged areas already dotted with tiny, creamy blowfly eggs, none yet hatched to larvae. A pinkish dried froth had discharged from the mouth—normal with initial decomp. Plant fragments— still green—on the tongue and teeth, grazing until its final breath. She stood and performed a slow pirouette. No noxious plant species in the vicinity. Maybe a toxic coating or spill? Accidental or deliberate? She'd take soil and vegetation samples.

Myrna focused back on the elk and sighed, fogging up the plastic of her mask. Poor thing. She pulled off her glove and squatted by his head. With great gentleness, she laid her bare hand on his neck and whispered, "I'll figure out what killed you. I promise."

She stood and continued her circuit, skirting huge antlers that rose to her chin in height, even with the animal on its side. The dark brown of the elk's neck and head and the thick beige hair of its body ruffled in the cooling breeze. But there was more move- ment: deeper, creeping, crawling shivers as fat black flies burrowed underneath the pelt and into dead skin to feed and deposit eggs. She deliberately blurred her vision to take in the wormy, squirmy motion. Uniform across the animal.

"Next, please," she said.

Jessup led her to the second elk, this one even larger than the first. Myrna propped her hands on her hips, mind spinning. How had they done it? How had ancient man with only stone points taken down such massive creatures, no bows or atlatls—although that was hotly debated—for a distance attack? They had to get up close with spears, using only cunning and stealth.

"What do you see?" she asked Jessup. He replied, she walked her circuit, and they repeated the pattern for the third animal.

The fourth bull had an odd antler configuration with one side well-developed and the other twisted and thick—an atypical. He'd fallen next to a large table-shaped rock, its flat top a dozen feet above the meadow, smaller stones crumbled around its flanks. Decomposition was further along, the bloat of the belly lifting a back leg parallel to the ground. The skin-crawling movements under its fur were worse, too. More bugs *and* they'd developed further: Some of the fly eggs had hatched into wriggling larvae— not unusual, but with the cold temperatures ... Then she felt the warmth of the air.

"The rock." Much of it now lay in shade, except for a cap of orange-purple light coating its gleaming top—the last of the sun's rays. She laid a hand against its rough side. Residual heat pulsed through her glove.

"West-facing. It catches the sun and stays warm into the night," Jessup said. "Careful of snakes. Myrna."

She started and blinked out of her almost trancelike concentration at the mention of snakes.

Or was it because of the caressing sound of her name on Jessup's lips?

Focus, Myrna, focus.... She stared at the beige fur along the elk's flank. Blurred her vision. Something was off—

Her gasp caught her by surprise, and only peripherally did she notice Jessup's sharpened gaze.

On an area near the rump, in a circular region maybe four inches in diameter, there was no movement of the animal's fur. Digging into her capacious pocket, Myrna pulled out a page of round orange stickers and affixed one next to the spot. She pressed her fingers around the area, feeling for an embedded projectile. Nothing. She dipped her hand back in the pocket and pulled out her magnifier. With careful fingers, she parted the fur, searching for a wound, blood, insects.

Again, nothing.

Why were insects avoiding this patch on the animal? Could it be important to the die-off? There was an easy way to find out. If she was wrong, no harm done. If she was right, she might solve this mystery in a couple of days, which might impress the Donavans, and then they might give her access to their stone points and the mammoth bones, which might—no, *would*—save her career.

Straightening she said, "I want this animal back at the staff compound for observation."

Jessup rubbed his chin. "We were gonna bury—"

"No. This animal, at the compound, placed this side up, a wire cage over the whole body to protect it. Two digital cameras, one pointed at its shoulder, here"—she pressed a second sticker into the fur—"and the other on its rump, here. A light suspended above. I want its decomposition filmed. Do you understand? I don't care how it gets done, but I will need *this* animal for *my* investigation."

Myrna propped her hands on her hips, awash with curiosity and a tingling happiness. "Now, let's take some samples for analysis. We'll start back at the first elk."

Seven

Myrna bent over the final elk, wielding the wickedly sharp blade with the quick slicing motions of a professional assassin to sever a chunk of tissue from the purplish-gray liver. It slithered into her bloodied glove, slippery and slick, but she didn't tighten her grasp. The key was to cradle the material gently so the sample wouldn't squirt out of her hand like wet soap. Been there, done that.

She rose, tissue in hand, her lucky knife in the other, gore splattering her white coveralls and splashed across her plastic face shield.

Done.

And just in time. While she'd worked over the dead elk, the day had retreated, the only light remaining in the sky a greenish glow to the west.

All three men—Jessup, Paden, and Webb—watched her, darkly silhouetted in the headlights so it was difficult to make out expressions. Each time she'd open an elk's belly to expose the offal, they'd retreat with the cooler. Understandable. Accumulated peritoneal fluids would gush out like a fountain of stink to soak into the ground. It made William Tell's pee on their boots seem benign.

Stepping back from the filleted carcass, she dropped the piece of liver into the labeled 50 mL conical tube. The bright headlights of the pickup truck garishly illuminated her bloodstained suit. There were very few clean areas left to wipe the blade. She found one, careful not to cut the material and expose herself to the butchery.

With a satisfied sigh, Myrna snuggled her sample in between the sublimating chunks of dry ice, white vapor spilling over the cooler's sides and onto the ground, spreading in a creeping carpet through the grass. She'd need to get these samples into a -80° Celsius freezer back at the Donavan compound to stop further decomp.

"Done?" called Paden.

At her yes, he jogged to the waiting bulldozer. It rumbled to life, and Myrna scurried away from the cooler. Jessup appeared by her side, grabbing a handful of Tyvek fabric from the back of her suit as the dozer maneuvered through the meadow. The machine was so noisy there was no way Paden could hear her, so she suppressed the need to remind him once again to be gentle when he lowered the massive bucket toward the elk.

Don't scrape the earth, don't scrape the ground, pleasepleaseplease.

She held her breath as Paden inched the bladed edge under the elk's back, bouncing its carcass up and into the scoop. Her excited "I think he did it" was almost buried in the rev of the diesel engine. Jessup's hand tightened, preventing her dash to the front of the moving machine, its bucket high off the ground, elk legs dangling over the sharp edge. The bulldozer rumbled out of the stark white headlights of the truck toward the open grave where Paden had already deposited the first two elk.

Almost dancing with impatience, Myrna surged forward, afraid if they waited too long, she might miss it. Jessup dogged her heels to the spot of ground where the dead elk had lain. Webb followed.

Relieved of the carcass's pressure, the earth seemed to pulse and move. Bugs, beetles, insects, worms, all drawn to death's cleanup, scurried wildly, startled by the truck's headlights and shock of cold air. Myrna dug out her phone for pictures.

"What are you looking for, Myrna?" Jessup asked. "What do *you* see?"

She snapped a pic, pointing before she moved and pressed the video icon. "*There*. That patch. It's vacant. No larvae, no worms. And the retreating insects, they're *still* avoiding it." She edged closer, wincing at the crunch of fleeing bugs under her feet. "Paden skinned the ground with the bucket when he picked up the first two elk." She zoomed in on the insect-free spot. "This time, he didn't. I need to take a soil sample."

Fishing into her pocket, she extracted clean gloves. Out came a test tube, Myrna peeling away its sterile wrapping as she waded through the bugs and crouched. Using its open mouth, she dug into the ground, scraping soil from the odd patch of bug-free dirt and writing on the label with an indelible marker before doing the same thing with fresh tubes at the three other carcass-flattened locations. "Controls," she murmured in explanation, though neither Jessup nor Webb asked.

"Ma'am?" Webb, hands shoved into the pockets of his jacket, shifted from one foot to the other. "The way you butchered those animals ... Seems to me like you've done this before."

Myrna froze, going back over her actions and chastising herself. It was her own fault, forgetting everything and everyone around her once she immersed herself in her work. She'd slipped back into motions that had once been so commonplace, they had their own muscle memory, reverting to what she once was instead of the aloof, white-coated, serious indoor laboratory scientist she needed to be to regain her reputation.

"Online videos," she said in a voice high enough to etch glass. She cleared her throat and lowered her tone. "There are dozens by survivalists, uh, hunters, and ... and cooks on how to disarticulate elk and deer and wild game."

She stood and, samples in hand, marched past the men and shoved the tubes into the dry ice. Spinning on the ball of her foot, she lifted her chin, looked down her nose, and channeled Eleanor. Myrna pointed imperiously across the meadow.

"I need Paden and that bulldozer to take the last elk—*my* elk—back to the staff compound. Webb, load up this cooler into the truck. And, Jessup, stake each area where the carcasses laid. I'll come back tomorrow to collect more samples."

She tromped with purpose toward the table rock, its side dimly illuminated by the truck's lights, the dark, heavy body of the fourth elk sprawled before it.

The stares of the men bore into her back like the sharp edge of her lucky knife.

EIGHT

Myrna stood at the open tailgate of the pickup, still dressed in her bloodied white suit, pretending to tidy her sampling kit and shooting quick surreptitious glances at Paden and Webb as they walked to the four-wheeler. The bulldozer idled down the road, the atypical elk she'd selected for the decomposition study hidden in the bucket scoop.

"Aw." Paden yanked the keyring from the ignition of the four-wheeler.

"You lost 'em again?" Webb shook his head. "Man, oh, man, Bard's gonna have your hide. He told you not to use that wire."

"The wire was just fine," Paden blustered. "It must've got caught on something, that's all. The gate key's gone. And the spare to the four-wheeler. *Fu—*"

"Paden. We have a lady present, son," Webb chided.

Paden pulled up short, eyes wide, cheeks glowing red in the vehicle lights. "Sorry, ma'am."

"Nothing I haven't heard before." The duplicate ignition key she'd taken seemed to burn in her jean pocket. Myrna pointed to the barely visible silver glimmer next to a front tire. "Is that one of them?"

Paden scooped the key out of the dirt, shoulders slumping in relief. "Now all I need to find is the extra—"

"Lose the keys again?" Jessup walked out of the darkness, rifle tucked under his arm, a mallet in his hand. "Bard's not gonna be happy." He stowed the tool and a couple of extra wooden stakes in the corner of the truck bed.

"Myrna already found one." Paden held up the key. "Right here on the ground."

Jessup swiveled to stare at her, but in the dimness, it was hard to see his expression. "Lucky. Well, give the keys to Webb. Myrna and I will head out first so we can make sure everything's prepped at the compound."

"I still need to clean up a little and, um, pee," Myrna said. A sharp yap came from the back seat of the truck. *Good boy*. He'd get an extra treat for that. "And I really need to let William Tell out, too. We can catch up. Right? Since it's going to take them a while." She nodded at the idling bulldozer.

Jessup stood quiet for a long moment. "Yep," he finally said. "We can do that."

Webb looked back and forth between Jessup and her before he zipped his heavy jacket, mounted the four-wheeler, and started it up. Paden and Jessup walked into the gloom, deep in conversation. A few minutes later, the rumble of the bulldozer and hum of the four-wheeler faded into the darkness along with the brightness of their headlights, until all around her was night.

Myrna bit her lip. *Two down, one to go.*

The crunch of Jessup's boots announced his presence. He was barely a shadow in the blackness of the forest behind him.

"There's biodegradable toilet paper in the passenger-side door of the truck. Have you ever had to, uh, use the outdoors? Make sure you bury it or tuck it in the biohazard pouch, and don't go far. I'll take the little guy for a quick walk."

"No!" It came out as a squeak. "He might pee on your boots again." She forced a chuckle, and his hard silhouette relaxed.

"Dr. Myrna P. Lee," he drawled. "You ever played poker?"

The laugh in his voice made her bristle.

"Actually, I ha—"

A brilliant pop of light flashed deep within the trees. She grabbed his arm.

"What was that?"

Jessup pivoted as a second bubble of light expanded and faded, this time accompanied by a crash of undergrowth and branches.

"Camera traps," Jessup said. "Camouflaged motion-detector cameras, which ranch security has strapped to trees. They're monitored at the staff compound. I've told Bard I don't want them because they spook the animals, but he says the higher-ups insist."

"Way out here?"

"Almost everywhere on the ranch."

She scowled. *That complicates matters.*

His phone dinged. He tugged it out of his jacket pocket, the glow of its screen harsh on his face. "Bard. Again. We need to get going. Call me when you're ready." He grabbed his rifle and strode into the darkness, phone pressed to his ear.

Myrna unloaded her pockets, stepped out of the rubber boots, and peeled away her suit, careful to avoid the gore as she balled it up and stuffed it into the biohazard bag. Then she theatrically patted her pockets and checked the toolkit and cooler with the samples. Careful to modulate her voice, she said loudly, "Darn it. My special knife. I think I left it somewhere on the rocks next to the last elk. I don't have my hiking boots on yet. Jessup?" She stared at the place she'd last seen him.

"I heard. We can get it tomorr—"

"Please, Jessup. My dear mother gave me that knife. It's about all I have left from her, and I don't want to lose it." Lies, most of it, especially the dear part. "Can't you go get it while I, um, use the facilities? I'll take William Tell out with me to save time."

A long silence. "All right." He flicked on a flashlight and walked away.

Myrna quickly tied the boot laces and opened the truck door. William Tell greeted her with an impatient snort. No licks or wags —they'd dispensed with PDAs a long time ago. He perched on the edge of the seat, deciding whether to jump to the ground.

Hurrying, she clipped on his leash and flipped on the blinking red safety flash that hung with his rabies and contact information tags. She lifted him off the seat with the harness so she didn't have to hold him and swung him to the ground at her feet. As soon as his paws hit dirt, he strained to the end of his leash, nose in the air, disappearing from the wedge of light shining from the open truck door.

Myrna grabbed her jacket from the back seat and shrugged it on. "Time for work," she said softly. William Tell scurried back into the light and sat, ears perked, his eyes weirdly bright and pinned to her face. She pulled another piece of old bone out of a pocket and let him sniff it.

"Find the mammoth bones, boy."

She tucked the leash into a special loop on his harness and let go. William Tell shot into the night.

NINE

The red light on William Tell's harness bobbled toward the cliffs, and Myrna chased it, fumbling to switch on her own small flashlight so she wouldn't face-plant on the rough terrain and mess this up. A quick look over her shoulder found Jessup's flashlight beam at the far end of the meadow. If he came after her, her wholly innocent excuse for running off would be a desperate worry that her dear little doggie would get eaten by a bear or something.

William Tell disappeared over the top of the slope. Myrna powered up the crumbling ridge of earth, but the rock under her foot slipped and her knee came down hard. She scrambled up, pain disappearing under her mother's angry voice shrieking in her head.

What good is it if I have to backtrack to find you? If you freaking hurt yourself? Control your separateness. Be part of the night, or they'll get you. THEY'LL GET YOU.

The dog's blinking light bobbled toward a jumble of rocks at the bottom of a cliff face. Myrna bolted after it. A waning moon had finally risen in the nighttime sky. It threw black shadows along her path. Her steps became surer as childhood instincts clicked in.

"Dammit. Myrna!"

The intensity of Jessup's bellow jerked her around. Her panicked pulse thumped loud in her ears. *They'll catch me. Rip me away from her. I'll be even more alone. I'll be—* Adrenaline spiked an overwhelming instinct to hide. Her head swiveled, swiftly cataloging half a dozen hidey-holes, expertly assessing each one.

There. She darted toward a dark tangle of fallen branches covering a thicket—

And stumbled to a halt. She drank in calming breaths. Jessup wasn't trying to kidnap her, to take her away. No one was *ever* trying to take her, because no one wanted her. All lies from the moment she could walk.

Ruthlessly banishing her compulsions back into their dark corner, she ran after the dog. He yapped high and sharp, and she sped up, nimbly navigating hillocks of bunch grass. A few minutes alone with William Tell before Jessup found them. That was all she needed.

Myrna pulled up short at the rocks the dog had stopped to investigate. Panting for breath, she leaned on a towering stone.

The hair on her neck rose.

Taking a step back, she flicked the beam of her light over the rock's vertical face. It was as slick as polished granite. It had been rubbed smooth by the fur and skin of something much bigger than any animal alive today. *A mammoth rub.* She laid her hand on a smoothly rounded corner.

"Is there more?" she asked in a hushed voice.

William Tell trotted away along the cliff face. She trailed behind him until they stood next to a gaping arroyo. It was recent, its crumbling walls cutting sharply into the sandy soil. She aimed her light at the far side—and couldn't breathe.

A huge set of ribs curved out of the sandstone. *Mammoth bones.* Eleanor said they had butchering marks. Were there stone projectile points, too?

"Myrna!"

Jessup was closer. She had to do this quickly. Her heart gave an excited jump.

She had to pick up the dog.

Myrna hurried back to the higher ground next to the mammoth rub, William Tell scampering beside her. She needed a good view of the land around the cliffs and the valley below—if William Tell worked the way she hoped he would. *That* was not a given.

"Here, boy," she said in her sweetest voice. She patted her leg enticingly, stooping a little and smiling.

The little shit just looked at her.

She tried musical and happy. "Come get a treat."

He sat and scratched at his harness.

"*Fine.* I'll get you a new harness. No more pink. Now, *come on.*"

He frisked toward her and play bowed.

Myrna knelt and took a deep breath, bracing herself. As if he'd decided to finally do his part, William Tell stepped in close. She put out a tentative hand and stroked him over his head, scratching his left ear. He sighed contentedly.

She rotated him until he faced forward and unclipped his leash, dropping it by her feet. She wrapped her fingers around his back and belly, making sure their contact—skin to fur—was at its maximum. And with eyes closed, Myrna lifted him as she stood and pressed him against her chest, beginning her countdown. *Three ... two ...*

The shock vibrated over her like the echo of a distant explosion. The unpleasant watery sensation traveled through bone and flesh. Shivery prickles stood the hair of her arms and neck on end. Around her, the fragrance of the forest changed, becoming colder, sharper. Freezing air wrapped her body, spatters of wet snow peppering her skin.

Clutching William Tell closer, she cracked one eyelid. Ice and snow crusted the ground. It was still night ... but different. Elation pumped through her veins.

It worked. William Tell had taken her back in time. Since he appeared to absorb clues from his surroundings and from the person who picked him up, hopefully, back to the Pleistocene. Back to the time of the mammoth in the arroyo. *Thirteen thousand years ago*.

Myrna didn't know how he did it. Only that he did, and that she could and had taken advantage of it for her career.

She and the dog were phantom spectators in a time when now-extinct animals like mammoths and mastodons and saber-toothed cats roamed the earth. And maybe this time she'd find evidence for her poison. Poison slathered on lanceolate stone points. Poison used to bring down a massive creature that would feed a clan of people and keep them satiated through the long, dark winter.

William Tell had made her one of the premier experts in Pleistocene megafauna before she'd royally screwed everything up. Maybe *this* was the night she'd recover her reputation with an amazing discovery.

Myrna gathered her courage, blinked both eyes open and, with a shaky breath, gazed toward the arroyo. Smooth earth replaced the black chasm cut into the ground. She frowned.

Where was the mammoth carcass? Where were the ancient Clovis people praying over it, thanking it for its sacrifice, butchering it with their sharp stone tools, bonfires alight and glowing fierce and hot with swirling sparks winking into a dull iron sky?

Nothing but the cliff loomed over the site.

The cliff. Was that it? Had the animal fallen from the plateau above? Bison jumps—places where first peoples had driven herds of animals off cliffs during hunts—weren't uncommon, although no mammoth jumps had been found yet. Cradling William Tell to her chest, Myrna tipped her head up, blinking as snow dotted her lashes.

A black shape hurtled over the edge toward her, plummeting to earth. Too small for a mammoth. And it wasn't going to land in the arroyo ...

It thumped to the ground, right in front of her. She jerked, even though she was in no danger. This animal in William Tell's vision—their shared vision—had fallen thousands of years ago.

Myrna crept forward, brows creased first in bewilderment, then in growing horror.

Her heart seemed to stop, then pound at a dizzying rate. It wasn't an ancient horse or camel or bison that lay dead.

A *man* lay face down in the dirt. And not from Paleolithic times, not from thirteen thousand years ago. A *modern* man, with spurs and boots and jeans, and a long-sleeved coat.

A ... a ... *cowboy*?

The clouds parted, allowing a beam of moonlight to sneak through. Something gleamed in the light. Myrna sidled closer, William Tell caught tightly against her.

An obsidian stone knife was buried in the man's back, its leather-wrapped handle dark with blood.

Robbed of breath, her muscles weakened, their energy drained by shock. Gorge rising in her throat, she sank to the dirt. William Tell struggled in her loosened grip. He leaped from her arms, and the vision—cowboy, sleet, snow, ice—disappeared in a blink. Myrna pressed a trembling hand to her mouth.

Hard crunching footsteps wrenched her head up. A dark figure ran toward her, rifle in one hand, flashlight in the other. Its circular beam raced over the empty ground up to her face.

"*Dammit*, Myrna, do you know how dangerous these woods are at ni—" His words cut off as the harsh light roamed her expression. Jessup stopped in his tracks. He stood right where the dead man had fallen.

A dead man who'd been murdered.

Ten

Ensconced in the front passenger seat, Myrna scooched forward. She peered out the dusty truck window as Jessup drove from night into an artificial dome of light over the ranch's staff compound.

"Solar-powered LED, 32000 lumens." Jessup offered up the information as if reading her mind. "Battery storage and backup in case the sun don't shine. No windmills. They kill too many birds. But otherwise, completely off-grid."

Off-grid with millions of dollars of hi-tech support. Solar panels and storage batteries stuffed with cheap rare earth elements dug out of foreign mines that devastate the environment. She'd seen it firsthand. Myrna couldn't hold back a derisive snort. Jessup shot her a side-eye glance.

She schooled her features to reflect interest and sat back to stare at Jessup's rugged profile. Unlike the false self-sufficiency around her, he looked like a man out of time, like he should be walking down the dusty street of a true Western town, not this weird dystopian Tombstone or Deadwood mock-up.

Jessup stopped the truck and rolled down his window as a four-wheeler rumbled up to the driver's side.

"Bard's fit to be tied," Webb yelled above the growl of the engine. "You know how much he hates to reset the lights."

"I radioed in—"

"Doesn't matter. He's ready to tear you a new one." Webb pushed his hat back and leaned around to speak to Myrna, his long, homely face pulled with worry. "Heard you had a scare. You okay, ma'am? And your little dog?"

William Tell took that moment to snore wheezily from the back seat.

"He's fine," Myrna yelled over the noise. "He slept the whole way back."

Visions did that. Drained him. They didn't seem to affect her physically unless it was to scare the bejesus out of her when dead bodies fell at her feet. She shuddered. "He was very brave, thinking he could go up against a bear."

At least, that's the story she'd told Jessup. She wasn't sure if he'd completely believed her, but he'd cocked his rifle and scoured the woods with his flashlight as they'd made their way back to the meadow and truck, William Tell trotting between them, dribbling pee on every available tuft of grass, fist-sized rock, and broken twig. The walk back had given her much-needed time to recover.

"Just hope that ol' sow and her cubs don't decide to follow the scent of that elk carcass, 'cause it's only gonna get more fragrant." Webb shook his head. "Bard's ticked about that, too. His stupid mutt's been trying to take a chunk—"

"No. Don't let Briscoe or *any* animal eat from that elk, please," Myrna said. "Not until I can figure out how it died."

Jessup laid his arm along the back of the seat, his body exuding heat. She unbuckled and shimmied along the bench seat toward him, using the perfectly logical excuse of yelled conversation to get closer.

"Where did you put the body, uh, carcass?" Myrna's skin prickled as Jessup's warmth enveloped her. "It needs to be completely protected, caged, around and above. Is the camera set up? I'd like to get the live digital feed on my computer."

"Paden's handling everything," Webb said. "You want to head over now?"

"We need to get the samples I collected put away first," Myrna said. "I don't want them compromised by any more delays."

Jessup's face was in shadow, but she swore he rolled his eyes. His low-voiced "And whose fault is that, Dr. Myrna P. Lee?" tickled her ear, barely audible over the four-wheeler.

Myrna slid back to her seat, nibbling her lower lip. Okay, make that Jessup *didn't* believe her about the bear.

Jessup leaned out the window, so she couldn't quite hear what he was saying over the noise. Webb nodded before he gunned his ride and accelerated down the street, turned right between two buildings, and disappeared. Jessup followed briefly but turned left down a narrow lane, then left again. There was less light on the backside of the main street and the buildings they passed were in shadow. He pulled up next to double doors in a long wooden and weathered facade with an overhang protecting a boardwalk. Myrna could just see a sign that read LABORATORIES in a stylized Western font. Beside it was a keypad.

"Your security code's in your handout materials. The freezer you want's in the back right corner." He hopped out of the truck and by the time she slid to the ground, Jessup was holding open one of the lab doors.

She stood on the threshold, the cool, sterile, positive-pressure air stroking her skin in a chill caress. Eerie glowing screens of hulking, humming equipment dotted the dark laboratory.

This would be her home for the next two weeks because she was a serious scientist soon to be accepted and admired and welcomed back by her community, where she belonged, not exiled out in the nasty wild wilderness.

Myrna hesitated.

"Where's the light switch?"

"No lights. Bard controls them at security. His way of punishing us for coming in so late."

She shifted her feet. "Do you need to go see him or anything?"

"What he has to say can wait." He was silent for a moment. "You going in? Or are you afraid of the dark?" His voice, supple and buttery soft, teased.

"Not for a long time." She peeped at him. "You think I lied about the bear."

"Something spooked you." Back at the cliff, he'd wrapped his arms around her and pulled her into his chest. She'd focused on the beat of his heart to calm her shock. It was the first time in a long time she'd felt truly safe.

He leaned his shoulder against the open door, a faint smile playing around his mouth. Behind him, a shining crown of stars dotted the night sky above the compound's buildings. "Care to explain, Dr. Lee?"

What could she say? *I have a magic dog that can transmit visions of the distant past*? That she'd breathed in the atmosphere of thirteen thousand years ago? Had literally *seen* Paleoindians from the Clovis culture use poison-tipped stone points to kill mammoths and other Pleistocene megafauna and just needed to find scientific proof?

Or, how about that a dead man fell at her feet about an hour ago, then—*poof*—disappeared as soon as she'd let go of William Tell? Myrna swallowed, throat tight.

"Minus eighty in the far-right corner?" She didn't need a light. Her eyes adjusted easily to the darkness from long habit.

Jessup studied her for a long moment before he straightened. He nodded and strode to the back of the pickup truck to pull out the sample-filled coolers.

Once, she'd explained everything—William Tell, the visions, her upbringing and past—to her mentor Tom Hutchinson. He'd believed her, accepted her. Made her part of his team and taught her everything he'd known. She'd learned to trust him, fallen in love with him. They'd become lovers, and for the first time, she'd felt like she'd belonged.

But it had all been a lie. He'd used and betrayed her, and her life and career had crashed and burned. No way she'd ever let her guard down that much for anyone ever again.

It was easier to do everything alone.

Eleven

It didn't take long for Myrna to stow her samples in the freezer and lock the lab up.

"Your elk's in the field west of the compound," Jessup said. "An easy walk from here."

But instead of walking, he opened the truck's passenger door for her before he climbed in and drove toward the security building, past her car, and into the open field behind it. Bright lights stationed at the perimeter lit up the space against the night sky. At one end, three men—Paden, Webb, and someone Myrna hadn't met yet—milled around a large square cage. A little farther out sat the bulldozer, the four-wheeler tucked by its side. Jessup bumped his truck through the bunchgrass toward them. William Tell's snores continued unabated from the back seat.

Jessup stopped the truck, and Myrna bailed out, scurrying closer to examine the setup that would record the elk's decomposition over the next week—if they let her keep it up that long. She pulled out her phone and leveled her screen for a long-range photo. The flash had the men's heads jerking toward her. Her next picture consisted of Jessup's hand, blocking her shot.

"Didn't you read your agreement? No pictures around the ranch compound, Myrna. You need to delete that. Now."

She stared at him, open-mouthed. "I took pictures at the die-off."

"I'm surprised Bard let you keep your phone. We'll need you to transfer those to a Donavan laptop and delete them on your personal device."

She dragged the picture she'd just taken into the trash and slipped her cell into a pocket. "No pictures around the compound?"

"Or anywhere else on the ranch. They've fired people for a lot less," Paden said. "Don't worry, I've already taken a bunch of shots and dumped them onto this." He gestured with his chin to a rugged field laptop he held across one arm. "It's yours while you're here. Come on, I want to show you the setup."

She fell into step beside Paden, Jessup flanking her.

The cold air dampened the elk's stench, but it was still pretty ripe, and the bright light suspended overhead attracted a hoard of flying insects. The cage was about six feet square, the brown body of the dead bull sprawled diagonally inside, two cameras suspended above it. She found a square area of wire, latched closed now, that would act as a door for sampling. A computer satchel rested on top of the cage.

"We had to saw the antlers off to make him fit." Paden canted the laptop's screen toward her. "The cameras are pointed at the target locations with a twenty-five percent overlap, live feed running to the computer."

Paden handed Myrna the open laptop, and she scrutinized the video. Camera angles were pretty good, the elk's rump with the odd bug-free area centered in one picture. She touched the icon for the camera focused on the control patch of hide. Its lens hummed faintly as it telescoped back then forward again. She pressed another icon and the camera angle shifted to a 30 percent overlap. "Remote adjustments?"

"Yep. Top-of-the-line everything for the Donavans." Paden nodded to a heavy-duty metal chest bristling with heavy-duty rubber-sheathed cords. "Cameras and light will run off batteries three days straight without a recharge, but I'm gonna ask Bard if I can deploy a couple of solar panels anyway. Whole setup's linked to the Donavans' satellite—"

"To *what*?" Myrna stared up at him. Who *were* these people?

Paden grinned. His front teeth overlapped the littlest bit. "Geosynchronous orbit."

"Where's Bard?" Jessup asked. He stood half in shadow near Webb and the old man.

"He's buried himself inside the security center, pouting because he has to stay late," the old man said. He had a deep, plummy voice with the rolling cadence of a native New Mexican raised speaking Spanish.

He hobbled toward Myrna. Clean-shaven, his face was as craggy as a mountain, eyebrows furry caterpillars. His black hair, wavy and thick, was only slightly peppered with gray. "Since these doofuses won't introduce me, I'll do it myself. Isaac Marín."

Myrna took his extended hand. His palm was smooth and dry. "Myrna Lee."

"Bienvenidos a Tesoro del Oro ranchero, Myrna Lee." He raised his eyebrows, a smile playing over his lips. "She's a pretty little thing, Paden. That last gal broke up with you, didn't she? You looking again?"

"Aw, Isaac." Paden's cheeks burned cherry red. Both Webb and Jessup chuckled.

Paden? Sure, he was cute, but he was just a boy compared to …

Her eyes darted to Jessup and away, her cheeks heating.

Isaac winked at Myrna, his wrinkles pulled deeper by a grin. "He's a good boy, que no? And he loves his mama."

Jessup's phone rang. He answered and said, "We're done and heading back now." He pulled the phone away from his ear. "Isaac? You need a ride?"

"Sure do."

Jessup was back on the phone. "We'll take the forest route. Isaac's been on his feet all day and needs to get home. I'll lead Dr. Lee in her car." He listened intently for another minute before he ended the call.

"Paden. Bard says there's been a black pickup truck nosing around all day. He wants you and Webb to leave through the main gate and check that everything's secure."

"That adds another hour before I'll get home," Paden said, a distinct whine in his voice. "Why can't he do it?"

Webb clapped Paden on the shoulder. "Let's get goin'."

Myrna handed Paden the laptop, and he shoved it into the computer bag. "Everything you'll need. No password." The four-wheeler rumbled to life. "Gotta go. If you have time tomorrow, I'll go over the programming. There's some really great stuff—" Paden dashed into the dark.

"Is he some kind of computer genius?" Myrna asked. She clutched the satchel against her chest.

"Graduated top of his class at nineteen years old, MIT," Jessup said. "Family's from around here, though. Been in New Mexico for generations."

"Wow. What about you?"

Isaac Marín threw his head back and laughed. "Me 'n' Jessup graduated from the school of hard knocks."

"Don't let him fool you, Myrna," Jessup said. "Isaac's a Cordon Bleu chef."

Isaac snorted. "Nah. Just a camp cook."

The lights flipped off at the compound. Wordlessly, they headed toward Jessup's truck. When Isaac stumbled, both Myrna and Jessup gave him their arms. He smelled like cake.

"Nobody's told me where I'm staying," Myrna said.

"Cimarron," Jessup said. "Small town north of the ranch."

"Means *wild* in Spanish, but it could come from the Taino

Indian word si'maran. Means *flight of an arrow*. Bard actually gave you permission to use the shortcut?" Isaac asked Jessup.

"Shortcut?" Myrna perked up.

"Staff-only dirt road out of the ranch," Isaac said. "No security, so—" He cut off abruptly and roughly cleared his throat.

Myrna would bet a hundred dollars Jessup squeezed Isaac's arm to stop him from saying anything else.

"I'll lead, you follow," Jessup said to Myrna. "Road's a little rough in spots, but your car should be able to handle it."

After helping Isaac into the passenger seat, she climbed in next to a still snoring William Tell. Jessup started the truck and kept up a low-voiced conversation with Isaac as he chauffeured them to her car.

Myrna eyed Jessup's profile speculatively. A secret back road into the ranch with no security, huh? Now wasn't that interesting.

Twelve

"What is this place?" Myrna unshouldered the computer bags—hers and the one Paden had given her—leaving them on the granite breakfast bar that divided a galley kitchen from the dining space. The small house they'd entered had an open floor plan that also included a living area with a fireplace.

She'd never stayed anywhere like this little house, so warm and welcoming it was like walking into an embrace. She wanted to explore, to touch, to absorb her surroundings. Myrna stroked the softest throw ever that was draped over the back of a weathered black leather wingback chair, its deep reds and burnt oranges echoed in the braided rug under the coffee table and the curtains covering the front window. It felt like a real home. Like it could be *her* home. It even smelled right.

Her mother's mocking laughter rang in her head, and she yanked her hand back. This was only temporary, like every place she'd ever lived, like everything had always been in her life.

Only. Temporary.

Jessup set William Tell's crate on the polished hardwood floor. The dog scratched to get out, but Myrna waited until Isaac closed the front door before she knelt to unlatch the wire mesh grate. William Tell poked his head out to sniff the air. He tilted his face up to Myrna, one bat ear twitching, eyes glistening under the light showered down by the old-fashioned glass fixture centered in the high, pressed-tin ceiling.

She gave him a mean *you'd better not pee on the furniture* look. If he even had one drop left. He had to be completely dehydrated considering the contributions he'd made during the multiple times she'd stopped along the back road out of the ranch. William Tell snorted and trotted out of the cage to investigate his *temporary* digs.

Jessup laid her duffle bag on a deep-cushioned loveseat—upholstered with the same distressed leather as the chair—that faced a wall-mounted flat-screen. "When the Donavan family expanded the ranch before the Second World War, they bought a couple dozen of these homes for their permanent employees."

"Mining and timber companies put these places up in the late eighteen hundreds for their workers. Even had a school para los niños—the kids. That's gone. Burned, oh, back in the forties during the war. The village of Cimarron is just up the hill." Isaac set her canvas bag full of William Tell's food and gear on the satiny dark wood of the dining table. "The Donavans gutted everything, que no? I don't know how many times. Electric, water, internet. But they managed to keep the insides right. Me recuerdo, you know when I was a kid, there was a gunfight right outside on the street. Such a scandal."

"I'm next door. Isaac's directly across the street." Jessup paused, his face a bland mask. "The dog's okay? You sure had to stop a lot for him on the way out."

"Thanks for being so understanding." Myrna gave William Tell a completely fake indulgent look. "The way he barks and carries on when he needs to be let out, it's hard to be in the same room with him, much less a car—"

William Tell took that moment to politely scratch the back door, sit, and sigh patiently. She narrowed her eyes at him.

Isaac limped to the door and turned the deadbolt. William Tell playfully gamboled around the old man's boots as he swung the door open and switched on the back porch light. The dog disappeared down the steps outside. "There's a fenced yard, so he should be fine. Jessup? Show Myrna Lee how the door locks work. They're coded with a keypad. This techy stuff, que no?" He shook his head, chuckling. "You set it so no one else can get in."

No one else except whoever controlled the techy stuff. She unclipped the flap on her computer bag and pulled out her laptop.

"Paden said there was a direct satellite connection. Do I use it for my personal gear?"

Jessup hesitated. "No. The Donavans' system is locked down. There should be temporary passwords for whatever they have in the house in that folder there by the toaster. Your cupboards and refrigerator are stocked, but if you need anything, there's a form for ordering and delivery. Maid service, too. Just check a time, and they send people in to clean."

Myrna smiled brightly. "How? I'm the only one who'll know the code to get in."

Jessup's lips thinned.

"I cook for the staff at the compound—breakfast, lunch, and dinner, if you don't want to eat alone," Isaac said. "Most of my supplies are produced on the ranch, from Dame Sylvia's regenerative farm."

"Local and self-sufficient. Their own little kingdom." Her smile was starting to hurt.

"More like mine owners with a company store." Jessup's dry tone bordered on sarcastic, but she couldn't be completely sure. He—like all the Donavans' personnel—seemed pretty invested in his job.

But she knew more than most how job loyalty could come back to bite you in the butt—or get you killed.

"About tomorrow," she said.

"I'll pick you up at six for a seven A.M. start," Jessup said.

"But it's after eleven now. I still need to unpack, get William Tell settled ..." That didn't sound like much, so Myrna laid a hand on his arm and raised her face to Jessup's with a doe-eyed look. "It's been *such* an exhausting day. Let me get some sleep tonight, then I'll be ready for early mornings and long hours till I figure out ..." His irises were flecked with the most amazing turquoisey blue. Her belly warmed and swirled. "Um ... Figure out ..."

The back door snapped closed. Myrna started and dropped her hand like she'd touched a red-hot branding iron. Nails tapping, William Tell walked across the wooden floor, heading through the open door off the kitchen. To cover burning cheeks, she followed him to the bedroom and flicked on the light. William Tell flung himself onto the area rug tucked under the end of the brass bedstead, chest bellowing on a contented sigh, and commenced snoring.

"That little ol' dog has the right idea." Isaac hitched his way toward the front door. "Jessup, help Myrna set her locks and let's get out of here and home to our own beds. I am sure we're all done for the night, que no?"

THIRTEEN

Myrna leaned over the steering wheel. "Unless I've made a wrong turn, we're almost ..." She grinned as her car's headlamps slashed through the darkness and spotlighted the large stones atop the elk grave. "There." She parked and swung open her door. William Tell snuffled in his carrier, watching her with beady eyes shining under the dome light. "I'll get you out in a sec, and don't give me that look. You're as curious as I am about that dead guy."

Talking out loud was more about buoying herself up than anything else. She was alone at close to one thirty in the morning doing something that would get her kicked off the Donavan project and fired from EcoNano if anyone found out. But after all the work William Tell put in peeing on the unsecured shortcut off the ranch so she could memorize landmarks, how could she *not* come back out to the meadow?

Myrna lifted the hatch to her cargo area and flipped a blanket off the half-moon hard case. She popped the latches, and with something close to reverence, unwrapped the short bow and quiver filled with stone-tipped arrows, checking to make sure they'd survived the rough terrain. She hooked William Tell's leash to his harness before she belted and secured her quiver and pouch, canting them along her lower back and hip. She lifted out her bow, expertly strung it, tested its draw, and made a quick adjustment. Clutching the smooth wood, Myrna closed the hatch, the dome light dimming ... dimming ...

Gone.

Once the pitch-black swathed her, she stood quietly, senses adapting, the darkness suffusing her being. She scented the loamy-woodsy essence layered just below the residual odor of the dead elk, acknowledged each insect's voice in the nocturnal chorus rising around her, and shook her curls, allowing the breeze to brush away her civilized constraints. She loved and hated the change that came over her. A shift she permitted only rarely because she was never completely sure she could force it back into the recesses of her ... what? Character? Behavior? Personality?

Such confining words. Her transformation was more primitive.

A coyote—*Canis latrans*—yipped in the distance, his pack joining in, followed by the staccato coos of a Western screech owl —*Megascops kennicotti*—bouncing gently through the dark. As a child, she'd learned the scientific names of animals and plants before she'd learned the common ones. And, to avoid her mother's hard pinches if she made a mistake, she'd learned them fast.

William Tell huffed at her feet, mouth open, head dropped between splayed front paws, drawing in the air of the forest, tasting its smells like a wolf. Myrna stared down at his oddly shaped head, his bat ears and stumpy tail. Dogs and wolves were the same species, no matter how much humans had fractionated their genes, parsed and spliced and chose traits that modified outward appearances and temperaments.

Nor was she all that genetically different from the prehistoric men and women who lived and died during the time of mammoths. And the sharp edge of her untamed self scared the bejesus out of her—sometimes.

Myrna faced the direction William Tell had led her earlier that day—the high cliff up to the tree-studded plateau from which the murdered cowboy had fallen. When the arrow-shaped tops of the pines became defined points against a sky decked in a glitter of stars, she breathed deep. Ready. She was good in the woods at night. She'd had to be. The consequences of getting lost when she was a child could've been deadly.

William Tell sensed her change and lunged to the end of his leash, towing her along behind him. Her soft moccasins left no trace.

She stayed out of the trees to avoid the camera traps, scanning for their telltale blocky structure strapped to trunks. She let William Tell guide her, keying in on landmarks she'd identified during her escape from Jessup a few hours earlier: the deadwood snag of a spruce, the heavy thicket she'd chosen as a potential hiding place, a waist-high, table-sized rock. Her heart rate ticked up. She halted the dog's headlong progress and tugged him to the flattened stone. The top was smooth to the touch, ground and polished by the muddy, gritty bellies of mammoths, giant *Bison latifrons*, and massive ground sloths—*Nothrotheriops shastensis*. The second rubbing rock she'd found meant the area had been a draw for these Pleistocene megafauna—and therefore a draw for predators, including Clovis People. When she found evidence of their presence, she'd use it to convince the Donavans her poisoned stone-point research was worth pursuing.

But tonight wasn't about the Pleistocene poisons project. Tonight was about the murdered man.

Myrna clicked softly to William Tell, and he darted toward the cliffside looming ahead of her. When they arrived at the stone rubbed glossy at a height Myrna could barely touch on tiptoes, she propped her bow within reach and tugged William Tell toward her. She studied the cliff, tracing its edge against the twinkling sky. She couldn't quite tell where the man had fallen from, but scuffs from her boots earlier that day marked where she'd stood—and where Jessup had been. Right where the body had landed.

"It's time." The dog sat on her foot. She rolled up her sweat-shirt sleeves, exposing her skin. The night air raised goosebumps.

Closing her eyes, Myrna bent and wrapped open hands around William Tell's chest. She straightened and shifted him until she'd secured a bare forearm under his belly and tucked him securely against her body. Maximum contact worked best for clear visions. She opened her eyes to begin her countdown.

Three.

The scene in front of her quavered, and Myrna braced. The night bleached brilliant white, then compressed into a painful point of light that shimmered for a single breath.

Two.

A rippling wave coursed through her, breaching the confines of her body, exploding with light. It spread in a mushrooming sphere, shredding away its own dazzling brilliance, accelerating outward, leaving in its place a blurred and darkened landscape.

One.

The temperature plunged. Snowflakes dotted her cheeks and the piney scent tickling her nostrils went winter-sharp. She blinked her vision into focus. William Tell normally brought her to about the same point in time when she needed more information—mostly. Almost fearfully, she dropped her gaze to her feet.

He was there. Myrna's breath left in a rush.

William Tell had missed the fall, but the body couldn't have been on the ground long. No snow dusted his clothes, so either he'd just landed—she gulped—or he was still warm.

The moon glowed an eerie silver from behind the now clouded night sky. Hugging William Tell reflexively, she edged nearer. The obsidian knife, buried in his back to the leather hilt, must've found its way between his ribs. The blood staining his jacket was only slightly darker in color than the heavy fabric. She began a careful walk around him, assessing his clothing for clues of the decade—or even century—of his death. His jacket rode up his back to show a blue shirt. Dark wool trousers, leather chaps. Scuffed boots, simple ball spur on one. No gun belt that she could see. A cowboy from maybe the late 1800s? Which would mean his murder would've occurred nearly 150 years ago.

Gathering her courage, she sidled to the man's head. His cheek pressed against the dirt. Thick black hair shot with silver lapped over his collar. It was parted on one side, a lock falling over a broad forehead. His skin was gray under clouds that seemed to glow above them. She knelt, readjusting the dog, unable to look away. Square-jawed handsome, not young—midforties?—with slashing black brows and a fan of spikey dark lashes resting on his cheek. His nose was bold over parted lips stained wet with frothy blood. The obsidian knife must have punctured a lung.

Myrna inched closer, deep sadness welling up, and studied the lines of his face. Almost involuntarily, she cradled William Tell against her abdomen and extended a hand. Her fingertips touched the man's cheek. She gasped in wonder as a tingle, like tiny bee stings, prickled over—

His eyes popped open. "*Please ...*"

FOURTEEN

Myrna squeaked and fell on her butt. William Tell struggled, but she quickly rewrapped her arms around him. This had *never* happened before. Mouth open, she stared into the man's dark, *living* eyes.

He stared right back. *He could see her.*

"Can't feel my legs." His voice was no more than a rasp of sound. "Think my back's ... broke." More blood bubbled over his lips and started oozing from his nose. He took a wet, sucking breath. "Tell my wife ... tell Elsie. The book's safe. Tell her I hid it where those ... boneheads ... will never find it. She'll know what to do. Tell her I love her forever." His lips twitched into a faint smile. "Even if she started out on the wrong side. And that ... I'm sorry."

Myrna rolled to her knees and sat on her heels, William Tell snuggled across her lap. Cold cedar and leather mixed with the metallic tang of fresh blood. With gentle fingers, Myrna brushed the hank of hair off his forehead. "Who did this to you?"

"They'll come ... to make sure," he said. "Hide, or they'll kill you, too." His bloody lips twisted into a small frown. "*Promise* you'll tell her. She'll worry so."

Myrna nodded. She cupped his cheek. "I promise."

That seemed to comfort him. He sighed out a whispered "Thank you."

The tingle of his skin against hers faded away. He stared at nothing now.

A raw burn built behind her eyes. *Promise you'll tell her.* How could she when the woman—Elsie—was probably already dea—

Cracking branches and rough voices jerked Myrna's head around. Hooves clicked against stones, echoing along the cliff. Tucking the dog under her arm, she bounded to her feet, grabbed her bow, and darted around the back of the rubbing rock. A quick examination showed crude stone steps. Arms aching, William Tell growing heavier by the second, she scrambled up to the top then hunkered down to peer over the edge. She couldn't let the dog go yet—not when she wanted to see the murderers.

One by one, five men on horseback materialized out of the night's fluttering veils of snow, their shoulders heavy in bulky winter coats. Dismounting, they gathered in a silent semicircle around the body, wide-brimmed hats shielding their faces. Horses stamped and snorted, the sound muffled as the snowfall thickened.

A short, stocky man at the group's center spoke first. "Search him."

Two cowboys pulled off their gloves and stepped forward, one prodding the sprawled body with his boot. "He's dead, all right." They fell on the fallen man like vultures, rolling him, yanking at clothing. When they finally stood, one held a sleek silver handgun. When the other man opened his hand, a gold wedding ring winked along with ... a *wristwatch*? Were wristwatches a thing in the 1800s? The round face glowed an eerie green.

"Strip him. Make damn sure he doesn't have it," the first man said. Myrna squinted. The guy wore round wire-rimmed glasses and sported a walrus mustache, but the shadows under his hat obscured the rest of his features.

One cowboy tugged at the dead man's jacket, but it was anchored by the stone knife. He grabbed the leather-wrapped handle and yanked it out. Blood and obsidian shone under eerily illuminated clouds. He turned his head toward a still-mounted man, knife held high. "Some pal you turned out to be. Remind me never to show you *my* back." He tossed it to one side before he pulled a Bowie knife from a sheath at his hip.

He sliced into the jacket, seams spewing cotton batting. He sliced through the thick trousers and woolen long johns. The second man ripped off the shirt, seams tearing, silvery buttons popping in glittering arcs. They handed pieces of clothes to the others, who patted and searched further before discarding them like trash next to the obsidian knife. When they'd finished, the dead man's pale naked body lay in an awkward twist of limbs.

The short man giving orders cursed. Myrna smiled grimly, satisfaction ballooning in her chest at his fury. "He must've cached the journal between the Corazón del Cimarron and the cliff top. It could be anywhere."

A man who'd been silent thus far spoke. "Then we must search more closely over his trail." His voice held a clipped foreign accent.

"In this weather?" One of the cowboys snorted. "Snow's already covered his tracks, our tracks, hell, any traces of the trail. He's led us away from the treasure."

Myrna's jaw dropped. *Treasure?* Oh, *come on.*

William Tell stiffened, ears perking. He twisted and bucked. The panorama before her collapsed and expanded, sound tunneling, men flickering. Myrna clamped him tightly. The scene came back into focus.

"... the cliff. Make sure no one'll ever find him."

The two cowboys who'd stripped the dead man grabbed him by the feet and hands, hefting him off the ground. His head lolled sickeningly. The mounted cowboy who hadn't spoken yet got off his horse and gathered up the clothes. Then, as if an afterthought, bent and picked up the obsidian knife. He wiped it on the discarded clothes, tucked it inside his coat, then jerked and shook his hand. He cursed, yanking off his glove, sucking at the junction between his index finger and thumb, before he turned to yell at the group.

"I cut my hand on that stone knife. Right through my glove."

"Hope you ain't been poisoned, too," someone called back. "Guess we'll find out soon enough."

Myrna blinked. Treasure *and* poison?

William Tell's chest bellowed. He released a growl so vicious it prickled the hair on Myrna's neck. And his attention wasn't fixed on the cowboys, but on the forest behind them. He writhed forcefully, this time squirming out of Myrna's tired arms. The snow and cold disappeared. Moonlight rained down through a clear sky.

No, no, no. She'd miss where they'd stashed the body. Desperate to recapture the vision, she reached for William Tell.

A camera trap flashed. Then another, closer. And another. A large dark animal crashed through the brush, snarling and growling. It tore across the clearing, heading straight for the rubbing rock, Myrna, and William Tell. Pulse thrumming, Myrna snatched up her bow. Up on one knee, arrow nocked, two others held in her hand, she drew.

William Tell bounced on front legs as he barked and growled furiously, the fur on his spine bottle-brushed.

She let out a slow breath, aimed—

William Tell drew in a huge snort of air ... and *roared*. It reverberated and echoed, amplifying off the cliff face. It rippled over her skin, shaking her to the core. Myrna tilted, releasing the tension on her bow string. Arrows clattered to the rock as she braced a hand on the surface. Tiny sharp stones bit into her palm. She curled fingers over a flake, pressing it into her skin.

"What the *fu*—?" A deep male voice echoed back.

The black hurtling shape froze in its tracks. The dog—not a wolf or bear—tucked its tail and whimpered, yellow eyes glued to William Tell.

Briscoe. It was *Briscoe*. That meant—

A man burst from the trees, handgun leveled at her. A second man appeared. He flung away a long black pole with an attached circle and shouldered a shotgun. Myrna shrank back into the shadows, except the moon and stars were so bright, there were no shadows. She was completely exposed.

"Don't shoot. Please." Her voice shook.

The two men approached cautiously, Briscoe slinking on his belly behind them. They raised their faces and moonlight bathed blue Jessup Page's familiar fine eyes and Dillon Bard's hard handsome visage. Disbelief stamped both men's expressions. They lowered their weapons.

William Tell gave a happy yip and frisked along the rubbing stone's edge, some ten feet off the ground. Myrna gritted her teeth. If the little idiot wasn't careful, he was gonna fall.

"Dr. Myrna P. Lee," Jessup drawled. "I thought your dog was afraid of heights. Guess you lied about that, too."

FIFTEEN

Myrna clipped the leash on William Tell's harness and gathered her backpack, bow, and scattered arrows. Bard lit into her as soon as she and the dog climbed down from the rock, his scathing tirade laced with threats and unpleasant promises. Jessup stayed calm, from what she could see of his moonlit expression. But when Bard stepped in close, William Tell suddenly decided he was a guard dog again. He advanced, projecting a deep, resonant noise that filled the space between Myrna and Bard and raised the hairs on her arms. It gave Bard pause long enough for Jessup to pull the big man away. They held a whispered conversation. William Tell sat on her foot, keeping one eye on the men and continuing to grumble at a skulking Briscoe.

Myrna eyed Jessup. She obviously wasn't the only person who'd faked wanting to go home and get to bed, then came back to prowl around in the dark without permission.

When the two men parted, Jessup ambled toward her. This time when William Tell stood, he wiggled and skipped to the end of the leash. Jessup bent to scratch his ears before he straightened and asked, "Why are you out here, Myrna?"

"Bones." She cleared her throat and dropped her voice lower. "Huge bones—potentially *Mammuthus columbi*—in that arroyo over there last evening after we were done taking samples. I have a funded project to study Paleolithic kill sites. Those bones were too extraordinary an opportunity to pass up, so I thought I'd check them out. On my own time. Away from ranch staff looking over my shoulder." A very believable and perfectly innocent cover story that increased her confidence. Eyes narrowed, she darted her gaze from Jessup to Bard and back again. "I didn't expect anyone else out here at this time of night. I mean, what are the odds?"

Face now completely shadowed under the brim of his hat, Bard crossed massive arms over his massive chest, cradling his shotgun. Jessup had holstered his weapon, but it sat dark and lethal on his hip.

The silence stretched between them. An owl hooted again, two short cries, the last one low and long. Leaves crackled near the cliff face. Two beady eyes shone like tiny, polished mirrors before they disappeared. Identification coalesced at the periphery of her mind —pack rat. Probably *Neotoma albigula*.

A curl of fear slithered up her back at her precarious circumstance. It would be too easy for these men to get rid of her, just like the men of the past had with the cowboy they'd murdered. She tightened her hand on her bow and raised her chin. She wouldn't go down without a fight. She was good with the bow. No, she was *great* with her bow. If necessary, she could take Jessup down with an arrow while moving out of Bard's shotgun range. It would be easy enough to disappear into this wilderness. Go to ground, hide, make up a story—

She clamped down on her spiraling paranoia because it was screeching like her mother had invaded her head.

"Dr. Lee? Where's your car?" Jessup's voice, low and resonant, wove sinuously through the velvety darkness. It penetrated her chest and spread an unwelcome warmth. "Myrna?"

Myrna shivered, suddenly *much* less afraid and much *more*—

"By the elk grave."

"Let's go." He fell into step beside her as she navigated the uneven ground. Bard walked behind them. William Tell pulled on his leash, back legs pumping as if he couldn't wait to get to his carrier. He had to be tired after that long vision session.

When her car was in sight, Jessup said, "Can you get back to your house by yourself?" She nodded, unable to hide her relief. "The three of us will talk about this tomorrow morning."

Only he hadn't said where. She decided the lab would be the best place. Her size and appearance gave her very little gravitas, but goggled and gloved and in her element, she might be able to muster a slight edge of intimidation. And it would remind Bard and Jessup that her investigation was very important to their employer.

Of course, they'd never explained why they were out on the ranch in the middle of the night carrying guns and metal detectors. That was what the long rod with the flat circle at one end Bard had tossed when he'd burst into the clearing had been.

She'd bet the Donavans didn't know about their nocturnal wanderings. It was a long shot, but it was the only chip she had to play to save her commission—and her future.

Although Myrna enjoyed nothing more than snuggling into a soft mattress swaddled in fluffy blankets, head tucked into a goose down pillow, she'd never needed much sleep. So it had been easy to close her eyes for a couple of hours and get up before dawn. Her plan was to be inside the lab working when Bard came in to fire her, if he hadn't already. Trying to explain to Eleanor would be a fool's errand. No way could she lose such an important commission and keep her job at EcoNano. Standing under a stinging shower, looking back at what she'd done, at her reckless curiosity about the murdered cowboy and its complete lack of connection to her job on the ranch, Myrna knocked the back of her head against the shower's tiled wall. *Ugh*. Why had she been so stupid?

A still groggy William Tell noticeably perked up when she let him out into the fenced backyard to do his business while she prepped his breakfast with kibbles she'd brought for him. Then she made herself a pot of sustainably sourced coffee, fried up a couple organic eggs from "Happy Pasture-Raised Hens," and toasted a slice of non-GMO cracked wheat sourdough bread. Packed with gourmet and preservative-free comestibles, her cupboards offered truth to the caution the security guard lobbed at her when she'd first arrived. No fast food. No junk food. No preservatives. All that did was make Myrna itch for a burger and fries to dip into a milkshake filled with more calories than anyone should consume in a week. Her stash of chocolate snack cakes gave her comfort.

A yellow-gray shade that prefaced dawn edged the eastern horizon when she snuck out of the house shouldering her back-pack, juggling a Donavan-logoed travel mug and William Tell's leash. The dog raised his head and sniffed the cool early morning air with his smushed black nose. He pranced down the front steps beside her and marked territory all the way to her car.

Myrna studied Jessup's house as she stowed her gear in the back. The *old man* would still be sleeping like a baby after his late night. She bit her lip, stomach curling with warmth. Except he wasn't that old, and he was darn attractive, and his eyes were stunning, and she had a terrible, horrible, no good, appalling weakness for—

She blew out a breath, firmly turned herself away from what she'd marked as Jessup's bedroom window, and pinched her lips.

His truck wasn't in the driveway.

Sixteen

"Your bladder's the size of a frickin' pea." William Tell's pathetic whimpers from inside the dog carrier compelled Myrna to accelerate her car down the dusty predawn streets of ... Did this fake Western staff complex have a name, or was it just called, portentously, *the Compound*? The dog's whines became more strident and demanding, such that when she saw the turn between buildings that led to the laboratory, she cranked the wheel of her car, braced as momentum drove her toward the center console, and smiled at the stomach-swooping recklessness of back-tire squeals. Tom Hutchinson had insisted that all members of his team take a tactical driving course before that dig in Yakutia because the goopy, muddy roads could be tricky to navigate. But the slimy tracks ended up being less of a problem than unfriendly mammoth ivory poachers who pursued outsiders with unabashed murderous glee for invading what they considered their territory.

She parked in front of the lab doors with a flourish, grabbed the leash, and hopped out to open the back. Unlatching William Tell's dog carrier gate, she clipped his leash to his harness and waited the three, two, one seconds it took him to scuttle to the ground. He bolted toward the field, yanking her arm into a straight line as his legs churned under him.

"All right, all right." He dragged her onto the main street, past her satisfyingly obvious skid marks, and past security, windows aglow. Ducking her head, she quickened her steps, but no one burst forth to confront her as she scurried by and into the large field that held her elk carcass experiment. Though the sun had not yet risen over the surrounding mountains, its refracted light ignited the sky in an ombre white-to-gray-blue from east to west that gave shimmering body to the air she breathed.

William Tell raised his face to snuffle every few steps. He'd proven time and time again that he had a preternaturally keen sense of smell, shortish face notwithstanding, mainly because he was better than a vacuum at finding the tiniest crumb of food on the kitchen floor. Right now, he was detecting the sweetish stench of decaying elk.

She, on the other hand, had great eyesight. But it didn't take a hawk to see someone crouched behind the wire cage, fiddling with the access door. Led by a growling William Tell, Myrna broke into a jog, then a run, a careful eye on the uneven terrain, the other on the squatting man. She slowed to scoop up a rock, cocked her arm, and aimed for the guy's forehead, except just as she released it, William Tell yanked hard on the leash. She stumbled forward, arms windmilling, into a jarring, stiff-legged recovery. The rock arched high in the air like a pop fly and fell harmlessly to one side of the cage. The guy didn't even notice.

"Hey," she called. "*Hey!*"

A man unfolded up and up, clutching something. He seemed frozen for the last few yards of her run before he literally shook himself and jerkily thrust his hand into his pocket.

William Tell hurdled a hummock of bunch grass, skidded to a stop, and released a single gruff bark. Myrna finished her run with two jarring steps, halting untidily beside him. The sweetness of decay she'd detected earlier had completely disappeared under the foul odor that draped the cage in an oppressive cloud.

Eyes narrowed, she ran a glance over the man dressed in dusty running shoes, roomy khaki slacks with slightly frayed cuffs, a narrow brown belt, and a Donavan-logoed polo, his name embroidered over the breast pocket. His neck penciled out of the collar to an elongated head with a wide brow and floppy brown hair. Either he was clenching his jaw oddly or he had an underbite that skewed to the right. Bespectacled, he blinked at her with clear hazel eyes, spaced just slightly too wide, giving him a space alien appearance that actually wasn't unattractive. He was likely in his early thirties, clean-shaven skin with a bronzed outdoorsy glow, even if his pocket protector, bristling with markers, mechanical pencils, and what looked like the jewel-toned butts of small screwdrivers, pigeon-holed him as a lives-in-the-lab nerd like her.

"Okay"—Myrna jabbed a finger at the name on his shirt— "*Buzz*. Why the heck are you messing with my elk?"

He gaped at her for a pregnant moment. Then his lower lip began to quiver. A snort turned into a shoulder-shaking giggle. He sucked in a breath. "My God, you looked like some sort of demented Kewpie Doll galloping over the ground. All you needed was a butcher knife." He raised his arm and made short, sharp stabbing motions in the air. He stopped and grinned. "Kidding. But your snack-sized attack pup doesn't help, you know. Not nearly as scary as Bard's vicious wolf-mutt. Does your dog still have his trouble puffs?"

His accent was charming. British, with a slightly exaggerated burring of the R's in "over," "scary," "Bard," and "trouble." A little slurred, though, like that oddly askew jaw interfered with his speech. Completely disarmed, it was her turn to gawp.

"His *what*?"

"Male accoutrements, accessories, paraphernalia. His naughty bits."

"Oh, uh. Yes?"

Maneuvering around the cage while slanting a wary eye at the snack-sized attack pup, the man extended a hand. William Tell followed his movements with a gimlet glare, spine fur-ridged. "You must be Dr. Lee. Another come to try and solve the puzzle."

Myrna hesitated before she took the man's hand. Not soft, but nothing like Jessup's or McJunkin's. Once she let go, the dog did that scratchy thing like a bull in the dirt, then trotted to one corner of the elk cage to lift his leg.

"I'm Harley Wakefield, by the way. Not Buzz. Hilarious nickname the ranch *cowboys*"—he said the word like it tasted slightly sour—"gave me because I'm the drone engineer, although I work with the anything techy on the ranch, actually. Like this setup for your field computer." He waved at the cage before he eyed William Tell, whose leg was still lifted. "I've never seen that much liquid come out of an animal that size. D'you think he'll deflate?"

Myrna frowned, still picking through his flow of words. "Paden said—"

"Yes, Paden. He called me last night for permission to use the cameras, which were secured in my lab—same building as your lab, by the by. We share an internal door. I gave him detailed instructions but noticed this morning he'd made a muck of it somehow. One of the cameras is pointing up instead of down, and it wasn't responding remotely. I came to fix it and lost"—he dug into his trouser pocket and pulled out a two-inch screwdriver with an emerald handle—"this inside the cage. Snagged it back when you and Rin Tin Tin came running to the rescue." William Tell dropped his leg and wandered to the end of his leash, snuffling the ground. "Ah! Finally done, I see. I was just heading to breakfast. Would you join me?"

"I've already eaten," Myrna said. "And what do you mean, *another one come to solve the puzzle*?"

Her words came out more truculent than she wanted because she couldn't for the life of her figure out why he was lying about what he'd dropped in the cage.

Seventeen

D illon Bard burst into the lab. Myrna's gloved hands stilled on the blood samples she'd found slotted in a blue wire rack. The security chief's face was tired and drawn, and no wonder. He and Jessup were out all night, wandering around the ranch ... For what? Somehow that hadn't been made clear.

Still, she knew she was in for it and had shielded herself with a pristine white lab coat, purple nitrile gloves, and stylish wraparound safety glasses. Professional and cool, with leg muscles the consistency of pudding. Outwardly bristling with specialized expertise and proficiency; inwardly, heart pounding hard enough to break a rib. Bard stomped across the lab and stopped way too close, glaring down at her with bloodshot eyes. He was trying to rattle her and doing a darn good job. Myrna suppressed a dry-throated swallow and casually pulled a single tube, pretending to read the handwritten label.

He spoke through clenched teeth. "You were supposed to wait at your house." His anger brought out a hint of a clipped accent.

Compared to Jessup, Bard was huge. As tall as Webb McJunkin but slabbed with muscle. And while his face was creased in fatigue, his khaki shirt and olive cargo pants were crisp and wrinkle-free, and he was carrying a holstered black gun on his hip. Most likely some cliché ex-special forces guy who had a tactical tattoo strategically placed on his body for maximum effect. He dressed and acted the part so rich people trusted he could keep them safe. And he probably could, except…

Except people like Dillon Bard always expected the threat to come from people like Dillon Bard. Not from someone half his size with a doll's face, guileless baby blue eyes, and puffy white-blond curls. Myrna had met his kind before—lots of them—through Tom Hutchinson. Tom used to say these people were tough, competent, and intimidating, but not very imaginative.

She, on the other hand, had a *great* imagination. Myrna breathed deep, steadier now.

"I don't recall any special instructions last night, and I have work to do and only a couple of weeks to complete it. Do you know who collected these blood samples?" Myrna transferred the tubes to a new rack to keep her hands busy. "I'd like to ask them some questions—"

"I don't care about any damn blood samples. I want the *truth* about why you were wondering the ranch last night. *Now.*" His hidden accent was even more prominent now. Eastern European? German? Not Russian.

He loomed over her, which was easy to do, but she'd been loomed over by people scarier than Dillon Bard. Like that stone-cold warlord with the soulless brown eyes who demanded payment for the permafrost frozen woolly rhino in the Magadan Oblast, or the hopped-up meth-head clutching a butcher knife at the dig in northwestern Nebraska who'd thought they were after her stash.

"Besides," he sneered, waving a dismissive hand over the samples, "what makes you think you're still on the project? When you decided to trespass on the ranch last night, you broke the provisions of your contract. One phone call and you're *gone*, Dr. Lee."

Myrna laid her gloved hands flat on the lab bench, hope rising in her breast. He hadn't made that call to get her fired.

Now wasn't that interesting?

"Yet, I'm still here. Why's that, Mr. Bard?" She narrowed her eyes and stepped in closer. Her gaze rolled up from a spot in the center of his chest, counting shirt buttons on its way to his face. "Is it because you and Jessup Page were doing something out there on the ranch, in the middle of the night, away from prying eyes, that you shouldn't have been doing? Something the Donavans don't know about?"

He checked, his expression suddenly wary. *Score.* Her confidence rose.

"What did Jessup tell you last night?" Bard asked.

Myrna picked up the rack of tubes and sashayed over to the glass-doored refrigerator, sliding one side open and placing the samples on the middle shelf.

"Absolutely nothing. And he was already gone when I left this morning." Myrna walked to the lab bench and leaned back against it. She crossed her arms and tipped her head to one side. "What were you doing out there?"

Bard answered too quickly. "We've had reports of trespassers, so we—"

"Decided to search for them, in the dark, carrying a metal detector." Actually, his excuse sounded pretty reasonable, except for the metal detector. "And you left me with Jessup because you had to come back to the compound and erase the camera trap photos of you two before someone saw them and started to ask awkward questions."

Bard's strong features firmed and closed off even more. He stared at her for a long moment.

"What metal detector?"

Myrna rolled her eyes. "The one you left—"

"—at the cliff," Jessup Page said.

Myrna jumped and Bard spun around. Neither had heard Jessup come in the lab.

He ambled toward them, detector tucked under his arm, turquoise-blue eyes pinning Myrna in place. His blond hair was mussed, and his craggy, handsome face was even craggier and handsomer with a treasure of gold and silver stubble across his jaw. She felt a sudden compulsion to lay her palm against his cheek and see if she'd feel the tingle she'd felt last night when she touched the man in her vision. Myrna shoved gloved hands into her pockets. Fingers found the piece of debitage she carried like a worry stone, fist clenching over it to stop from reaching out to him.

William Tell—who'd been sleeping like a baby in the dog cage she'd set up—pressed himself against the side of his wire pen and yipped happily, his whole body waggling in greeting.

"Two, actually." Jessup propped a pair of metal detectors against the bench. "I dropped mine in the forest when Briscoe caught your scent and went off half-cocked. Took me a while to find it. We use them to look for artifacts for the Donavan Ranch museum. Mostly we dig up handmade nails and saddle and bridle metal."

Myrna raised a brow. *Mostly* she'd bet they were after the *treasure* the murderers talked about in William Tell's vision and hunting for it under cover of darkness.

"You know, those are some pretty big bones in the arroyo," Jessup said. "There's a tusk, too, so your little foray onto the ranch last night rings true."

She smirked. Trying to distract her with the mammoth bones. *Amateur.*

"I also found this." From a square pocket of his camo cargo pants, he pulled a folded handkerchief and laid it on the bench top. With careful hands he opened the cloth.

Inside was the dirt-encrusted remains of a six-inch red-agate Clovis point—two inches of the tip snapped off.

Eighteen

Myrna stared at it until her eyes burned, mind spinning dizzily. "The tip could still be lodged in a bone," she whispered.

"Is that important?" Jessup asked.

Her gaze flew to his. "Oh, *yes*," she breathed. "*Exactly* what I'm searching for. It could revive my whole career. Restore my scientific reputation. Things I want more than ..."

Jessup's brows raised high. Bard's expression couldn't have been smugger.

Her excitement hit the floor with a splat. Why couldn't she keep her big fat mouth shut?

"More than what, Dr. Lee?" Bard leaned his elbows on the countertop, relaxed now.

Myrna straightened to her full, completely unimpressive height and curled her lip in what she hoped was a menacing snarl. No way to recover the ground she'd just lost except to charge straight in. She'd seen William Tell do that plenty of times.

"Cards on the table, boys? *You* don't report that I was on the ranch last night, and *I* won't tattle about your metal detectors and extracurricular activities to the Donavans. You know, I have a scheduled appointment to talk to Mrs. Donavan in a couple of days ..." She trailed off threateningly and swaggered to the counter, pressing open hands on the cool surface and pinning them with her meanest sneer. "That way, we all keep our jobs, capisce?"

Bard blinked, his face slowly turning red. His first snicker shook his shoulders. He dropped his head, torso bobbing with chuckles. Jessup's fingers rubbed his mouth, but she could tell he was laughing, too. *Laughing*.

Dang it. She hated not being taken seriously, but sometimes that was the only direction left to go.

Quickly shifting strategy, Myrna lifted widened, helpless eyes. "Let me finish my investigation into the elk deaths, and in my spare time, let me check out the mammoth site for my own research. Come on, guys. *Please?*"

Jessup's smile dropped. He studied her, then clapped his hand on Bard's back. The men retreated and spoke in undertones she strained to hear. Heads nodded, and they turned back to Myrna, decision obviously made.

She drew in a nervous breath, stomach swarming with bumblebees.

"You can stay, but you'll forget you saw us last night," Bard ordered. "And Jessup here is going to stick to your side whenever you travel the ranch. You will drive in with him in the morning, you will go home when he leaves work. Where you go, he goes." He paused and narrowed his eyes. "Capisce?"

Wow. So much scarier when Bard said it. He had the intimidation factor *down*. Maybe once they got to know each other, she'd ask for a few pointers. Myrna pushed back.

"Jessup has his own job. What if he's busy when I'm done with my lab work and I want to—"

"Then you wait." Bard set his jaw. "We're done here." He pivoted gracefully for such a big man and headed toward the door. Myrna willed him to trip and fall on his face. "Coming, Jessup?"

"Gotta talk to Dr. Lee about heading back out to the die-off site today."

"For my official dead elk investigation," Myrna called after Bard. "I'll need to study the meadow for the next few days. Officially."

"*Officially*, I want that elk carcass you dragged back here buried soon. It's stinking up the whole compound," Bard said as he yanked open the heavy door.

"Just a little while longer!" Myrna said. The door closed behind him. "Or maybe I'll need the rotting carcass to stay there forever."

Jessup's laughter wasn't silent this time. It was deep and rich. "Don't push him. He holds quite a bit of power around here and doesn't have much of a sense of humor."

"No kidding."

Jessup walked over to William Tell's pen and leaned in to scratch his head. The dog snorted a blissful sigh.

Myrna eyed Jessup. "So you're going to be my babysitter?"

"Bard wasn't lying about people on the ranch illegally, doing we don't know what."

She turned away, hiding surprise at his statement. When Bard told her about intruders on the ranch, Jessup wasn't present. Had they played her? Planned their strategy before Bard bulldozed into the lab?

She dismissed that thought. Bard had probably told Jessup during their whispered conversation. Slipping open the cooler's doors, Myrna pulled out the blood samples.

"Do you know who collected these?"

"I did, soon as we found the carcasses. Those elk hadn't even gone stiff when I sent Paden back here to get those tubes. We use them to draw blood for sick livestock. Hope they help."

"I'll process and run them though the mass spec today. I just wish I had some controls." She looked up. "These intruders. That's why the camera traps flash white light instead of infrared. It's a warning."

"Yep, but it hasn't stopped them so far."

It was quite possible Jessup was lying. But living wild as a kid for as long as she had had opened her eyes to all the illicit activity that went on in the wilderness.

"Do you think these people are dangerous?"

He hesitated. "I don't know. But if they are, it's a good reason not to be exploring the ranch after dark."

"You and Bard were out at night," she countered.

"We carry weapons." *And we're big scary men* was left unsaid.

Jessup squatted down and rubbed William Tell's tummy. The little dog was a tan puddle with protruding black legs.

"I had a weapon," she said.

Another laugh. Myrna shivered as the sound slid over her skin.

"A short bow and a few crude arrows. That's not going to scare anyone, and neither are you." It was said kindly. And dismissively.

She raised her chin. "It might catch people off guard."

He stood, studying her. The dog puddle breathed in a gusty breath but otherwise remained boneless.

"Are you any good with that bow?" Then his eyebrows shot up his forehead and he glanced down. "William Tell," he murmured.

"I could have named him Robin Hood or Hawkeye," she said. "Or Katniss Everdeen."

He furrowed his brow at the third name. She didn't imagine he would be familiar with that last reference.

"We guide bow hunts in the fall on the ranch, so we have butts set up for practice. I'd like to see you shoot, Myrna."

Pleasure glided through her at his use of her name. She stomped on it. She had no time for handsome cowboys who twisted her insides into tight, hot ...

"And I'd like to have a few evenings at the mammoth arroyo. You take me out there after work—after all, it's on the back road to our houses in Cimarron—and I'll put on a dazzling archery display and shoot an apple out of Bard's mouth. Jessup, please. I really, *really* need to explore that site."

He smiled, but it faded quickly, and his expression became troubled. He stepped closer.

"Funny thing, Myrna. Both times I chased and found you, you weren't at that arroyo with the bones. You were by that rubbing rock. I keep asking myself, why?"

The tight, hot knot in her stomach chilled.

Jessup dipped his hand into another pocket. When he pulled it out, he scattered four tarnished silver buttons on the countertop.

Myrna stared, astonishment making her mute. They were *his*. The dead cowboy's. They had to be. Because when the murderers had stripped him, they'd torn open his shirt and glittering buttons had flown in all directions.

"Metal detectors aren't just for coins," he said. "Do you know anything about those?"

She shook her head vehemently and squeaked, "Uh-uh. No. Absolutely nothing at all."

Nineteen

"Myrna?"

Myrna locked her panicky gaze on Harley Wakefield. He stood at a closed door that connected to what she assumed was his lab. In a quick nonchalant motion, knuckles white, she covered the buttons with a lab book.

"Ready for coffee?" Harley studiously avoided looking at Jessup.

Metal scraped the floor like nails on a chalkboard. She cringed and glanced over her shoulder at William Tell. He'd pushed two hinged panels of his cage out and sat in the V peering through the wire. Jessup had stiffened at the sound of Harley's voice but didn't turn around. The already high level of tension in the room doubled.

Harley cleared his throat. "You said nine o'clock."

She hadn't, but he was offering a perfect opportunity to escape and get her story straight.

Harley hesitated before he stepped toward Jessup, his hands bunched deep into his trouser pockets. He nodded, face a bland mask. "Page."

The silence between the two men lasted an uncomfortably long time.

"How ya doin', Mr. Wakefield?" He pushed back the brim of his cap and quirked his lips. He swung around and extended a hand. "Haven't seen you in an age."

"Busy. Hunting season starts— Ah. You know that, of course." Harley gripped Jessup's outstretched hand but disengaged quickly.

Myrna shucked her lab coat and laid it over the back of an ergonomic lab chair, hurried around the bench, and bolted toward the front door.

"We'll talk later, Jessup," she chirped. "I'm sure you have work to—"

"The little dog, Dr. Lee. You gonna leave him?"

Myrna stopped in her tracks. *So close.* She pivoted on her heel to get William Tell.

"You can't bring him into the café," Harley said. "Maybe tie him on the porch?"

Yeah, no. Who knew what kind of mischief he'd get into? She opened her mouth to tell Harley she couldn't go, when Jessup stepped in so close she caught his scent—the tang of sweat, leather, something spicy. Her body heated.

Dang it. She was in *so* much trouble. Myrna raised her eyes to his.

His expression was blandly pleasant, but she could tell. He was laughing at her. *Again.* That smothered the fire his scent had kindled. Almost.

"I'll take him for a walk," Jessup said. "Paden wanted to meet me by your elk experiment, anyway. He found fresh bear scat at the far edge of the field."

"Yes. I saw that this morning," Harley said.

Jessup's brows rose. "You were out by the carcass?"

"It's where we met," Myrna said. "Look, Jessup, don't—"

"Pick up the dog? No. Cross my heart." And he swept a finger over his dusty shirt.

Chewing her lip, she gave him a tentative nod. "Thanks. He likes you, you know."

Jessup's tired face softened. "I like him, too."

She gulped, pivoted on her heel, and barreled past Harley.

"Thirty minutes, Myrna," Jessup called, his voice a warning.

She hit the double doors, scurried outside into bright sunshine that struck her like a shovel, and headed into the alley connected to the compound's main street.

"Myrna!" Harley called. "Café's this way."

Without breaking stride, she changed course. Harley waited until she walked beside him, one step for every two of hers.

"Why can't Page pick up your dog?"

"Contact dermatitis. William Tell has very sensitive skin."

"Ah." For a moment, his brows pinched in confusion. Then he shrugged and touched her elbow, directing her toward an adobe building. Multipaned windows flanked weathered wooden doors fitted with old-fashioned iron handles. Skipping up two steps to the covered boardwalk, Harley gallantly ushered her inside.

"The Donavan Ranch café and dining hall. Check your weapons with the proprietor. Just kidding."

Myrna stepped over the threshold and into the past. The long narrow room could have doubled for a saloon in any self-respecting Hollywood Western. A beautifully polished bar with brass fittings ran along one side. Behind it, an elaborately framed mirror hid behind a wall of glassware. Scattered over the spur-scarred plank floor were eight wooden poker tables, each encircled by six heavy chairs. Glassy-eyed elk and deer heads hung on burnished wood walls. Swinging saloon doors divided off an opening to what must have been the kitchen based on the scent of bacon wafting into the room. The only things that weren't true to the era were the little chromed racks of homemade jams in the middle of the tables, and that the usual painting of a plump, reclined, and scantily draped lady had been replaced with a Bierstadt—one of his Yosemite Valley paintings. Knowing the Donavans, it was probably real.

Harley pulled out Myrna's chair and they sat.

A young man dressed in jeans, boots, and a blue plaid shirt, white apron wrapped around his hips, emerged from the swinging doors carrying a tray with an antique silver coffee service. He poured the coffee into thick-walled glossy brown mugs before he set plates and silverware before them.

"Uncle Isaac told me to tell you there's hash brown casserole and assorted pastries," he said before he disappeared back into the kitchen.

"Uncle Isaac?" Myrna sipped her coffee.

"Something you come to realize rather quickly on the ranch. Not only have the Donavans been on this land for generations, but so have many of their employees' families. I believe Isaac is the eldest of his clan still alive and working here, whilst that young man"—Harley nodded toward the kitchen—"is the youngest. Hispanos, you know. Some even have homesteads within the Donavan acreage, although that has been a teensy bit problematic recently." His focus shifted behind her, and his face brightened. "Ah, breakfast."

The young man deftly placed plates of casserole and pastries on the table, topped off their coffees, and faded away. Harley helped himself to an eye-popping pile of food and dug in.

"Hispanos?" Myrna said.

"New Mexicans who trace their lineage back to the Spanish conquistadors and imperial land grants. Ancestors here as early as the sixteenth century. Both Paden and, uh, Jessup Page's families are included in the mix." Harley waggled a finger at her. "And don't be fooled by their appearance. Northeastern New Mexico is filled with enclaves of blond, red-headed, blue-eyed, fair-skinned, freckled Hispanos. Of course, Dillon Bard is not one of them. Although his family has long been in the area, it's associated with the Maxwell-Beaubien land grant. His direct line is more recently descended from Germany."

"Did I hear Germany?" The swinging doors to the kitchen clacked rhythmically back and forth behind Isaac Marín. Wrapped in a white bib apron over a chambray long-sleeved shirt and black canvas trousers, he limped to the table and held out a gnarled hand to Myrna. "I was stationed in Germany after the war. Mind if I sit?" He pulled out a chair and braced his hands on the table as he slowly lowered himself down. "Not World War II, o' course. Not that old. Korea. Army sent me to Paris for my chef training. For a kid who'd never been outside the state, *that* was a trip."

Brows knit, Harley swallowed a bite of pastry. "I thought you were stationed in Korea—"

"You ever been to Europe, Myrna?" Isaac pushed the plate of pastries toward her.

"For scientific meetings, but I've mostly traveled ... east."

"Try that cherry one. Fruit's grown right here on the ranch. Far East Russia, Siberia and around there, right?"

Myrna's bite of pastry turned to dust in her mouth. After Tom Hutchinson's ... disgrace, the agency he'd worked for had literally scrubbed his research from the internet. Since she'd been closely associated with him, that included most of her work, too.

"With my earlier research group," she replied. They obviously didn't have the whole truth, otherwise she wouldn't be here. "How did you find ...?"

"The Donavans have deep backgrounds on all the people they hire—even contractors," Isaac said.

"Leverage, they like to call it. And they've been known to use it." Harley helped himself to a third pastry. "Isaac, here, is on the board of directors of the Donavan Ranch Initiative—their nonprofit. So was his eldest brother, who saved old Charley Donavan's skin once or twice. The Donavans aren't the only ones who use leverage to get ahead."

There was a sneer in his voice. Myrna took another bite of pastry, darting a glance from Harley to Isaac.

"You'd know all about that, wouldn't you, Buzz?" Isaac said.

Harley's face flushed.

"My brother was great friends with Charles Tres Donavan's granddaddy, Charley Primero. They fought together during the Second World War. Sent a bunch of men from the ranch over there together. Same in the Great War." Isaac propped his elbows on the table, hands clasped. "A lot of us go way back on this ranch. *Way* back."

"Siberia? Aren't you a poisons expert?" Harley asked her. "What had the Russians done that they needed you?"

"Nothing," Myrna said too quickly, voice too high. She deliberately slowed her speech, dropping her pitch. "I was working with a paleontology team interested in Pleistocene megafauna— mammoths, woolly rhinos, steppe bison. I did sample analysis on both the animals and plants they found." Not a complete lie.

"Aren't some of those groups trying to grow frozen cells of extinct animals for cloning?" Harley asked. "Did you do that?"

"Hardly." Best to cut off that line of questioning since that research had pretty much ruined her career and reputation, as well as led to Tom's ... demise. Speaking of deaths, maybe Isaac knew something about her cowboy at the cliff. "Isaac? Your family has been on the ranch for a long time, so I imagine you know the area's history."

"My people first came on Don Juan de Oñate's expedition in 1598. It was hard, que no? Traveling to a new world. Knowing you'll never again see those you left behind but craving a better life." Isaac shook his head, expression sorrowful. "We didn't know how to live off this land and so many perished. Indian attacks, starvation, sickness. But the strongest survived and adapted. Grew deep roots. We came here for gold, but we soon learned that nuestro oro—our gold—was in la tierra—the land."

"Is that why you called this place tesoro del oro ranchero?" she asked.

"Nah." Isaac leaned back, hands rubbing his thighs. "I called it that because of the treasure buried somewhere on the Donavan Ranch."

Goosebumps swept Myrna's arms. "Treasure?"

"Oh my God, not that again." Harley's eye roll was almost as good as any teenage girl's. "According to legend, a bell of pure gold cast by Spanish padres was lost after the Native population attacked them. A perfectly reasonable response, in my opinion, because your people stole their land and chopped off their limbs for minor offenses."

"Buzz, you are surely an Imperial British ass. The treasure I'm talking about is worth a million times more than the gold in that old bell." Isaac laced his fingers over his chest, grim-faced and solemn. "And in their quest to find it, men have done some truly horrible things."

TWENTY

Myrna's skin prickled. Like a cowboy stabbed in the back and pushed off a cliff? Isaac could be just the resource she needed to unravel that mystery.

Isaac's nephew appeared. "Tio? Dame Sylvia is on the phone."

Isaac grimaced. He grabbed a cloth napkin and wrapped up a couple of pastries. "Take these to Jessup, Dr. Lee. It'll sweeten that boy up. Better yet, let ol' Buzz here hand 'em over since he's so good at pissin' everyone off." He pushed himself up and hitched back through the swinging doors, his nephew a step behind.

"Let's get out of here before Isaac Mentira comes back and tries to sell you Royal Albert Hall," Harley muttered.

Myrna grabbed the pastry bundle, gaze lingering on the kitchen doors. A little more information might lead her to the dead cowboy's identity. But then what? Not like she could really do anything with it. Not that there would be anyone left to contact unless it was some great-great-great relative. Would they even want to know what happened? Would they care?

She nibbled her lip. She could just as easily have died when she lived wild. Lost, never to be found again. *Would anyone have cared?* A knot formed in her chest because she knew the answer.

No one.

Myrna firmed her jaw. Well, this poor cowboy wouldn't be an unsolved mystery. She'd made him that promise.

Harley thumped down the boardwalk toward the lab. This time he didn't measure his steps against hers and she had to trot to keep up.

"I thought his name was Isaac Marín," Myrna said. "You called him Isaac *Mentira*."

"Mentira means *liar*. Another nickname from the ranch cowboys, this one well-deserved. The man's notorious for exaggeration, if not outright fabrication. That's the first time since I've worked on the ranch I've even heard about this elusive treasure. I don't believe for one moment he was *ever* stationed in France or Germany or Korea." Harley stuck out his crooked chin. "And he's *mean* to me."

Myrna's heart just about melted on the spot. She'd endured bullying, too, in that stupid prep school she'd been shunted off to after she'd been rescued.

The theme song to *The Good, the Bad, and the Ugly* emanated from Harley's trousers. He heaved a long-suffering sigh, stopped, tugged out the phone, and held it to his ear. "Yes? All right." He disconnected. "Dillon Bard. I am wanted at the elk carcass to help Paden with the misbehaving camera. He said to tell you to get back to the lab and get to work on your samples. Cameras everywhere, Myrna. Cameras everywhere."

Myrna frowned. "In my lab, too?"

He shrugged.

"Harley? You said earlier that others had been brought in to solve the die-offs. Do you know what they found?"

"You weren't given their— Ah. Of course not," he said under his breath. "Obviously no one has come up with the correct cause for the deaths, thus far. You've already done more than any of the others with your recorded observation of the elk carcass. I ... *we* are all counting on you to solve this puzzle."

"Why? Are people laying down bets or something?"

Harley's gaze snapped to hers, eyes bugging out behind his glasses.

"*Of course not.* That would be—" He cleared his throat. "Ah, Myrna? If you'd like to do coffee again or ... or a meal, I'd love to hear about your preliminary data. My lab is literally right next door to yours. You can't just come in, though. I have some very delicate projects and equipment, and ... erm, let me give you my phone number. We can text."

Juggling pastries, they exchanged information. Harley hesitated after they were done.

"Look, I know you might not want to hear this, but be careful of Jessup Page. In fact, be careful around all the cowboys in that clique. They and their families may have worked at the Donavan Ranch for generations, but their loyalties lie ... elsewhere."

"I'm only here for two weeks."

"I know, just be careful." He looked like he wanted to say more but, instead, spun and hurried away.

Myrna keyed in the code for the lab and stepped inside. She closed her eyes and inhaled the faint stink of organic solvents tinged with a whiff of plastic, allowing it to wipe away the perfume of wildflowers and the fresh scent of pines. Who needed birdsong or wind shirring through the trees when there was the underlying buzz of refrigerators and -80°C freezers? She wended her way through benches, snagged her discarded lab coat, and shrugged it on.

"Jessup?"

William Tell wasn't in his doggy cage. Instead, he was sprawled on his belly underneath Jessup's blue jean-clad legs. Her minder was tipped back in a desk chair, boots crossed at the ankle and propped on a desk that held an empty coffee mug and a curled leash and harness. Jessup's chin rested on his chest, his arms folded, fast asleep.

Sleep didn't take years off Jessup's face. If anything, the lines and wrinkles were more pronounced, craggier and rougher. His lashes, blond and thick, rested like wings on cheeks tanned golden from the sun. A man who'd lived his life outdoors, content with who he was. Confident, kind, genuine. Longing rose inside her.

This man is perfect for me.

She froze. Where the hell had *that* come from?

Shaken, Myrna dropped the pastry packet on the desk and spun away from the sleeping man and dog. She marched to the high-pressure liquid chromatography–tandem mass spectrometer and opened the cover that protected the columns. She was being paid to solve the mystery of the elk deaths, and by God, that was what she was going to do. She had no time for handsome cowboys, either living or dead.

With quick efficiency, she made her adjustments, mixed her solvent and wash buffers, and started extracting the collected blood and tissues.

Two hours later, samples running through the analyzer, Myrna sat in front of the laptop she'd been assigned during her commission. She launched the recordings of the elk carcass decomposition and found the exact moment the camera glitched.

Myrna leaned in closer, face scrunched. She rewound and ran it again. And again. She caught her breath.

"What do you see, Dr. Lee?"

Jessup's rich baritone, rough with sleep, rippled through her.

"A tremor in the video, like something bumped it. See? The video flickers and the camera rotates to the sky." She rewound again. "Harley and Paden are out there now trying to fix it, but it's taking them forever."

"Why'd you pick this elk to watch?" He bit into one of the pastries she'd brought back from breakfast.

Myrna leveled a finger at him. "No eating in the lab."

His cheeks flagged red, and he dropped his hand. "Sorry. I didn't know."

Tan and black flashed, and William Tell dolphined to snag what was left of the cherry Danish from Jessup's fingers. He disappeared at a scrabbling run.

"Catch him!" Myrna screeched. She leaped from the lab stool and dashed after the dog. "If he eats anything other than his special food, it upsets his tummy."

But by the time she and Jessup got to William Tell, he was snuffling crumbs.

"Aw, *don't lick the floor*." Myrna stomped up to the dog, leaned down, and made sure to close her eyes as she lifted William Tell into his cage. When she straightened, Jessup stared at her.

"Why do you do that?" he said.

Myrna's throat choked. He was asking about her closed eyes, but she chose to misinterpret his question. "Caging him while I work is for his own safety. Otherwise, he gets into all sorts of mischief. Now. Why did I choose this elk for observation?" She brushed past him and beelined to her computer.

"Yesterday, at the die-off site, I noticed a patch on this elk that was devoid of insects. I saw the same type of spot on the ground underneath the elk by the rubbing rock." She queued up a short video she'd taken at the die-off and transferred to the computer. "See? These sterile patches could be evidence of where the elk were shot—"

"They weren't shot," he said flatly.

"Not by a bullet, but by some type of dart or pellet. Something that barely made a mark but might have delivered a poison."

Jessup shook his head. "These animals are wild and savvy. I told you, even if someone got close enough to pop something into one of them, that would've spooked the others."

"I haven't quite figured out delivery yet. That's why I wanted visual evidence, which I'm obviously not getting because of the stupid camera. This sterile patch could be where the poison is concentrated. And if it can drop an elk, it could easily kill insects, so they avoid it."

"But if poison killed those elk, it must have spread throughout their bodies. Why don't all these flies and larvae drop dead once they start feeding?"

"Excellent question. Flying insects could buzz off and die in midair. But the larvae obviously aren't dying." She rubbed fingers over her lips, thinking out loud. "Why? Without dilution from the circulatory system, movement of the toxin would be by diffusion. A gradient effect? Insects could be susceptible to the toxin at higher concentrations, but not lower? Cellular metabolism has stopped, and decomposition is advancing apace." Her hand dove into her pocket to worry the stone fragment. "Is the poison degrading by inactivation to something more benign?"

"Camera's back up," Jessup said. "Would you look at that?"

The video on the screen focused on the rotting elk, split skin revealing black putrefied tissue covered with a creamy rippling carpet of blowfly larvae.

And in the center of this disintegration, a ragged circle of fur—maybe four inches in diameter—stood pristine. Myrna smiled in relief.

"Now that the camera's working, I want a few hours of this recording as evidence. After we get back this afternoon from the die-off site, I'll harvest that patch."

Since she was 99 percent sure analysis of this elk would solve the mystery of their deaths, she'd be the hero. The Donavans would be so appreciative, they'd let her excavate the mammoth and analyze their stone projectile point collection. With a little luck, she'd find her poison and revive her flagging career.

Myrna tapped the screen, her reflected expression smug.

Piece of cake.

Twenty-One

Myrna stared longingly at the cliff half a mile away from the field where the elk had fallen. Her mammoth was there, and the stone points and tools used to kill and butcher it, some possibly covered in residual Paleolithic poison. Would Jessup give her time to explore after she finished gathering samples?

She shrugged disposable coveralls over her shoulders then rummaged through her toolkit, dropping cryotubes, markers, scalpels, tweezers, scissors, extra gloves, a trowel, thin metal spatulas, tape, and fluorescent sticky dots into her pockets. Since her disposable face shield was way too gore-splattered from yesterday's harvest, she instead slipped on goggles, a surgical mask, and the hood of her suit over her hair, pulling it tight with a drawstring.

Jessup leaned against the truck, long gun tucked under one arm. He'd showered and changed into soft faded jeans, his belt sporting a large, engraved silver buckle. His long-sleeved Donavan-logoed shirt hugged his leanly muscled chest and shoulders.

Harnessed, leashed, and alert, William Tell sat at Jessup's feet, bat ears twitching.

Myrna held out a blue paper surgical mask, but Jessup shook

his head and pulled a neck gaiter over his mouth and nose. She stilled, chest suddenly tight. He looked just like the outlaws who'd killed the cowboy at the cliff. She pivoted and marched into a buzzing insect cloud hovering over staked ground. Agitated flies pelted her suit with hard pops.

"How many die-offs has the ranch had?" Myrna scooped up soil soaked with decomposing elk juice and wriggling with insects, depositing everything in a tube.

"In the last few years, a dozen or so. At first, we thought maybe we were seeing an increase in illegal hunts. This ranch holds some pretty incredible trophy elk and deer. But it's easy enough to tell if the animal's been poached because of the wounds. We can use metal detectors to find the bullet. If a bow's used, most of the arrows go through. Not like those stone-tipped arrows you carry."

She sniffed as she labeled her tube. "My arrows cause just as much damage."

"Sure, Dr. Lee."

Her lips compressed at his mocking tone. "What kind of die-offs can you explain?"

"Lightning strikes, disease, infection, parasites, avalanches and slides, age, even natural poisoning. Algae in stock tanks killed about a hundred elk on a nearby ranch a few years back."

"*Anabaena flos-aquae*. Its toxin depolarizes and blocks acetyl-choline receptors, which leads to respiratory arrest in a very short period of time," Myrna said. "Are there tanks or troughs in this area? I'll need samples to rule it out."

"A couple of seeps along the cliff face, and we get run-off from the mesa top during monsoon season." He waved away a large and persistent black fly. William Tell wandered behind him, sniffing the ground, casually-on-purpose wrapping the leash around Jessup's legs. Myrna gave the dog a baleful look.

"The other die-offs. The ones you can't explain. Tell me about them." Myrna tromped to the next site, digging in her pocket for a fresh tube.

"Most were single animals—deer, bear, elk. Even had a cougar a while back. Didn't think much of them. Animals die. But a few years ago, we noticed groups of two or three elk—bulls only—dropping dead in their prime, and that the deaths skewed into the late-summer months before the rut." He untangled himself from the leash. William Tell started his slow revolution again.

Bulls only, huh? Right before mating season ... She squatted down and scraped dirt and bugs into her tube.

"If these die-offs have been going on for years, why do the Donavans suddenly care about them?"

"We figured it had to do with Charles Tres Donavan deciding he might run for president. We think he'd like to get this mystery solved so it can't be used to drum up bad publicity," Jessup said.

The same thing Eleanor had told her. Myrna labeled and pocketed the sample. "Harley said I was *another one* hired to solve the puzzle. How many others?"

Jessup's lips twisted. "Harley Wakefield. Worthless piece of— He's just as poisonous as whatever killed these elk."

"Why? Because he's an outsider? Because he's not part of your group and never will be?"

She'd been an outsider. The one the snobby girls at prep school never accepted, never invited to join in their study groups or come to their rooms to gossip and laugh and watch movies. But she'd showed them. She'd become the best at everything she did, worked the hardest, got the highest grades, bullseyes at every competition, graduated summa cum laude, finished her PhD, traveled all over the world as part of very important paleozoological digs, and published dozens of research articles.

Then, when she'd finally opened up enough to love someone, Tom Hutchinson proved it was all a lie by stepping off that cliff and shattering her heart.

He'd left her alone to pick up the pieces of her life. Just like her mother.

"Harley told me how he's bullied by some of the other cowboys," Myrna said. "Does that include you?"

William Tell stopped his meandering to stare at her.

"Sore subject, Dr. Lee? You won't want this advice, but it's best to stay away from Wakefield."

"He said the same thing about you."

"Doesn't surprise me. Why do you want to know about the other labs the Donavans hired? Didn't you get their reports?"

"Nope." She waded through the tall grass toward the pickup. "I don't know who they hired or any of their results. And the lab instruments and computers have been wiped clean of any past data." Which she found odd, like someone was trying to severely handicap her investigation.

"That a problem?"

"Not for me. I expect to have this commission solved *way* before my two weeks are up."

William Tell, in a last underhanded attempt to trip up Jessup, darted between his legs, bounding toward a butterfly. Jessup adroitly stepped over the leash and Myrna threw the dog a taunting smile. She opened the cooler and lodged her sample tubes between dry ice chunks. William Tell ambled closer to her, sniffing at her disposable suit-covered boots.

Jessup pulled his gaiter off his face. "It took experts months to solve the algae deaths of those elk. What makes you different?"

Myrna propped her hands on her hips and raised her chin. "Because I'm the best."

William Tell lifted his leg and peed on her foot.

Twenty-Two

Myrna sat on the open tailgate while Jessup stowed the cooler with her samples in the truck bed. She'd stripped out of her blood-and-urine-stained disposable suit and shrugged on a sweatshirt against a rising breeze that stirred the pine boughs and teased her curls. William Tell was in the back seat, gnawing on an old bone, all windows down.

"Um, Jessup? Could we please visit the mammoth before we head back to the lab?" She gave him the same wistful look William Tell gave her every time she grilled hamburgers. "I won't take long —maybe thirty minutes to poke around?"

He propped his hands on his hips. "Dr. Lee, I bet you had your daddy wrapped around your little finger."

She probably would've, if he hadn't been some one-night stand her mom picked up from across a craps table in Reno.

"So, yes?" She grinned.

"Yes. But it's my turn to ask you some questions."

Myrna's grin dropped. "I don't know anything about those silver buttons. How could I? They're probably over a hundred years old." She avoided eye contact by shifting her butt to the tailgate's edge and extending one leg toward the ground.

Jessup stepped between her knees, captured her waist with strong hands, and swung her down.

Myrna's stomach swooped, but it had nothing to do with the drop and everything to do with the heat emanating from Jessup's body. She tipped her face to his. The turquoise flecks of his irises, spiky lashes, and planes of his beard-peppered cheeks were disconcertingly close. When his eyes fell on her mouth, all thought evaporated like raindrops in a hot iron skillet.

"*Wrapped.*" He lowered his head, warm breath brushing over her parted lips, fingers caressing her back. She gripped his forearms and leaned in, breasts pressed against his chest ...

William Tell yapped high and sharp from the truck's back seat. Jessup's hands dropped, and he stepped back as if he'd been slapped. Myrna grabbed the tailgate, desperate to find *terra firma* under liquid knees.

Jessup stilled, his fists clenched, cheeks red. With a jerky movement, he washed a hand over his face.

"I apologize, Dr. Lee." Myrna shivered at the rough edge in his voice. "If you'd like to file a complaint, I can take you back to the compound." He sidled around her and closed the tailgate, then strode to the passenger side and opened her door.

Myrna followed, castigating herself a dozen different ways. Hadn't she already established she had no time for this man? What she had was a job to do, a reputation to revive, and a prehistoric poison to discover.

But she'd wanted that kiss. A lot.

"No. I, uh ... I don't want to file a complaint. Let's just forget about it."

She clambered into the truck and plunked down in the seat, staring straight ahead. Jessup climbed into the driver's side and turned the ignition. He pointed the truck toward the cliff in the distance. The two-track dirt road continued along the line of trees, bumpy and washed out in places, the cliff looming up in front of them. It wasn't that tall—maybe forty or fifty feet—topped by a thatch of brush and pines. The forest flanking the trail fell away as they drove into the strip of land devoid of trees and vegetation that ran parallel to the cliff face. To the west lay the arroyo and mammoth bones; to the east, the mammoth rub protruded from the rock wall.

Jessup turned toward the mammoth rub and parked. He climbed out of the truck and opened the rear door for William Tell, then used the back tire as a step to access the bed.

William Tell scampered up the little hill to sniff some loose dirt, probably where Jessup had dug up the silver buttons. Jessup followed, a metal detector over his shoulder. He swung the detector into place and began long arcing sweeps over the ground. Discordant whines and beeps echoed off the cliff.

Myrna grabbed her pack from the back seat, climbed out, and slammed the door shut behind her. She shrugged on the pack and clipped the strap across her chest.

"William Tell should be leashed," she said.

"He'll be fine." Jessup continued his sweeps. "Tell me about those rubbing rocks. I need to know."

Myrna stared at him, brows pinched. Why would he *need* to know?

"They're enormous scratching posts Pleistocene megafauna used to remove undercoats and mud. Grit and dirt in their coats ground them smooth over the millennia." She reached upward, fingertips just on the edge of a polished area. "But there's more than just this. Follow me."

Myrna skirted around and climbed the chipped-out steps set into the cliff, William Tell on her heels. Jessup propped the detector against the rock and followed.

On top, she had a view of the trees bordering the cliff and the valley spread out beyond. The dog padded to the rock's edge. Front paws braced wide, he lifted his head to scent the air, king of his domain.

"This was the perfect place for early man—Clovis, Folsom,

Archaic—or more modern Native people to scout for game, watch for enemies, maybe guard an encampment. It's high and up against the cliff."

"So they wouldn't skyline themselves," Jessup said. "A silhouette makes a perfect target."

"It also gave them time to knap." Myrna knelt and brushed away pine needles and leaf debris. "See? Debitage. Flint chips, obsidian, chert flakes. Leftovers from making arrows, scrapers, knives, spear points." She picked up a flake and held it in the sunlight to display sharp edges and the warm translucence of the red-brown stone.

Jessup went down on his haunches beside her and sifted through the scattered chips. "I've seen this a dozen times on top of rocks and bluffs. Even picked up one or two broken arrowheads."

"Knapping isn't easy. It takes years to learn."

"Who did the stone points for your arrows?"

She frowned, peeved. "I did."

Jessup smirked. "Sure."

Myrna held out her hands. "See these scars? Cuts from working stone. Go ahead. Feel."

It wasn't until he took one of her hands in his that Myrna realized maybe this wasn't a good idea, but he said nothing as he ran gentle fingers over the tiny white ridges of skin.

"Doesn't mean you can shoot straight, Dr. Lee." Jessup released her hand and stood to leave. She scrambled to her feet and trailed after him. William Tell hopped down the stone steps and darted to the metal detector, where he lifted a leg—

"No," Jessup said almost casually. The dog swiveled and marked a clump of bunch grass instead. He then scratched the ground like a bull, kicking up arcs of dirt and debris before he looked up at Myrna.

"I can't believe you mind *him* and not me," she grumbled, scowling.

Jessup clicked the detector on, swinging and walking at a

steady pace toward the arroyo. She hurried after him and searched the cliff for more polished stones, but rock falls made it difficult to get a closer look.

They were near the arroyo when the metal detector whined with a hit. Jessup squatted down and dug in the ground with his hand, William Tell bounding over to help.

Myrna extracted a trowel from her backpack. "Use this."

Jessup didn't need to dig very deep before tarnished metal glimmered in the shallow hole. He pried loose a grayish disk and rubbed off clinging dirt before he held it flat in his palm.

"What is it?" Myrna dropped to her knees beside him.

"Silver dollar. Morgan, 1881." His thumb rubbed over a circular depression.

"Has it been ... shot?"

"Yeah. Looks like it might have saved someone's life. Wonder how it ended up here?"

Myrna didn't. She'd bet everything in her backpack that, like those silver buttons, this coin belonged to her murdered cowboy.

TWENTY-THREE

Myrna eyed the tumbled rock falls at the bottom of the cliff. Had the murderers hidden the cowboy's body in a crevice and piled stones over it? At least the coin had solved the approximate date of the murder: 1881, *if* the coin was the dead cowboy's. She could ask Isaac if he knew of any disappearances or stories from around that time.

Yep, she could ask Isaac *or* ...

She shot a furtive glance at her minder. Jessup had resumed his metal detecting by the arroyo's edge, his back to her. William Tell sat on her foot. He rolled his face up to look at her, his black eyes unblinking. She could do this fast. Pick up the dog, get a vision, find the body ...

Except there'd be no wife to contact and repeat his poignant last words to, no one to punish for murder.

His wife, *even if she started out on the wrong side*. What had he meant, *the wrong side*?

Tell Elsie the book's safe. *Tell her I hid it where those boneheads will never find it.*

The outlaws had searched their victim for a journal—the book he'd hidden. One that could lead to the treasure. *He must've cached the journal between the Cabeza de Bacas and the clifftop.*

Still, a quick peek into the past wouldn't hurt. She bent, curled her fingers under William Tell's belly—

Jessup's voice drifted up from the arroyo. "You comin', Dr. Lee?"

Myrna straightened, sweeping her hands behind her back. Besides, finding a human skeleton would only add to an already complicated situation of elk deaths and mammoth kill sites.

The dog bowed in a long stretch, then trotted to an area next to the cliff where the arroyo wall had collapsed to a slide of sand. He disappeared down the slope. Myrna followed him, surfing to the bottom and landing with a little jump. A film of water slicked the cliff face, dried white at the edges, ending in a brackish puddle surrounded by animal tracks, including elk. She made a mental note to take samples. William Tell sniffed the pool before bounding down the arroyo, nose in the air. With anticipation fluttering in her chest, Myrna hurried after him, around a shallow curve ...

And there they were. Bones scattered here and there in the arroyo's wall. A massive femur jutted from the earth, while part of a huge skull protruded farther down.

They were *beautiful*.

She rushed to the skull, reverently touching a cracked, elongated socket that would have held an ivory tusk. Unclipping her pack, she swung it off and dropped it at her feet. Scrabbling inside, she removed a brush and swept away dirt and sand to reveal the Holy Grail of Pleistocene paleontologists. Her head swam dizzily. "*Butchering cuts*. They chopped out the ivory from the dental alveolus."

"I found the broken spear point by that rib," Jessup said. He nodded to William Tell. "Should he be chewing on that?"

"You've heard of cadaver dogs? He's trained to find Pleistocene megafauna burial sites. Mammoth is his favorite." Myrna knelt in the dirt next to the femur, magnifying glass in hand, shivering in delight. Jessup, sans metal detector, stood beside her.

"Look at this. It was shattered peri- or postmortem." She stood and stared at a V of earth at the top of the cliff. "A mammoth jump?"

"Like a buffalo jump? Native hunters herding bison over a cliff —but for mammoths?" Jessup asked.

"Except mature animals were too smart. Unless— Is there more than one set of bones?" With deliberation, Myrna stepped back, gaze searching the arroyo's wall.

She squealed in delight, then clamped her hand over her mouth as if to contain and save her joy. "Oh, my gosh! *A juvenile.* Up there. A smaller rib. And vertebrae!"

But a completely different stratum of earth divided the adult and juvenile mammoths.

Myrna ran down the arroyo until she found a place to scramble out and turned back to dash toward the cliff, stopping above Jessup and the juvenile's rib. Her gaze probed the dirt around her feet. "Bones protruding? This is wrong, so wrong." Jessup passed her the trowel.

She worked without speaking, careful but rapid, exposing bone after bone, articulating them in her head. The air grew colder, and shadows lengthened as Myrna sifted through the distant past, her mind wandering into another time and place. When she finally sat back on her heels, Jessup, by her side again, handed her a water bottle. She drank, lost in the juvenile—no —*infant* mammoth's last moments of life.

"What do you see, Meerkat?" Jessup went down on one knee.

Myrna smiled. She didn't need William Tell for this vision. She could see, even *hear*, what had happened as clearly as if she'd been a witness.

"Two *Mammuthus columbi*—a mother and her newborn calf. They were up there, somewhere on the mesa. A sheltered spot to give birth, a few days to regain strength before she rejoined her herd and introduced her family to her new baby." Her smile faded. "Instead, they were hunted. First People knew mammoths used this place because of the rubbing rocks. One kill, and they'd have food to fill their bellies for months. So they pound hollow log drums, wave pitch torches, and jam more torches into the ground to form a funnel of fire. They drive the mother and her baby toward the cliff."

Myrna closed her eyes. Her day became their night. The scent of pine and loam turned acrid and sharp and mixed with the muskiness of the mammoth's thick, matted hair. She swallowed against the tightness in her throat.

"They back her to the edge. Her calf is bawling in confusion, his cries tearing at her. He's under her, between her legs, his little trunk curling into her fur. He's so afraid. She trumpets, calling for her herd, for help, eyes rolling in fear and fury. She would fight them. Charge, trample. Sweep her great tusks to decapitate, to cut her enemy in two.

"She could have killed them all, saved herself and her infant—but for the poison. From behind a blind, they launch spears, their stone points smeared with poison. Even though they barely penetrate her coat and skin, it's enough. It seeps into her blood, makes her sick. She staggers, woozy. Her foot slips and the ground crumbles. She falls, not afraid for herself, but for her baby, screaming for him." Myrna opened her eyes. "They say that kind of energy fuses with the rocks, becomes embedded in time as deeply as bones or artifacts."

Tears cooled her cheeks, and she clutched Jessup's hand. "But the calf didn't fall. Maybe she pushed him away, tried to save him from her fate. In her desperation, she didn't understand. The First People caught and killed her child up there because there aren't enough bones down here. No skull or scapulae. No humeri, radii, no ulnae."

Jessup stared up at the notch in the cliff. "No skull?"

Myrna released his hand and pushed to her feet. "Over time,

flooding washed away part of the cliff. That's why these bones are down here. But some are practically on the surface, so the washout that cut the arroyo washed these over, too."

The sound of pattering pebbles jerked Myrna's gaze toward the cliff. William Tell dug into a section along the wall, the earth above him cracking and collapsing, showering him with dirt and creating a fissure. The newly opened gap arrowed up to a darkened lip of stone arched like a rainbow.

"*Jessup*. Those black marks are *soot*. This dirt plug could hide a cave! The people who killed these mammoths could've had their camp in there." And it could hold vessels filled with the poison they used and she needed to make a career comeback. Myrna pressed both hands against her mouth. "I need to get into that cave."

Jessup rubbed his jaw, his gaze tracing the arch.

"Yeah. I guess it's possible there's a cave behind all that fill, but there's no guarantee you'll find anything from the mammoth's time. And lots of people have lived and worked this land over the years. Natives, Spanish, trappers, miners, cowpunchers—"

Myrna's jaw tightened in frustration. He was going to say no. But it didn't matter. She'd sneak away from him, pick up and point William Tell in the direction of the cliff face, and get a better picture of what was behind that wall of dirt.

"—losing light fast. We have an hour, tops, to make any headway."

She spun, mouth agape. "We can excavate? Now?"

Jessup's expression gentled, the lines at the corner of his eyes crinkling in a smile. "You're hard to say no to, Meerkat. I've got a shovel and pick in the truck—"

His cell phone rang.

"Paden. What's up?" Jessup's smile melted from his face as he listened. He handed the phone to Myrna. "Bard got orders from the top to bury your elk. We won't make it back in time. Tell Paden what you need."

Myrna's stomach dropped. She'd gotten distracted again, lost sight of what should be her top priority: the elk die-off. She pressed the phone to her ear. "Paden? Why—?"

"No time, Dr. Lee. What do you need me to do?" His words were choppy, breath interfering. The vibration of a heavy engine grew louder.

"Cut out a fist-size chunk of tissue on the elk's hindquarters. The area with no bugs where the fur and skin are still intact. Put it in the freezer in my lab."

"Walk as you talk, Myrna." Jessup released a piercing whistle. William Tell backed out of his hole, his black face powdery with dirt and sand. He frisked at Jessup's feet as they hurried back toward the truck.

"Can you do that, Paden?" Myrna asked. "Just cut around—"

"Hey. *Stop!* Aw, *fu*—" The growl of equipment and strident beeping drowned out Paden's words.

"Paden?" Myrna's feet stuck to the ground. She grabbed Jessup's arm, needing his support.

The phone transmitted the fading rumble of the dozer's engine.

"Sorry, Dr. Lee," Paden said, tone hollow. "Too late."

Twenty-Four

Bard had evaded Myrna last night, but she wouldn't let him get away this morning. She dogged his heels—three skipping steps to each one of his—as he stomped into the field behind the staff compound that had become her elk's graveyard. An enormous earthen mound covered her experiment.

But that wasn't her biggest problem.

Colorful dome tents dotted the field and dozens of assorted Girl Scouts and leaders cooked breakfast over merrily crackling campfires in the early morning light.

"Why didn't you tell me about this? I would've harvested before—"

"I didn't know until their vans arrived yesterday that they'd be staying *here* instead of the meadow by the lodge." Bard scowled over his shoulder, dark circles under bloodshot eyes, a whiff of—alcohol?—on his breath. "I had thirty minutes to get that field ready last night, so get off my back."

Webb McJunkin raised a hand in greeting as he drove a UTV hauling a train of linked flatbed trailers piled with archery target butts. At the far end of the field, ranch hands milled about, including Paden and Isaac. Jessup held William Tell's trailing leash, the dog sitting on his boot, ears perked.

Myrna skipped to Bard's side, determined to stay in his line of sight. "Whatever killed those elk is in the tissue I was watching with the camera."

"Then you should have chopped it out sooner instead of waiting until the only way I could get rid of the *stink* was to bury it under a ten-foot-high pile of dirt."

The cool morning air did have a crisp flowery freshness to it.

"But I needed the digital footage to confirm the lack of insect feeding and weird tissue preservation," she said.

"And I don't care." Bard halted and waved in his crew. He turned his back on Myrna to address the gathered staff. "I want the butts placed fifty feet from the tree line. Paden, after you're done, grab Webb and set up a roping station in the stable yard then prep tack for the trail rides tomorrow. We'll dig the fire pits they'll need for cooking over there. Isaac, you're in charge of that. Use the backhoe if you need it." Bard scowled and side-eyed Myrna. "Jessup. Get rid of that dog. You're supervising geocaching and wildlife forensics. Sanchez, Begay ..."

Myrna scurried to Jessup as Bard continued to bark out orders. "Forensics?"

Jessup held out the leash to Myrna. "Disarticulated animal skeletons buried in a sandpit. Kids dig them up and see if they can reassemble the bones for one of their badges. These little girls may hate hunting and see Bambi in every deer, but ask them to be animal detectives and they light up." He raised an eyebrow. "You're no different with your mammoth bones, Dr. Lee."

The mammoths. "You didn't tell—"

"You can trust me, Myrna." His slow smile warmed her.

"I can still get my tissue from the buried elk, but I need help because there's too much dirt. Bard won't listen to me."

"You could try blackmailing him again."

She gave him her best, wide-eyed pleading look. His smile only deepened.

"Can you talk to him, Jessup?"

"Don't get your hopes up. He's pretty ticked about Miz Donavan's sudden change of plans. Best take the dog back to your lab and work on the samples you have. I'll have Isaac deliver breakfast and coffee."

The sun broke over the building tops, filling a slice of air above them with thick, honeyed light, illuminating the concentric circles of yellow, blue, and red, vivid on the white background of the archery butts.

"Jessup," Bard bellowed. "Where the he—*heck* is Buzz? He's supposed to have the drone station up and running by eight o'clock."

William Tell trotting by her side, Myrna skipped off to her lab, scowling at Bard over her shoulder. She'd get that elk dug out from under all that dirt and get her samples, even if she had to make a deal with the devil.

TWENTY-FIVE

Myrna studied the thin digital trace against the black background of the computer screen. The levels of pesticides and herbicides in the elk tissue weren't a surprise. When wildlife and humans coexisted, exposure was well-documented. The amounts weren't enough to kill the elk by any means.

Samples from all four die-off elk each had a peak which the chemical database identified as testosterone—again, no surprise—but all the testosterone peaks had an odd shoulder bulge that bothered her. Her fingertips flew over the keyboard, zooming one of them larger on the monitor.

She touched the screen, and the electrospray ionization mass spectrometry/mass spectrometry results popped up. Preliminary findings indicated glycosylations—sugar additions—on an oxygenated steroid derivative which was extremely toxic to mammalian cells, except that these derivatives were only found in Pacific marine corals. Why would these elk have this weird hormone in their blood? How did it get there?

Was this what killed them?

She started at Jessup's touch.

"I heard from Isaac you ate a late lunch," he said.

He was very dirty in her nice clean lab, his jeans and shirt streaked with grime.

"You talked to Bard?" Her fingers stretched over the keyboard. "Will he let me excavate my elk?"

"'Fraid not. Miz Donavan is heading out to the camp with some big money donors for her husband's campaign. Rotting elk can't compete with a passel of cute Girl Scouts. Take a break and come outside. They're starting their archery badge."

Myrna shrugged off her lab coat. "Is that why you insisted I bring my bow this morning? You still don't believe I'm any good with it."

"Prove me wrong." He nodded to where William Tell hugged a huge knuckle bone with his front paws, happily gnawing. "Is he okay to stay here?"

"So long as no one picks him up."

Mellow sunshine bathed the deserted streets of the compound, and light, high voices and laughter drifted in a pleasant caressing breeze. A four-legged shadow skulked around the corner. Briscoe. Whenever Myrna and William Tell went out for a walk, he'd be slinking around, giving William Tell mean looks and scent marking over William Tell's territorial pee-mail. The big dog disappeared into the shadows when he realized William Tell's absence.

Jessup and Myrna passed the partially excavated sand pit as they headed for the field.

He nodded at partial skeletons of a deer, badger, and raccoon laid out on a tarp. "Very enthusiastic kids."

In the distance, the mounded earth and an orange caution barrel prominently marked her buried elk. Myrna eyed it then slid her gaze toward the lines of Girl Scouts. "Enthusiastic about animal forensics, huh?"

A row of Scouts stood twenty feet from the butts, arrows nocked in pink-camo compound bows or gleaming wooden recurve traditionals. They let fly and most hit within the circular target, a few even landing in the middle yellow circle. Girls cheered and bounced on their toes in excitement as a second group stepped into place. Guided by leaders and ranch staff, they nocked arrows and aimed.

Jessup led Myrna to tables set up under a huge cottonwood. Webb sat in a chair, adjusting the draw weight on a bow for one of the scouts, while Paden gave lessons to a girl whose arm shook as she pulled back the bowstring. Near the northernmost edge of the large field, Harley knelt between two scouts, controllers in their hands, helping them fly small black drones up and down, left and right. He lifted his head and grinned when Myrna caught his eye. She waved at him.

"I put your bow and arrows over there," Jessup said. A whistle's shrill cut through the chatter. "Come on when you're ready." He jogged toward the butts, haloed by dust puffing from his clothes.

Myrna threaded through a knot of scouts to retrieve her weapons. She shrugged on her leather quiver and strapped on her wrist guard.

Two girls, probably eleven or twelve, one large for her age, the other one very pretty and she knew it, planted themselves in front of her. She'd encountered girls like this before. Sweet around adults who mattered, but otherwise unsubtle bullies who ruled by popularity and force of personality. Myrna eyed the big girl. Or threats. They'd made her life hell when she was twelve and new to prep school, when all she wanted was a friend after having nobody.

The pretty girl glanced around casually—looking for a troop leader, most likely—and found none. Her innocent expression twisted with disdain. "Paden and Webb said you made that. I don't believe it, and no way it works." The cluster of Girl Scouts at the table went silent.

The pretty girl's lack of respect was astonishing, especially when confronting an unknown entity.

Myrna's mother had taught her to study her prey before she attacked.

Understand it, girl, weigh its strengths and weaknesses. It makes you less likely to get hurt if your target turns on you. Her mother's eyes had dulled, and she'd drawn inward. *And they always turn on you.*

Eyes narrowed, Myrna turned on the pretty girl and her minion—

"*I* believe she made it. Just because you can hit the bullseye doesn't mean you know everything, *Imani.*"

Two more scouts, slim and athletic, obviously identical twins, stepped forward, arms crossed, chins lifted. Everything about them matched, even the colorful badges studding uniforms different from Imani's and her friend's. Dusty braids of dark hair draped over their shoulders and dirt streaked their clothes—like Jessup's.

"You're just mad because *I* hit more bullseyes than both you and your clone put together," the pretty girl, Imani, said. She pointed at Myrna's quiver. "And *I* knew those arrowheads were made of red-banded yellow chert. Jealousy doesn't look good on you, Leia."

"*She's* Louisa. Yeah, but you and the Hulk didn't know an ulna from a humerus and thought the badger skull was a *fox,*" said the second twin with a spectacular eye roll.

"Shut up, Clone." The large girl behind Imani pushed forward, fists balled.

The cluster of Girl Scouts around them shuffled and shifted, dividing into distinct packs behind each pair of combatants.

Myrna assessed her prey, realizing this wasn't about her and her homemade bow and arrows. This was about a rivalry between warring factions. She glanced at the pile of earth covering her elk. Maybe she could use their division to her advantage.

Since the twins had stepped up to defend her, Myrna chose Team Leia and Louisa. Now all she needed to do was bend them to her will to get what she wanted.

Except she was actually much better at pissing everyone off.

Best to start with her strength.

"I made my gear all right, including flint-knapping the arrow-heads. And I can guarantee my bow shoots better and I shoot straighter than anyone here, including you, and I'll prove it." Myrna stared pointedly at Imani, lip curled in a faint sneer. "Teams. Me plus Leia and Louisa and their troop against you and your troop in an archery contest."

Imani eyes widened at the challenge. She'd expected Myrna to be the adult, to back down. But she'd started it, and Myrna was not above being just as juvenile as she was.

The girls behind Imani shifted uncomfortably, their gazes darting back and forth between each other. Even the large girl looked unsure of herself. But not their leader.

"Whatever." Imani crossed her arms. "Is there a prize for winning?"

"See that dirt pile over there?" Myrna said. "Buried underneath is an elk. Someone poisoned it and we need to figure out how, or more animals could die. Whichever team wins will help excavate the body and gather samples to identify the poison." No way Bard would stop a passel of adorable Girl Scouts from digging out her elk. And if he tried, she'd coach them how to cry on command.

"So this wouldn't be some fake excavation," Leia said. Or was she Louisa? "We could actually make a real difference?"

"Yes," Myrna said simply.

The girls exchanged excited glances.

"Okay, that's a pretty cool prize," Imani said. "But it's not fair that your team has a grown-up, and ours doesn't. We should get to pick an adult, too."

Myrna recognized cunning, and this kid's face was filled with it. The girls who'd backed away stepped in tighter, spines straightened and faces defiant. Imani had a ringer stashed somewhere, and her team knew it.

Myrna lifted her chin. "It won't matter who you pick. My team's still gonna win. We'll meet you at the butts. Come on, girls." She marched toward the tables holding the archery gear, Leia, Louisa, and the rest of their troop clustered around her. "Who can shoot?"

A blond girl with chubby, freckled-spotted cheeks and round wire-rimmed glasses skipped forward. "Leia and Louisa, but Imani did beat them pretty bad this morning—even though the leaders don't allow competition with winners and losers. Maybe three of us can hit the bullseye if we're close, but the other three are completely hopeless, including me. I can barely pull back the string." There were nods of assent all around.

Single elimination would solve that problem. Myrna would let attrition take the weak and still win because she was the best.

"How about Imani's team?" she asked.

"Imani's really good," said Blond Glasses. "We go to the same school, and I think her family bow hunts, like, real animals. Angelica—the one who backs her up—she's pretty good, too. The others are like the rest of us. Some okay, some not. But you have to be careful with Imani. She cheats."

There was a murmured swell of agreement from the surrounding girls.

Blond Glasses suddenly gasped, eyes huge. "Uh-oh. That's not good."

"What?" Myrna asked.

"The adult Imani chose for her team. It's—"

"I have *just* been informed that you're planning an archery contest—*with teams*." A frowning scout leader planted her hiking boots in the grass in front of Myrna, hands on her hips, in her "Girl Scout Strong" T-shirt, baggie shorts, and her hair pulled back so tightly it looked like someone spray-painted her scalp brown. "Don't you understand that competitions set up our girls for failure? Scar their delicate psyches? And you weren't introduced as staff, so you aren't authorized to be around these children."

"Dr. Lee's been background-checked," said a melodious voice with a hint of a posh British accent.

A smug Imani and a veritable Amazon in crisp safari khakis stopped beside the jabbering troop leader, who retreated double-time. The Amazon pinned Myrna into place with the lightest, clearest green eyes she'd ever seen embedded in a generously freckled face. But the freckles didn't stop at her cheeks. They bathed her throat and arms, complimenting thick strawberry-blond hair pulled into a high ponytail. In her late thirties and over six feet by a couple of inches, she had the graceful leanness of a thoroughbred racehorse. Unease trickled over Myrna's skin.

"Imani has chosen me to be the, ah, *adult* on her archery team. What are the rules?"

"If you miss a bullseye, you're out," Myrna answered. "Last one with a team member standing wins."

"I agree, with one slight modification. Single elimination, but the winning team must collect the highest total number of bullseyes. That way no one person dominates the competition." She gave Myrna's custom bow a pointed glance. "We'll start in half an hour."

Myrna's eyes followed the woman as she crossed the field with her team.

"Told you Imani would cheat," said Blond Glasses under her breath. Her fingers crept into Myrna's, hot, sticky, and ... *trusting*.

Myrna stared at their linked hands. Was this little girl using her as an anchor, for comfort and support? She didn't even know the kid's name.

She should let go of the girl's hand. Instead, her fingers tightened.

"How is Imani cheating?" Myrna asked. "And what's your name?"

"I'm Rhea, and she's cheating because that's Dame Sylvia, the lady who owns this ranch. Imani picked her because she won a silver medal in the Olympics—for archery."

TWENTY-SIX

Myrna's archery team—they'd decided to call themselves the Dire Wolves because it sounded a lot meaner than just the Wolves—shifted on nervous feet. Arrows Myrna had carefully selected from the ranch's supply packed their quivers, and they held bows Jessup had adjusted for easier draw and control. Webb McJunkin had done the same for Imani's team —who'd named themselves the Wild Cats.

Gourmet snacks appeared from Isaac's café, and the clot of men and women who'd arrived with Dame Sylvia sat as an audience, murmuring and munching under gilded afternoon light filtered through towering cottonwoods. Scout leaders encouraged or harangued the girls not on the archery teams to work on other badges, including at Harley's drone station. But it was obvious everyone's focus was on the archery butts.

"You sure you know what you're doing, Dr. Lee? With Dame Sylvia's background ..." Jessup bent over Rhea, helping her tighten her wrist guard.

Myrna waved her competition's experience away along with a large black bee—*Xylocopa mexicanorum*—that buzzed around her head. "Have you seen the precision equipment and specialized stadiums used in those competitions? Nothing like these simple bows and arrows and the raw outside." Where she had the advantage because of her raised-wild background. "Dame Sylvia holds power over Bard. Once we win, I'll demand the bulldozer to excavate my elk. I won't even need the girls' help anymore."

Jessup and Rhea stared at her.

"But you said we were going to help save animals from poison if we win," Rhea said, face dawning with hurt.

Jessup patted the girl on her shoulder. He strolled over to Myrna, disappointment etched into the lines around his eyes. "No one likes to be used, Dr. Lee."

And Myrna braced for the lecture she'd heard about a million times before. How a burden shared is lighter, how she's a terrible team leader, how she needs to trust other people.

Like she'd trusted her mother not to abandon her at a hospital when she got sick. Like she'd trusted her grandparents and aunts and uncles and cousins and sister to love and accept her instead of shipping her off to boarding school. Like she'd trusted Tom Hutchinson not to try and steal William Tell after she'd told him to pick up the dog.

Like trusting anyone had ever worked out for her ever.

Myrna curled the fingers Rhea had held on to, her conscience prickling, and peeked at Jessup. He looked like he'd been struck by lightning and shocked into place. She knitted her brows in confusion.

"And maybe I don't have the right to throw stones," he said, almost at a whisper, almost to himself. He rubbed a hand over his mouth and sighed. "Right now, the rest of your team needs to feel like they're important. How are you at pep talks?"

Horrible. "I'm great at it."

He smiled, but lingering turmoil swirled deep in his eyes. "Dire Wolves! Your team leader has something to say to you."

Butterflies fluttered in her stomach.

The girls, bows in hand, crowded around in a circle, their

expressions ranging from determined and eager to worried and scared. Myrna's butterflies morphed into burning, bouncing meteorites. If only she could do this alone without having to rely on anyone else. But she couldn't. She had to trust these unknown girls fidgeting around her.

Myrna latched onto the confidence in Leia and Louisa's faces. "Do you want to say something?"

The twins exchanged a look.

"Yeah. We do." Leia met the eyes of each girl. "Imani's been a pain since first grade, and you all know it. We need to show her she can't go through life thinking she's better than us."

"Sometimes you play because you love the game," Louisa continued. "Sometimes you play for a prize. We're playing because we're a *team*. If one of us misses a target, we all miss the target. If one of us gets a bullseye, we all get a bullseye. When we work together, we try harder. We can beat Imani because she doesn't care about her team. She only cares about herself. Hands in!"

Jessup stuck his in first. Grubby hands layered on top of it.

Myrna clutched her bow, sifting through Leia and Louisa's words. Was she like Imani? Thinking she was better than everyone else? Not caring about other people's feelings?

But she'd had to be the best because she'd been so alone.

Right?

"Dr. Lee?" Rhea smiled up at her. "You need to put your hand in, too. You're one of us."

Myrna surveyed the circle of bright, trusting faces. *You're one of us.* The meteorites shifted to bubbles that floated up and around her heart. She laid her hand right on top.

"Okay? And break!" Leia said.

Arms flew up. "Go, Dire Wolves!"

A whistle blew. Myrna, the first to shoot, nocked an arrow. A hush fell as she drew, only birdsong interrupting the silence. Fingers curled at her cheek, she sighted the target. With a slowly exhaled breath, she released. The arrow flew true and buried itself into the center of the yellow circle. Bullseye number one. Her girls cheered and high-fived.

Dame Sylvia moved into place. The woman had chosen a compound bow, an advantage because of its power. Her arrow embedded itself in the center circle of her target, buried almost to the fletching. She turned and gave Myrna a saccharine smile. Leia stepped up to the line. When she struck the yellow center, her grin was beautiful. Imani shot next, her face smug when she hit the bullseye.

Dire Wolves: 2; Wild Cats: 2.

When Rhea stepped up, she looked to Myrna and licked her lips nervously. Myrna mimed a stance, fingers curled at her cheek, held, and released a pretend bowstring. Rhea nodded. Lips firm, brow puckered in concentration, she mimicked Myrna's actions ... drew back her arrow ... held her aim ... released—

And hit the center circle.

The surprise and joy on the girl's face made Myrna's eyes burn.

Leia and Myrna's self-assurance held their team together through three rounds. They only lost one girl compared to two lost by the Wild Cats, which gave Myrna's team a single bullseye advantage. But in the next rounds, more girls peeled off when their confidence made them careless or their arms tired. When Rhea hit the wrong butt during her turn, it meant, for the first time, the Dire Wolves fell behind by one bullseye. She trailed to Myrna, head down, bow tight in her fist.

"I'm sorry," she said. "If I'd picked the bow you told me to take, maybe this wouldn't have happened. But I wanted one like yours. Now I've let everyone down."

Myrna's heart melted. Instead of berating her teammate—something she'd done a million times to grad students and lab techs who'd messed up because they thought they knew better—she knelt in front of Rhea. "You haven't let me down. We all learn in different ways about how to get better at something."

And it made her feel good inside. Different from the overweening triumph of proving someone wrong when she was right.

More rounds, more eliminations, until there were only two left on Imani's team—Imani and Dame Sylvia—and three on Myrna's team—the twins and Myrna. But Louisa's arm was shaking. She barely hit yellow her last turn—the two teams were tied.

Leia stepped up to shoot, set herself, pulled back the bowstring in one smooth motion ...

A buzzing black drone swooped down into the path of her shot. She jerked her release and her arrow arced over the target. The drone zipped back to Harley's station.

"I'm so sorry!" A scout with the same uniform as Imani's troop ran over, controller in hand. "It got away. I didn't mean—"

Leia stormed to Imani, shaking with anger. "You are such a cheater! You had Beverly do that on purpose."

"I haven't even spoken to her!" Imani and Leia stood nose to nose, fists clenched. Myrna and Dame Sylvia pulled the girls apart.

"Let her shoot again," Myrna said.

"No way." Imani pushed her lip out. "The rules say you're out when you miss, no matter what. What if that had been a bird?"

"People can't control birds," Leia yelled.

"Is that what you want, Leia? To break the rules—to cheat—for a second chance?" Dame Sylvia said. "Then go ahead. Shoot. Everyone! Step back for Leia's second chance."

Leia stared up into Dame Sylvia's face, jaw set.

"No. I'm out." She strode back to her team, disappearing into the huddle of girls.

"Still tied and we're losing light. You're up, Miz Donavan," Jessup called. "Then you, Dr. Lee."

The Dame stepped up to the line and nocked her arrow, aimed ...

A second drone, compact and fast, darted into her path right as she released. The arrow hit blue, two rings out from the yellow center. The drone spiraled upward until it was a buzzing black dot overhead.

"*Harley!*" Dame Sylvia screeched, her expression a mask of ire.

"What's good for the goose," Harley called back, a lopsided grin on his crooked face. "Just thought I'd even the odds."

Myrna's turn. She stepped up to the line, drew ... and released her arrow straight up.

The hovering drone shattered in a shower of black plastic. *Bullseye.* A cry of awe went up from the crowd.

Jessup jogged to Myrna. She grinned. "Told you I could shoot."

"You just eliminated yourself."

"I know. Maybe this should've always been about the girls, not me."

"Maybe. But Miz Donavan doesn't like to lose."

"And she probably won't. Louisa's arm's tired. I don't know how much longer she can last."

Imani stepped up to the line. Her arrow hit yellow. Wild Cats up by one.

"Louisa," Imani called with a smirk. "Your turn."

Louisa broke from her team's huddle and trotted to the line. She nocked her arrow and let fly. *Bullseye.* She grinned and waved at the applauding adults before she walked up to Imani and said, "Guess my arm wasn't as tired as some people thought. We're tied again. No pressure, Imani," before jogging back to her cheering team.

Dame Sylvia frowned and leaned down to whisper in Imani's ear. Whatever she said seemed to rattle the girl.

Arrow in place, Imani darted a glance to Dame Sylvia, before she swallowed and aimed. The arrow hit just outside the center circle. The last member of the Wild Cats was eliminated. Louisa stepped up and nailed the final bullseye.

A cheer went up from the Dire Wolves. Myrna and her team ran to Louisa, enveloping her with hugs.

"That was stone-cold, Louisa. And I was worried your arm was too tired—"

"It was." The girl glanced at her twin, eyes sparkling. They grinned at each other.

Wait. Had they—?

"What about our prize?" Louisa asked. Or was she Leia?

"Prize?" Dame Sylvia stood a short distance away. A smile played over her lips, but her eyes were icy.

"I, uh, promised to let the winning team help me excavate the elk Dillon Bard buried last night. I need to retrieve an important tissue sample for my analysis."

"Without getting permission first? How underhanded of you, Dr. Lee. And since I'm the only one who can give you said permission to dig up that elk—"

"No, you're not, Sylvia."

Dame Sylvia Donavan's face froze. Both irritation and chagrin flickered in her eyes.

A short, stocky man dressed in a business suit with a bolo tie bisecting his shirt appeared beyond the crowd of girls and adults. Bright white lights switched on behind him. Their glare washed out Myrna's vision and made his face featureless under a deep blue shadow thrown by the brim of his ten-gallon hat.

"That was quite a display of marksmanship, Dr. Lee."

Myrna frowned, searching for where she'd heard the man's gruff nasal voice before and coming up empty. The girls and gathered crowd had gone silent.

"I believe that drone you destroyed cost about a thousand dollars. I'll make sure half of it comes out of EcoNano and Eleanor's commission, while Buzz there"—he shot a thumb over his shoulder—"will have to eat the rest, since he pulled that stupid stunt. About your prize, Dr. Lee. Sometimes Sylvia can be a little—"

A gurgle of laughter interrupted him. Sylvia Donavan sidled to his side and laced an arm around his back.

"Now, Charles. Don't make me look any worse than I already do. You know how much I hate to lose."

Charles. The silhouetted man was Dame Sylvia's *husband.* Myrna measured the couple's height difference in feet.

Leia—or was she Louisa?—stepped up to Charles Donavan and squared her shoulders. "We can help Dr. Lee excavate her elk?"

"You bet, young lady. Since it's almost dark, I had my staff set up some lights for you. Dr. Lee? Tell Jessup if you need anything else."

He touched the brim of his hat and turned away. He and his wife headed toward the compound, their hands clasped. The crowd of donors followed.

Myrna saw Charles Donavan's intervention for what it was— avoidance of bad publicity. Still, she sympathized with Sylvia Donavan, taken to task—embarrassed—in front of their guests. She'd experienced that kind of reprimand plenty of times with Tom Hutchinson and Eleanor. It was never pleasant and could cause—*had* caused—lingering resentment.

Had she just made herself a powerful enemy?

As the couple disappeared into the dusky light, Myrna straightened.

"Girls? Let's suit up."

With a nod to Jessup, Myrna scurried back toward her lab, a gaggle of excited scouts in her wake.

Myrna looked up and found Jessup at the edge of the stark white light holding William Tell. The dog strained at the end of his leash, lungs bellowing as he tasted air infused with rotting elk. Girls in puffy white hazmat suits troweled dirt from what was left of the carcass, heads covered with elastic-banded white caps, N-95 face masks over their noses and mouths, and underneath, mentholated jelly smeared on their upper lips.

"We're at fur! This is *so gross*," Rhea said with relish.

Myrna waded to the elk's exposed rump. She held out a gloved hand. "Brush." One of the girls slapped it into her palm.

They crowded in close. Myrna gently swept away the remaining dirt ...

Gasps rose around her.

"What?" Jessup said.

"It's gone." Myrna stared astonished at the hole in the elk's flank rimmed with dirt and blackened flesh. "Someone stole my sample."

TWENTY-SEVEN

Myrna knocked on the door of Isaac Marín's home after her nighttime walk with William Tell. Except *walk* implied she got exercise instead of stopping about a million times as he left his doggie version of breadcrumbs throughout the quiet, quaint neighborhood just in case he ever needed to find his way home.

Home. She stared back at her little house with something approaching longing. It was nearly perfect—cozy, warm, welcoming. So much better than the converted garage furnished with yard sale cast-offs she rented in Socorro. With a sigh she wished—

The front door opened. Mellow light mixed with the fragrance of cinnamon and apples burst into the cool night air already laced with the scent of wood smoke.

"Hi, Isaac," Myrna said. "I got your note to come over for pie. I hope you don't mind that I brought—"

William Tell bounded up the steps, pulling the leash taut.

"Let him go. Jessup'll unhook him so he won't get tangled." Isaac put his hand over his heart. "De verdad."

Myrna dropped the leash. It snaked inside, and ecstatic whining and cute little happy yips ensued. Her pulse rate shot up.

Those were his *I'm-adorable-pick-me-up* whines and yips.

"*Don't pick him up!*" Myrna dashed past a startled Isaac and skidded to a halt on the polished wood floor.

The room was laid out similarly to her little house, with the path to the kitchen bounded on one side by a wall and on the other by a cushy blue sofa. A well-used recliner angled toward a large flat-screen TV, and a table and chairs that looked like they'd been rescued from a 1950s diner were tucked by the back door. Jessup stood next to the closed bedroom, harness and leash dangling from his hand, the dog foursquare at his feet. Both stared at her, Jessup's brows pinned to his hairline.

"He might have, uh, mange—possibly—just a—a small spot on his belly." Her voice squeaked, and her face burned.

Silence stretched for excruciatingly uncomfortable seconds. Then William Tell gave a tremendous shake and trotted toward the warmth of a small fireplace with whole logs burned to glowing red coals. He plopped down on the hearthrug and rolled to expose his completely blemish-free, adorable, tubby pink tummy before he relaxed into a snoring sleep.

She pivoted on the ball of her foot to face Isaac, curving lips into a bright smile. "You said there's pie?"

Isaac hobbled into the most gorgeous modern compact kitchen Myrna had ever seen, all gleaming stainless steel and hanging copper pots. Jessup ambled to the sparkly red laminate kitchen table and pulled out a chrome and vinyl-upholstered chair for Myrna. She shrugged out of her backpack and looped it over the chair back, then tried to catch his attention, but his sharp gaze followed Isaac, who appeared to studiously avoid any eye contact with his friend. Jessup sat next to her, half-eaten pie topped with melting vanilla ice cream and a mug of coffee in front of him. Next to Jessup's dish rested an open plastic zipper bag containing the silver buttons he'd dug out of the ground near the mammoth rub. Myrna's eyes widened, and she flashed him a sharp look.

Isaac plunked down a huge piece of pie: thinly sliced apples speckled with spices and stacked between flaky layers of crust, topped with a perfect scoop of ice cream. A mug of coffee followed.

"But I can't eat—"

"What you can't finish, leave. Not that you will." He cocked her a half smile.

She took a bite. It was really good. She'd definitely put on weight if she stayed on the ranch—

Myrna shook that thought away. Even if she got permission to excavate the mammoth, it would only be temporary. Not a real home.

Isaac clasped gnarled hands around his steaming mug. "Jessup here tells me you're interested in those big stone spear points. You know the Donavans have some up at their ranch museum? Well, they aren't the only ones. I found a bunch, too, long time ago. Have 'em right here in the house. Jessup said you might want use 'em as part of some project?"

She swallowed her mouthful of pie. "For a grant on Pleistocene poisons. I'd love to take some surface swabs."

"To find those poisons you talked about at breakfast with that pendejo, Buzz, er, Harley, que no? Bueno. Let me go get 'em." Isaac set down his coffee and shuffled to the bedroom.

Myrna leaned toward Jessup. He'd showered and changed since the Girl Scout elk debacle earlier that evening and smelled as good as the pie.

"Why did you show Isaac those buttons? If he tells someone where you found them, they'll find the mammoth bones, and—"

"Why are you so worried?" Jessup sat back, arms crossed.

"It's a pristine mammoth kill site," she hissed. "With associated lithic artifacts and butchering marks. Every tin-horn Paleoindian archaeologist from here to the Smithsonian will converge on this ranch like a plague of locusts when they hear about it."

"I didn't tell him where I found the buttons. And I didn't tell him or anyone about the mammoth bones. I promised you that, Myrna."

"Well, somebody else knows because my boss heard it from some stupid secret contact she has on the ranch." Frowning, she broke off a piece of pie crust and munched it. "Why'd you show the buttons to Isaac?"

Jessup turned in his chair and looped an arm over the back. "They're pretty distinctive. Thought maybe he's seen an old photo or heard a story about how valuable silver buttons disappeared."

"Valuable?" Myrna's eyes narrowed. "That's why you and Bard were sneaking around the other night, wasn't it? You were looking for that lost trea—"

As fast as a striking snake, Jessup's hand shot out to cover hers. He leaned forward, eyes intent. "Not lost. It's somewhere on the ranch. The buttons prove it."

Rattled by his touch, Myrna blurted, "How? Those buttons came from—" Oops. Time to shut up. She clamped her lips tight.

"From what?" Jessup's expression animated and his eyes almost glowed. His hand tightened over hers. "What do you know?"

"That those buttons ain't from the treasure, unless that treasure's Navajo, and it ain't as far as I know." Isaac stepped out of the bedroom, a rectangular glass-topped wooden case in his hands. "They got a maker's mark on the back."

Jessup dug into the bag and picked up a button. He turned it over, squinted. "I didn't even ..."

Myrna unzipped her pack and pulled out a lighted magnifier. Heads together, she and Jessup studied the flat tarnished underside. A tiny word was stamped in the silver but it was barely legible.

"R-O ...? Rosehouse? Roan?" she said.

"Maybe E? Red? Redhouse? Redhorse?" Jessup grabbed another button.

"You're more interested in those things than these rocks?"

Isaac sounded put out. He sat down and shoved the glass-topped case across the table.

"Oh. No." Myrna gave Isaac her full attention as she picked up the box. Nestled in yellowed cotton batting were five lanceolate points, the largest at least six-and-a-half inches. Classic Clovis projectiles with bifacial percussion flaking and longitudinal flutes that ran one-third the length of the stone.

Except one, which was a pretty good fake. She touched the glass over it.

"Where did you find these?" Myrna asked.

"Out assessing damage from a big flood that ran through a logging camp, oh, long time back. When Charles Junior started running the ranch—this Charles Donavan's pop. Water swept away everything." His eyes focused in the past. "Me and my brother, Joe—he was a lot older than me. Fought in Europe during the second war. Roads washed out so we had to go in on horseback. Houses collapsed, cars overturned. Clothes and furniture scattered everywhere. Even found a rocking chair hung high in a tree. Well, we rounded a corner, came up on a washed-out dirt wall chock-full of bones. Thought first a herd of cows must've been buried in some earlier flood, but the skulls weren't from cows. Some kinda ancient bison. They got one at the museum at the lodge, all put together, now. Me and Joe picked through the bones and those"—he gestured to the box—"were mixed in."

A beautiful story, rich in detail, which was how she'd been taught to lie by her mother. Because it was a lie. The basic elements of Isaacs's story came from the 1908 discovery of Folsom artifacts by a ranch foreman and former slave. And the bison Isaac described—*Bison antiquus*—had never been associated with Clovis culture, so he was lying about the provenance of the points, too. Was this what Harley meant by *Isaac Mentira*?

"May I open it?" At his nod, Myrna lifted the hinged top, and the subtle earthy tang wafted out. She sighed in pleasure. Jessup turned off the magnifier's light and propped his elbows on the table. Digging into her backpack, she pulled out a handful of sterile cotton swabs and a rack of test tubes filled with her special preservation solution.

She snapped on gloves and cradled the first flute in her palm, breath held in reverence. A tool created by a person who'd lived, hunted, and died thousands of years ago. She swabbed the stone, the cotton tip picking up faint gray-brown color.

"This point was hafted onto a spear or atlatl using tar or a sap mixture to adhere the binding. I'll take a small sample." Fresh scalpel blade in hand, she scraped a minute amount of adherent into a tube.

Myrna repeated the process on the next two fluted stone points —inspecting, swabbing, scraping—all with a running commentary that was more for herself than the men, a habit she'd fallen into as a child to lessen her aloneness—and loneliness. But on the last authentic flute, the umber-black of residual blood stained the swab.

She held the stone up. "Did someone cut themselves on this one?"

"Couldn't it be from whatever they hunted back then?" Jessup asked. At some point, he'd leaned back in his chair, coffee mug cradled with both hands on a flat, hard stomach, half-closed eyes watching her.

"This blood's not that old."

"My brother, es posible. I seem to remember some loud cussing and a bandaged hand. You almost done?"

At Myrna's nod, Isaac creaked to his feet. Jessup stood and swiped up his and Myrna's plates. Both men ambled to the kitchen, holding a low-voiced conversation.

Myrna shot them a quick glance and picked up the box. Handmade with fine dovetailing. Cedar, from the faint scent of remaining oils in the dried wood. The pane of glass slotted into a wooden frame. Two small hinges on one side and a hasp latch on the other. She trailed a finger down a smooth side and bit her lip. Weirdly, the box was so ...*familiar*.

Quickly, she pulled out all the stones and cotton batting. Its origin was branded into the wood underneath: *Second Chance Trading Post, Route 66, New Mexico.* Myrna reassembled the cotton and points and closed the box.

"Done."

"I'll walk you home." Jessup whistled and William Tell went from a dead sleep to on his feet in an awkward twist.

He trotted to the front door and docilely cooperated while Myrna threaded him into his harness. "Thanks for the pie, Isaac."

"Anytime, 'jita. Nice having a pretty girl around. Ain't it, Jessup?"

His knowing chuckle followed Myrna as she and Jessup stepped out into the cool, clear night. Their steps crunched on fine pebbles interspersed with the bunch grass that made up Isaac's lawn, a million stars speckling the velvety black sky above.

"Anything interesting, Dr. Lee?"

She liked how his eyes, even shadowed with darkness, always seemed to smile when he said her name.

"I won't know until I process the swabs. But I'm pretty sure Isaac's story isn't true. I think he might have bought those flutes from a Route 66 trading post. And one of them was fake." They stopped on the path to her front door. "I guess they don't call him Isaac Mentira for nothing."

Jessup faced her. He smelled of apple pie and very good coffee. A sudden yearning to taste him enveloped her. "Who called him that?"

"Harley."

"I've known Isaac a long time. His *pequeñas mentiras* have never hurt anyone."

"*Peck-en-ya—*?"

His attention moved to her mouth. He hesitated, stepped close. Her heart rate accelerated as the night wrapped around them. Jessup's hand rose to cup her cheek, hard calluses tender on her skin. Myrna's breath caught.

"Little lies," he said. "Very different from *una pequeña mentirosa*."

With maddening slowness, his lips descended. Her face rose to his, anticipation piercing her chest. But at the last second, he turned his head and whispered, "*Pequeña mentirosa*. Little liar." He stepped back, lips smirked, and tapped her nose with a gentle finger.

"Goodnight, Myrna. Be ready by six o'clock," he said, and pivoted on his heel.

Myrna, outraged and *extremely* disappointed, rushed after him, managing to grab his shirt sleeve before the leash pulled tight, William Tell an anchor.

"Hey. *Hey!* I am not some ... some *child* to be patted on the head and told to go to—"

Jessup hauled her into a crushing embrace, the press of his lips evaporating her thoughts. Swept away by a bone-melting lassitude and bursting pleasure, she wove her fingers through his hair and plastered herself tightly along the hard heat of him, head spinning, deepening the kiss until she didn't know where he ended and she began.

When he thrust her away, her shock and disappointment returned with the cold slap of night air.

Jessup spun, fist clenched, body rigid. He looked up at the sky, his breathing harsh.

"I know you're not a child, Dr. Myrna P. Lee. And, God bless it, that's a big damn problem." He strode to his house without a backward glance.

William Tell suddenly remembered he had legs and barreled after Jessup, only to be yanked short. Myrna, stunned she still held the leash, strained back as much as the dog tugged forward.

Jessup surged up the porch steps. "Six o'clock." He disappeared inside his home.

Throat tight, Myrna stared dully at the closed door. She was a *big damn problem*. Nothing new there.

Myrna hiccupped a sigh and gently reeled in William Tell. "Come on, boy. Time to get some sleep."

William Tell let out a poignant yip-howl, like so much doggie crying.

She knew exactly how he felt.

TWENTY-EIGHT

Jessup's truck traveled over the smooth blacktop road rolling comfortably through the Donavan Ranch. Myrna absorbed the passing forest and the dapple of sunlight amid the trees as if only in appreciation, but skills sharpened by hard lessons seared distinctive landmarks into her memory—just in case she got lost. A barely discernible animal trail, a distant rockslide with a single pine growing out of the peak, a ramshackle log cabin decaying for more than a century. William Tell marked his way home with scent; she marked hers with vision. Taking mental snapshots, absorbing the land, the changing scents, shadows, and silhouettes as the day and night waxed and waned.

Not that she'd ever get lost. Although the Donavans had declared thousands of ranch acres as wilderness—no mechanical or motorized vehicles—the scenic byway to their renowned and celebrated lodge probably had human guides strategically placed behind trees to lead the disoriented back to the comfort of a three-star Michelin restaurant, luxury cabins, or, if guests didn't want the drudgery of having to venture outside, a suite in their five-star hotel.

A stealthy side-eye in Jessup's direction revealed the same

detached manner that had greeted her at six A.M. when she and William Tell stepped out the front door of her little house. He'd dropped her off at her lab with a pleasant, distant, "I'll pick up you and William Tell at nine thirty."

If he wanted to ignore the kiss they'd shared last night, she could, too. Mixing work and pleasure had already tanked her career once. She refused to let it happen again. She tucked Isaac's Clovis point swabs into the -80°C freezer, prepped more elk tissue, and read all about the lodge on the Internet in preparation for her first *official* meeting with Dame Sylvia Donavan.

Jessup braked across from a laser-cut black metal sign that directed drivers to head right to the Donavans' Elk Bugle Lodge or left to Woollywood Regenerative Farm.

But didn't "regenerative" equal "organic"? Then why had her elk tissue showed detectable levels of both pesticides and herbicides?

Jessup turned left.

"Wait! My meeting with Dame Sylvia's at the lodge. In ten minutes. I don't want to tick her off more than I already have."

"I got new instructions about a half hour before I picked you up. Miz Donavan's at the farm giving campaign donors the two-bit tour. She wants to talk to you there, show you around." For the first time since the kiss the night before, Jessup thawed. He shot her a lazy half smile. "I think you intimidated her, and she's ready to take some back."

She goggled at him. "*I* intimidated *her*?"

"You intimidated me, too, remember? Not at all what I was expecting, considering the package you're wrapped in." He chuckled. "You're a lot like that little dog. Fearless."

Myrna twisted in her seat to hide heated cheeks. "Are there animals on this farm? Sometimes William Tell thinks he's a sheepdog."

"That would be something to see since the Donavans keep a

few bison up here for their breeding program. He can stay with me. I'm supposed to come get you after lunch, anyway."

"Just don't—"

"Pick him up. I know." He gave her a quizzical look as he pulled into a pea-gravel parking area bordered by hitching posts and water troughs. Jessup tipped his head toward a sleek silver passenger van under the shade of a huge cottonwood. Dame Sylvia closed the sliding side door on a passel of blue-jeaned and booted men and women, and waved goodbye as the van backed out of the lot. She walked to the truck and peered into Jessup's driver-side window at Myrna.

"Too bad about your elk disinterment. It's almost like someone doesn't want you to succeed." Her clipped British accent lent a mocking edge to her words. "Mr. Page? One thirty at the lodge to pick up Dr. Lee."

William Tell stood, and his carrier wobbled. He barked once, curious and high.

Dame Sylvia craned her neck. "That little thing's been terrorizing Bard's monster dog?"

"Oh, I've seen a badger best a grizzly bear, Miz Donavan," Jessup drawled. He winked at Myrna. "Sometimes all it takes is attitude and a willingness to face up to what scares you."

"Ah. How folksy." Faint distaste stamped her features. "Dr. Lee? I hope you wore comfortable shoes. We have quite a bit of ground to cover." And she strode off.

Myrna snatched her backpack from the floor, about to hop out of the truck when Jessup grabbed her hand. "Be careful. That woman sure as hell will go grizzly on you if you turn your back."

She nodded before closing the door, and half jogged down the gentle slope of a grassy meadow toward fields of mixed crops, glinting greenhouses, and sturdy fences surrounding huge, placid bison.

"Try to keep up," the Dame said over her shoulder. "Now,

what do you know about regenerative agriculture? Not much, I'm sure. Let me explain ..."

Myrna shrugged on her backpack and muttered under her breath, "*Be the badger, be the badger.*" It was gonna be that kind of day.

Twenty-Nine

Myrna stood in a furrow of matted plant litter surrounded by squash, bean vines running up criss-crosses of twine, and stalks of corn, all literally bursting with late-summer fruit and grain. The three sisters—*las tres hermanas*—Dame Sylvia called them.

"Which makes perfect sense nutritionally," Myrna said.

The Dame's eyes brightened. "Complex carbohydrates, essential fatty acids, and all nine essential amino acids. What one plant lacks is made up by another. We also use a variety of heirloom cultivars which tend to carry more insect resistance. And notice the squash. The hairy stems and leaves provide a natural pest deterrent. Everything we grow is completely organic, of course. No pesticides, no herbicides."

Myrna kept her expression neutral. Her preliminary results on her elk tissue samples directly contradicted Dame Sylvia's statement. "You don't worry about drift from farms surrounding the ranch?"

"Our large acreage acts as a buffer to outside contamination."

Myrna touched a bright pinkish-purple flower on a stalk sprouting spiraling trifoliate leaves.

"*Cleome serrulata*. Rocky Mountain bee plant. Indigenous cultures use it to attract feral pollinators for the squash and beans, but we've also supplemented with honeybees. *Apis mellifera*." Dame Sylvia's expression became pained. "Unfortunately, colony collapse has devastated our hives, so we've come up with some rather novel fixes. Come, Dr. Lee. I have so much to show you before we're picked up for lunch."

Myrna hurried to follow the woman who'd morphed from cold and arrogant to one as passionate about regenerative farming as Myrna was about Pleistocene megafauna.

Dame Sylvia pushed open the door to a state-of-the-art glass greenhouse and waved Myrna inside. Flowers of every color, shape, and size grew in profusion, and she breathed in the most amazing cacophony of scents.

An odd buzzing overhead drew her attention away from the rainbow of blossoms. Large black insects filled the air above the foliage. Myrna's whole body shuddered. Her curly, fluffy hair easily trapped flying bugs, and she *hated*—

Her jaw slacked. The bees or flies or whatever all hovered at the exact same height.

Myrna caught a movement at the back of the greenhouse. Harley Wakefield held a tablet in a heavy black case, his focus on the swarm. A finger swept over the tablet's surface, and the bees swung into a humming ring that circled in the air.

"Oh, my gosh." Myrna's eyes widened. "*Nanodrones*."

Dame Sylvia beckoned Myrna to a plant sprouting sweet-smelling apricot lilies. "Watch."

A single drone broke from the circle and dropped toward them. It perched lightly on a petal, crept with precision toward the flower's flute, and telescoped a bristled protrusion inside. When yellow pollen coated the fine hairs, the drone retracted its probe and flew back to the circling mass, soon lost in the swirl.

"They take no nectar, and only a fraction of pollen that bees do," Dame Sylvia said.

Myrna's mind spun at fast as the nanodrones. "How do they recognize flowers ready for pollination? How far is their range? How do you—?"

"Secrets, Myrna," Harley said. "I could tell you, but then I'd have to kill you. Kidding." His off-center jaw twisted his grin. He tapped the tablet to open a live video. "They're equipped with tiny cameras which allow for flower recognition via algorithms. Watch."

The tablet's video swooped as a drone pollinator dropped toward a Colorado blue columbine, the bright yellow of its pistols and stamen cupped by a delicate five-petaled lavender shell. Bristle extended, it picked up fresh pollen before it zoomed to a second flower, then a third.

"Hold out your hand."

Myrna did. One of the tiny drones hummed down from above, hovered, and dropped onto her palm. "I can barely feel it."

"Titanium legs. Incredibly thin and strong," Harley said.

"But it's wings—"

"Aren't normal rotating propellers. We have better maneuvering with actual flapping," the Dame said, an almost maternal smile on her lips. "A spider silk and Mylar blend—light and extremely durable."

Myrna brought the tiny drone closer to her face.

"*Ouch!*" She jerked her hand away. The drone tumbled toward the floor before its wings started up. It fled to its circle of friends. A tiny drop of blood welled up from her palm. "What did you do?"

"Nothing," Harley said. "It must have felt threatened, and the needle deployed."

"They can *defend themselves*?"

"Against birds, mostly." Harley shoved a hand in his pocket and pulled out a small flat packet. "Alcohol wipe."

"What's their power source?" Myrna pressed the wipe against the sting.

"Their bodies are coated with a special polymer that absorbs both heat and light. They only work about fifteen minutes in the dark but can be revived by the warmth of a hand, say, or a flashlight's beam." Harley's grin was smug. "Sometimes I amaze myself."

"How do you clean the pollen off?" Myrna asked.

"See that metal block over there?" Harley sidestepped around her. He tapped his controller, and the swarm of bee drones dove to the block, docking in uniform rows. Another finger tap, and each nanodrone deployed its pollen-encrusted needle into a tiny slot below its body. "They'll be rinsed and the pollen or whatever else they've collected—like your blood—will be analyzed individually if so programmed."

Myrna ran a finger over the spot where the drone stung her. It had stopped bleeding and she could hardly see the sting. "What else can they do?"

Dame Sylvia frowned. "What do you mean?"

Harley grinned, arching a single eyebrow. "Yes, Dr. Lee. What *do* you mean?"

"Can they collect blood or a tissue punch from animals in the wild?"

Or, Myrna thought, *reverse the process and inject wild animals with toxins or poisons?*

"What an interesting idea," Harley said at the same time Dame Sylvia asked, "Why?"

Myrna raised innocent eyes. "I need control elk blood and tissue for a baseline sample comparison against the die-off elk tissue."

Harley's smile was sly. "Let me see what I can rig together."

Dame Sylvia's phone chimed. "Transport is here to pick us up for lunch at the lodge, Dr. Lee." Back to cold and arrogant.

As Myrna exited the greenhouse, she could've sworn Harley whispered, "*Knight takes Queen pawn.* Check."

These two were playing some kind of game with each other, and she'd bet her entire stake she was a pawn.

The question was, why?

THIRTY

In the lodge restaurant, the blue-jeaned and booted investors Myrna had glimpsed in the van earlier that day laughed and talked at a large oval table bristling with wine bottles. Her attention lingered on their sunlit silhouettes before she skimmed her gaze around the lofty room. The bank of floor-to-ceiling windows held a spectacular view of heavily forested mountains and granite bluffs under a rich blue sky studded with puffy white clouds. Rustic slate floors kept the restaurant cool, while huge river-rock fireplaces warmed it in the winter. Mounted on silvered wood-planked walls, trophy elk, deer, bison, mountain goat, and bighorn vied with more exotic animals like oryx, Barbary sheep, and ibex. A display of nineteenth-century western landscapes and antique firearms tacked between the glassy-eyed heads rounded off the assemblage.

She still needed permission to sample the Donavan lithic arti-fact collection and dig up the mammoth bones, and conversation had been practically nonexistent thus far. Maybe admiring the dead animals …

Myrna sipped sparkling water from a crystal goblet and said politely, "Are all those heads your husband's?"

"No. Some were slaughtered by Charles's bloodthirsty predecessors." The distaste stamped over Dame Sylvia's face was epic. "Nothing like shooting an animal from three hundred yards with military sniper technology. The sport of kings."

Myna thumped her water glass down in surprise. "You don't like hunting?"

"There are other ways to maintain healthy animal populations." Sylvia flicked a dismissive glance at an enormous atypical elk. "I don't see why I can't change the trophy-hunting culture. After all, I've converted the soullessness of modern farming back to more sustainable natural practices here at the ranch. We grow over ninety percent of what we serve, purely organic, as I've said."

Which was definitely reflected in the prices tattooed on the menu. Myrna figured if she had to eat at this restaurant every day, she'd go broke halfway through tomorrow's lunch.

Dame Sylvia plucked a snowy white linen napkin from the table, shook out its intricate folds, and smoothed it over her lap. "The cuisine here is outstanding and reflects the amalgam of cultural influences, including a unique blend of Hispanic and Puebloan recipes. I'll take the stacked red enchiladas," she told the suddenly hovering waiter. "Dr. Lee?"

Myrna had gone hungry as a child if she or her mother had failed to hunt or gather enough food, so she wasn't a picky eater. Still, everything sounded delicious. She selected the blue corn chile rellenos, calabacitas, and mixed beans—pinto, bolito, and Anasazi —cooked in a micaceous pot.

"Before we talk about your progress, I want to remind you that you're prohibited from speaking, writing, or revealing through any source what you have seen or heard on this ranch during your employment." Dame Sylvia's gaze was direct, polite, and cold. "Thus far, no one we've hired could give us a definitive answer to the die-offs. Do you know what killed those elk?"

A raucous bout of laughter from the investors' table punctuated her last words. Myrna let it die down before she hedged, "I have my suspicions."

Dame Sylvia perked right up, lips faintly curved in what was almost a triumphant smile. "You don't know."

"Not yet." Myrna lifted her chin and held the Dame's gaze. "But I'm the best at what I do. I believe it's more complicated than simply poison. That's why I asked you about the use of agrichemicals on the ranch—"

"We don't use them. I'm not sure how I can make myself clearer."

"My tissue samples are contaminated with agrichemicals. Not at levels that could kill the elk, but ..." She had a theory, except she didn't have enough evidence yet to voice it. "Were pesticides and herbicides found in the earlier studies?"

"Unfortunately, a lightning strike severely damaged our servers. That data was lost."

Myrna didn't believe her. She narrowed her eyes. "And lightning somehow reached into the lab computers and wiped them out, too?"

Dame narrowed her eyes right back. "I'm sure none of that will be a problem as you are *the best at what you do*."

Their food arrived, stopping Myrna from saying anything stupid enough to get her fired. She cut into the rellenos, the feeling of being sandbagged growing stronger.

They ate in silence, but after a few bites, Dame Sylvia sighed and laid down her fork.

"No one else we've hired looked for agrichemicals because they're banned on the ranch. But if you've found them, it's a problem for my Woollywood organics brand. I could lose my certification."

"Were pesticides and herbicides used on the ranch in the past?" Myrna asked.

"The families that occupied the old logging and mining camps grew their own food." The Dame shifted in her chair, her forehead etched in worry. "They used the mines to stockpile some pretty nasty stuff. I was assured it was removed and destroyed decades ago."

Except the synthetics Myrna found in her samples were more modern, produced recently, not decades ago.

"Maybe something was missed. I'd like to visit those mines and do a little exploring for myself."

The Dame's lips tightened, but she nodded her assent and picked up her fork.

The investors finished with lunch, and the group of men and women drifted away from the table. Two men, one tall and one very short with a cowboy hat in hand, headed toward Dame Sylvia. The sun took that moment to light up the room and halo the men to silhouettes.

Their hostess dropped her linen on her plate and stood.

"Finn!" She embraced the taller of the two men, giving him the both-cheeks European air-kiss. "Charles didn't tell me you were here. Is Lina with you?"

"Not this trip. My business included an in-depth review of the reclamation projects." The man Finn spoke perfect English, but there was something clipped and foreign about it. "I'll be outdoors with my men, and you know Lina and outside don't mix." The light kaleidoscoped through fast-moving clouds, allowing Myrna glimpses of a striking man: gray eyes; sharp, clean-shaven cheeks; a square jaw; and salt-and-pepper hair cut short. Wide shoulders capped a lean torso and narrow hips, and his trousers molded long legs. He wore a single silver earring.

"Ah, those mines." Dame Sylvia's face sobered. "We were just talking about them. Finn Posse, this is Dr. Myrna Lee, a visiting toxicologist. Finn owns the company in charge of mine-site cleanup on the ranch. And you've met my husband, Charles."

The sun burst from behind the clouds as Charles Donavan stepped around his companion to square off next to his wife.

"Good afternoon, Dr. Lee," he said courteously. "I heard you didn't get the results you expected from your excavation last evening."

Myrna raised a hand to shade her face. "I'm afraid not, but it won't stop me from figuring out—" Clouds blocked the sun once more. Her words died on her tongue.

She hadn't gotten a good look at him last night, but she got an eyeful now. Pale blue eyes set in tanned skin met hers through round gold-wire spectacles. Below his potato-shaped nose, a thick walrus mustache draped his top lip and drooped cowboy-style to bracket his mouth. He resembled Teddy Roosevelt, but that's not what choked off Myrna's speech.

Standing in front of her was the twin of the man who'd led the outlaw gang she'd seen in William Tell's vision.

The man who'd ordered the fallen cowboy's murder.

Thirty-One

White coat buttoned to her neck against the cold laboratory air, Myrna sat at the humming HPLC. She touched an icon on the screen to trigger a high-pressure system purge, scouring away leftover residue and contaminants. Purification of the precisely engineered machinery gave her a deep satisfaction, a fresh start with each experiment. If she wasn't precise and thorough, her results would be tainted. Worthless. In the analytical processes she oversaw, cleanliness was next to scientific godliness.

Myrna checked the level of solvent, her holy water used to purify her flock of machinery. Organic absolution. With the dawning of a new day, her equipment could go on with their analyses as if her past experiments didn't blot their internal workings anymore. And if the columns and tubing became gummed up with the residuals, she could replace them with new parts.

Too bad it didn't work that easily with living organisms.

She stopped the pump and closed the purge valve. She'd already figured out part of the *how* the elk died. Like she'd told Dame Sylvia at lunch that afternoon, what caused the deaths was complicated, but contamination by pesticides and herbicides had contributed. Once she found the contamination's source, she'd start to explore the *why*, although she had a theory. Especially after she'd seen the drones at Woollywood Farms.

Except more time outside in the wild searching for rogue agri-chemicals diverted her away from her clandestine actual prize: discovery of a Paleolithic poison and the absolution she craved from her peers. Then, after proving to everyone and herself she wasn't a disaster, maybe she could forgive herself for falling for that rat, Tom Hutchinson.

Exploration of the mammoth kill site was vitally important, as well as sampling the cache of Clovis points Eleanor had told her existed in the ranch museum. She'd meant to ask for access at lunch, but that had been blown to kingdom come when she'd seen Charles Donavan's face.

On autopilot, Myrna switched out the solvent mixtures with fresh bottles of filtered mobile phase.

Charles Tres Donavan wasn't the man she'd seen in William Tell's vision. She knew that. But the likeness was uncanny. So, a genetic great-great-great relative.

The buttons Jessup found could help pinpoint the decade. She needed to ask him—

No, she didn't. Investigation of a past murder would only fritter away more of her precious time on the ranch.

The lab door swung open with a flash of sunlight, a swirl of fresh air, and William Tell's loud, juicy panting. The dog powered past her bench, his leash taut in Jessup's outstretched hand, like he was a largemouth bass pulling the angler who'd hooked him into the depths. He dove into the water dish and lapped noisily, dribbling more than he drank, before he snuffled his empty food dish. He sent Myrna a reproachful look.

Jessup unclipped the leash and closed the little fence on the pen. He leaned over to give the dog a pat before facing her, eyes smiling.

"I swear he got plenty of water. He also might have eaten half of Paden's turkey sandwich."

"He pants open-mouthed like that because he's tasting the air to figure out what's going on," she said. "It supplements his sensory inputs. And, given the chance, he'll eat garbage."

Jessup leaned his elbows on the black countertop between them. It made his body longer and leaner. Myrna gulped and turned her back to him.

"We had a good day together," he said. "Outside."

She fiddled with the purge valve.

"You should try it. Not in a paper suit or pursuing your mammoth bones. Just … out there." His voice was much closer. She glanced over her shoulder and her stomach swooped. He stood near enough that she thought about panting open-mouthed, too. "How was your day, Dr. Lee?"

"I learned a couple of things from Dame Sylvia that need follow-up. And I confirmed pesticides and herbicides in the elk blood you collected. The levels aren't high enough to drop them dead on the ground, but it's possible they had an indirect effect."

"The Donavans don't allow—"

"Yes, yes, I know." She faked a terrible British accent. "The ranch is completely organic."

Myrna snapped off her gloves and beckoned him to follow her to a desk at the back of the lab. She sat, and Jessup pulled up a chair as she tapped the laptop on. "I did two-dimensional isoelectric sodium-dodecyl polyacrylamide gel electrophoresis—

"Meerkat, I barely made it out of high school."

She frowned impatiently. "Then I'll *teach* you. Like I was saying, I did 2D-SDS-PAGE on the liver samples I harvested. For the control, Isaac found some old elk liver in the café's deep freeze—it's not ideal. Too much degradation, but it's all I have for comparison. The experiments measure the number and amount of individual proteins in the tissue, separating them by charge, then mass, to give results that look like this scattering of spots we see on the screen. Notice that some proteins in the die-off samples are elevated compared to the control. The database identified the elevated proteins as enzymes that chemically modify xenobiotics, an adaptive detoxification mechanism. I'll come back to that in a sec." Myrna waved a hand at the screen. "Do you see the difference? I mean, it's completely obvious. Even *you* ..."

When she received no response, Myrna turned to him.

He was looking right at her. His eyes held embarrassment, anger, and disappointment, emotions she'd incited on the faces of countless students and scientists she'd worked with over the years. Except for the disappointment. Somehow, that stung the worst.

Heat crept up her neck, but she refused to acknowledge shame or discomfiture for the way she treated him. This was who she'd had to be, her arrogance and bravado the only way she'd been able to gain control over her chaotic past. Over people who underestimated her, who dismissed her.

Who abandoned her.

"I know this is above your level," she said. "But I need you to understand the results because I want something from you."

He shifted back in the chair and folded his arms. "Then you're goin' about it all wrong."

"It's the way I do it with every other individual I work with. Like I said, I'm *teaching*."

"No. You're pushing me—and all those others—away." The disappointment on Jessup's eyes morphed to pity. "Didn't you learn anything yesterday with those Girl Scouts?"

She had. And it had felt good to be a part of such trusting innocence. But she'd discovered the hard way that relying on other people—her mother, friends, lovers—was for chumps. Because no matter how much she'd tried to be who they wanted her to be, they always let her down.

Myrna lifted her chin, lips pressed into a hard line to stop them from trembling.

"I don't need your judgment or pity." She grabbed the mouse, zooming in on a specific region of the experiment. "I've already had enough in my life to fill an ocean and drown in it."

"And I don't need your attitude, young lady," Jessup's voice was stern, commanding.

Oh, no. Myrna's body gave a delicious shiver as goosebumps trickled across every inch of her skin. Her stupid daddy complex raised its snakelike head, offering her a bite of the poison apple yet again. The ridiculous yearning for the father figure she'd never had as a child that Tom Hutchinson had mocked and laughed about more than once during their relationship.

"I've admitted that you intimidate the hell outta me because you're so smart and so young. But treat me with respect, and it'll be returned." His voice gentled. "Myrna? I won't be like those people who hurt you in the past."

William Tell's quiet snores and the hum of the equipment filled the silence.

"How do you know?" She grimaced and fixed unseeing eyes on the computer screen. "I mean, how do you know about my ... past?"

Jessup's hand covered her hand that covered the mouse. The skin of his palm was callused and warm, the top of his hand and wrist dotted with white-blond hairs and a galaxy of sun freckles, his fingers blunt and strong. Another shiver coursed through her.

"Maybe you're not the only one who had it rough as a kid." His hand squeezed and slid away. "How about we start over, and you tell me what you want from me."

Myrna chanced a quick look at him. He was focused on the computer, but there was a telltale red stain across his cheeks, and his arms were once again folded over his chest, like he was trying to restrain them. She cleared her throat.

"The elk had both pesticides and herbicides in their bloodstreams. Not enough to kill them, but their exposure appears to be chronic. Ingestion increased the levels of certain proteins or enzymes that help detoxify chemicals. Higher levels of these detoxifying enzymes *usually* change xenobiotics and contaminants into compounds that can be excreted out of the body in the urine. But sometimes they create compounds that stay in the body longer and are actually *more* toxic." She paused. "Which brings me to another question. Do you inoculate your animals against disease? Use antibiotics in the water, give them supplemental feed with any type of drugs or hormones to stimulate antler growth? Anything like that?"

"No." His voice was firm.

"No? Or not that you know of?"

"I mean no." Jessup's brows lowered. "What do you mean, not that I know of?"

"It's part of my theory. Have you ever heard of a prodrug?" At his head shake, Myrna continued. "It's a medication that relies on cellular metabolism for activation. For example, the body uses specific enzymes to convert codeine, a prodrug with little activity, into morphine, a compound ten times more potent. I think something like that is happening to these elk."

"The elk are turning pesticides and herbicides into something that kills them?"

"No. Those compounds induce certain enzymes to high levels. Then *those* enzymes ..." Myrna weighed her words carefully. "What if the elk had some *other* drug in their body—not a prodrug, but a pro*poison*, and the pesticide-induced enzymes turn it into a substance that kills them?"

Jessup frowned. "But to get those four animals to literally drop dead at the same time—"

"This propoison would've had to be introduced to them at the same time." She swallowed. "Like, maybe by nanodrones?"

Jessup's eyebrows shot to his hairline. "*Harley's* drones? Why would that *idio*— Harley Wakefield want to kill elk?"

"Not intentionally. Unintentionally."

He made a scoffing noise. "Unintentional killing. Right. Dr. Lee, there's an old cowboy saying: If you hear hoofbeats drummin' outside the bunkhouse, they're probably not comin' from a zebra."

Except people hired her to solve unsolvable poisonings, and *lots* of zebras inhabited her world.

"Anyway, wouldn't it be more likely this propoison is in the weed killers?" he asked. "Or the pesticides?"

Myrna nibbled her lip. "Possibly."

"And since these four boys were hanging out together in a bachelor herd, maybe they ate or drank something that was contaminated with this propoison around the same time that could've triggered their deaths."

"Sure, but—" She hesitated. Jessup's simple explanation made the rest of her theory seem like she plucked it from an internet conspiracy site. She drew one last card. "Has there ever been any use of birth control drugs to lower the elk or deer population so hunting on the ranch can be eliminated?"

Jessup barked out a laugh. "Charles Donavan's head would explode if he knew you were even asking that question."

Her expression fell. That's what she'd been afraid of.

"Are those elevated spots in your experiment the only evidence you have for your theory?" he asked.

If she didn't count the tiny quantities of the deadly steroid-like neurotoxin she'd found in her samples, or the perfect drone drug delivery system she'd been shown at the greenhouse. Or Dame Sylvia Donavan, who might hate hunting enough to implement a birth control program under her husband's nose. But to accuse his wife without more evidence ...

"If I took my preliminary results to Mr. Donavan, do you think he'd be angry enough to shoot the messenger?"

Jessup scratched his chin. "Charles Tres Donavan is a fair and honorable man—much more so than his predecessors. But if this notion of yours makes him feel even half the way I do, I wouldn't count on staying to finish this commission, much less dig up those mammoth bones."

She deflated on a breath. "That's what I figured." So maybe she'd wait to break into Harley's lab for evidence *after* she got permission to test the Donavan museum stone projectiles.

"Myrna?" A gentle finger ran over her jaw. Her attention snapped to Jessup's baby blues, thoughts scattering like marbles.

"You said you wanted something from me. What do you want, Myrna?"

Heat flashed through her. Loaded question, and she figured her first answer would be considered *extremely* inappropriate.

She gathered up her marbles and went with her *second* answer.

"To find the source of the pesticide and herbicide contamination. Prove it's originating from the ranch. You know this land, and I don't have the time to explore it on my own." Especially with only ten days left of her two weeks. "But I don't just want your help. I—I need ..."

Myrna broke their gaze to stare at her fidgeting fingers. She wanted to trust him *so much*. Was it worth the risk? Was he—*Jessup* —worth the risk?

Because somehow, this seemed like more than a simple trip with him into the wilderness.

She straightened her spine, dipping into her well of courage. When she raised her eyes to his, she faced him as an equal. A partner.

"Jessup? I *need* your help," she admitted. "I—I can't do this without you."

His blossoming smile shot straight through her heart. "We'll leave tomorrow morning."

For the second time in two days, the icy ball of betrayal and mistrust, served to Myrna her whole life by people she'd loved, thawed a bit more. And hope for a future where she didn't have to be alone started to germinate.

Thirty-Two

The next morning, Myrna pouted in the passenger seat of Jessup's work truck, arms crossed, bottom lip pooched, except the roughness of the two-track dirt road severely tested her ability to maintain her posture. She kept having to brace for ruts so she wouldn't be thrown around the cozy cab that smelled of bacon and egg breakfast sandwiches and coffee—offerings from Isaac because she and Jessup had left Cimarron so early on their back country search for the agrichemical contamination. He'd also packed their lunch in an insulated cooler that sat on the floor behind them.

Right below *William Tell's doggie carrier.*

Myrna darted a peevish glare at the snoring dog, then to Jessup. "He'll be nothing but trouble."

"Mm-hm." Jessup, his face shadowed by the brim of his ball cap, slowed to negotiate a crumbling section of track just visible in the lightening dawn. He'd stopped responding verbally three or four complaints ago.

Myrna hunched a shoulder. She stared out the truck window, determined not to utter another word. Nope. Not a sound. Quiet as the grave.

"You like him so much," she sniffed, "he can stay with you at night. That way I can get some sleep, because he snores."

"I like you even more, Meerkat, so you could stay with me at night, too. But I can't promise you'd get any sleep." Jessup sent Myrna a smile that curled her toes. The pleasure of his words trickled through her.

They'd driven in on the unsecured back road to the ranch but turned onto a second branching track about ten miles in. Twenty minutes later, Jessup navigated the truck into a narrow gap cutting through the pines and stopped. He hopped out and opened a three-rail gate, rusty twists of barbed wire securing a red NO TRESPASSING sign. They drove onward, signs with the same message nailed to trees every quarter mile, until the truck emerged into a valley tapered to a V at the far end by steeply rising mountain slopes. Myrna craned her neck, interest piqued by the electric and telephone wires draped on short poles alongside the road.

"Someone lives out here? Isn't this Donavan land?"

"Not this valley. All the surrounds are, though," Jessup replied. "A few families remain who wouldn't sell or refused to be driven off by earlier generations of Donavans. Most are hanging on by their fingernails because their children leave. This family hasn't had to face that ... yet."

The sun capped the mountaintops with cheery morning light, illuminating a jumble of rocks that Myrna would've sworn was a ginormous cow skull with a darkly shadowed eye socket and a long, sloping nose. On the valley floor, black-bodied cattle dotted the tall grass, white faces popping up to watch the truck as they drove by.

What was left of night rolled down the far mountains, rushing toward them until the truck burst from shadow into the light that sped across the valley. A house appeared in the distance, made of the same gray and red stone of the cliff that rose behind it. It sat squat and unobtrusive, its only sign of life a trickle of smoke unwinding from the chimney. Trucks, cars, and farm equipment in various stages of disintegration decorated the dusty yard. A large garden nestled between the house and a barn whose grayed patina revealed its age. Except ...

Myrna leaned forward. Blond planks of new wood replaced some of the old, and pyramids of deer fence and bundles of posts lay stacked near the garden.

Jessup stopped the truck about a hundred feet from the front door, engine idling. He rolled down his window and propped an elbow on the sill. Long seconds ticked away as the chill morning replaced the cab's warmth. William Tell stood up, wobbling the dog carrier. He sniffed the cold air and gruffed.

"Aren't you going to get out and knock on the door?" Myrna asked. A curtain flickered in the window.

"They know we're here."

"You don't seriously think that garden is the source of the herbicides."

"I doubt they can afford those kinds of chemicals. The only money coming in is from selling spring calves and their landowner elk tags."

Myrna caught movement in her side-view mirror. A huge late-model midnight-blue pickup punched out of the forest behind them, going fast enough to jar the teeth out of its driver. It roared past and swerved to a halt, blocking the front door.

"No money, huh?" Myrna said. "Then how'd they pay for *that*?"

Jessup didn't reply, but all traces of the good-natured cowboy were gone. He opened his door and stepped onto the hard-packed road. William Tell yipped. Myrna shushed him, so he resorted to scratching the plastic insides and whining. He felt the tension as much as she did.

When the blue truck's driver's-side door finally opened, a man about Jessup's age got out and hurried to the passenger door. Myrna's eye's widened as Paden, the young ranch hand who'd set up the computer system for her elk carcass, slid out of the backseat.

"Paden's family lives here?"

"Goes back on this land longer than the Donavans," Jessup said. "That's his dad, Arthur."

Paden snuck a glance at Jessup before he fished something out of the truck bed. He unfurled it into a fancy walker with a cushioned seat and wire basket. Arthur swung open the front passenger door to help a third person out with careful hands, and the oldest human Myrna had ever seen grasped the walker's handles. Bookended by Paden and Arthur, the old man rolled with shuffling steps toward Jessup, who didn't wait but trotted forward. When he reached the group, they exchanged stiff handshakes and nods. A woman hurried from the house, pushed through the men, and gave Jessup a hug. After she released him, Jessup headed back to Myrna as Paden's family trailed inside their home. He opened the back door and unlatched the dog carrier.

"We've been invited in," Jessup told her. "I said we needed to walk the dog first."

Myrna jumped to the ground and scurried to meet Jessup. William Tell strained at the end of his leash, nose up, mouth open, padding back and forth and sniff-snorting the air, alerting to something only he could smell.

"What would happen if I dropped the leash?" Jessup asked.

"Are you kidding? He'd head directly for whatever he's scenting, even if it's halfway up the mountain, and he can be *very* hard to catch, so don't—"

Jessup dropped the leash.

Thirty-Three

William Tell bolted straight for the barn. Well, not straight. First, he dodged the rolls of deer fencing and posts. Then he ducked around a pile of brand-new shingles stacked by the side of the house before he dipped between the garden and a shiny olive-green UTV. He slowed as he approached the barn. Myrna, hot on his tail, dove for the trailing leash, only to have the dog find a hole under a broken board and dodge inside. He started up a furious barking.

Jessup, already at the barn's double doors, lifted the bar that secured it and threw it to the ground. Myrna grabbed one handle, Jessup the other—

"Don't you go in there, Jessup Page!" The rack of a shotgun punctuated a woman's voice. A man pleaded, "Trini, *please.*"

Myrna flipped and plastered her back to the door, heart pounding hard enough to jump out of her chest. She stared into the two dark eyes of the double-barrel tucked into the shoulder of the woman who'd hugged Jessup. Arthur and Paden stood like statues behind her. Jessup didn't turn around.

"What you gonna do, Trini? Shoot me in the back? Bury our bodies in the family cemetery? I've always wondered about those blank headstones." He had to yell over William Tell's unremitting barks. "Got a call from Oliver Chavéz y Chavéz."

Paden's stiffness melted to a slump. "He knows, Mom. Give me the gun. *Please.*"

"We needed the money, Jessup," Arthur said. "All he wanted was the mount. He let us keep the meat. The carcass is hanging in the tack room. We set it up for cold storage."

The shotgun muzzle sagged. Paden tugged it away from his mother and cracked it open. He pulled out two shells.

"Who, Arthur?" Jessup pressed.

"One of them Germans cleaning up the mines. Said he wouldn't be here in the fall for a legal hunt because they're close to finishing."

That turned Jessup around, his expression a deep frown.

Myrna put it all together with that last piece of info—almost. "You let one of the guys cleaning up the mines poach an elk, and the carcass is hanging in the barn. Who's Oliver Chavéz y Chavéz?"

"He runs the grocery in Cimarron, along with being the best taxidermist in this part of the state," Jessup replied. "They dropped off the cape and head this morning before light."

"Stupid Oliver," Paden said.

"He's afraid of losing his license," Jessup said.

Trini snorted. "Never bothered him before."

"You're lucky he didn't call Game and Fish. Or Charles Donavan. How much?"

Trini and Arthur exchanged a quick glance before Arthur let out a long sigh and stuffed his hands into the back pockets of his jeans. "Twenty. It's already spent."

Jessup narrowed his eyes to slits. His demeanor hardened. "If I had to total up the truck, the UTV, fencing, roofing, barn repairs ... Adds up to more than twenty thousand dollars."

William Tell's steady barking continued to fill the air. He was getting hoarse.

"Arthur's disability finally came through ... and Paden's bonus," Trini said.

Jessup jerked his gaze to Paden, who turned beet red and dropped his gaze. His hands fidgeted along the shotgun.

"I—I've been doing an extra, uh ... *project* for Dame Sylvia."

Jessup snatched off his cap and slapped it against his thigh. "*Dammit*, Paden. You're sleeping with that woman?"

"*No!*" Paden choked and got redder still if that were possible. He swallowed before he looked at his mother. "I'm not, I swear."

Trini's face was as white as Paden's was red. When she spoke, her voice was strained. "Why don't you get your dog and come inside for coffee. You wanted to talk to Mike, right?"

Jessup nodded. He waited for Paden's family to turn back to the house before he opened the barn door and stepped inside. Myrna followed. William Tell stood at a closed door to the tack room in the back of the cavernous space, body jerking with each bark. A muffled hum of electrical equipment emanated from the room.

Myrna grabbed the end of the leash as she looked around. The barn held the comforting scent of fresh hay and dust, and a metallic hint of blood. "When did they shoot the elk?"

"Couple days ago, according to Oliver. Why?"

"More control tissue for my analyses. Take William Tell." Myrna handed him the leash, pulled out her knife, and opened the tack room door, a wash of cold air flowing past her. "I won't be a minute."

Elk tissue and soil samples from the garden tucked into the lunch cooler, Myrna knocked on the front door of the house. Paden let her in, unwilling to meet her eyes. Was he embarrassed by his mother's behavior? Because *her* mother made Trini look like a saint, shotgun and all. Trini had defended her family. Myrna's mother had abandoned hers.

She patted his arm and stepped into the home's warm embrace, wishing she could be a part of a family like Paden's, one that had obviously lived there a long, long time.

A low-ceilinged room made up the front of the house. On one side, two built-in bookcases jammed with paperback romances, spy thrillers, and dozens of movies flanked a large rock fireplace. In front of it, a comfortable and well-used leather sofa and two rocking chairs perched on a huge, colorful rag rug. Side tables stacked with magazines and lamps were tucked here and there. At the other end of the room, a wall of cabinets made up one side of a seriously old-fashioned kitchen, a camp coffee pot percolating away on a wood-burning enamel stove. A bowl full of eggs sat on a faded yellow Formica countertop and the scent of baking biscuits teased Myrna's nose.

Dividing the kitchen from the living area was a round table with six wooden chairs. The old man from the truck sat closest to the kitchen, one thin leg draped over the other, arm crooked on the table next to a heavy-walled mug of coffee. He studied Myrna with brown eyes faded to gray. Jessup sat next to him, the old silver buttons he'd found resting in a plain white saucer. William Tell lay at his feet, chin on his paws, but alert.

"You're sure, Mike? You've never seen buttons like these before," Jessup pressed.

The man picked up his coffee with a desiccated brown hand and the unsteadiness of the very old and took a sip.

"They're marked with a name," Jessup pressed. "Redhouse or Rosehorse. Probably Navajo. That ring any bells?"

"Them biscuits done, Trini?" Mike asked in a wavering voice. "Get this gal a cup of coffee. I remember a girl, just like you, in France, near the German border. Skinny. Alone. Living like an animal in the woods. Me and my squad fed her C-rats—canned rations—and gave her a warm blanket. Talked that night about taking her with us to turn over to the authorities. She'd disappeared by morning."

Trini placed a cup of coffee and a jug of milk on the table.

"She would've been scared." Myrna spoke with conviction and experience. Only six or maybe seven years old, she'd been terrified standing at the edge of that Idaho hunting camp, hair in a wild tangle, her clothes faded and dirty, watching the group of men joke and laugh in the firelight.

Her mother had left her alone for a week—or maybe forever. Myrna never knew. In her absence, Myrna had consumed all their meager provisions, scavenged for more, but hunger gnawed her belly something fierce. The scent of meat cooking over the campfire had overcome her fear—mostly. She'd been so attuned to the wild, so alone in herself, the hunters hadn't even noticed her. Finally, knees shaking, voice a whisper, she'd stepped forward and asked, *"May I have something to eat?"*

When she couldn't eat another bite, they'd zipped her up in a tent with a cozy cot thinking she'd fall asleep and they would hand her over to the authorities the next morning. She'd used her knife to slice through the heavy canvas, not the first time it had gotten her out of a jam.

"Scared even of your kindness, if she'd been living wild." Myrna traced the deep lines on old man's face with her gaze. "I imagine she stayed hidden, watching until you were gone."

And wishing they wouldn't leave her alone.

Mike frowned. "I don't think we've been introduced." With old-fashioned formality and creaky grace, he stood. And in his eyes, Myrna glimpsed a once charming and shy young man behind the haze of age—a lot like Paden. "Miguel Cabeza de Baca. Arthur over there is my youngest grandson, his wife Trini, and my great-grandson, Paden. Got how many greats, Arthur?"

"Sixteen. Four great-greats with Juana's new baby."

"Myrna Paula Lee." Myrna shook his fragile, cold hand.

"Please call me Myrna." Still holding his hand, she helped him back into his chair and sat.

Mike noticed the buttons anew and picked one up. "Where'd these come from?"

"I found them on the ranch, up near the bluffs," Jessup said. "You ever seen them before?"

Mike dropped the button on the leathery palm of his hand. He pursed his lips, beetled eyebrows bunched as he brought them close to his eyes. He shrugged and placed it in the dish again.

"Used to run with a wild bunch when I was a kid." Mike nodded to Jessup. "Your great-uncle was one. No harm in us, but after the war ..." He took another sip of his coffee, losing focus as he stared across the room. "Things were different."

"I'm sorry," Trini murmured. "He gets this way."

Jessup nodded. He scooped up the buttons into the baggie and stood, tucking it into pocket on the thigh of his camos. "Mike? Could I show you one more thing?"

Jessup dug into his pocket again. He deftly spun a large coin on the table, which quickly wobbled to a lopsided stop. The bullet-deformed silver dollar.

The old man paled. "Where'd you get this?" he rasped.

"Hey, Grampo. Don't you have one of those? Like the one up at the lodge? 'Cept yours isn't ..." Paden's voice faded. "Grampo?"

Jessup answered Mike's question. "Same place I found those buttons. But you already knew that didn't you?"

Mike exploded, his face choleric, gray replaced by red. "Get out of this house. Get out!"

Myrna, who'd been watching the interplay intently, pushed her chair back and stood. William Tell scrambled to his feet. Jessup didn't move.

Mike turned to his grandson, hand outstretched, pleading. "Arturo?"

Arthur, his expression a mask of worry and confusion, placed a hand on the old man's shoulders. "You need to leave, Jessup. He can't have this upset. It's bad for his heart."

Before Jessup could take the coin, Mike's claw-like fingers swept it up and slipped it into his shirt pocket.

"No. You can't ... That's not—" Myrna started, but Jessup raised a hand to silence her.

"We're heading through the canyon, up to the Corazón del Cimarron. Anything we need to know?"

Brows puckered, Arthur shook his head, but Trini turned away.

She opened the oven. "Damn. I burned the biscuits."

THIRTY-FOUR

Myrna buckled herself into the passenger seat and shot quick glances at Jessup's stern profile. He grabbed William Tell's harness handle, lifted him into the backseat, and secured the dog in his carrier. He climbed into the truck beside her and powered the vehicle forward in an engine-revving, gravel-scattering surge before gaining traction. He drove along a two-track dirt road around the far side of the barn and straight toward a funneling canyon, steep cliffs on either side.

"You checked the garden?" he asked. A white-faced cow hurried across the road ahead in a jarring trot. She stopped under a lone tree to watch the truck.

"I took plant and soil samples, but no way the contamination I found is coming from that homestead. You knew that." Myrna licked her lips, suddenly very unsure of him. "So why did you bring us here?"

"Fastest route to the mine reclamation site is through this canyon. That's part of your investigation."

"Visiting that ranch wasn't. This wasn't about the poached elk in the barn. It was just a convenient excuse to show Mike those buttons and that coin. Why did you think he knew who owned the coin?"

Other questions smoldering in her subconscious bubbled up. Why had Bard assigned Jessup as her minder? Why not some other, less important staff member?

"Are you using me?" she blurted.

Jessup's hands tightened on the steering wheel. "What's the matter, Dr. Lee? It's only okay when you do it?"

Myrna chewed her lip. She deserved that.

Jessup navigated the truck past a sun-bleached wood fence surrounding a tombstone-peppered cemetery. Lashed in the middle of a metal entry gate was a cow skull. On top of two tall poles above it was a rough sign that read CABEZA DE BACA. Mike had introduced himself with the same last name.

Time to defuse the situation, because she needed Jessup to help solve her riddles—exactly what he'd accused her of. Myrna shrugged off her niggling guilt and dug into the sack of food at her feet, half unwrapped a breakfast sandwich, and handed it to him. Modulating her voice to make it contrite, she asked, "Where are we headed?"

He took the sandwich with a long, indrawn breath and visibly relaxed.

"A logging road that runs along the bluffs above your mammoth kill site. We'll have to hike, though. No motorized vehicles—road's been closed over twenty-five years—the Donavans' nod to wilderness. A mile or so in, then a half mile of bushwhacking to the cliff." He shot her glance. "You up for that?"

She nodded and swallowed a bite of food, deciding not to ask why.

"After that?"

"To the mine reclamation site. Charles Donavan called last night to clear a visit with the overseer."

Jessup bit into his sandwich to the sound of William Tell's *I-*

want-bacon whine. The relative silence—this time companionable —lasted as they wended their way up the side of a forested road. He halted the truck in a grassy clearing facing a wall of evergreens, birch, and aspen. The road continued between the trees but was barricaded by logs and stones. A posted sign declared, WILDER-NESS—No Motorized Vehicles Allowed.

Myrna opened her door. The sharp, pine-scented air tingled over her skin. She slid to the ground. Her boots sank into rich, loamy earth, and her toes curled. Her gaze darted hungrily into the warren of trees as her wild side drew up from the depths. She'd lived in old growth forests in the Northwest, survived in wilderness so pristine she might have been born ten thousand years ago. Whenever her mother felt like it, they'd hitchhike across hundreds of miles, just to be dropped off in the middle of nowhere to disappear into undergrowth so thick they had to crawl on their bellies over beds of moss and ferns, beneath thickets and deadfall.

She'd loved and hated those times. Loved them for the feeling of belonging. Hated them because the wilderness wasn't as isolated as everyone thought. Dangerous and deadly, animals and humans lurked in the gaps. Jessup knew it, too. He slotted a handgun into a concealed holster on his hip before he leaned in to open the dog carrier. With seasoned practice, Myrna secured her quiver and bow to her backpack.

Leash snapped onto William Tell's harness, they hopped the barrier logs and headed into the forest.

William Tell snuffled and pulled after smells only he could detect. Myrna ruthlessly kept him moving. If he marked every tree —which he was on track to do—they'd be out here for hours.

The road they walked had been destroyed for vehicles— trenches dug, trees felled, and boulders rolled as barricades. But it would take years for the compacted soil to loosen up enough for anything other than surface grasses and forbs to grow. They'd hiked for half an hour when Jessup angled into the forest on a well-defined game trail. William Tell and Myrna followed single file. They tromped between trees that periodically opened into clearings stacked with jumbled islands of boulders surrounded by a sea of denuded soil.

At a particularly large hill of rocks, William Tell leaned hard into his harness, plowing furrows into the sandy dirt with pumping back legs, intent on pulling Myrna's arm off. She staggered after him up a couple stone tiers and crinkled her nose at the strong scent of urine.

Packrat scat, piles of twigs, bits of aluminum, shiny bottle caps, chewed pieces of insulated wire, even a shell casing or two lined a large black opening. Big enough for her to disappear down into, much less the beseeching dog at the end of the leash.

When William Tell finally realized Myrna wouldn't let him explore the burrow, he lifted a leg and left an impressive puddle on a flat rock.

"You can mark it all you want, but we are *not* coming back." Tugging the dog behind her, she hurried after Jessup.

Jessup finally stopped at a ragged arroyo four feet wide and shoulder-deep that funneled over the cliff's edge.

"The mother mammoth kill site's below." He smiled. "You said the rest of her baby's bones were up here. Thought you might want a look, Meerkat."

This detour was all for her? Myrna's heart warmed.

"Thank you."

And she'd accused him of using her for his own purposes.

She handed him William Tell's leash and climbed down into the arroyo. The bottom was sandy, the side walls strung with tree roots. Bent double, Myrna began a slow perusal. A dozen feet in, a broken scapula protruded from the arroyo's wall, difficult to distinguish in a jumble of small stones nearly the same color. Her heart rate soared. She crouched, scanning for more bones—

And found a partial boot print. Recent.

Casually, she backtracked, expression relaxed, eyes sharp. Someone had been digging. Skillfully covered up, but she'd been to too many illegal excavations—even participated in a few—not to recognize the signs.

"Find anything?" Jessup asked.

Myrna forced a smile and pointed to the protruding bone.

He nodded, his fingers fidgeting with the leash. "Do you see a skull?"

He'd mentioned the skull before. She pretended to do another sweep. "No, but excavation might turn one up." Myrna paused. "Why?"

"Let's follow the arroyo, see if we can find the water source."

A nonanswer to her question. He took off, William Tell's nose stuck to the ground, and quickly disappeared into the undergrowth.

Myrna dug into her pack for sample tubes and filled them with sand and soil before she hurried after Jessup, sticking to the arroyo as her path.

About fifty yards up, she found the first plastic bag snagged on water-bared roots. Though torn and tattered, Myrna could still read the warning label: PHOSPHATE FERTILIZER, 40 LBS. Her heart began to thump, painfully this time.

She continued up the narrowing arroyo. More labeled plastic—preemergent herbicide, shredded black trash bags spilling food wrappers and fast food garbage, beige grocery store sacks, empty cans, a torn shirt, and *shit, shit, shit*—a dead pine marten. She knelt by it, hand pressed to her mouth.

They're baiting for rodents, not caring about collateral damage.

Myrna scrambled up the arroyo's side. At a sprint, she leaped deadfall and dodged trees, her *wild* bubbling up and seizing control in her urgency.

She halted at the edge of the old logging road. A trench dug across it had washed out to form part of the arroyo, a perfect flume for whatever water system she knew she'd find on the other side.

But where were Jessup and William Tell?

Because if she didn't stop them, they'd walk right into a hornets' nest.

THIRTY-FIVE

With quick fingers, Myrna released her bow and arrows from her backpack. Arrow knocked, she skittered along the forest's edge, blending into shadows, tree trunks, and brush, her footfalls cautious. Around a bend, she found Jessup squatting above a log laid in one of the road trenches to make the track drivable. William Tell snuffled the dirt. Farther down the road, trees had been bulldozed to form a lane disappearing up the mountain slope on the other side. The ground was torn up with both truck and UTV tracks. *Fresh* tracks.

William Tell noticed her first. He bounded to the end of the leash, ears perked. Jessup stood, and she caught his gaze.

"We need to go," Myrna said, tense as her bowstring. "*Now.*"

"We need to find their camp," Jessup said, expression inflexible.

"Are you *crazy*? They'll have just as many trail cameras as Bard has, maybe booby traps, and they'll be armed to the teeth." Myrna glared at him. "*You knew.*"

"I suspected. So did you from the contamination."

She had. Illicit marijuana growers weren't subtle. Since they didn't care about the devastation to wildlife or their customers, they dumped ridiculous quantities of poisons on their product and around their camps. Legalization didn't stop the devastation, and lawmakers only paid lip service to the pollution because they were in it for the money, too.

"Come on." Jessup started up the hill, and Myrna dashed to cut him off.

"You can't take him," she hissed. "He'll bark."

"I trust him to be quiet." William Tell waggled his butt adoringly at Jessup.

Myrna rolled her eyes. She stowed away her bow. "Count to ten, then follow my trail. And *no* talking."

She slipped into the trees, ignoring Jessup's "Myrna, *wait*."

Sixty yards in, the understory had been cleared, the debris and deadfall and cut trees used in berms and dams that trapped the water needed for the grow site. A dam burst had probably cut the arroyo down to the cliff. Enough water had spilled to unearth the mammoth bones, meaning the operation was large. Lots of product worth lots of money. It would be well-protected. She scanned the tree trunks for trail cameras, spotting one up the slope.

A twig snapped behind her. Myrna held out a restraining hand. She caught Jessup's eyes and pointed to the camera. He nodded. William Tell, playing the role of "best-est doggie ever," sat obediently at his feet, blinking soft, liquid eyes at her. Yeah, well, she wasn't fooled. Myrna scowled at him before she crept forward to inspect the camera. Motion-triggered, but not wireless. The SD card had to be retrieved for viewing, so whoever ran the grow couldn't respond to immediate threats. Dumb. She unbungeed the camera and let it fall to the ground. In short order, she disabled three more.

Her path ended at a massive, naturally terraced rock formation that rose to a huge crown of stone. The cow skull formation she'd seen from Paden's homestead that morning. PVC pipes ran down the side, connected by valves to heavy-duty black hoses snaking over bare ground and disappearing into the forest. The terraced stones would act as catchments for the water needed at the grow site. From where she stood, Myrna couldn't see any plants, but their musty, pungent scent permeated the breeze.

She paralleled the hoses, keeping to the trees. A loud *thwack* and increasing trash around her feet alerted her to the campsite as did the stench of human waste, wood smoke, and charred meat. The low thrum of a generator blended with masculine voices. Myrna darted behind a jumble of stones, avoiding the gnawed green block bait scattered near a dark burrow opening. She raised her head and peered over the rocks. What she found chilled her.

A concave cliff rose steeply from the back of the cow skull rock formation, sheltering half the clearing at its base like a curved awning. Towering pine trees with old growth girth protected the other half. Myrna counted half a dozen dirty dome tents and a couple of small storage sheds within the trees. Filtered sunlight dappled the whole campsite, creating natural camouflage. A perfectly situated operation for an illegal grow, virtually undetectable by everything in the sky—from satellites to airplanes to drones.

But it was the dozen men who populated the trash-strewn clearing that sent her pulse into overdrive. Half stood in a semicircle awaiting their turn to heave a hatchet into one of the huge pines, cheering or jeering when the glinting blade struck. Others sat on bent folding chairs around battered camp tables, AR-type long guns propped beside them. And, honest to God, two men stacked green pineapple-shaped hand grenades into a wobbly pyramid like they were building a house of cards. Sweat broke out on her brow.

Shrinking low, Myrna drifted back until she'd dropped below the camp's sightline. The laughter and voices disappeared under the throb of the generator until only the thwack of the biting axe echoed through the trees.

It wasn't until she was a dozen yards from Jessup that she heard William Tell's low growl. She whirled and pointed to the dog, making cutting motions to her throat. Jessup reached down to pick him up—

"No!" Myrna clamped a hand over her mouth, eyes so wide they burned. She whipped around when music blared off the rocks above her. Someone had turned on a boombox, covering the sound of her outburst. She grabbed Jessup by the hand and pulled him down the slope, dodging trees and veering in the direction of their parked truck. Calm crept into her breathing with each step.

"Semiautomatics and grenades," she whispered, hardly louder than the noise of their footsteps. "We need to get back to the truck and—"

William Tell barreled to the end of his leash, barking furiously. An unkempt young man with long, dirty-blond hair, eyes astonished and open-mouthed, frantically hiked up his jeans even as he fumbled for the gun propped against the tree.

THIRTY-SIX

"*un!*" Myrna bolted, Jessup beside her, William Tell leaping and bounding as if it were a game. Gun shots shattered the air. Voices rose and brush crashed behind. She glanced back quickly to see a dozen armed men filtering through the trees and pounding down the slope, ready to commit murder.

She jumped a fallen log just as Jessup and the dog ran around either side of a tree. Both man and dog yanked to a stop, Jessup slipping on pine needles and going down, William Tell dragged backward by Jessup's momentum. Jessup scrambled to his feet and pulled his gun. Myrna veered back, fingers clumsy and shaking as she unhooked the dog's leash before sprinting down the hill with Jessup. William Tell, tongue lolling, followed with a speed she didn't usually see unless there was steak involved, running faster and faster until he passed between her and Jessup.

They dashed across the road and into the trees on the other side, angling toward the parking lot. Bullets slapped trunks and tore branches above their heads. To get to Jessup's truck, they'd have to parallel the cliff. If some of those men followed them into the trees while others ran down the road ... Myrna did the geometry in her head. No way they'd make it. And if they continued their trajectory, they'd go right over the cliff to their deaths like the mammoth and the cowboy.

If she died, who would mourn her?

No one.

If she disappeared, would anybody search for her, try to solve the mystery?

No.

That sucked.

A spray of gunfire ripped up brush on their right. She veered left, Jessup beside her, William Tell looping ahead. They were being herded. But she'd been in worse spots.

Okay, maybe not this bad.

"Is there a trail down the cliff?"

"Not for miles," Jessup panted.

"We could try and hide."

"They're too close." He crashed through a bush. "I say we follow the dog. He seems to know something we don't."

William Tell ran ahead, nose elevated, mouth gaping, tasting the air.

"*The packrat burrow*," Myrna puffed. "That opening in the rocks. We can fit."

Gunfire from behind. Then more shots, but this time ahead of them.

"If we can fit, so can they." Jessup's profile was grim. "Hurry, boy."

As if he understood, the dog shot ahead. He broke through the tree line and bounded up the jumble of boulders he'd marked on their way in. William Tell stopped, his tan chest bellowing. Myrna stumbled into the open, Jessup grabbing her shoulder to steady her. The dog yipped once then disappeared. Myrna and Jessup scrambled up the rocks after him.

Voices and crashing behind them grew louder.

"Go!" Jessup shoved her toward the opening in the earth then took cover behind a big stone, watching the trees behind them. He squeezed off a shot just as Myrna lunged headfirst after William Tell. She crawled, elbows and knees, over slides of dirt and twigs, down, down until she was at least two body lengths from the light. More shots popped.

"Jessup! *Hurry!*"

Everything went dark as Jessup dove in behind her and clambered inside.

"Keep going," he ordered. "Out of the line of fire."

Myrna wriggled and slithered as if her life depended on it—which it did—Jessup at her heels. The sloping tunnel narrowed, widened, narrowed. About thirty feet down, it opened to a low-ceilinged space. She twisted to the right. Jessup, hands hitting the dirt and sticks at the bottom, rolled left as the first shot ricocheted from above. William Tell stood in a puddle of light and barked furiously.

Myrna swept him to her side, closing her eyes as bullets pulverized rock. Cordite, packrat urine, and dust bit into her nose. She pushed William Tell to the ground, held him down, and opened her eyes. Excited voices echoed as one of the bad guys climbed into the tunnel, blocking the light. Jessup moved, twigs crunching under his knees, and squeezed off a shot, the crack making Myrna jump.

A yelp, and light streamed back into the hole. A distinct, "I'm not going in there. If you want 'em that bad, *you* go."

"He didn't hit anything."

"I don't give a *flying fu*—" Furious infighting streamed down the hole.

"Shut up. *Shut up!*" Quiet reigned above, before a low murmur resumed.

"Jessup, look." Myrna peered into the semidarkness behind them. "The cave goes back—"

He held up his hand, eyes focused on the light above. "I don't like this."

Something thumped into the tunnel and rolled on rock, before it thumped, thumped, thumped. And stopped.

Myrna's breath froze as she met Jessup's wide eyes.

"Grenade!"

Scooping up William Tell, she and Jessup plunged into the opening at the back of the burrow—

The whole world exploded.

THIRTY-SEVEN

A concussive wave of pressure and sound, stinging sand, and smoldering twigs blasted through the opening. Myrna curled into a fetal position, William Tell cowered in the hollow of her belly and thighs, Jessup draped over them both. Light from the burrow's entrance blinked out, only to be replaced by the glow and crackle of burning wood and leaves.

Jessup rolled off her. "Go."

His voice bit into Myrna's panic. She scrambled to her hands and knees, spitting dirt, and scuttled after William Tell into the tunnel at the back of the burrow, straight into darkness. William Tell yelped, and Myrna stopped. Jessup plowed into her behind.

"*Go!*" he barked.

Myrna did.

Right off the edge.

She tumbled down a steep sandy slope, her yelp just as loud as the dog's, and somehow rolled into a sitting position at the bottom, dizzy but unhurt.

Jessup's "*Oh, sh—*" jolted her to scurry out of the way until she bumped into a furry body and a rock wall.

Another boom rumbled above them as a second grenade went off. Shivers of sand rained down and a shaking William Tell scrambled into her lap. She cuddled him close and closed her eyes.

"Jessup?" she said plaintively into the darkness.

The shush of movement, the snap of twigs, and Jessup wrapped his arms around her and pressed her face into his chest.

They waited for what seemed like forever, silent, ears strained, tense.

Nothing.

Jessup's arms still holding her, Myrna raised her head.

"Do you think they're gone?" She pulled William Tell tighter, opening her eyes to a squint.

And was knocked silly with wonder.

A stream of men dressed in sinew-stitched leather and furred pelts treaded warily up a passage, carrying blazing pine-pitch torches that danced their shadows on worked rock walls. They followed a heavily caped shaman—sha*woman*—with long gray hair who scattered glittering green powder from a mittened hand, lips moving in a chant, but all sound of their trek was lost to the past. The old woman sent a side-eye glance at Myrna, fear pinching her white-gray brows, before she moved on. Myrna's gaze skittered along the line of people, collecting details of their clothing, trying without success to place them in time, until ...

The final man carried a spear. And atop the straight heavy shaft, tarred and wrapped tight with the thinnest gut, sat a luminous chalcedony Clovis point. Her skin shivered with goosebumps.

These were the mammoth people.

Sudden brilliant white light smothered the flickering oranges and yellows of the torches. The Clovis people's bodies shimmered and faded, then morphed into ... *cowboys*? Boots, wide-brimmed hats, heavy waxed jackets and dusters, leather gloves. Each man carried bulky canvas sacks slung over their shoulders, and gas masks hung from their necks. Hissing like a hard rain on a roof emanated from lanterns carried by the first and last man. She read the lettering on the fuel fount—COLEMAN.

The black-hatted cowboy at the front raised his hand in the universal sign for halt and placed the lantern in the dirt at his feet. He readjusted his sack before he fished a large chunk of charcoal out of a capacious pocket and marked a circle on the stone wall. The face of his wristwatch glowed green in the harsh light and silver buttons glinted down the front of his black shirt. He put away the charcoal and motioned for the men behind him to continue, a hollow *"We're almost there"* echoing around the passage.

Then he lifted his face—and looked directly at Myrna. She squeaked. *The man from the cliff.* Eyes widening, his gaze slid over her head. He stared in shock, his mouth falling open.

Oh, crap. Jessup.

Myrna unceremoniously dumped William Tell onto the dirt floor. The light winked out, and Jessup let her go like she burned.

"What the hell was that?" The words exploded from Jessup's lips.

"Nothing." Her screech even scraped her ears. She scurried away from him, blinking against the tunnel's darkness.

"You're *lying*. I saw ... I saw ..."

A giggle bubbled hysterically. A *shared* vision? That had never happened before.

She needed light. With quivering fingers, Myrna slipped off her bow—amazed it was still intact. From her backpack, she pulled out a mini tactical flashlight, switched it on, and turned the head until diffuse light brightened the distance between them. Jessup's sky-blue irises pierced her from a face powdered with dirt. He'd lost his hat. William Tell leaned against his legs, eyes and ears droopy, drained from the visions.

"Should I pick him up, Myrna?" Jessup asked quietly.

She swallowed. "Please don't."

Jessup shifted. He placed a hand on William Tell's head and stroked the dog along his back. William Tell lay down and exhaled an enormous, snuffly sigh.

"What did I see?"

Myrna searched for an easy explanation and drew a blank. She tucked up her knees and circled them with her arms. "The past. At least, that's what I see. Others have experienced ... different."

"The people in the tunnel. Who were they?"

"Clovis people. Mammoth hunters."

"And the second group?"

Myrna shook her head. Sand showered from her hair. "I don't know."

"The man at the front saw us. He saw *me*."

"So did the woman in the first group. Or sensed our presence. It happens sometimes."

Myrna stood and brushed herself down, sick to her stomach. This had happened twice before, where people had picked up William Tell and seen ... something. Both times ended badly. She might have to disappear for a while. Again. It all depended on Jessup Page.

She dug her water bottle and a collapsible silicone bowl out of her backpack, filled the bowl to the top, and put it in front of William Tell's nose. He wobbled to his feet and drank, lapping loud and wet in the tunnel. She piled a handful of kibbles on the floor.

"It drains him," she explained. "Drink?"

Jessup shook his head and stood, extracting his own water bottle from a large pouch in his cargo pants. He pulled out two protein bars and passed one to Myrna. "You hurt?"

"Bruised up a little, that's all." She pointed the flashlight up. Rubble blocked the hole at the top of the slide. "Looks like we can't go back the way we came."

"There has to be a way out." Jessup gave her a strained smile.

"Otherwise, those ... visitors wouldn't have been wandering around down here."

"Those visitors were down here over thirteen thousand years ago. Things change." She bit into the power bar.

"But the second group was no earlier than the mid-1950s," Jessup said.

Myrna stopped mid-chew and swallowed. "How do you know that?"

He hesitated. "I recognized the lanterns."

Jessup pulled a second flashlight from his cargoes, spotlighting the barely discernible charcoal circle. His fingers brushed over it. "Hopefully these will take us to an entrance. Our best bet is to backtrack instead of follow. Neither group looked like they'd arrived at their final destination."

Myrna pointed toward where the cowboys had headed. "That guy said they were close, and I want to see—"

"No." The word came out hard.

Alarm bells clanged in her head. Normally, that tone of command made her melt in all the right places, but Jessup had been acting sketchy all day.

She smiled disarmingly. "Okay."

But she *would* come back and *would* explore further. And she had a better way of marking the route than faded charcoal circles.

"Just let me give William Tell a little more water and fashion a leash. I don't want to lose my little sweetie down here." Her voice rose to baby-talk level as she leaned down and scratched William Tell behind one bat ear as he munched kibble. Other than an annoyed twitch, he completely ignored her.

Myrna rifled in her backpack and pulled out paracord to loop into the dog's harness. She also slipped out her pace beads before turning off her flashlight to conserve battery, leaving only Jessup's light pointing in the direction from which the mammoth people and cowboys had appeared. She picked up the dog's empty water bowl as William Tell padded to the end of his makeshift leash. He stopped and lifted his face to sniff the air. His ears perked. One more long, snorting inhale, and William Tell started off, tugging her behind him.

He'd caught the scent of something. Myrna hoped it was a way out.

Thirty-Eight

Silently counting her steps, Myrna slipped a pace bead over the string when a muffled explosion reverberated above them. An ominous rumbling followed, and the thud and click of rocks echoed from the corridor ahead. Dust and dirt billowed toward them accompanied by the intense musk of feces and ammonia punch of urine. William Tell sneezed.

"Our boys are still up there." Jessup covered his nose with a sleeve.

"I know that stink." Myrna blinked back the burn in her eyes. "They're blowing up more packrat burrows, trying to seal us underground."

Jessup swung his flashlight beam through the settling dust as they inched along the tunnel. Rounding a curve, they found a section of wall newly collapsed into rubble, exposing a hollow behind it. Jessup shined his light inside, and it glinted off a large, hard honey-brown column that climbed up a crevice in the rocks.

"*Amberat*," Myrna said in a hushed and worshipful tone.

"What?"

"*Neotoma*—pack rats—don't drink water, so their pee is super concentrated. In dry climates, it crystallizes into this stuff." She waved a hand at the lumpy formation. "Amberat. It acts like a time capsule. An organic cement preserving whatever the pack rats bring into their midden—sticks, seeds, bugs. Generations of *Neotoma* live in these burrows, so deposits have been dated to the time of the mammoth people. Some even before that."

"No light coming in. The explosion sealed the burrow," Jessup said. His flashlight beam dropped to the fist-sized rocks, gnawed sticks and twigs, and shattered amberat carpeting the dirt floor. Iridescent green glittered from within.

Myrna waded through the rubble and squatted down. She pulled out her flashlight, adjusted the beam narrower and brighter, and bent closer to study the encapsulated green glow. She hefted up the chunk amberat, stood, and fitted it into a ragged hole like a three-dimensional puzzle piece. Running her light over the reassembled amberat, she lit up dozens and dozens of glinting green dots in the same area.

"What are they?"

"Beetles? Maybe an infestation. Look." She lifted the light up the amberat. "The bugs are pretty far down, which means they were probably captured thousands of years ago. It's amazing the color has lasted this long."

The old shawoman had scattered iridescent green dust. Was it connected?

Jessup picked up a thumb-sized lump of amberat. "This one's got a beetle in it."

Myrna dug in her pack and pulled out a sterile plastic test tube. She opened the lid, and he dropped the sample inside. "Can you find a couple more?"

Jessup bent and probed with his light, kicking away debris. Metal glinted. He leaned over to pluck something out of the litter.

"Another button." His tone was awed. "From the set I dug up."

Myrna peered at it. "The ammonia must have kept it from tarnishing."

"Do you think we're near the cliff?"

"Maybe." She held up the pace beads. "Two hundred steps per bead. The burrow we dove into was about half a mile from the arroyo over the mammoth kill site. We've been angling in that direction the whole time we've been walking."

"Ranger beads? That's serious backcountry stuff, Dr. Lee." Suddenly, his face was hard, and his tone wasn't nice. "And here I thought you were just a prissy science girl with your white paper coveralls."

"Good. That's just what I wanted you to think." Myrna dug into her backpack again and retrieved a head lamp. "I'll take the lead now. And it's *doctor* prissy science girl to you."

Chin raised, she marched toward the tunnel opening, and immediately rolled her foot over a piece of debris, landing with an *oof* on her butt. William Tell crowded in to jump up and lick her face, his way of doggie laughing.

Jessup hurried toward her. "You okay?"

"I'm fine." Myrna pushed the dog away, snatched up the stupid chunk of whatever tripped her to throw—

And stopped. She turned it over in her hand. Even though it had been gnawed at either end, one side still showed gold paint over an intricately carved pattern. The other side was flat, with an almost indecipherable design burned into the wood.

"It looks like a piece of carved furniture or ... picture frame?" Myrna said. "Amazing what these animals find out in the middle of nowhere."

Jessup stilled. "Can I see that?"

She handed it to him. Expression blank, he turned it over and over before he pocketed it and helped Myrna up.

They continued down the passageway, Myrna letting William Tell pull her forward. She counted steps and moved beads. Jessup pointed to another circular smudge, but she excitedly found scorch marks from torches darkening the ceiling above them right before the tunnel opened into a large domed cavern. It had been cleared of rocks and debris, except for one wall that consisted of sand and dirt that sloped to the ceiling.

"I think that's the backslide that overlooks the mammoth kill," she said. "It might have been open during the time of the mammoth people."

"But it doesn't look like those cowboys came through it. There must be another way."

She and Jessup fanned out to explore the dark crevices, cracks, and rocky folds of the cavern. Her headlamp brightened a passage entrance. Just inside, a black circle smudged the wall.

"Found it! I found the way out!"

"Me, too," Jessup replied, voice grim.

Myrna trotted toward him, tugging a snuffling William Tell behind her.

"And this way. And that way." His flashlight pointed up to two passage openings above a rocky ledge.

Myrna shook her head. "They're *all* marked with soot?"

"And probably booby trapped."

"*What?* Why would they—" Realization hit her like a ton of amberat. "This is about the treasure, isn't it? The one Isaac talked about." She grabbed Jessup's arm. "*Isn't it?*"

Jessup, his expression impassive, said, "It's safer if you don't know."

"*Safer?*" She sputtered. "Safer than dodging bullets and grenades while being chased by drug lord minions?"

He smiled. "Got me there."

"Do you know which passage will get us out of here?"

"No." His look into her eyes was gentle, but his voice steel. "Myrna? We have to pick him up."

Two beams of light, one from Myrna's headlamp, the other from Jessup's flashlight, slid to William Tell. He sat, his back leg straight up, licking his—

"Dogs are so gross," muttered Myrna.

Thirty-Nine

"That wasn't very helpful," Myrna said after she and Jessup released the dog. She sat in the dirt and opened her backpack, William Tell sprawled beside her, head on his paws. The mammoth hunters had ghosted through the vision for only seconds, then disappeared, then ... nothing. "But I was right about the cave in the cliff. It was open in the past. Maybe we could dig ourselves out."

"With what? Our hands?" Jessup sat against rock, legs extended, ankles crossed, his arms folded over his chest. "Who knows how much sand and rock are in that collapse. It could take us days."

"What we need is a couple of those grenades." Myrna poured water into the dog's bowl and gave him another handful of kibbles. William Tell heaved to his feet to eat and drink.

"You don't seem too upset that we didn't see the cowboys so we could follow them out of here," Jessup said. He flipped on his flashlight.

"I *told* you. It's not like tuning in to your favorite TV show. Sometimes picking him up works. Sometimes ..." Myrna sniffed, stroking William Tell. "How do you know about the booby traps?"

"Rumor, mostly. From stories we—I've collected."

We. Dillon Bard. Was that his only partner? Were there others?

"Did those rumors tell you how to disarm them?" she asked.

"No." He hesitated. "There's a diary or journal hidden somewhere. It has the locations of the traps and keys to the treasure."

He finally admitted it. This *was* about the treasure.

"William Tell can get us out of here. At least, I'm pretty sure he can." Myrna stood and stretched, sucking in a deep breath of the chill dry air. "I found him in Siberia. Ivory hunters were using him in ice caves and permafrost tunnels to locate mammoth tusks. They're worth up to fifty thousand dollars apiece. Money like that can support whole villages for a year. But they weren't taking good care of him. He was cold and skinny and hungry, so I sort of..."

"Stole him?"

"*Rescued* him. At the time, I didn't know he could"—Myrna waved her hand—"you know. I just figured they'd trained him to find ancient carcasses or mammoth ivory underneath the permafrost." William Tell finished his water, and she tucked the bowl away. "Tusk hunting is mostly black market. Pretty lawless. Those drug dealers above us are like a pee-wee baseball team compared to ivory hunters. William Tell's extracurricular abilities in those ice caves were probably why they came after us with a rocket launcher."

"So not a prissy science girl," he said.

Myrna smirked. "We should get going."

She made kissy noises interspersed with, "Come on, boy, let's go outside. Outside." William Tell perked his ears. She walked him around the cave to each of the soot-marked passages. He showed no interest until they got to the bottom of the ledge. He studied the rocks, and, gathering himself with a butt wiggle, bounded up to examine the openings in the wall. Myrna had to drop the leash so he could reach the far-left threshold. Once there, he lifted his nose and sniffed before padding into the darkness.

Myrna clambered up to the ledge, her eye on the trailing leash. "He was pretty deep inside those caves when I snuck in to get him. I had, uh, borrowed a jacket and hat from their camp, and figured we'd walk out of the caves like we belonged, and everyone would leave us alone. Except I got lost—it was just a hive of tunnels. But once I let him take the lead, he guided me out. I think he smells the fresh air." She adjusted her backpack and bow and held out a hand to Jessup.

He stared at her for a long moment. Did he suspect there was more to her William Tell ice cave rescue story? 'Cause there was. A *lot* more, and she was coming to realize he was ridiculously perceptive. She widened her eyes to their most innocent. He took her hand and climbed up.

"Switch off your headlamp to conserve batteries." His flashlight beam found the end of the leash, and he picked it up. "I'm behind the dog, you're behind me. Stay close."

William Tell moseyed along a natural fissure that had been chipped larger by hand in some areas, stopping periodically to sniff a crack or branching passages, or lift his leg to pee on the wall. Each time he led them into a new gap in the rock, Jessup drew a small circle about a foot from the dirt floor using chalk he'd pulled from a pocket. Just in case they had to backtrack, he told her.

Right. Or in case he came back to look for the treasure by himself or with Dillon Bard and whoever else was involved.

The problem with his chalk signs were that anyone could use them.

About twenty minutes later, they found a faded charcoal circle.

"He seems to be going in the right direction. Hold him while I check for traps." And Jessup and the light disappeared before Myrna could get her heart out of her throat. It was a very long five minutes in the dark before he returned with the all clear.

Another careful half an hour passed before they crept through an arch into a cave that looked like it had been carved by water. Drips still seeped here and there from a slab rock ceiling low enough that Jessup reached up to touch it. He ran his light around the dark expanse, illuminating a honeycomb of dark openings in the surrounding walls. Myrna knelt and dug out the dog's bowl. She poured a little water into it, and William Tell lapped thirstily.

"All the passages look the same, probably by design," Jessup said. "Makes it harder to choose the right way in or out. I'll do a quick check, but if they're true to form, they'll have marked them all."

His flashlight beam painted a moving white pool on the cave floor, leaving Myrna and William Tell in shadow. On impulse, she grabbed her own stash of chalk from her backpack and snuck soundlessly into as many passages as she could, marking each one to muddy the route back. It would be her insurance that Jessup would have to bring her and William Tell with him to find the final destination of the mammoth people and cowboys, because she wouldn't need chalk marks.

Her insurance that he wouldn't leave her behind.

She hurried back to William Tell, tucking the chalk into her jacket pocket for easy access, listening for the scuff of Jessup's boots and the melodic drips of water into small puddles. But as she waited for his return, the justification she'd felt with her trick seeped out of her. Somehow, what she'd done now felt like a betrayal, even though her underlying unease remained.

"You have to learn to trust," she whispered.

The dog crunched kibble and ignored her.

Jessup came back with the news that all the passageways leading from the cave were marked with soot. "We'll need the dog to get us through."

William Tell led them along the cave's edge, bypassing half a dozen openings before he gazed alertly into a dark passage. He darted inside and took an immediate ninety-degree turn, yanking the leash from Jessup's hand.

"Don't lose sight of him!" Myrna screeched. She flipped on her headlamp and bolted past Jessup. As she ran and ducked down the passage, her bouncing light illuminated the dog's piggy behind skidding around a corner.

She lost him only once—at a confluence of tunnels—frantically shining her light into each. Jessup slid to a stop beside her. He pointed to a dark splatter of wet sand inside an opening just as a low *ruff* echoed from the same direction. Myrna darted toward it, Jessup on her heels. More growls drove them into a maze of side passageways, chasing pee splotches and sound. Bursting through an archway, Myrna crunched to a halt on a pile of moldering leaves and twigs, gulping smelly air. William Tell stood in a refractive pool of sunlight, his face pointed upward, his ears cocked.

They stood in a cylindrical cave that rose high above their heads like a natural well. Ledges and darkly shadowed niches punctuated the soaring rock walls, the areas in between chiseled smooth. A protruding jumble of boulders at the top blocked the view but allowed sunlight to filter in. Myrna dropped her gaze to the cave floor. The crunching under her boots wasn't from twigs. It came from scattered, partially articulated bones, crispy brown skin attached—

Her light caught a dented white-and-red cardboard bucket listing against a rock.

"*Fried chicken,*" she hissed. An excited William Tell bounced to a trash pile and scooped up a drumstick, chomping it loudly. Myrna dove for the dog and grabbed his jaw, prying it open with her fingers. "No. No! *Drop it.*"

And the moldering leaves weren't moldering leaves at all. They were actually moldering, stinky garbage.

"Look out." Jessup grabbed Myrna's arm and William Tell's harness and tugged them away from the center of the cave as trash rained down. A white plastic bag floated to land at Myrna's feet.

She snatched it up. Rodentacide. Male voices, loud and frantic, echoed after it.

"*Shut up.* You two are staying right here until someone relieves you. Boss said we have to keep eyes out until we know if those two hikers escaped and reported us. The plants are too valuable. And we got to get rid of *those.*" The man's voice faded.

"The drug guys," Myrna whispered, staring skyward. "They're talking about us. We must be right below their camp."

"Below the Cabeza de Baca formation. This must be the Corazón del Cimarron."

"What?" Her light skittered down the wall—and her jaw dropped. "Jessup. *Look.*"

Above the arched entrance they'd just run through were dozens of handprints diffusely outlined in red and yellow paint. Above them was a barely discernible pictograph of a bulbous head, two curling tusks, and a long trunk.

"The mammoth people," Myrna breathed. "They were *here.*" She grabbed her phone and took a series of quick pictures.

Hanging on a rusted metal peg just below the pictographs was a dusty Coleman lantern.

"And the cowboys," Jessup said. "We can't get out this way, not without ropes, and especially not with armed drug guys up there."

Suddenly, he pivoted in a circle, the flashlight beam jerking around, searching frantically.

"Where the hell is that dog?"

FORTY

The flashlight beam zigged and zagged between the snaky leash drag marks and the dark wet pee stains in the dirt. When they finally caught up to William Tell, Jessup grabbed the end of the leash to stop the dog's forward momentum.

"Could we take a break?" Myrna slid down a wall and jumbled around in her backpack, pulling out a packet of chocolate snack cakes. Tearing it open, she handed one of the two cakes to Jessup, who slid down beside her. He used his flashlight beam to highlight the snack's completely delicious lack of any nutritional value. "Miz Donavan would have a conniption fit if she ever saw these. It could get you fired," Jessup said, a smile in his voice. As he chewed, he zipped open a pocket of his cargoes and extracted his water bottle. He uncapped and offered it to her while William Tell danced around, snuffling for crumbs.

He switched off his flashlight, and Myrna doused her headlamp. Utter darkness fell. She shivered and inched her body toward Jessup's warmth until they sat pressed together from shoulder to knee. Realizing the cakes were gone, William Tell heaved a deep sigh and plopped his head on Myrna's lap. She played with his ears.

"Jessup? That silo was obviously one way the cowboys entered these caves. Is there another way out?"

"According to rumors, these tunnels hook up with one of the old gold mines—the one you're supposed to take samples from this afternoon. But that's at least another couple of miles as the crow flies from the Cabeza de Baca formation. I don't even know if we're headed in the right direction."

"If there's another way, William Tell will find it. He found the Calzone de Cimarron."

Jessup chuckled. "Corazón. Means *heart* in Spanish."

Myrna frowned, something tickling her memory, but her thoughts scattered when Jessup shifted and slid his arm around her. It only seemed natural to lay her head on his shoulder.

"I'm worried about our light, Myrna."

Sitting up, she switched on her lamp and opened her backpack, fishing out her baggy of extra batteries and a bundle of snap glow sticks, dropping them in Jessup's lap. "If we're careful, we'll be okay for a few days."

His sudden laughter warmed her. "My God, Meerkat, what else do you have in that bag of tricks?"

She snuggled back into him, and his arm tightened.

After another hour of walking, desultory talk petering out to exhausted silence or periodic excited utterances when they found a charcoal circle on the rocky walls, William Tell ambled to a halt and plopped his butt in the dirt. A jagged pile of rocks blocked the tunnel.

"*No.*" Air whooshed out of Myrna. "This *has* to be the right way."

"It is." Jessup's flashlight illuminated a dark square timber that ran up the wall, then swung up to the gaping hollow in the ceiling above the rock pile. "A stabilizing beam. The mine starts here."

Her heart leaped. "We can squeeze through— What is *that*?"

The edge of the bright circle of light had caught grotesquely twisted wire tacked into the stone, the ends blackened and frayed. Jessup followed the wires down the wall until they disappeared behind the rubble.

"Booby trap." His light probed the rock pile's perimeter. "Sprung."

A skeletonized arm covered by tattered, dusty fabric reached from the rock heap, a wristwatch, face shattered, still strapped over bone. A gold wedding ring circled a flesh-denuded finger. Jessup flicked off the light. The watch face glowed an eerie green.

A zing of shock snapped Myrna straight. The murdered man at the cliff had worn a watch like this.

Or it was the *exact same watch*, and *this* guy was the one who took it? The *friend* who'd betrayed him.

"*Damn*," Jessup whispered. The word was imbued with what sounded like despair. He knelt, touching the ring, then the watch.

Jessup's identification of the Coleman lanterns had readjusted her timeline of when the cowboy was murdered from the 1800s to the mid-1900s. Which meant it was possible Jessup had heard more than just secondhand rumors. What if he'd gotten his information about the treasure from a *primary* source? Someone who'd been alive during that time—

Or still was.

"Do you know who that is?" Myrna asked.

He sent her a sharp look. His *no* was curt.

Liar. He didn't trust her. Myrna's heart squeezed then hardened. Teeth on edge, she said, "If he got in, we can get out."

She whistled to William Tell and pointed at the rock pile. The dog heaved a long-suffering sigh, scrambled up the blockage, and slipped through to the other side. Myrna, driven by anger and disappointment, followed, shoving rocks out of the way as she climbed. At the top, she pushed at the rubble to make the opening larger, then glanced back at Jessup. He had the watch and ring in his hand, expression desolate.

She shimmied through the hole and climbed down to the mine floor, catching William Tell's leash. Rusted mine car rails led away from the blockage into the dark tunnel. She waited until Jessup was by her side, then marched off with William Tell, who trotted ahead of her.

The dog wove them through a maze of decrepit tunnels and skirted black-hole mine shafts, still peeing at every turn. There were no more charcoal marks on the walls. Jessup continued to make his own with chalk.

Another thirty minutes passed before Myrna stepped over a knee-high barrier of rubble and sighed in relief. A string of lights ran along the ceiling and the tunnel widened and braced with metal beams. The old mine car tracks had been pulled up, and crushed gravel lay over the floor. Everything was all new and shiny and ...

"Didn't Paden's dad say the reclamation project was almost complete? Then why—"

"—are they shoring up this tunnel?" Jessup finished.

Bad men in permafrost caves and on pot farms sprang into Myrna's brain. She sucked in a breath. "What if what they're doing isn't official? What if they're after the treasure? That booby trap proved someone thought it was worth killing for."

Jessup frowned. "Wait for me. I need to ..." And he disappeared back into the mine shaft.

Myrna peered down the tunnel. Her eyes adjusted to the darkness enough that she could just make out a graying of the light—and bulky canvas overcoats and hard hats hanging on hooks pounded into the rock wall.

A plan—brazen and stupid—formed. Leaving her backpack, bow, and William Tell's leash looped over a heavy rock, she crept toward the coats. Vague noises began to filter down the tunnel, louder with each step. The *rat-tat-tat* of a jackhammer, the whine of a generator—

She plastered her back against the wall as two men walked past in a perpendicular passageway about fifty yards ahead, the harsh cadence of their voices rising in competition against the echo of rumbling equipment. When they disappeared, she grabbed two overcoats and hardhats. Finding safety glasses underneath, she plucked those up and hied back to the waiting dog. She burrowed into a coat, welcoming its warmth, and sat, chin on her knees, to wait.

After what seemed like forever, Jessup stepped over the rubble barrier.

"Where'd you find that coat? I thought I told you to stay put."

"I have a plan," she whispered, and handed him the gear. "Put this on. You erased your chalk marks, right?"

"As far back as I could. I added a few for misdirection, too. And I found a second passage and another booby trap. This one live. If they dig parallel to this tunnel, they'll hit it." Jessup frowned as he shrugged on the coat. "What's your plan?"

"Pretend like we're part of the mine crew and walk right out of here."

William Tell took that opportunity to stroll over and sit on Jessup's hiking boot.

"With a dog?" Jessup's voice shook the tiniest bit. He was laughing at her. "If I remember correctly, that didn't work when you stole—"

"*Rescued.*" Myrna sniffed. She settled the hardhat on her curls and slotted on the safety glasses.

"Charles Donavan called to let them know we're coming. Let's just say we were supposed to meet someone inside the mine, and no one showed."

While his plan lacked panache, it was maybe the *teensiest* bit more logical than hers. She was about to ungraciously concede as much when the string of bulbs tacked to the ceiling popped on one by one, scalding the cave in dazzling white. William Tell bounded to his feet, hackles raised, and began his *what-the-hell-is-going-on-I'm-going-to-kill-you* barking. Myrna wrapped the makeshift leash twice around her wrist to stop him from charging the two men who stood gaping at them at the end of the tunnel.

Heart banging against her ribs, Myrna forced a bright smile. "Thank *goodness*! We thought you'd *never* come! Are either of you Peter, uh, Piper? We were supposed to meet him here for a tour and got lost."

In answer, one of the men pulled out an ugly black gun.

FORTY-ONE

A silent security guard ushered Myrna and Jessup through a threshold into a swanky office on the ground floor of the Donavan Lodge. The wood-paneled walls and Western antique desk could have been that of any self-respecting cattle baron a hundred and fifty years ago. The contents of her backpack and everything else she and Jessup carried when they were caught —well, almost everything—had been placed in meticulous order on a large table just to her right, including her bow, arrows, and quiver, her survival gear and snack cakes, and Jessup's pistol, the bullets lined up like little soldiers. A fancy silver ice bucket held her test tube samples, including the amberat. Missing were their phones, the silver button, the gilded, gnawed wood they'd pulled from the packrat's burrow, and her knife, tucked away in a secret pocket at her thigh. A typed page listed all the items and lay squared at a corner of the table.

Jessup wore the jewelry he'd taken from the dead man in the tunnels: the gold ring around his finger and the green glowing watch strapped to his wrist.

Finn Posse stood by a sumptuously curtained window, hands clasped behind his back, his single earring glinting under vintage

Edison bulbs screwed into antique pendant lights. Above them, the high ceiling was paneled with elegant copper botanical swirls set in enameled turquoise. A thick Persian rug woven in medallions of reds, golds, and black covered a glossy wood-plank floor. Everything was warm and inviting, except the icy blue eyes in Posse's face.

"Mr. Page," Finn Posse said, his clipped accent even more pronounced. "Your very clear instructions stated you were to wait for an escort into the mines. Yet you proceeded. Why is that?"

Myrna wasn't completely sure about Jessup's capacity to lie convincingly under high-pressure conditions, especially if his job could be on the line. *She*, however ...

Widening her eyes and softening her face into confusion, she said, "But we *did* follow instructions. We walked into the site and introduced ourselves to ..." She screwed up her face, "John?"

"João," Jessup said.

"That's right. And he seemed very busy, so he sent us to a trailer for dusters and hard hats and told us to meet ..." Myrna nibbled her lip, pulling her eyebrows tight over her eyes. "Paul?"

"Santiago," Jessup corrected. His eyes started to dance.

"Yes. But when we got to the opening, George—"

"Martim."

She side-eyed Jessup. "*Martim* told us we couldn't take William Tell into the mine. At least I think that's what he said. He was very difficult to understand, and I don't speak Spanish—"

"Portuguese." Now Finn Posse was correcting her. "My company is based out of Brazil."

"Brazil? Funny, the people at the mine didn't *look* Brazilian," Myrna said innocently.

Posse's mouth twisted. "You Americans and your obsession with skin color and race."

Jessup raised his eyebrows at that. He widened his stance and crossed his arms, his demeanor shifting to hostility.

"We had permission from Mr. Donavan to be at the site today, to take samples." Jessup nodded at the test tube in the ice bucket. "Instead, when we went down the wrong tunnel, we were met with guns drawn. What's goin' on out there, Mr. Posse?"

"First, we need Dr. Lee's assurance that any pictures she might have taken inside the mine will be deleted," a rich, plummy voice said. "We've already checked your phone, Jessup."

Startled, Myrna peered around Jessup. Charles Donavan stood in a doorway that had earlier been part of the paneling.

"I didn't take any pictures in the mine." The truth, although she'd snapped a few in the cave. "The men who *held us at gunpoint* can attest to that. I don't remember their names."

"Ringo Starr and Pete Best? Or maybe Peter Piper?" Finn Posse murmured acidly.

Charles Donavan chuckled. "Well, Dr. Lee, from the stories I read about you and those ivory hunters in Siberia, this encounter should have been a walk in the park."

A chill trickled down her neck. How much had he actually found out about her past?

"There've been reports the reclamation is almost done, Mr. Donavan," Jessup said. "That's not what we saw. Looks like they're shoring up tunnels, not sealing them closed."

Charles Donavan sighed. He exchanged a glance with Finn Posse as he strode across the room to Myrna and picked up her hand. "Dr. Lee? If you head right down the corridor to the end of the hall, you'll find your little dog tied up in our ranch museum's patio. He's been well taken care of, I promise." The man's eyes twinkled above a smile.

It was hard not to smile back. But charismatic leaders were like that, and this man was preparing a run for president.

"Can I get my stuff?" she asked.

He patted her hand avuncularly and nodded before he let her go to gather her things. With all three men watching, Myrna hurriedly filled her backpack. When she grabbed her snack cakes, Charles Donavan said, "My wife sees those, and she'll fire you. But

I promise I won't tell if you give me one and *you* promise not to tell." He grinned, for real this time.

Myrna handed him a pack. The only other reaction from the men was when she grabbed the amberat samples and Finn Posse took a single step toward her. Charles Donavan shook his head at him.

With one last look at Jessup, Myrna left the office and hurried to find William Tell and fix whatever havoc he'd wreaked in her absence.

And she worried how much havoc Jessup would wreak when he was alone with Posse and Donavan. She wished she'd told him to keep quiet about the pesticide and herbicide contamination. If they picked that thread, everything else would unravel, including the caves that led to the mine, her possible access to the mammoth kill sites, and whatever else was at the end of the *other* tunnel that led from the packrat midden. How much would he say? Probably everything, because when you got right down to bedrock, Jessup Page was a good person and loyal employee.

Sadness squeezed in her chest. In fact, he was nothing like her.

Forty-Two

Myrna found William Tell in a lovely walled courtyard off the museum, happily gnawing to dust a leg bone he'd torn from a fully articulated *Bison antiquus* skeleton. The makeshift leash had unraveled from his harness and trailed back to an ornate iron bench under a small stand of carefully landscaped dwarf aspen. She glanced around furtively. No one else was in the museum, although the tink of silverware and murmured conversation filtered over the wall. It was a warm evening. The huge glass bay doors must be open for outside dining at the Donavans' lodge restaurant, as were the museum French doors that led to the little courtyard.

The dog lifted his head, eyes bright black marbles under a long necklace of globe lights strung overhead.

"Give me that." She snatched the bone from between his front paws and hurried inside the museum, quickly wedging it back into place. Myrna stepped back and eyed the whole skeleton. Whoever had curated the animal for display had made a bunch of rookie mistakes: ribs on the wrong side, vertebrae flipped backward, front hooves on the incorrect feet. Her critical gaze ran over some of the other articulated skeletons on display, noting more errors, then down a line of shelved animal skulls. She tsked and switched labels between a badger and a raccoon.

But as the minutes ticked away, Myrna glanced out to the hallway that led back to Donavan's office too many times to count.

Silently berating herself for worrying about what Jessup might say, she shifted her focus back to the museum. She'd been wanting to explore the Donavan stone points collection since Eleanor had told her about them. No time like the present—*if* she could find them.

Myrna wandered to the middle of the room. It was high-ceilinged, walls painted an antique beige, and about the size of the Blackwater Draw Museum in Portales. Glass-topped display tables ran in long columns, the artifacts inside arranged in what appeared to be no particular order, some with provenance, some with personal stories either handwritten in faded brown ink or typed by a manual typewriter. Old black-and-white daguerreotypes and photographs of people who'd lived and worked at the ranch over the years hung on the walls: trappers, First Peoples, explorers, soldiers, cowboys and trail herds of cattle, miners, and pioneers. Myrna studied a photo taken inside a mercantile, the proprietor in profile, his customers blurred because they'd moved before the exposure was complete. Another picture showed children lined up by height in front of a wooden schoolhouse. The schoolmarm, young and stiff in mutton sleeves and a long, dark skirt, closely resembled Paden's mother. An ancestor? Jessup said some of the families had lived in this area hundreds of years.

Myrna knit her brows. The present Charles Donavan had an uncanny likeness to the man who'd ordered the death of that cowboy in William Tell's vision. Maybe his photo was in the museum, too. She stepped toward a wall of color-washed portraits.

William Tell blocked her path.

"What?"

He scratched the wooden door to the cupboard underneath one of the display tables. His *I'm-hungry* signal.

"I don't have any treats," she said, and realized her mistake as soon as it left her mouth. His ears folded back, and he started to wiggle, his doggy eyes smiling at the word *treats*, then stretched up to press his paws into her leg.

"You ate all the kibble in the caves." William Tell dropped to the flagstone floor and scratched at the cabinet front again, harder, more demanding.

"*Stop.*" Myrna squatted and rubbed at the faint scores from his nails. "See what you did?"

He wiggled up to her again, being adorable. Myrna rose and plopped her backpack on a glass-topped display case, unzipping the pouch. "You are such a pain. Fine, I'll see if anything fell out of the baggie—"

She stilled, gaze riveted. Under the glass, in a simply framed photograph laid flat, Charles Donavan's doppelgänger looked down a line of men—*uniformed soldiers*—all grinning tired, youthful grins. Next to him, cigarette tucked behind his ear, a shock of blond hair slanted over his forehead, was a young man who could've been Paden Cabeza de Baca. It had to be his great-grandfather, Mike. She'd bet the farm on it. The Black soldier under Mike's arm was a Webb McJunkin double. Two men, brothers by their resemblance, she didn't recognize. But the next man was obviously someone from Isaac Marín's family. And the last man in line ...

She pressed her hand over her mouth. *It was him*. The handsome black-haired, square-jawed cowboy at the cliff. He wore a different uniform than the others—the insignia patch on his jacket a shield with a flaming sword topped by curved stripes. And he and Charles Donavan's ancestor—*the man who'd ordered him murdered*—grinned at each other, somewhere in time.

Her shocked eyes slid to the silver dollar next to the photo. A typed rectangle of card stock read:

.　.　.

One of the lucky silver dollars given by
Xavier Donavan to his son, Charles, and any
man who served from the ranch when they left
for the European theatre. And they worked! All
our boys came back in one piece.

Only to be betrayed.

Myrna turned away, nausea pressing into her throat. She leaned over the case behind her, head down, seeing nothing, eyes blurring with tears.

"It's a pretty horrific story."

Myrna spun, blinking. Before her vision cleared, she could have sworn that the Charles Donavan she'd seen in the photo and at the cliff stood before to her.

Horrific. Did Charles Tres Donavan know about the murder? Did he know the motive? About the treasure the man was killed for?

"You forgot your phone." He held it out and she took it with nerveless fingers. A smile fanned his brushy mustache. "I didn't mean to startle you. I just figured you'd be examining the Clovis points. Don't look so shocked. Our background check brought up your grant. I've been waiting for you to ask about our collection." He nodded at the display case. "Not that I'm surprised to find you standing over this table."

Myrna frantically gathered her scattered thoughts and turned back to the display underneath the glass. Pictures of an excavation, broken crockery, suspender buckles, and cat's-eye marbles. A charred Bible was propped on black velvet. And next to the artifacts lay a cloth topsy-turvy doll in pristine condition.

"Best guess, the old miners' cabin was torched, oh, a few years after the end of the Civil War. The whole thing was turned into a show on cable. *History's Supernatural Mysteries* or some such nonsense. My wife set it up. Good publicity, she said." He eyes twinkled benignly behind the oval Teddy Roosevelt glasses he wore. "Not so sure about that. Murder never garners good publicity."

Myrna's gaze snapped to his. "Murder?"

"That was the conclusion. There were at least a dozen people in that cabin—men, women, and children. They'd all been poisoned, except one. He burned to death." Charles Donavan pointed at the doll. "That was found clutched in a little girl's skeletal arms. Not a scorch mark on it. Guess that was the supernatural part. Now. Let me show you our stone tool collection." Donavan headed toward a table across the room, near the bison skeleton.

With one last glance at the photo of the soldiers, Myrna asked, "Who's your curator?" William Tell trotted at her heels, nails tapping on the flagstone floor.

"No one. Too far from the bright lights of Santa Fe and Albuquerque." He threw a wink over his shoulder. "We invite undergraduates from Eastern New Mexico University for summer internships. They do their best."

"That bison has some pretty blatant mistakes, and so do these." Myrna touched a finger to the glass over a display of arrowheads underneath. Her head had cleared, finally. She stared at the spectacular arrays of stone projectiles before she turned back to Charles Donavan and took a deep breath.

"What happened today wasn't Mr. Page's fault. If you're going to fire anyone, it should be me." She swallowed, hardly believing what she'd just done.

"Dr. Lee, you're not getting fired. Besides, I've heard you're close to solving our elk die-offs. What do you think of those stones?" He smiled proudly.

"They're magnificent, and I'd like the opportunity to take samples—swabs—for my project."

"I read your grant. It's quite ... creative." He twinkled again. This time she smiled back. "And I know about the mammoth bones near the elk die-off meadow. Nothing stays secret for long on my ranch."

You'd be surprised, Myrna thought. She straightened to her full height and rolled the dice. "After I've completed the die-off investigation, I'd like permission to excavate that site for projectile points used in the hunt. And"—she swallowed—"for the Donavan Foundation—you—to front the cost."

Charles Donavan chuckled, the sound deep and rich. He didn't have much of a belly, but this was a man who'd probably make a great Mall Santa when he was older.

He drew in a breath, a grin spanning his face. "By God, girl, you remind me of me. I'd need a full action plan with a budget. And you must successfully complete the die-off project we hired you for in the first place."

"Done and done. And I'd like to analyze these points while I'm here."

He gave her a smug, assessing look that started a small twinge of worry in the back of her brain. What had Eleanor said about the Donavans and control?

Screw it. This opportunity was too good to miss.

"Done," he echoed. "What do you need?"

"Access to these points in the case and"—she raised an eyebrow—"any less than perfect points or worked stones you might have tucked out of sight."

Charles Donavan nodded and bent to open the cabinets below. A rush of musty air spilled out.

The hair on William Tell's spine bottle-brushed. He backed away, the low growl in his throat erupting into a series of punctuating barks, sharp and alarmed.

Charles Donavan stood, a large, flat, glass-topped case in his hands, and frowned. "What's wrong with your dog?" He had to raise his voice to be heard.

As if in answer, a packrat dove out of the cabinet, ran across Donavan's boots, and dashed through the open courtyard doors to disappear into the bushes. But William Tell didn't even acknowledge the animal, continuing to bark, hard sounds that hurt her ears.

Charles Donavan shoved the case into Myrna's hands and pulled out his phone.

"Get someone from wildlife down to the museum *immediately*." He listened to the response, his face turning purple with inchoate anger. He bellowed, "Then call him. I have a problem, and I want it dealt with *now*."

The murmurs of the diners next door suddenly turned to squeals and cursing.

"Dr. Lee. Go to the front desk and tell them you need a driver to take you home." The avuncular, chuckling Santa Claus had vanished. What was left was the ruthless cattle baron. He anticipated her question. "Jessup isn't at the lodge. He left to get his truck. *What?*" he barked, just as loud as William Tell when he read another question in her face.

"The box of points?" She held it out, then glanced down through the glass top, her breath catching.

"*Dammit*, then find someone else," Donavan bellowed into the phone. Lens flashing, lips tight, nose blowing smoke, he snapped to Myrna, "Take it with you and get your samples. Just remove your *damned* dog so I can fix this *damned* problem."

Myrna scurried to the door, William Tell dogging her every step, barking frenetically. She slammed her hip into the corner of a display table then pinballed her shoulder into the door jamb. She hardly noticed, her eyes fastened on one of the artifacts tucked in the box. Pulse thrumming, she cataloged the traces of a brown tar-like substance that sparkled with green iridescent flecks, and the mottled residue of dried blood staining the leather-wrapped handle.

Nestled inside the box she held in her hands lay the obsidian knife used to kill the cowboy on the cliff—the same man as the soldier in the photo with the sword insignia on his uniform.

Forty-Three

Myrna knocked on Jessup's front door, fidgeting with William Tell's leash. The truck in his driveway looked like a personal vehicle, not the official Donavan one they'd left parked on the mountain.

A light breeze chilled her still damp hair. In the black sky above, the stars and a moon shone blue. Her toes curled in her fuzzy slippers, stomach flipping and twisting. After their time in the cave, it felt like they were in this together, even though she wasn't quite sure what *this* was yet. William Tell sat and stared at the door then at the bundle tucked under Myrna's arm. He was still edgy, ears perked straight up, head lowered, black eyes intent.

She'd been sure Jessup would knock on her little home's door first, come in, and brief her on Donavan, Posse, and the mine. Then she could tell him about ... She squeezed her eyes shut, screwing them up tight against her internal fears.

Trust. She had to trust. Right? The twist in her stomach moved up into her chest.

Why hadn't he come to her?

A chair scraped. A shadow fell over the curtained, diamond-paned window. The handle turned, the door swung open. Behind the screen, Jessup stood, camo T-shirt stretched tight, faded jeans low on his hips, barefoot, his wet hair backlit by soft, honeyed light. He hadn't shaved and the blond stubble on his cheeks seemed to glitter.

Myrna's stomach and toes curled for a completely different reason.

"Did you get fired?" she blurted, clutching the rolled towel tight against her belly.

"No."

She sagged in relief. "Can we talk?"

William Tell gave a yip and waggled his butt. He scratched politely but insistently at the screen door. After a hesitation, Jessup pushed it open. The dog darted inside, his leash towing Myrna in behind him. She unclipped from his harness, and he made a swift sniffing journey of discovery around the room before plopping onto a braided rug by the hearth. He rested his chin on his paws, but his eyes were bright as he followed Myrna's movement.

Myrna did her own detailed examination, trying to divine from the house more about the man who silently watched her, his expression closed and shadowed. It was laid out exactly the same as hers, except the kitchen cabinets and floors were darker. Bookshelves flanked the rock fireplace, filled mostly with paperback Westerns—from Zane Grey, Louis L'Amour, and Tony Hillerman to Larry McMurtry, Molly Glass, and CJ Box. The overstuffed loveseat upholstered in blue jean material looked supremely comfortable, as did a matching chair. A silvery barnwood coffee table held an open manila folder. Her photo smiled up at her.

Jessup had her file.

Myrna's arm hair prickled. Had he asked for it? Was it given to him? It couldn't hold her deepest secrets. If it did, she never would've been hired for this job. Or any other.

She walked past Jessup to the dining table, smoothing her fingertips over the satiny wood. A laptop displayed a familiar survivalist website. Next to it, a cut-glass tumbler holding a half inch of amber liquid anchored a sheet of paper—her backpack's inventory from Charles Donavan's office.

Jessup still stood at the door, hands shoved in his pockets. A thin line of pale skin peeked between his shirt and the waistband of his jeans. Myrna's cheeks heated as she tore her eyes away.

"I thought I was a pretty good outdoorsman. Thought my wilderness skills were second to none." He ambled to the table and tapped the list. "What's in your backpack, Meerkat, is high-level bug-out gear. Disappear into the wild and never come out stuff."

He tapped a key on the keypad. A list of her publications popped on screen.

Jessup moved behind her. Heat rolled off his body, sparking a shiver that had nothing to do with cold.

"I don't pretend to understand your research, but a couple things jumped right out at me." His breath was bourbon-warm in her ear. "You really are an expert on mammoths."

"One of the world's top living specialists." Myrna winced. She hadn't meant to say it that way.

"Living." Jessup reached around her, hard muscles of his arm brushing hers, his chest pressing into her shoulder for a brief hot second. He slid his finger in a slow circle over the touch pad and opened another tab.

A photo of Tom Hutchinson. And she was smiling up at him like he'd hung the moon. She'd been told the Russians had done a pretty thorough wipe. Guess not.

"He's on most of your articles," Jessup said.

"He is, *was*, the world's top expert on mammoths." Myrna chewed her lip. "And my mentor."

Jessup gently turned her to face him. The darkness in his eyes held uncertainty now. "More than that."

It wasn't a question.

She nodded. Without moving, he seemed to retreat.

Then he did retreat, picked up the glass, and downed the last of its contents with a grimace.

He gestured toward her, a half-smiling mask in place, opened his mouth, then closed it. He shook his head, his wry expression slipping for a moment. "You wanted to talk."

Myrna laid her bundle on the breakfast bar.

"The truck?" she asked.

"Tires slashed, side-view mirror broken off. Easy to explain away. I left it at the motor pool and picked up my personal vehicle."

"Did you tell Finn Posse or Mr. Donavan about the marijuana grow?"

"Not yet. I have to clear up a few things first."

Because he had to protect someone. Probably Paden's family. Myrna had been thinking about how such a large encampment could be up on private land, and the only thing she could come up with was that those men had help from someone associated with the ranch, and Paden's father had a brand-new pickup truck.

"What did Charles Donavan say about the mine?" She paused. "Can you tell me?"

Bare feet making no sound, Jessup rounded the breakfast bar into the kitchen. Turning on the faucet, he rinsed out his tumbler. "No. Donavan was pretty explicit about that, but I'm going to anyway. Donavan says Finn Posse found a rich vein of gold in one of the shafts after they dynamited to close it. I think Donavan—or Posse—is lying, because if it's true, someone would've let it slip— at some bar, to a woman. Rumors fly fast out here."

"What are the rumors?"

"Just that everything is on schedule for closing the mine."

Which was also a lie. Which meant the men spreading the messages in the community were disciplined. Like soldiers under orders. Or professional mercenaries. Something she'd encountered before.

"Do you believe Posse and Donavan are in this together?"

He dried his hands on a towel, brows bunched in a frown. "In what together?"

"The treasure."

Jessup's face darkened. He wasn't going to be receptive, at least, not about Charles Donavan. She'd need to come at this from a different direction.

"The cowboy in the cave. From the vision. Do you know who he is?" she asked.

His eyes turned wary. "Why?"

"I ... I've seen him before," she confessed. "I saw him today. In a photo, at the Donavans' lodge museum, in uniform. World War II, with someone who looked like Charles Donavan, and someone who looked like Paden—probably Mike, I think—and people who looked like Webb and Isaac. And there was a silver dollar, like the one you found at the cliff, and a card that said a man named Xavier Donavan gave one each to his son and all the men who served from this ranch."

"Xavier Donavan." Jessup braced his hands on the edge of the sink. "This Charles Donavan's great-grandfather."

Myrna fidgeted. "That's not all."

Jessup's gaze was sharp as an eagle's.

"Those silver buttons you found at the mammoth rub and in the packrat midden."

"The ones that cowboy was wearing in the cave?" he answered dryly. "You think I didn't recognize them?"

Myrna squirmed a little. "Did you find out anything about them?"

"I got an email today." He pivoted and strode to the closed bedroom door, swinging it open. A bright ceiling light shone over a packed duffle resting on his bed, a battered leather shaving kit next to it. "I'm heading out tomorrow to meet with someone in Albuquerque who might know the maker, see where that leads me. I'll probably be gone overnight. I was going to tell you when I dropped you off at the lab in the morning."

Albuquerque. Just an hour north of Socorro and Eleanor's lab. She nibbled her lip as a plan formed.

"I need to show you something." Myrna peeled back the towel she'd placed on the breakfast bar to expose a plastic bag encasing the obsidian knife, and a sterile package of nitrile gloves.

"After he was done with questioning you, Charles Donavan came to the lodge's museum," she said. "He gave me permission to analyze the stone points and tools they've collected from the ranch for my poisons project."

"He might seem like a nice man, but Charles Donavan never does anything out of the goodness of his heart," Jessup warned. "You'll be in his debt if you accept."

"I know. But that may backfire on him spectacularly." She slipped on the gloves and opened the bag with the knife. "The night you and Bard found me on the mammoth rub, I, um, used William Tell to try and see a vision of the mammoth kill site. Instead"—Myrna swallowed on a dry throat—"the silver button cowboy, the one from the cave and that picture in the museum, fell off the cliff. He landed at my feet. He was still alive, and I ... I spoke to him. And he spoke to me. *That's* never happened before. Later, someone who could have been Charles Donavan, and a bunch of men on horseback, rode up. The man from the cliff was ... dead by then." She pulled out the obsidian knife. "They'd stabbed him in the back with this and forced him over the cliff. They murdered him."

Jessup reached for the blade, but she pulled it back.

"The brown tar? I think it's dangerous. Maybe even poisoned." With deft fingers, she untucked and slowly unwound the stiff leather wrapping the handle. "They stripped him—the silver buttons went flying—searching for a book—"

"The treasure journal," Jessup said.

She nodded. "They carted the body off, but not before they took his watch and wedding ring." Myrna paused to see if he would say anything about the watch and ring he'd taken off the skeleton under the rocks. Jessup only stared at her with narrowed eyes. "When one of the men pulled this knife out of his back, he cut his hand on it. I've taken samples. DNA analysis might be a way to find the dead cowboy's identity *and* the identity of the man who cut himself. But I don't want to do the analysis at the ranch lab or on Donavan computers. I don't trust—"

She didn't trust anyone from the ranch. Maybe not even the man in front of her. There were too many secrets here—the elk deaths, the marijuana grow, the mines, and this elusive treasure. Myrna took a deep breath.

"If you're leaving the ranch tomorrow, I want to go. I want to drop off the samples at Eleanor's lab, so we'd need to detour to Socorro, and ... one other place." She flipped over the leather strip she'd unwound from the knife. Branded into it were the words *Second Chance Trading Post, Route 66.* "The same name was burned into Isaac's box of stone projectile points. Is Isaac part of your treasure team? Because there's more than just you and Bard, right?"

Jessup lifted a shuttered gaze to hers. She sighed internally but couldn't fault him for keeping his secrets when she held tight to her own.

"One of the men in that museum picture could have been Isaac's brother, and if he owned this knife, Isaac may know more than he's telling." She rewrapped the leather, tucked the knife back in the bag, and stripped off her gloves. "I have a couple more questions, then I'll take William Tell and go and pack if you'll take me with you." The dog was still on the hearth rug, now sprawled and snoring.

Jessup nodded.

"How did you know about the treasure journal?" she asked.

"Rumor, old stories, odd bits of gossip. We pieced together fragments and figured out the treasure was more recent than the gold bell, and that the journal was linked to a mammoth skull."

Mammoth skull? But the one in the arroyo had only recently been exposed after thousands of years, so it couldn't have been stashed there.

The dying cowboy's whispered words played in her head.

Tell her it's hidden ... it's safe. She's safe. That those boneheads *will never find it.*

Boneheads. Myrna's knees wobbled. *The baby mammoth.* They hadn't known there was a second skull until she'd found evidence of the baby mammoth. *The journal is in the missing baby mammoth's skull.* They just needed to find—

Jessup stepped in front of her and slid his hands up her arms. "Myrna. Why do you care, sweetheart? All you need to do is finish your commission, and you're done with all this craziness." His mouth curved to a tender smile, his blue eyes like balmy seas.

She stood still beneath his hands, absorbing his closeness.

Why did she care? Because she wanted to be present in a world where she'd been trained by her brilliant paranoid mother to be invisible? Because she'd climbed to the highest point in her field but had been unceremoniously toppled off because she'd trusted the wrong man? Because she wanted someone to need her, to think highly of her, to *see her.*

Like the cowboy in her vision. He'd seen her. She'd held his hand, and, without her, he would've died alone. And alone could be a terrible place, one she'd experienced all too often in the wild and in civilization.

She licked her lips. Jessup's gaze dropped to her mouth. "The murdered man. He asked me to help him. To tell his wife she's ... safe. I can't do that unless I find out who he is. Find out his name and why they murdered him."

Oh, *God,* she wanted Jessup to see her for *who* she was, not what she was. Not Dr. Myrna P. Lee, disgraced scientist, mammoth and poisons expert. But the little girl in tattered clothes and a too-large backpack who'd had no name until a clerk at a convenience store gave her a package of chocolate snack cakes and a kind smile.

"What's your name?" she'd asked the lady.

"Myrna, like meerkat, not mermaid. What's yours, sweetie?"

And she'd answered, "My name is Myrna like meerkat, too."

And Myrna like meerkat wanted Jessup to kiss her.

"I'd better go." She tugged away from him, gathering up the knife in the towel.

"Myrna?" She closed her eyes, her body savoring the rough edge of his voice. "Stay with me. It'll make it easier to leave early tomorrow if we wake up together."

Once she could breathe again, she said, "I've only known you for a few days."

"Sometimes, that's all two people need."

Her belly simmered with heat. "I—I'm not on the pill or anything."

"I have ... protection here. When I bought it, I thought ..." Jessup made a rueful face. "Never ended up needing it."

She searched his eyes. "You have ... had someone else in your life?"

"Not for a long time. But I'd like ... *love* for you to be in it now." He blew out a shaky breath. "Stay."

Heat and happiness and something like *relief* writhed under her skin. She'd been with no one with whom she'd felt such *connection* since Tom Hutchinson. That relationship had ended so wrong, but *this*—

Trust.

Myrna pressed up on tiptoe to kiss him. "Okay."

FORTY-FOUR

The truck was packed: Jessup's duffle on the floorboards in the back seat, Myrna's single change of clothes in a spare bag tucked next to Jessup's, her backpack on the passenger's side floorboard. William Tell gamboled about the yard, too excited to mind until Jessup took control of him and stowed him in his carrier strapped into the back seat.

Took control. Myrna's shiver had little to do with the predawn chill. She stood on the stoop of his little house, more content than she'd been for what seemed like years. She refused to give in to the fear and panic that skulked in the darkest, most primitive recesses of her brain. Not this time. Her wariness had sabotaged too many relationships in her past.

"I forgot the buttons." Jessup's eyes, crinkled in a smile, met Myrna's in the residual light from the truck's interior. "Must've been distracted or something."

She swayed over to him and cupped prickly cheeks, rising to plant a lingering kiss on his lips. Warm hands slid around her waist. "Or something. Where are they? I'll get them."

"On my bureau in the bedroom, there's a box. Lift out the

insert and they're underneath." Jessup pecked her lips again. "Hurry. We're burnin' daylight."

Myrna laughed. They were more than an hour away from dawn. She skipped into the house feeling lighter than air and quickstepped to the bedroom, only to stop and stare for a moment at the made-up bed, breathing a satisfied sigh. The dresser was tucked by the curtained window; on top, there was a flat rectangular wooden box with a hinged lid. The divider tray insert held a pair of tarnished silver and coral cufflinks, a high school ring with a sapphire blue stone, two watches—a man's and a woman's —and a blue velvet box. Myrna shot a quick glance at the bedroom door. She opened the box and found an old-fashioned diamond wedding set, along with a man's gold band, worn thin on one side by wear. His parents'? Heart touched, she closed the box and lifted the insert.

Underneath was the chunk of gnawed picture frame from the packrat nest. Her brows creased. It hadn't been on the table in Charles Donavan's office. Jessup must have hidden it so they wouldn't find it. Weird. The watch and wedding band Jessup had taken off the dead man in the tunnel were there, too. The baggie of silver buttons lay to one side, five total, so plus the one they'd found in the cave. She lifted the watch, running fingers over the tightly woven olive-green band—very military—and read the face: Panerai Radiomir. The back was a thick glass circle that revealed the workings, maker's marks around the edge. No personal inscription. Pensive, Myrna rotated it to stare at the face. If that group with Charles Donavan's grandfather had been ex-soldiers, it was possible that all those men had similar military-issued watches, and that one of them had tried to find the treasure with disastrous results.

She laid the watch down and picked up the gold band, holding it up to the light diffusing through the curtains. Inscribed on the inside was one word: *Schatzi*. A last name? She'd run it through the internet to see what she could find. Jessup probably already had. Myrna stilled.

Then why hadn't he told her? She bit her lip, shifting her feet. Maybe he would on the drive.

Myrna put the ring back and picked up the chunk of gilded wood, once again studying the burn marks on the flat side.

In an impulsive decision, she decided to take the wood and the watch with them. She scooped up the bag of buttons, but somehow snagged a credit card-sized piece of plastic, flipping it out of the box and onto the dresser top. Pulling a face, she picked up the card. The front was a swirled bronze background with THE LODGE stamped in gold. The back was white with a black magnetic stripe and directions in four different languages on how to use the card to get into the hotel room. She shrugged, slotted the card back into the box, slid in the top tray, and shut the lid.

Myrna closed the front door behind her, hopped down the steps, skipped to the truck, and jumped inside. Jessup wasn't there, but movement under the porch light of Isaac Marín's little house had Myrna craning her neck. Jessup was on the stoop, holding the handle of a bulky cooler. Isaac stood in the threshold and ... Myrna squinted at the third man who stood between shadow and the yellow light from the porch. Paden. He and Webb McJunkin took turns driving Isaac into work.

Jessup stepped into Isaac's front yard and jogged to the truck.

"Took Isaac my house key just in case," he said as he stowed the cooler in the back seat. "He gave me enough food for an army. Where are your samples?"

"In my bag. I don't need a cooler. They're stable at room temp."

Jessup maneuvered the truck to the road running between the line of houses, lifting his hand to the two men as they drove off.

Myrna nibbled her lip, pushing down creeping worry. "Did you tell Isaac and Paden we were leaving the ranch?"

Jessup hesitated. "I said you had to visit your boss's lab to drop off samples. That you didn't have the proper equipment at the ranch lab."

"What if the Donavans find out?"

"I trust those men."

"Did you tell Bard?"

Jessup's hesitation was longer. "He'll cover for us if we need him to."

"So now, pretty much everyone knows we're not on the ranch," she said, her worry growing.

The truck pulled onto the road that ran through Cimarron. Lights from oncoming vehicles brightened the cab, early morning ranch hands and laborers on their way to work.

"Does Bard know about the cave?" Myrna asked once they left the lights of the town behind them.

"Yeah. He took me up to get the truck. He had to know about the pot grow and how we got away. He won't tell the Donavans, I promise."

"So he knows there's access to the cave through the gold mine, too?"

"It doesn't matter, Myrna. I erased the chalk going back half a mile. I'm not even sure I could find my way back in if I had to."

"Were you going to tell me about this?" *Or anything else you've found out?*

He released the steering wheel with one hand and extended it to her, palm up. Biting her lip, Myrna placed her hand in his warm, rough fingers, and he brought it to his lips for a kiss. She could feel his mouth pulling into a smile.

"Like I said earlier, I was bit distracted, but I'm glad you brought it up now. You can trust me, Myrna."

Trust. She squeezed his hand. Okay. Then she would.

"I can get us back to the packrat midden," she offered. "Without your chalk or the charcoal circles."

In the cab's darkness, she could feel Jessup's puzzlement. "How?"

She shifted in her seat and glanced back at William Tell. He wasn't asleep but listening, black eyes shining in the low light, ears perked high on his head.

"I have a confession. That water William Tell drank in the cave? He basically turned it into scent markers all along our trail he can track," she said. "Essentially, William Tell *peed* our way back in."

Jessup stared at her in astonishment. Then he burst out laughing.

Forty-Five

Myrna's gaze swept over the single- and multi-story shops and restaurants with their huge glass display windows that lined both sides of downtown Albuquerque Street. Old West-style brick facades were fused with the sleek modern redesigned businesses, which then morphed into the Art Deco-Pueblo revival architecture of the next shop. A style mixture that was both charming and jarring at the same time.

She staggered a couple of steps as William Tell's paws dug into the sidewalk and dragged her to a scraggly tree planted in a cement cutout. Cars ambled by on Central Avenue SW—Old Route 66— stretching east to west, creeping to the next red light.

Ball cap brim cocked up, his blue plaid cotton shirt open a single button at the throat, Jessup trotted around the back of the truck. He'd managed to capture a parallel parking spot a few doors up from their destination: the Silver Sky Trading Post and Pawn. A brightly painted neon sign of a bucking horse against a turquoise background dangled over the front doors.

"I emailed every silversmith, trading post, and pawn shop from Gallup to Tucumcari that had roots before the 1940s or '50s,"

Jessup said. "Got a few responses, but this one seemed the most promising."

Myrna read the stylized Art Deco script painted under a long mural of traditionally dressed dancers. "Navajo owned and operated since 1940. You sure they won't mind William Tell?" The little dog tipped his head up at her.

"Look inside."

Through huge windows filled with painted clay vessels, leather goods, and layers of colorful blankets, Myrna spied a yellow dog curled up on a large pillow at the back of an aisle.

"The owners fund a shelter for rez—reservation—dogs." Jessup led her around a curve of glass that funneled them between displays crammed with Katsina dolls, sand paintings, and dream catchers of every size and color. The front doors opened into a room lined with case after case of silver jewelry. Knotty pine walls rose to a ceiling overlaid with stamped copper sheets and hung with wagon-wheel and antler chandeliers. The cacophony of art, hand-woven rugs, saddles, bridles, and chaps, quivers, moccasins, belts, knives, primitive wood carvings, santos, feathers, pots, masks, and taxidermy—one area held half a dozen jackalope mounts—was even more overwhelming than the mix of architectural styles along the street outside. Leaving Jessup waiting for an employee to finish with a customer, Myrna retreated to the back corner of the store where a man wearing dark-lensed glasses worked with a small torch, creating small silver beads.

The dog they'd seen from the window lay next to the silversmith booth. She lifted her head, her muzzle grayed with age and eyes blurred milky blue with cataracts, to smell the air as William Tell trotted toward her. He gently touched noses with the old girl, who beat her tail on the bed. And when she rose unsteadily to her feet, William Tell held absolutely still while she blindly sniffed him. When she finished, she plopped back down with a tired sigh. William Tell shook his whole body and sat on Myrna's foot. Myrna turned her attention back to the man—

"Don't look at the flame." The man's voice rose over the sound of the torch. He jutted his chin toward the yellow dog. "They exchanged their stories."

"What?" Myrna blinked, dots burned on her retina.

"Now she knows your dog's stories, and he knows hers."

Myrna gave the man a skeptical look. "She wouldn't be sleeping if she knew his. His life has been somewhat ... harrowing and unique."

"So's hers." The man turned off the torch, leaving a dozen silver beads to cool on a charred rectangular brick. Standing, he stretched, bull-chested, with salt-and-pepper hair buzzed short. He slipped off the welding glasses and slipped on wire-rimmed aviators over eyes that looked like they'd squinted against the light for so long they were stuck half-closed. Unlatching a swinging door at the back of his booth, he strolled around to her. "*What has been will be again, what has been done will be done again. There is nothing new under the sun.*"

"Ecclesiastes," Jessup said, stopping next to Myrna. A smile tugged at his lips and his eyes twinkled. "I think you'd be surprised at what that dog's seen. Lady at the front sent me back here. You must be Herman Roanhorse."

"And you're the feller with the ol' silver buttons." Mr. Roanhorse extended a dry, callused hand, knuckles thick, his fingernail beds stained silver-gray.

"Yes, sir. Jessup Page. This is Dr. Myrna Lee."

"A real doctor?" Roanhorse asked, taking her hand to shake, too, winking down at Myrna. "'Cause I got this pain in my shoulder—"

"Doctor of philosophy in forensic paleontology," Jessup said, and Myrna was touched by the pride in his voice. "She studies Pleistocene megafauna."

"Ah!" Roanhorse shimmied behind a glass counter that housed hundreds of carved stone fetishes. He slid open the back of the case and extracted one. "*And a chief monster with a long arm coming down from his shoulder that he uses as we do ours."* He opened his palm. Nestled inside was a small figure carved in red jasper.

"An Algonquin historical story that could be describing mammoths," Myrna replied. She picked up the little figurine. Fine bone tusks extended downward from a bulbous head, its body carved as if shaggy with hair.

"Made by a very talented Naskapi Innu craftsman. An exchange of stories from him to you," Roanhorse said. "Now, about these buttons."

Jessup tugged the plastic baggie from his shirt pocket and spilled the buttons onto a piece of polishing felt on top of the case. Roanhorse pulled a loupe out of his jeans and switched on a swing-arm lamp. He studied one of the buttons, then turned to pick up a sheaf of yellowed onion skin paper behind him. A black-and-white photo was clipped to one corner.

"My grandmother did the books for years. Quite a packrat. No one ever got around to dumping the boxes of old contracts and receipts. When my daughter took over, she realized what a treasure trove they were. Pictures, signatures. History. She's been scanning them into the computer, maybe to write a book or something. That's Uncle Cecil's mark on the buttons." Roanhorse slid the pages across the glass.

Jessup laid a button next to the photo.

"Looks like he originally made six," Roanhorse said.

"We found five," Jessup offered.

"My grandfather's uncle made them after he came back from the war, 1946 abouts. He didn't make much stuff, but it was good. The store tried to handle anything he brought in." Roanhorse leaned his elbows on the case. "I don't remember too much about him. I was just a kid when—" He waved a hand. "From the paperwork, we displayed them for a year before they were bought by another trading post in '47. According to my daughter, Silver Sky did good business with the proprietor. The post's stamp and the owner's signature are on a bunch of our old paperwork."

Jessup flipped the page and found the stamp. *Second Chance Trading Post, Route 66.*

Myrna's astonished gaze met his.

"I can't make out the name from this signature," Jessup said. "It could be important. You said you did good business with this trading post. Maybe we can look at some of the other receipts?"

Roanhorse straightened. "Hey, Carl. When's Rita gonna be in?"

The man who answered didn't even look up from the tray of squash blossom necklaces he'd laid out before a customer. "Check your phone, Herman. She sent a text."

Roanhorse tugged a cell out of his back pocket. "Can't get used to these things." He held it at arm's length and scrolled with the side of a blunt finger. "That's right. She's out at To'Hajiilee today. Look, we get requests like this all the time. People sending us pictures of old Indian-made jewelry, asking for provenance or how much it's worth. The only reason she took the time to pull this paperwork was because yours wasn't the only email we got."

"You received more than one email about *these* buttons?" Myrna said.

"Three. And when one of them hinted at a major purchase for the Donavan Lodge boutique"—Herman Roanhorse raised his eyebrows—"that's enough to make anyone sit up and listen."

Forty-Six

Myrna held the jasper mammoth fetish in the sunlight streaming through the truck's windshield. It was beautifully wrought and *extremely* expensive. Not something her bank account could really handle until after she finished her project at the Donavan Ranch and was paid her commission.

And left the ranch. She'd have to. Even if she drew up the proposal to excavate the mammoths Charles Donavan had asked for and it was approved, with winter approaching, the dig season was coming to an end. Jessup would be busy guiding hunts on the ranch, and she had a job in Eleanor's lab that paid her bills. She might not see him until next year.

She clutched the fetish tight in her fist and flashed a quick glance at Jessup, not sure if the heaviness she felt was because they were headed to Socorro to drop off her samples and she'd have to deal with her *team*, or because she didn't know if she and the man next to her would ever ... *could* ever have a future. Together.

A crazy, desperate wish.

Jessup looked into the rearview again, eyes scanning the traffic behind them.

"I'm as paranoid as the next guy," she said. "But I doubt anyone's following us. You turned off your phone's location monitor, right?"

"Yes," he said, his reply clipped.

"Maybe we can stop by Silver Sky Trading Post on the way back to the ranch. Speak to Rita Roanhorse about who sent those other two emails—"

"Or I could text her for the information *right now*," he interrupted.

"Not a good idea. If one of those emails to the Silver Sky was from the Donavans, then someone on the ranch accessed your information. I mean, they did yesterday when they checked your phone for pictures at the mine. I have some experience with electronic spying—" Myrna thinned her lips. That certainly wasn't a road she wanted to map right now. "If you want to contact Rita Roanhorse, you can use a computer at the lab, but keeping your messages verbal is the only way of not allowing more information to escape."

She shifted in her seat to face him. "And you need to stop asking people on the ranch about the buttons or anything else. Isaac, Mike and his whole family. Bard. Webb? They've all heard about the treasure. Maybe they sent the emails. Greed is a powerful motivator, besides possibly wanting to cover up the murder of that man."

"Cover up? I doubt anyone cares anymore. It happened close to seventy years ago."

"Charles Donavan might make a run for the presidency. Clearing the family closet of skeletons is on his priority list. I mean, someone on his team is worried about elk dropping dead and bad publicity." Myrna sat back and fiddled with the mammoth fetish before laying her fist on the center console. "Who else have you told?"

"Only people I trust."

Whoever else was on his and Bard's team, but he wasn't going to tell her who that was. Myrna's heart squeezed, past betrayals rearing their ugly heads. "Even those closest to you can burn you alive."

He shot her a look that carried both sympathy and guilt.

"We only connected the buttons to the Second Chance Trading Post today," Myrna said. "No one else knows about that."

Jessup drove another few miles in silence. Then his right hand dropped over her fist. Very deliberately, he interlaced his fingers with hers, trapping the mammoth fetish between their palms.

Almost her whole life, she'd been alone, her relationships hollow—whether it was with her family, men. Her mother. But with the heat of Jessup's hand, the solid strength he willingly shared, the silent connection between them, it was as if she was finally part of something larger than herself. Couple, team, pairing, whatever it was called, it felt ... right. Myrna melted inside, happiness fluttering up despite her disquiet.

"No one should know." Jessup squeezed her hand and negotiated a turn. "Unless we're being followed."

Myrna sat in Eleanor's office, lit golden by the late afternoon sky, Jessup beside her, William Tell dozing between them. She fidgeted, hating she had to push up on her toes so her feet wouldn't dangle like a child's. Jessup had been quieter than even his usual laconic cowboy self. Probably intimidated by everything—the building that housed the lab, the lab itself, her white-coated colleagues busy performing experiments in the lab. Although "colleagues" *was* stretching it. Other than disdainful looks, they'd pretty much ignored her presence when she breezed in with a careless wave and nervous smile. It kind of made her sick to her stomach that she'd cavalierly torched so many bridges in the past, since she really needed them now.

The door flung open and Eleanor stepped through, breathy

and flushed, hair artfully disheveled, her sparkling eyes running over Jessup, who rose to his feet. Eleanor's gaze settled on Myrna then dropped to the floor. She clasped her hands, bent over, and bared her teeth in a smile. Myrna almost recoiled. It was like watching Cruella de Vil count Dalmatians.

"Oh, my! There's the little puppy dog. *Dr.* Lee"—slight emphasis on doctor. She straightened and glanced around the floor —"he hasn't, um—"

Got it. She wanted to play it professional in front of the client's representative.

"Oh, no, Dr. Kelly. Not this time," Myrna said formally. "This is Mr. Page from the Donavan Ranch."

Eleanor extended a toned arm, her mouth widening into a lovely smile. "Of course, Mr. Page. *Very* nice to meet you."

Myrna frowned. Eleanor was gushing. She didn't gush.

Jessup took her hand with a murmured, "Dr. Kelly."

"Please sit down. I was across campus advising the dean"— now Eleanor was boasting. She did boast—"when I received Myrna's surprise text that you and she were here." She swept around her desk and settled gracefully in her chair. "The question is, why?"

"The Donavan lab is well-equipped, but it doesn't have the instrumentation I needed for a more in-depth analysis of my samples." A logical reason for traveling to Socorro.

"From the projectile points in the lodge museum? I'm impressed Charles Donavan gave you permission."

"How did you know that?" Myrna asked. "Oh, that's right. Your spy at the ranch. Is that why you haven't checked up on my progress—no calls, no emails, no texts—the whole time I've been up north?" She hadn't meant to sound so accusatory. Okay, maybe she had.

"With you, Dr. Lee, I figured no news was good news," Eleanor said dryly. She leaned her elbows on her desk and clasped her hands to rest her chin on folded knuckles, studying Myrna before one hand fell on the glass-topped box, fingers smoothing over the wood. "What about the mammoth kill site? Any progress?"

"Um, yes. Charles Donavan said he'd fund the dig, but that I'd have to submit a written proposal." Jessup snapped his head to stare at her, and guilt itched a little. She'd neglected to tell him in case things didn't work out on either the scientific or the relationship fronts. "There are actually two sites—a cow at the bottom of the cliff and a calf at the top."

"A potential mammoth jump and the possibility of two skeletons for display. Wonderful. How complete are they?"

"Skull for the mammoth cow, disarticulation cuts on exposed bones. I won't know the full extent until I excavate. Some of the baby mammoth's bones have washed over from the top. No skull yet."

"That's disappointing." Eleanor's eyes flickered to Jessup. "I apologize for not including you in our little discussion, Mr. Page. This mammoth site was Myrna's main enticement for taking the commission. Now, Dr. Lee." Eleanor stood. "My assumption is that you wish to secure your samples?"

Myrna's brows knit. Eleanor hadn't even asked about the elk die-off project. "Actually, I'd like to start the analysis tonight—"

"Which will take you—what? A couple of hours. Leaving Mr. Page at loose ends." Eleanor sauntered around her desk, smiling. Myrna, Jessup, and William Tell stood. "We have a top-notch brew pub in our little town, Mr. Page. I'd love to catch up on our mutual acquaintances at the ranch." She reached for Jessup's arm.

Now Eleanor was poaching. She did poach.

Myrna stepped in front of Jessup. At first, she thought maybe she was the genesis of the growl she heard until she realized William Tell stood next to her, hackles raised, too. Her boss pulled her hand back and retreated a step, eyeing Myrna and the dog warily.

"*Actually,*" Myrna drawled with a tight smile. "Mr. Page would like to use the phone and computer in my office for some business related to the elk die-off. I'll take him there and make sure he's logged in before I start my analysis."

Eleanor's eyes hardened to marble. "Mr. Page? Could you wait in the hall? I need to speak to Dr. Lee. *Privately*." Her voice held all sorts of menace.

"Why?" Myrna asked, astonished. "I didn't do any—"

"*Dr. Lee*," Eleanor snapped. "Mr. Page. Would you leave us?"

At Jessup's quiet "Sure," Eleanor smiled down at Myrna in triumph.

Myrna waited for Jessup's steadying hand on her waist or shoulder, for a reassuring touch or squeeze that would calm her confusion at Eleanor's odd confrontational behavior.

But leash in hand, and without a backward glance, Jessup headed to the door. William Tell set his legs stubbornly, refusing to budge, but after some gentle tugging, he reluctantly followed. Fingers on the handle, Jessup finally turned his head and caught Myrna's strong and brave gaze. At least, she *hoped* it was strong and brave, and not like that of a seven-year-old who'd huddled in a casino bathroom stall while her mother gambled away what little money they had.

All her life she'd stood alone with a few exceptions: the woman —Paula—who'd rescued her from the wild and nursed her back to health, only to ship her off to snooty relations who didn't want her; her undergraduate mentor—Dr. Medici—who'd nurtured her passion for old bones and exotic poisons, but who threatened to take away her grant money; and the first man she'd ever loved— Tom Hutchinson—who'd stepped off a cliff in Yakutia's Orulgan Range and left her with William Tell, a stolen motorcycle, and only her wits to get her back to the States. Myrna had learned over and over the hard lesson her quixotic, unreliable, unstable mother had hammered into her from the time she could walk: She could only truly rely on herself.

But hope kept getting in the way.

With all her soul, she didn't want Jessup to leave her. She wanted him to stake a claim, to signal to Eleanor that Myrna was a part of his life even if they hardly knew each other, had only started to be together. That *she* was special to *him*.

It was a stupid thing to want.

Her blaze of courage oozed out of her. She dropped her gaze to the floor.

Boots appeared in her line of sight. Callused fingers touched and lifted her chin. With heart-melting tenderness, Jessup pressed his lips to hers. He drew away, never breaking her gaze, and smiled. Creases fanned around his intense blue eyes.

"If you need me, Meerkat, I'll be right outside that door."

And *right then, right there* she knew he meant something more, that he would be there for her, stand beside her, maybe even step in for her when things got tough. Her heart swelled.

Jessup stepped into the hallway and started to close the door when Myrna tipped her chin defiantly at Eleanor. "Please excuse me, Dr. Kelly. I have work to do. I will meet with you after I've processed my samples."

Myrna marched past her boss. Back ramrod-straight, she led Jessup and the dog down the hall, feeling a spike of satisfaction when Eleanor slammed the office door behind her.

FORTY-SEVEN

After dropping off Jessup and William Tell in her office, Myrna marched to the lab. She swept up her samples and wove through the benches until she stood next to Dr. Kent Sheffield, Eleanor's analytical entomologist and the person who'd taken over Myrna's Khyber project.

Kent continued racking glass vials into the HPLC. He didn't even look up.

There was no love lost between them, and maybe she hadn't always treated him fairly. Okay, she hadn't *ever* treated him fairly. She needed him now, but it was more than that. While she could accomplish a lot on her own, being part of a team could increase success exponentially by pooling expertise. Of course, she'd *known* that, but had to rely on herself so much in the past that she'd disregarded it.

Then she'd seen teamwork and trust in action watching the Donavan Ranch hands work together—and with her—with the elk carcasses, and then at the archery contest when those girls folded her into their team with such confidence and innocence.

Myrna was also willing to concede that she'd been less than

generous to everyone else in the lab, too. Remorse scrabbled up her spine.

She licked her lips. "How's it going?"

Kent lifted his head, brown eyes wary in his narrow face. "Fine. You're done with the Donavan commission?"

"Not quite." Myrna hesitated. "I'd love to see your Khyber project results."

"Why? So you can tear them apart?"

A glib, sarcastic response jumped to her lips, but she hesitated. When she'd attempted to teach Jessup about her elk-death findings, he'd accused her of trying to push him away.

Maybe it was time to stop doing that. Maybe it was time she *trusted* her colleagues.

"Maybe, but science is a second pair of eyes," Myrna said, halting and unsure as she searched for words that tasted strange coming from her lips. "It's finding better ways to do what we do. So when we publish, someone else can use our results like a stepping stone to go forward."

Kent stilled but made no response.

"Look, in the past, maybe I've been too harsh—"

He snorted. "*Maybe?*"

"And I'll try not to be going forward, but criticism makes what we do better. A lot of people out there think science is infallible. It's not, because humans are arrogant and—and *fallible*." Myrna stared down at her clasped hands, knuckles white. "Sometimes, we're even afraid we won't be taken seriously."

Kent darted her a sharp look.

"Dr. Sheffield? Kent. I really need your help." He literally gawped at her. Myrna's cheeks burned, and her hope dropped right to the floor.

All of Eleanor's lab personnel, who must have been shamelessly eavesdropping, stopped what they were doing and wandered in Myrna and Kent's direction.

"Don't trust her, Kent," said Noemi, her fiery mane of red-gold hair glinting under the fluorescent lights.

"It's probably a trap," piped up Rohaan. He'd shed his lab coat and was garbed in his gray track suit striped with silvery reflective tape that flashed with the tiniest movement.

"Maybe she's in love or something." Jeannie crossed her arms, her pretty face frowning. Myrna eyed her, wondering for the millionth time about the genetics that gave someone so scarecrow-skinny so much ... bosom.

"We can make this collaborative if you want." Desperation threaded Myrna's words. "A team effort."

"Team?" Kent said. "Like coauthors-on-publications team?"

"Yes. Plus, this." Myrna opened the cooler and extracted the tube containing the amberat-encased beetle. "Possible Pleistocene origin. It could be all yours to analyze and publish. And I have other samples: human DNA, swabs from Clovis points, contaminated soil. I could use everyone's help."

Kent held the green beetle up to the light before he gave Myrna a narrowed-eyed look. He handed the tube back at her. "I don't believe you."

Noemi and Jeannie turned away. Rohaan pulled out his phone, his expression bored. The hope flopping around Myrna's feet like a fish out of water gave up the ghost.

Throat tight, she shoved the sample back in the ice.

Whatever. She didn't need their help. She didn't need anyone. She'd do it all by herself. Alone.

But alone didn't feel right anymore.

Her negative thoughts acted like a shroud, blocking out the light. But she pushed those thoughts aside, took a deep breath ...

And took responsibility, reaping what she'd sowed and every other cliché she could think of.

"Kent? For what it's worth, I'm sorry I've been such a ... you know."

She picked up the cooler and wandered to her bench space,

settled on the lab chair, and began to catalog the tubes, soon losing herself in the quiet hum and beeps of equipment.

The tap on her shoulder made her jump.

Kent had materialized at her side, Jeannie, Rohaan, and Noemi arced behind him, their arms crossed, their faces neutral. "Dr. Lee? Uh, Myrna? Okay."

Myrna frowned. "Okay, what?"

"We'll help you, but we have a few demands."

His face—all their faces—blurred a little as Myrna blinked away the stupid weird happy tears that started after Kent said *we'll help you.*

He stopped, mouth open. "Hey. Uh. Are you okay?"

"Yeah," she replied. "I think I'm going to be fine."

Forty-Eight

By the time Myrna's samples had been divided between her colleagues, the only remanent of the sun was an orange highlighter strip that separated the mountains from a midnight-blue sky. They'd worked together to get everything readied for analysis bright and early the next morning with a promise from Kent that he'd call her with results. Warmth still swirled in Myrna's chest at their teamwork, even though she knew the wounds she'd created needed more time to heal.

Eleanor hadn't bothered them at all. Hadn't even poked her head in the lab. When Myrna, Jessup, and William Tell finally left the building, her office was dark, and her car was gone. She must've thought better about whatever dressing down she'd saved up for Myrna. At least for now.

Jessup trundled his pickup slowly along narrow roads that ran through an older residential area of Socorro, Myrna ensconced next to him.

"Turn right at the stop sign. Fifth house down on the left." She pointed him to a dirt alleyway between backyards, its darkness unrelieved by streetlights unless the homeowner erected their own. Luckily, a nearly full moon hung over the river valley. Tires popping on rocks scared up a cat that darted across the headlamps only to disappear into a jumble of garbage cans and dried weeds. The alley meandered past small rectangular pink and yellow houses until the truck's headlamps lit up her rental, a detached garage converted into her one-bedroom apartment. Stucco bubbled and cracked away from the base, and a waist-high chain-link fence surrounded a patch of pebbly dirt yard. A green hose snaked from a spigot to a spindly tree, the ground around it soaked dark.

"You live here." Jessup's statement sounded like an accusation.

"I've lived in worse." Myrna strove to keep defensiveness from her voice. "We can stay the rest of the night and head to the trading post early in the morning."

Jessup turned off the truck. Myrna opened her door and slid to the ground, backpack over one shoulder, hand tight on the strap. When she opened the back, William Tell whined and scratched at the carrier. She shot a glance at Jessup, who still stared at the garage, before she unlatched the carrier and snapped the leash on the dog's harness. He bounced off the seat to the floor to the running boards then the ground in a blur and strained toward the little yard, his butt waggling ecstatically. The driver's side door slammed, Jessup finally out of the truck.

Myrna unlatched the gate and unclipped William Tell. He darted to the tree—

Then stopped. He stood still in the heavy moonlight, before pressing his nose to sniff the ground around his feet, stutter-stepping as he followed scent along the square cement pavers that lined the path to the front door. Myrna retrieved her house key from her backpack and hurried up the path when a low growl rumbled from the dog's chest. The hair on her neck stood.

The front door to her converted apartment, a black rectangle under glowing blue moonlight, was open.

Myrna extracted her knife from her secret pocket, pulse spiking.

"What?" Jessup, behind her.

She raised a hand to silence him. William Tell quivered, his growl rolling louder. Knife ready, Myrna took a careful step forward. The dog lunged at the door and disappeared. His furious barks echoed from inside the house.

"Someone's broken— Why in hell don't you have a porch light?" Jessup said, low and seething.

Myrna pointed silently to the shattered bulb on the ground. William Tell had gone quiet. A few seconds later, he snuffled out and stood half in shadow, half in moonlight before disappearing inside again.

"Whoever was here is gone now." Knife still clutched in her hand, she took a step, but Jessup grabbed her forearm.

"I'm not afraid," she said.

"I know." He squeezed her wrist lightly and treaded around her to push open the front door, Myrna behind him. She flipped a switch on the wall. A single overhead light planted in the middle of the ceiling glared on.

The room was trashed. It was like a gut punch.

Jessup gestured to a half-open door along one wall. "Bedroom?"

Throat tight, Myrna eked out a croaky, "Bathroom, too. And closet."

Jessup vanished through the door. A light switched on. Myrna pocketed her knife and surveyed the damage.

The kitchen counter ran along the wall to the left of the front door. Cupboards ajar, pots and pans pulled out and scattered across the yellowed linoleum floor. Her refrigerator stood open. The small Formica table and two plastic patio chairs had been shoved to one side, but not upended like the secondhand loveseat, cushions strewn, or coffee table, tipped on its side. Books spilled from a shelf pulled away from the wall. William Tell rooted dejectedly around a tattered, flipped-over dog bed, pawing at crumpled dog blankets. She knew what he was looking for.

"Can't find Tan Turtle?" Myrna asked softly.

Tan Turtle, the disgusting rag toy that stayed gross no matter how many times she washed it. The toy she'd forgotten to take with them to the Donavan Ranch. The toy he spent countless hours flinging up into the air only to pounce and retrieve and toss it again and again. She sat cross-legged amid the blanket carnage and ran a hand over William Tell's drooping head. His eyes shone liquid, like he was ready to cry. She might beat him to it. "It's probably under my bed."

"Nothing's under your bed anymore. Or in your closet." Jessup walked to the kitchen and picked up a can of soda that had rolled against the kick board. "Still cold. Whoever broke in did it while we were at Eleanor's lab."

Myrna barely noticed his casual use of Eleanor's name. Her home had been invaded and wrecked. It made her sick to think about it. "I don't have anything anyone would want."

"No," Jessup said quietly. "You keep everything you need in that backpack in case you have to leave in a hurry, don't you? Why is that, Myrna?"

William Tell chose that instant to snuggle up next to her and plop his head onto her knee. The dog heaved a huge, shuddering sigh. She curled to press her cheek against the top of his head, not knowing if she was comforting him or he her.

"You really do love him."

Jessup stared at her from the kitchen, still clutching the soda can. She shrugged a shoulder and continued to gently stroke the little dog.

"Should we call the police?" she asked.

"A police report could be picked up by the Donavans' security systems. Since they think we're both on the ranch working, it might get us fired."

"Then let's go."

"Where?"

"To the Second Chance Trading Post."

He hesitated. "Myrna, I think this was about the treasure."

Myrna knuckled nascent tears from her eyes. "I only found out about that stupid treasure a few days ago. Why would they target me?"

His lips curled in disgust, and his eyes went flat. "Because someone has a big mouth."

FORTY-NINE

The headlights of Jessup's truck smeared over a jumble of midnight-black buildings scattered ahead on either side of the lonesome two-lane road. Myrna squinted, trying to pick out anything that resembled a trading post from the hard-edged silhouettes. Odd the way the smothering blanket of clouds seemed to illuminate the air around what was once a tiny town while the actual structures sucked in the night like dilapidated black holes.

"I thought Route 66 paralleled the highway." She glanced through the driver's side windows. No moving headlights shone from Interstate 40. No light shone from anywhere.

"This isn't exactly on Route 66. It's an auxiliary spur off a spur. Far enough out that it doesn't make the off-road travel sites people look for online. And it's on private land. But from what I've heard, it was busy with tourists in its heyday." Jessup swerved around scrubby bushes that had broken through the pavement, their branches clawing the truck. "At least we'll know if someone's following us," he said. "We'll see lights coming for miles."

"Maybe they got what they wanted from my place and are gone."

She could literally feel Jessup's skeptical gaze across the dark cab.

With one last bump, the road smoothed. Jessup rolled the truck past splintered split rail fences, falling-down sheds, and the hulk of what could've been a barn, roof half-collapsed. A small adobe home sat back from the road, walls melting into the earth, doors and windows gaping hollowly. Once they passed, darkness devoured it again. Myrna shivered.

The truck's headlights carved out a tunnel down the center of the town, its wash lighting up a tiny building with POST OFFICE stenciled in flaking black paint above the weathered wood doorway, a boxy clapboard home behind it. Farther down, the lights caught a flat-roofed building guarded by the rusted skeleton of a neon motor court sign and—

Myrna sat forward, hands pressed against the dash. "Are those ... *teepees*? Like those drive-up teepee motels?"

"Looks like," Jessup said. "Garage and filling station over there. For when cars got only a few miles to the gallon. A big reason these little oases sprang up and down the Mother Road."

"But where's the trading post?"

Jessup drove past a weedy picnic area, the tabletops and benches warped and cupped, a swing set hung only with off-kilter chains, and a tall metal slide, no ladder. Turning into a large dirt and gravel parking lot, he flared his brights to illuminate a long L-shaped structure sitting a hundred feet off the road, its back to the mountains. Single-story wings constructed of rectangular stones, flat roofs, and rough vigas bracketed a central two-story section of the building. Leaving the headlights on, he turned the truck off. "The Second Chance Trading Post and Pawn."

Myrna counted eight long boarded-up windows set deep and perched high on the outside walls. Hitching posts that ran the length of the front acted to funnel travelers and tourists toward huge central double doors that split the building into two halves. The right-hand portion of the structure eventually folded ninety degrees and ran up to the road, paralleling the truck on Myrna's right. On the far-left edge, a dozen huge, leafy cottonwood trees clustered, dropped branches no one had cleaned up for a long time piled around their trunks. A gust of wind fluttered night-dark leaves.

Jessup leaned over the steering wheel, arms crossed along the top. "Those trees mean a spring or well. I imagine this was once a pretty place to live."

Out the passenger window, backwash from the truck's headlights allowed Myrna to read the faded paint on an elaborate shingle hung on the stone wall. CAFÉ AND GROCERY OPEN 6:00 A.M. – 9:00 P.M. SODA FOUNTAIN. C'MON IN!

Jessup cut the lights, and the world outside faded to darkness. Clouds strobed with lightning in the distance, followed by the rumble of thunder.

"Whole thing was owned by a family named Chance," Jessup said. "Opened right after the Civil War and stayed in the family. Closed in the 1950s, about a year before I-40 was finished. They also ran a zoo and had a Wild West show. These kinds of places usually had some odd attraction to get traffic to their doors."

"Sounds like you were busy today in my office." Myrna slid out of the truck, immediately enveloped in an atmosphere heavy with the scent of rain. She opened the back door to get William Tell leashed.

Jessup walked around the truck to stand by Myrna. "Actually, I already had quite a bit of information. William Tell and I may have taken a little nap. Didn't get much sleep the other night," he drawled, slow and warm. It was too dark to see if he was smiling, which was surprising since her cheeks were hot enough to glow.

She bent down and fake-adjusted William Tell's harness. "Eleanor didn't bother you while I was in the lab?"

There was a pause. "Not really. Got your flashlight?"

He flicked on his light and dragged the brilliant white beam over the walls of the buildings around them. Myrna snapped on her light to spotlight the motel across the street where it reflected weakly off the grimy picture windows around the office. She flicked the beam to a huge metal teepee painted in washed-out earth tones, then to its tightly closed entrance.

"It's like people just locked it up one day and left, never to come back. I mean, there's still intact glass in the windows ..." She drew in a sharp breath. "*Graffiti*. There's no graffiti. Or vandalism. Abandoned for dozens of years, but completely intact. How?"

"There may be a couple of things I didn't mention."

This time she could see his smile. Smirky and intimate, it shot straight through her heart.

"One, there's always been an aggressive law enforcement presence not afraid to arrest trespassers. And two, the locals out here say this place is haunted. And the ghosts inside aren't all that nice."

FIFTY

Myrna snorted. "What locals? There're no lights anywhere." Still, she rolled William Tell's leash around her wrist to take up the slack and keep him close. When the leash tugged his harness, he ambled to sit on her foot.

"There's a few ranches in those hills, and we're fairly close to the Laguna and Fire-Sky Pueblos." Jessup walked to the café door to probe a rusted padlock with his light. He grabbed the lock and rattled it, but it held. "Let's try the others." He led Myrna down the building, examining windows along the way. All three doors into the trading post had the same heavy padlocks.

Jessup stepped back and exhaled. "I didn't want to have to break in. I'll get the crowbar from the truck."

He jogged to his vehicle while Myrna and William Tell rechecked the doors and re-tugged the locks. At the café entrance, William Tell alerted, ears perked, and stared at the bottom of the door. He scratched the wood, leaving furrows in the flaking turquoise paint.

Myrna tugged him away. "Don't *do* that." She automatically squatted to assess the damage—

The padlock fell at her feet with a clunk. Myrna picked up the lock and stood slowly, turning it over in her hands. Still snapped shut. She spotlighted the heavy latch on the door and casing. Completely intact.

The door creaked open about a foot, and a cool dusty air wafted over her.

"Uh, Jessup?"

The dusty scent transformed to a faded perfume, floral and feminine followed by woody cedar and tangy spice, darker and masculine. William Tell backed away from the door to press against her leg, a low growl emanating from his throat. Myrna's arm hair prickled.

"Jes—*sup*." The last part squeaked as a hand came down on her shoulder.

"Guess we won't need this. Good job, Dr. Lee."

He propped the crowbar against the outside wall, pushed the door wide, and went inside. The air bloomed icy white with the flashlight beam.

"But I didn't—"

"You comin' in?" His question sounded hollow and distant. "You gotta see this."

Myrna took a fortifying breath—the perfume and cedar had disappeared from the air, if it was even there in the first place—and tugged William Tell over the threshold behind her. Jessup had switched on an LED lantern and hung it from a hook in the low ceiling.

"Oh, my goodness," she breathed, and stepped into another era.

A long counter ran the length of the room, an old-fashioned black cash register stationed at the end. Stacked on shelves behind the counter were pyramids of fluted glasses and a hand-painted sign: SODA, EGG CREAM, ICE CREAM SODA, MILKSHAKES, CHOCOLATE MALTED, ICE CREAM—VANILLA, CHOCO-LATE, CHERRY. Sandwiches topped a second column: PIMENTO AND CHEESE, BOLOGNA AND CHEESE, MUTTON AND

CHEESE—*yuck*—then INDIAN FRY BREAD, NAVAJO TACOS, TWO EGG BREAKFAST, and STEAK AND EGGS, all at ridiculously low prices. At the very bottom: HOMEMADE PIES (APPLE, PEACH, CHERRY) and NATILLAS. Three wooden stools bellied up to the counter, and three round tables, each with four chairs, graced the open space. Grocery shelves lined the far wall, all empty.

A newspaper lay folded on a table. Jessup gently picked it up, creating a small whirlwind of dust, and read, "January 28, 1956. Weather report's circled. Rare blizzard conditions predicted throughout Central and Northern New Mexico and West Texas."

"Maybe they evacuated and never came back. Seems no one's been in here since. Not even animals." The only tracks marring the grubby wooden floor came from William Tell. He'd gotten over his growling and leaned into his harness, sniffing the closed door at the end of the counter.

"I doubt we'll find trading post records in the café," Jessup said. He grabbed his lantern and strode to the door William Tell was investigating, his boots thumping hollowly. Twisting the doorknob, he pushed it open on barely creaking hinges. He stepped through, taking the light, and Myrna scuttled after him.

They stood in a well-equipped kitchen, dishes stacked in piles, pots and pans hanging on hooks. Jessup opened an old white enamel refrigerator. Empty.

"Wherever they disappeared to, they took the food with 'em."

A door at the back of the kitchen led to a long hallway lined with a series of small storage rooms: first one empty; second one tacked with wooden shelves, upon which sat a single can of SPAM; the last room contained boxes of Borax, dust rags, brooms, buckets, and mops, stacked and organized like someone had anticipated returning, but they never did.

The door at the end of the hall opened into a large corner room. On the right side, a pot-bellied stove seemed to guard a handmade loom. A moth-eaten rug was woven into its warp, natural dyes faded to gray. Heavy rectangular wooden tables lined the back and left-hand walls, turning the corner to end at a wide threshold, its lintels almost two feet thick. It opened into another pitch-black room.

"Rug and blanket room. Still smells of wool. Those pictures?" He gestured to a series of photos above the tables before he stepped in close to the loom. "Weavers. They would have set it up like a show. The weaver would sit there, and tourists would surround her in a semicircle while a someone described the work." Thunder cracked. "Storm's getting closer," he murmured.

Myrna pointed her light at a photograph. Two Native women stood, eyes averted, unsmiling, their hair slicked back and knotted elaborately. They wore traditional garb and tall moccasins and held geometrically patterned rugs over their arms. Myrna moved around the room, studying each picture, William Tell snuffling at her feet. All the women held the same pose, with rugs over their arms and painted clay pots at their feet.

The final photo stopped her in her tracks. Not black and white like the others, but vivid technicolor. Two women, pretty, both young—maybe midtwenties—their friendship clearly on display, sat on a split rail fence. One woman was First People, costumed in Hollywood Native American garb with a colorful beaded headband holding back raven wings of long hair. The second, an All-American girl, white cowboy hat tipped back on shining strawberry-blond curls, her freckled face wreathed in a grin as big as the outdoors. She dressed as a Hollywood cowgirl: fringes and silver conchos on a turquoise Western shirt with elaborate piping and cactus flower embroidery. She'd strapped a two-pistol rig around her waist, the ivory handle of one gun peeking out of her holster, the other pistol pointed to the sky. Behind them was the Second Chance Trading Post sign and a ... zebra? Part of the zoo and Wild West show Jessup mentioned? Who were these two and what was their relationship with the trading post? Maybe their names were written on the back.

Tucking the flashlight between her shoulder and neck, Myrna reached to take the picture off the wall—

The growl that issued from William Tell stood her hair on end. She'd heard that sound from him only twice: when they'd come face-to-face with a blood-covered polar bear feeding on a dismembered seal, and when she and William Tell somehow landed between two opposing groups of mammoth tusk hunters ready to recreate their own version of the OK Corral with Avtomat Kalashnikovas.

Slowly, she turned, spotlighting William Tell's tan body. The hair on his back stood up straight and wide. He stared into a darkened area behind the loom, feet spread, head down, white canines glistening. With trembling fingers, Myrna pointed the beam into the shadows.

A man's stocky silhouette appeared at the edge of her light. He took a menacing step toward her.

Frantically, Myrna stumbled back as William Tell barked furiously, front paws coming off the floor. "*Jessup!*"

Boots pounded, the shadow man grew larger—

Myrna spun and landed in Jessup's arms.

FIFTY-ONE

"What's wrong?" Jessup tightened his arms around her. Myrna took comfort in the thumping of his heart.

"I saw— *We* saw—" But William Tell had stopped barking and sat casually at their feet. He scratched at his harness. How *stupid*. They'd seen Jessup's shadow from his light in the next room. She'd been so focused on the color photo she hadn't even realized he'd left. Myrna scrunched her nose, cheeks hot. "We thought there was a—never mind. Did you find anything?"

"Come look for yourself." He slid his arms from her but anchored her hand in his, then tugged her—and she tugged William Tell—into the central room of the trading post. Light from the lantern he'd looped over a hook penetrated every corner.

"This room's called the bullpen. Glass cabinets shaped in a U along three walls with just enough space behind for the proprietors, shelves everywhere else. Iron stove right in the middle for warmth during winter. And look up."

Myrna craned her neck. Woven baskets and bowls hung from the latilla and viga ceiling.

Jessup drew her to a shelf, the floor creaking with each step. He picked up a dusty rectangular box with a glass window in the top.

"Like the one Isaac has with the stone points, and ..." Myrna furrowed her brows. She'd seen the same box somewhere else, too.

"Looks like tourists could buy it empty and fill it with artifacts." Jessup grinned. "Mostly fakes, I'm guessing. One of those glass cases has a bunch of stone arrowheads and spear points, a few bear claws and stone fetishes. There's some beaded jewelry left, but no silver. Leatherwork, *ojos de Dios*, feathered headbands ..."

As he talked, Myrna handed him William Tell's leash and shimmied behind a glass-fronted cabinet to peruse photos and small paintings hanging on the back walls. The same strawberry-blond showed up here and there, her age varying from early twenties to midthirties. But in two places, the knotty pine wall had lighter areas where pictures must have once hung, but now were gone.

"This isn't the pawn shop. That's where they'd keep their paperwork." Jessup pointed to a wooden door behind the middle section of glass cabinets. "I'm hoping that'll lead to it, or we'll really have to take the crowbar to an outside lock."

Myrna pushed through the door and followed her flashlight beam into a long, narrow corridor that ran the length of the building, all its windows boarded up. To the right, steep wooden steps led to the second floor while two separate doors graced the left-hand corridor. Lantern held high, William Tell's leash looped on his wrist, Jessup headed left and opened the first door.

"Here's the real pawn."

Myrna followed Jessup inside a room filled with pottery, baskets, saddles, blankets, clothes, pots and pans, crates of Ball jars, kerosene lanterns, a butter churn, a large selection of iron and steel tools, stacked bolts of cloth and notions, horse collars, an old camera with cracked bellows, leather jackets, suitcases, and even a few acoustic and electric guitars.

"Imagine heading to California to try your luck in Hollywood, and not having enough money for gas or food." Jessup touched the neck of a ukulele before he maneuvered around tables and shelves to a desk and two four-drawer army-issue file cabinets, a wooden table between them. He rolled the top drawer of one cabinet open. Full of files and paperwork.

"I'll take William Tell," Myrna said. "Have a look around."

"Be careful." He kissed her distractedly, then turned to rifle through the files in the drawer.

Myrna hurried to the final room in the wing. She opened a wooden door, the top half a covered window, and probed inside with her light. A well-equipped infirmary with two beds and a movable curtain wall. The chairs and beds were old army issue, she guessed. In one corner below a dusty oval mirror, a white enamel sink hung on a wall. Next to a firmly closed front door, amber phials and paper boxes of medicine crowded the shelves of a tall glass case along with rolled bandages, glass syringes, rusting scalpels, and a couple of bottles with discolored tubing next to pliers. A desk sat against the short wall by the hallway door, on its top a blotter and manual black typewriter, a blank page of paper fed into the spool.

Myrna touched the *M* key in an almost childish need to leave something of herself behind in the trading post. The spoke whipped up to hit the black ribbon with a smart dry *snap*. No *M* adorned the paper—the ink had evaporated a long time ago—but she could make out a faint impression of the letter on the page.

She picked out her name, the *snap-snap* of the keystrokes loud in the silence.

"Myrna?" Jessup's voice, hollow through the wall that separated the rooms.

"It's an infirmary," she called back. She typed Jessup's name, then William Tell's. "With an old typewriter."

"I guessed that." His voice held a laugh.

She gathered up William Tell and stepped back into the hallway, closing the door behind her. It didn't latch. She tried again, but it swung open. "Forget it," she murmured, and headed down the hall. She peeked into the pawn shop. Jessup sorted through a pile of papers. "Find anything?"

"Nothing so far. Files are organized by date, and I'm walking back from 1956—that's the end of the paperwork."

"Any names?"

"That's the weird part. The signature is the same scribble we saw at Silver Sky Trading Post, and nothing else. Like there was a conscious effort to erase or hide—" He shook his head. "Doesn't matter. I'll keep looking for the buttons' sales receipt. But I'm wondering if this is a fool's errand."

"It's still our best lead at figuring out who the murdered cowboy is. I'll go upstairs, see if I can find anything."

Myrna headed down the hall and up the steps, the door at the top closed. She opened it and stepped into an apartment above the trading post's bullpen that included a tiny kitchenette with a vintage curved-edge ivory refrigerator and slender two-burner matching stove—not unlike her garage apartment setup. A wire dish rack next to the enamel sink held a single dish and a single coffee cup, but a table with two chairs was pushed under a boarded-up window facing the front parking lot.

Myrna left the door open a crack and tucked William Tell's leash into his harness so she could explore.

"Do *not* pee in this room," she admonished. He pinned his ears back and smiled a wholly innocent doggie smile then darted to the kitchen area to snuffle for prehistoric crumbs.

Wooden floors creaked underfoot as Myrna played her flashlight beam around the room. A woven rug divided the kitchenette from a sitting area. She spotlighted two chairs upholstered in a tweedy fabric, both flanked with side tables holding heavy glass ashtrays, a standing lamp with a tasseled shade between them, and an oval coffee table at the foot of the chairs. The chairs faced wooden double doors to the balcony. Along the far wall was a console stereo, a liquor trolley with a single empty bottle labeled ASBACH URALT, and a closed door.

Lighter squares and rectangles on the walls where pictures had once hung again caught Myrna's eye. She approached the largest rectangle and touched the edges. They weren't sharp, but diffuse, like the frame had been elaborately carved. One of the faded squares of wall in the bullpen had the same blurred edges.

No photographs graced the living area, nor did there seem to be anything personal lying around. She made a quick search of drawers and cabinets—empty except for a few *Look* and *Life* magazines dating from the 1950s.

Maybe the bedroom would yield a clue. William Tell already stood at the closed door, ears perked, head cocked. Myrna grabbed the doorknob and turned. Locked. William Tell lifted a paw to scratch—

"No!"

But when he touched the wood, the door creaked open. He darted inside.

"I wish this place would stop *doing* that," she muttered crabbily, and pushed the door wider.

A double bed against the far wall with a cute-kitschy desert scene painted across the headboard sat on a thick rag rug. But the mattress had two shallow dips in it, which meant two people, not one, like the single dish and cup suggested. Two side tables bookended the bed, each with a ceramic cactus lamp festooned with fussy fringed shades. The side table farthest from the door held a cobalt-blue jar of cold cream—her side—the one nearest the door, a pipe turned upside down in an ashtray—his side.

A dresser leaned against the wall that held the door, with a round mirror hanging above, its silver backing peeling off in places. Myrna's light glinted over perfume bottles, makeup containers, and a dozen ceramic figurines of—she wrinkled her nose—*skunks*. She picked one up and blew off the dust. Bashful, blue-painted eyes looked back at her.

She put the skunk down and picked up a classic rectangular bottle. Chanel No. 5. An amber residue coated the inside. Myrna popped the stopper. A punch of the scent she'd detected when the café opened hit her square in the nose. Next to it stood a bottle of Chanel Pour Monsieur, its scent citrus with woody notes.

They'd lived here. But who *were* they?

She pulled open the drawers. Empty. Same with the nightstands. Bathroom next, but she found no clues to the couple's identity in the small medicine cabinet or tiny tiled shower.

The closet bumped out from the wall next to the bathroom door and had two sliding wooden panels. Myrna hooked her fingers into the round notch and slid the door open.

Three outfits hung inside. A spangled ivory silk evening dress with padded shoulders, and two military olive-drab uniforms—one a woman's, the other a man's.

She sucked in a breath.

The patch on the arm. A flaming sword with a rainbow. Like the one the murdered cowboy wore in the photograph at the Donavan Lodge museum.

William Tell scuttled to the open closet and began to bark.

"*Shush-shush-shush.*" Fishing in her pocket for a treat that would make the dog *shut up*, Myrna encountered her mammoth fetish, the military watch, her knife, and the chunk—she sucked in a deeper breath—*of extremely carved and ornate wood she'd found at the packrat nest.*

No way. If this was a piece of frame, no way it could be—

Could it? Everything had led Jessup and her to this place.

Pick up the dog. Chewing her lip, she assessed the agitated animal at her feet. It was a long shot, but her whole life had been a long shot.

You can't win if you don't play. Her mother's laugh cackled in her ears.

She definitely couldn't do it on the second floor because there was no guarantee their shared vision would include the trading post. She'd tried that once from the top of a rusted-out Soviet-made LuAZ 969, hoping for a distant view of the landscape. But because cars obviously hadn't existed back when mammoths roamed Siberia, she'd dropped to the frozen tundra, landing hard on her butt and jarring William Tell loose from her arms. When the vision vanished, she was still on top of the vehicle, but with a sprained ankle and ticked-off dog. Lesson learned.

The trading post's bottom floor was probably less than a foot off the ground—not that far to fall. If she picked up William Tell downstairs, and *if* his vision placed her in the trading post at the opportune time—which was always a crapshoot—then *maybe* she could find what she needed on the walls of the bullpen. If not, she could trundle upstairs.

Myrna tugged the leash from the harness and dragged a now-hoarse William Tell back into the living area—he immediately stopped barking. At the top of the stairs, she paused, listening closely. A file drawer rolled, and paper rustled. Jessup was still searching.

Padding down the steps, she slipped through the door into the bullpen and pulled William Tell into the middle of the quiet room. She turned off her flashlight and placed it on the potbelly stove. In darkness, she rolled up her jacket sleeves for maximum contact, then reeled William Tell to toward her.

"Ready, boy?" she whispered.

Myrna closed her eyes and picked him up.

FIFTY-TWO

The silent force hit Myrna hard. She staggered, clutching William Tell tightly. The eerie silence of the deserted trading post drained away to be filled by the warm mixture of conversation and shrill voices of excited children, their feet drumming on the wooden floors. Myrna's lashes fluttered, opening to a room burgeoning with honeyed sunlight.

A soft drink calendar pinned behind the glass case read SEPTEMBER 1955. Relief relaxed her shoulders.

The trading post was filled with families in vintage clothing: men with open-necked shirts and casual trousers, others with loosened ties, hats tipped back on their heads. Women wore cotton dresses, wrinkled from the drive, and easy flats, their hair short and softly waved. Two children, obviously siblings, ran from the rug room, the boy in cowboy boots, blue jeans, and a green-plaid short-sleeved shirt; the girl had a ribbon pinned in her curly brown hair and wore a yellow-and-pink checked dress with yards of rick-rack and polished white shoes.

"Paige. AJ. Stop running this instant or no ice cream," a pretty, petite woman admonished, but her tone was kind. She bent to peer into a case chock-full of turquoise and silver jewelry, tugging a little at the scarf covering her shining blond hair.

"Aw, *Mom*. That man in there said that lady is a *real* Indian." The boy, a cowboy hat perched over a shock of brown hair, pointed at the woman Myrna recognized from the rug room's Technicolor photo.

"Are you?" the girl asked shyly.

"I am." The woman went down on one knee in front of the girl. "What's your name, sweetie?"

The girl bit her lip and stared at the floor. "Paige Iris Viggiano. What's yours?"

"My American name is Dehlia, but my Indian name is Dancing Rain."

"That's pretty," the little girl whispered, lifting bashful eyes.

"You gonna scalp me?" the boy asked boldly.

Dehlia stood and dusted her green velvet skirt. She raised her eyebrows. "Today's Tuesday, right?" The boy nodded. "I only scalp little boys on Thursdays."

His eyes widened. "*Golly*. Mom! Can we come back here Thursday?"

Dehlia let out a light laugh and tucked herself behind the glass case, where she was immediately approached by a man who asked about one of the items inside.

A curtain over the door at the back swept open, and the strawberry-blond stepped through, a wide band with a bow holding back her hair and a spotted kerchief tied at her neck. She wore a tan Western shirt, its yoke placards embroidered with rearing horses. Her gaze landed on a man in a suit and tie looking into a case draped with gorgeous squash blossom necklaces.

"Mr. Bryant?" she asked. When he nodded, she moved with a graceful swinging step around the case. "You're interested in one of our silver pieces?" Her voice was clear as a bell with a Western twang. Laugh lines fanned blue eyes and a field of freckles peppered her cheeks and nose, her face slightly older than the one in the rug room picture. She laid her hands on the case, a gold band circling her ring finger.

"I sure am, but only if it's made by the Navajo Cecil Roanhorse."

Myrna almost dropped William Tell. *Cecil Roanhorse had made the silver buttons.*

"We have a two of his creations. This ..." The woman opened the back of the case and pulled out a necklace. She leaned down again. Myrna held her breath. "And this bracelet."

Not the buttons. *Dang.* Arms tiring, Myrna secured a grumbling William Tell and inched closer as the woman and the man in the suit haggled over the price.

Five minutes later, the strawberry-blond wrapped up the necklace on the counter behind her. The man said, "Well, Miss Chance, you sure as heck got the better of me."

"Elsie, please. And why do I have the feeling you knew this necklace's value before you came in? I'm going to throw in one of our handmade cedar boxes for free." She turned, and her smile faded. "Mr. Bryant? Is something wrong?"

Mouth opening and closing like a beached fish, he pointed to a small elaborately framed oil painting of a beautiful young woman holding white flowers, black hair elaborately curled on top of her head. Dark sloe eyes stared defiantly out at the world, chin set in a softly rounded face. Her ears dripped with pearl earrings, and the dramatic play of light and shadow in the painting arrested the eye.

"That's—that's a—*Caravaggio.* An honest to God Caravaggio."

Elsie Chance paled, her freckles standing out on skin turned paper-white, her pupils dilated with shock. Or was it fear?

"No! No, Mr. Bryant." She forced a laugh. And her voice changed. The twang disappeared, and her English turned clipped and accented. "It's a reproduction. The original was lost. Burned in Berlin. My husband, he bought it from a street artist in Italy after the war—"

But Mr. Bryant wasn't listening. He bulled his way around the case, yanked the painting off the wall, flipped it over, and laid it down on the counter. "Don't lie, Miss Chance. These"—he jabbed a finger at the back of the elaborately carved and gilded frame— "are exhibition marks, and this"—he pointed to a black inked number in the back corner of the frame—"is an inventory number. Munich Central Collection Point. Not lost. Not burned. *Stolen*. By *you*."

"Not stolen," Elsie whispered. "*Rescued*." The woman's eyes shimmered with tears as she stared at Mr. Bryant.

"I have to report this to the authorities," he said gravely. Then his expression turned crafty. "Unless ... Unless you hand this over to me. Now."

"I don't think so." A large, tanned, masculine hand sprinkled with black hair grabbed Mr. Bryant by the shoulder. Eyes wide, Myrna gaped. Around the man's wrist was the watch in her pocket. On his ring finger, the gold wedding band in Jessup's box.

Both Myrna and Elsie Chance whipped their eyes up to the man who stood menacingly over Bryant.

Dear God. It was *him*. *The murdered cowboy*. And the buttons on his shirt—

"*Ron*." Elsie Chance released a sob.

Bryant turned gray. His lips moved, a single word slipping out —started with a "P"—but his voice was almost inaudible above the noise in the bullpen.

"So you do remember me, Sergeant," the man named Ron said. He stood six feet tall, broad-shouldered, with classic Hollywood movie-star looks. "I remember you, too. Florence, 1945. Let's go to my office and talk about old times."

He shoved a dumbfounded Bryant down the back aisle before he enveloped Elsie Chance in an embrace. She buried her face in his chest as he murmured, "It'll be okay, *Schatzi*. I'll take care of everything." He kissed her forehead and released her. Elsie and Myrna watched him escort Bryant, none too gently, behind the curtain. Elsie grabbed the painting and slipped it behind the counter before she ran to Dehlia. The two women, Dehlia's arm wrapped around Elsie's sagging shoulders, walked into the rug room. No one else in the trading post appeared to notice the drama that unfolded.

Myrna, stunned, tucked William Tell under one arm and stepped behind the case. The painting lay face down, as if to hide its worth. With her free hand, she pulled out her gnawed chunk of the gilded wood found in the packrat's nest. She laid it, flat side up, next to the black inventory marks on the painting's frame.

Marks that matched perfectly.

FIFTY-THREE

Myrna stared at the fluttering curtain that led to the hallway, poised on the balls of her feet. Should she follow the men? Or the women?

She pivoted toward the rug room.

And met the unsmiling black stare of a stocky man, faced creased with age and decades of exposure to sun and wind. Dressed in scuffed boots, black canvas trousers rolled at the ankle, and a patched and faded chambray shirt, he blocked the opening to the next room.

Myrna gulped. *He could see her.*

A smiling dark-haired man coming out of the rug room walked *right through him.*

Locals say this place is haunted.

Myrna swayed dizzily, fear crawling with cold, prickling feet. She sidestepped to the stove to retrieve her flashlight and knelt to put William Tell on the wooden floor, gaze trapped by the apparition's piercing eyes, praying that when she let go of the dog, the old man—ghost—*whatever*—would disappear.

She released William Tell. The sounds of the tourists' voices cut off like a switch had been flipped. Darkness dropped over her.

She stood and flicked on her light. The dog yipped. Nails tapping, he trotted across the dusty floor and disappeared into the rug room. No one, *no ghost*, blocked his path. She took a step after him, then hesitated. There was no way for William Tell to get out. Jessup had closed both the door from the café's kitchen and the door to the outside. He'd be fine.

Her residual fear receded, replaced by excitement.

Myrna grabbed the chunk of picture frame and darted to the back of the bullpen. Double-timing it down the hall, she burst through the pawn shop doorway.

"I picked up William Tell and you will not *believe*—" Myrna skidded to a halt by the desk. Jessup was seated, his lantern shining on an open file and short stack of papers. She pressed the hand clutching the flashlight on the surface of the desk, the second hand still clutching the chunk of gilded wood, words streaming from her mouth. "Her name is Elsie Chance. She's one of the women in the photographs and she must own the place. I mean, Second *Chance* Trading Post? Makes sense. And she's married to a big man"—Myrna raised her arms up and wide—"named Ron something starting with a 'P,' like Pay or Payne, and he's the one I saw murdered at the cliff, the one in the tunnels we both saw. He had on the watch and wedding ring, and he was *wearing the silver buttons. It's him.* And the calendar said September 1955!" She ran out of breath and sucked in more air. "And a man named Bryant came in and said he recognized an old painting of a woman on the wall, and the piece of frame we found in the packrat midden *matched the painting's frame.*" She held out the wood spotlighting it with her light. "And these marks are numbers from the"— Myrna paused and searched her mind—"from the Munich collection point, or something like that. Munich. *Germany.* And I think when Ron was murdered, one of the men at the cliffs was German, and now Finn Posse and the men doing the mine cleanup *speak* German."

As did Dillon Bard, Jessup's partner.

Myrna's thoughts stumbled for a moment before they righted themselves and began filling in the blanks of the murder mystery inside her head, each answer chilling her to the bone. But on the outside, she kept up her manic, excited babble and kept her expression awed by her discoveries.

"And Mr. Bryant threatened Elsie Chance about the painting, and Ron came and threatened Bryant right back—they knew each other and someone named Florence in 1945. And Ron called Elsie *Schatzi*, just like the inscription on the ring. Then he took the man Bryant out the back of the bullpen, and I was going to follow. That's when I saw the ghost. Or I *think* I saw a ghost, but he's gone now." She paused for another breath, fixing Jessup with a bright smile. "Then I came back here to tell you. What did you find?" she asked, voice chirping high, and leaned in to tap the pages.

He stared at her, and for an instant Jessup felt like a complete stranger. Her stomach muscles tightened, and cold sweat prickled on her upper lip. She casually wiped it away with a clammy hand.

"Elsie Chance is the name on some of these papers. Her parents' and grandparents' names—Chance—are on others that go back to right after the Civil War when the trading post was established. Nothing about the buttons, but if you say you saw them on this man—Ron?"

"Yes. Ron Pa—" No. It couldn't be. She blinked at him, her throat closing, heart slamming painfully. "His uniform is upstairs in the second-floor apartment. The patch in the museum picture—a flaming sword topped by a rainbow—was sewn on the sleeves."

Jessup looked down at the paperwork in front of him, one hand curling into a fist. "Anything more about the woman—Elsie?"

"Nothing," Myrna answered brightly. "But we should be able to find him now, and her, in online records or—or a marriage certificate. And tell the next of kin what happened. If they already don't know."

Jessup closed the folder. He stood slowly. "The painting, Myrna. The one this man Bryant recognized. What did he say about it?"

"That it was stolen." Myrna swallowed when Jessup wrapped his hand around hers and the piece of frame. "That it was a ... Caravaggio." His hand tightened over hers. She lifted her face to his. "What does *Schatzi* mean?"

"Treasure," he said. "It means *treasure* in German."

Thunder rumbled as they stared into each other's eyes. Then his hands slipped up her arms, over her shoulders, to circle her neck, the rough skin warm. His thumbs gently lifted her chin, blue eyes shadowed. He tensed, hands tightening. She slid the flashlight into her pocket and wrapped her hand around her knife.

"Myrna." He swallowed. Then his lips hitched up into a small smile. "*Schatzi*. I need to tell you—"

Snap.

Myrna stiffened. Jessup's head swiveled toward the sound.

Snap-snap ... snap.

It came through the wall.

"The typewriter," Myrna whispered, eyes burning. "In the clinic next door. But no one else ..."

Jessup dropped his hands to pull his gun. They both sprinted to the door, checked the hallways in both directions. Nothing.

The snap of typewriter keys quickened.

Jessup ran down the hall and swung around the infirmary's door jamb, gun leveled, Myrna at his heels, knife in hand.

No one was there.

They searched the room, shoving away the curtained screen, clearing the tiny bathroom, checking under the beds.

Nothing.

Myrna rounded the desk to stand in front of the typewriter. She stowed the picture frame piece in her pocket, exchanging it for her flashlight. That, she pointed at the machine. She switched it on.

Black letters marred the sheet of paper. She rolled the carriage until the words cleared the top, and read:

```
He has the little dog
```

FIFTY-FOUR

A roll of thunder merged eerily with William Tell's distant, furious barks. But instead of his sharp gruff yaps, rising high with each explosive cry, they ended with a howl.

Myrna gripped Jessup's arm. "I know that bark. He's afraid. *He's terrified.*"

Darting out of the room, she pounded down the dark hallway and into the shadowy bullpen, chasing the sound. She swung around the cabinets, beelined into the rug room. A jerky, blue-white light lit the hallway to the café. Someone in camo, face covered, yanked on a leash, dragging William Tell down the floor as he struggled to back out of his harness.

Myrna screamed, *"Let him go!"* Jessup barreled into the room behind her.

The camo-man froze but recovered and raised his brilliant white flashlight beam right into Myrna's eyes. Jessup grabbed at her shoulder, but she ripped free and charged down the hallway into the vision-obscuring light, screeching like a banshee, a plan blossoming.

Without a weapon, she'd never fight him off long enough to get the dog, so she trailed her hand along the wall until the second opening and zigged inside. Her mother had taught her how to stun small prey animals—rabbits, birds, squirrels—with well-thrown rocks. A can of SPAM would work the same way.

Myrna leaped out of the room, arm cocked. The dognapper pulled William Tell into the café, almost to the front door and home-free. She rifled the SPAM.

It connected with a meaty *thunk* to his shoulder. The man released a pained *oof* and staggered but didn't let go of the leash. He raised his arm. A loud *click*-flash. Wood splinters showered down. With a huge heave, camo-man yanked William Tell out of the café and into the night.

"*No!*" Myrna sobbed. She ran through the kitchen, the café—

Another *click*-flash, a buzz, and *pop* into the wall behind her.

Jessup grabbed her away from the open door. "*Gun!*"

She didn't care. She fought Jessup with all her might, with every dirty trick she had, sobbing, crying, pleading. But he was too strong and shoved her to the floor, pinned her face down.

"Stop. *Stop*. Listen."

Cheek pressed into grit and sand, she felt him lift his head and flung hers back, catching his chin. Stars sprinkled the darkness.

"*Dammit*. Myrna. *He's got a gun, and the storm's right on top of us.*"

The room lit up in a brilliant flash, lightning so close that charged air raised the hairs on her arms. Deafening thunder cracked above them, the room trembling as if the earth quaked. Jessup rolled off Myrna and turned her into his arms, protecting her with his body as dirt and debris showered from the rafters. She hid her face in his shoulder to ride out the storm's wrath, only to be struck by the sharp metallic tang of rain sweeping into the room as the skies let loose. The deluge pounded furiously on the roof.

William Tell was gone.

Myrna sobbed, tears absorbed by Jessup's shirt. She'd saved him from the tusk hunters, and he'd saved her from the emptiness after Tom Hutchinson chose to leave her. She'd beg, steal, lie to get the dog back—or die trying.

After what seemed like forever, the rain slowed to a comforting shush. Thunder continued to rumble, but more distant. Myrna raised her head and opened blurry eyes to blue and red lights tumbling around them through the open café door. Jessup loosened his grip, and they both sat up.

A woman's stern voice boomed over a loudspeaker: "Cubre Country Sheriff. Come out slowly, with your hands on top of your head."

~

Myrna stood, knees unsteady. Jessup pulled his sidearm and laid it on the nearest café table. She followed suit with her knife. He raised a hand to cup her cheek. She closed her eyes, more tears welling, and leaned into his work-roughened palm.

"There's a ninety-nine percent chance that's really law enforcement, but I want to be prepared for the one percent," he murmured. "Follow only if I call your name. Otherwise, take the gun. Can you shoot?"

"Not really. I'm better with my bow. And rocks. Or SPAM."

He chuckled. "That guy's gonna have some bruise," he said, and leaned over to kiss her sweetly, then laced his fingers on his bare head—he'd lost his hat somewhere. "Coming out," he called and walked through the open door.

Myrna laid her hand on the gun. It would be easy to fade back into the trading post, slip past whoever was out there, and go after whoever took William Tell.

But when Jessup walked out of the café door, he wasn't leaving. He was putting his life on the line.

For her.

No one she'd cared about had ever done that.

Not her mother. Not Tom Hutchinson. Not Eleanor.

She had a crappy track record, but maybe this time she'd chosen well.

She wouldn't abandon Jessup.

"Myrna?" Her cue.

She let go of the gun and placed her hands on her head. She walked out of the café and into a gentle warm rain, blinking as it beaded her eyelashes, and stood next to Jessup.

An SUV, headlights fuzzy in the rain, its light bar pulsing, idled on the road. A single dark figure wearing a Western brimmed hat stood behind the hood of the vehicle, gun drawn. She straightened, her rain poncho fluttering.

"Jessup Page," she called. "You armed?"

"No, ma'am. I left my gun inside on a table." There was relief in his voice, and his face, washed clean by the rain, had softened. A worm of jealously wound tight in Myrna's stomach.

The woman tilted her head at Myrna. "How about you?"

"No weapons." Myrna looked at Jessup. "You know each other?"

"Guided her husband on an elk hunt a couple of years ago."

The sheriff swept aside her poncho and holstered her weapon. "Keep your hands on your head." She moved behind Myrna and patted her down, then shifted to Jessup before she strode around and into Jessup's arms for a hug. "That damn elk mount is on the wall in my den. Did you have to harvest one so enormous?" A gust of wind molded the poncho over her very pregnant belly.

Myrna dropped her arms. "Did you see a man dressed in camo come out of the café?"

"'Fraid not. I was on my way home when I saw lights in the trading post and a truck driving away."

"Which direction did it go? Please. He—he took my dog."

"Tan and black? Looks sort of like a French Bulldog?"

The sheriff strode to her passenger-side door. She opened it, and William Tell leaped out. He streaked to Myrna, who fell to her knees, tears of joy mingling with the rain. William Tell dropped

Tan Turtle, pushed her to the ground, and they rolled in the mud, whining and crying together.

Jessup knelt, his grinning relief completely focused on Myrna and William Tell.

But the officer froze, staring at the open café door. One hand pressed to her belly, she inhaled a shaky breath and dipped her hat, touching the brim in acknowledgment.

A stocky man, face craggy with age and decades of exposure to sun and wind, stubbled cheeks and shaggy gray hair, his eyes a black void, nodded in return.

Sheriff Martinez invited Myrna and Jessup to stay the rest of the night at her ranch in a high green valley northwest of the trading post. And when they finally left the next day, it was closer to dinner than lunchtime.

Jessup drove back to the Donavan Ranch, the sun in their rearview mirror. In his crate, William Tell had Tan Turtle securely tucked under his chin, a doggy smile on his dozing face.

Buckled into the passenger seat, Myrna's fingers fretted with her mammoth fetish, questions roiling. Who had followed them? Who had tried to dognap William Tell using his favorite toy, obviously stolen from Myrna's house? And how had he known the significance of Tan Turtle?

Her stomach cramped at the answers she'd come up with, but she held doggedly to the trust she had in the man who sat beside her. He'd put her first, stepped out of the café and into the unknown to keep her safe. That had to mean something.

She startled when he spoke.

"The Martinezes have a nice little spread. Reminds me of the Cabeza de Baca."

Myrna shot him a questioning glance.

"Paden's family ranch," he clarified.

"It was nice." She stared at her fidgeting fingers, unsure how to start.

"Myrna, I don't know how that man found out about the dog toy."

"But you're the only one I told." She nibbled her lip. Actually, now that she thought about it ...

Jessup stared at the road ahead. "Does anyone in Eleanor's lab know?"

She laughed. "Are you kidding? No one has been to my house for any reason, not even Eleanor. She barely tolerates William Tell. In fact, yesterday was the first time she's shown any interest— Are you okay?" His cheeks had turned brick red.

"Yep. I don't think it was your boss at the Second Chance Trading Post."

"Not a chance. Eleanor wouldn't be caught dead in camo."

Jessup turned his head, the crystal blue of his eyes glinting in the fading light.

"You try to be like Eleanor, don't you? Act like her, dress like her. Even talk like her. Why?"

"She's successful. She's taken seriously by her colleagues. Maybe not loved, but respected. And valued. She's confident, and I wanted ... *want* that. But now Bard doesn't trust me, and I got Dame Sylvia on the wrong side of her husband in front of a lot of people. And William Tell found that poached elk in Paden's barn, which could get his family in trouble." She blew out a deflating breath. "I've managed to mess up a lot of things in my life, and I thought that maybe by being someone else ..."

Jessup pulled to the side of the road and turned off the truck. She checked her phone. No bars. Geographic and digital isolation. It was how she'd spent a good part of her life, both as a child and in remote digs as an adult. A great way to hide from who she was.

Maybe it was time to stop hiding.

Myrna stared past her translucent reflection in the passenger-side window at a herd of cows, mixed with a dozen pronghorn, grazing peacefully in the syrupy dying light. She shifted in her seat, met Jessup's serious eyes in his serious face. He smiled faintly before he spoke.

"You were just another stuck-up scientist, lording your education over us all, like Eleanor, afraid to break a fingernail. Then you use a homemade arrow to shoot a drone out of the sky and make friends with a bunch of little girls like you've known them forever and wrap every ranch hand around your little finger. I thought the closest you'd even been to the wilderness was a city park, then I watched you disappear into the forest and dive into a packrat burrow without a second thought."

Slowly, carefully, he took her hand in his. He turned it over, exposing her palm, moving his thumb across her calluses as if reading her past.

"I thought you would be soft and weak. Then you put your bare hand on the neck of that elk and vowed to figure out what killed him." He brought her knuckles to his lips before he released her hand. The heat of his touch lingered.

"I thought it would be so easy," he whispered, and she caught sadness and regret behind his words. "Myrna. Who are you? Your file. The one Charles Donavan gave me—"

"Lies. At least for my formative years. Everything after middle school is true. Sort of." What she was about to do, to say, was stupid. To expose herself for the freak she was. She didn't think she could bear it if he rejected her.

Because she'd fallen in love with him.

Not that sappy hero-worship she'd had with Tom Hutchinson. What she felt for Jessup could be the real thing, the for-as-long-as-you-both-shall-live love. Dumb. She'd only known him for a few days.

Myrna swallowed, prayed she wouldn't hit the bottom and break her neck, and dove in.

"I don't know how old I really am. I don't know exactly where I was born. Wait. I'd better start earlier. My mother was brilliant. I mean Isaac Newton, John Nash, Stephen Hawking brilliant. But she got pregnant at fifteen. Apparently, she was pretty wild, already showing early signs of instability, and her parents couldn't handle her. When the baby was born, they gave her to an aunt and her husband to raise. My mother seemed to straighten up after that. Went to college, got a degree, went to graduate school, got another degree. Settled into academia. Then her beautiful mind broke. She began to gamble incessantly—baccarat, blackjack, all kinds of poker—and she won because she could count cards. She abandoned her job, her life, hopped from casino to casino, one-night stand to one-night stand. She got pregnant again, fifteen years after she'd had her first child, and, again, her parents decided to take that baby—me—away from her. They didn't realize or care how much they'd traumatized her the first time. When she refused, they froze her bank accounts. Took away her trust fund. And she ran. Six months pregnant."

Myrna glanced at Jessup, but he was gazing into the distance.

"She hid from private investigators, trackers, bounty hunters, anyone and everyone they sent after her, and lived off the land. I don't know how she did it with an infant. From the time I could walk I learned to forage, hunt, stay hidden. She'd break into cabins and steal food, clothes, paper and pencils, books. She taught me to read and write and do math. She really loved math." Cold seeped into the pickup's cab. Myrna hugged her arms around her body. "I don't think I spoke to another person until I was maybe four years old. That's when she started gambling again."

Myrna sat back in her seat. He was pulling away from her. She could feel it. He finally spoke.

"How did you ... Were you ..."

"Rescued? I got really sick when I was around twelve. My mother abandoned me in an emergency room in Idaho Falls with information they needed to contact her family in Boston." Myrna forced a smile to her lips. "They didn't believe who I was. I had to take a DNA test. They were never family, you know? They bought a birth certificate to legitimize me, set me up at a boarding school with tutors. I caught up quickly, went to college, grad school. That's where I met Tom Hutchinson. He became my family." She'd been desperate to connect. Attaching herself to Tom had been the best and worst thing she'd ever done in her life.

"I loved him," she confessed.

"And he committed suicide and left you alone again," he said. "Abandoned you."

Myrna nibbled her lip. What *really* happened to Tom Hutchinson danced on the tip of her tongue. But the threat of federal prison and another possible international incident made her swallow her words. Not knowing would keep Jessup safe.

"How did you end up with a job in Socorro?" he asked. "Not a place many people know about."

"My Boston relatives might have helped me get out of Russia, but they didn't want me around, so they pressured Eleanor to hire me."

"They knew about Eleanor and her work? Why her and not some other place?"

"Well, first off, I think they wanted me as far away as possible, but in a place where I couldn't cause more problems for them. And second of all, the first baby they took away from my mother? It's Eleanor. She's my half sister."

Jessup sat in the waning light, silent and unmoving for what seemed like forever before he started up the truck and drove into Cimarron. Myrna stayed quiet, desperately hoping nothing would change between them. Hope that leached away with every silent mile.

When he finally parked the truck between their two small homes, she spoke, needing to be honest with him about the future.

"I'm pretty sure I know what caused the elk deaths, but I want validation from the samples I left with my colleagues"—it felt good to say that word—"in Socorro. I've already written most of the report. All I need to do is dot the Ts and cross the Is. Then I'm done."

Jessup draped his arms over the steering wheel.

"I need to report in early tomorrow morning," he said.

She deflated. "Okay. Maybe I'll see you later—"

He turned, half illuminated by the porch light. "Will you stay with me tonight?"

Myrna's heart soared.

Jessup's truck rolled to a stop in front of her lab. Myrna released her seat belt and shot him a swift glance.

"Can you keep William Tell? I have some, er, delicate work to do today and might not have the time to walk him." She could hear the hesitancy in her voice, feel an odd desperation between them.

They hadn't gotten much sleep. She'd awoken with a happy smile that had faded over breakfast and been completely lost during their drive to work, but she couldn't quite put her finger on why.

He looked her directly in the eye, something he hadn't done since she'd poured herself a cup of coffee in his kitchen that morning.

"No problem, Meerkat."

She nibbled her lip. "You know I've spoken to Charles Donavan about excavating the mammoth, so I'll probably be back up here after I wrap up some work down in Socorro."

He nodded.

"Maybe I can help with your treasure hunt then. Use William Tell to smell his way back to where we saw those men with the sacks and gas masks."

Briscoe appeared from in between two buildings and trotted to one of William Tell's favorite cottonwoods. He sniffed the trunk, then proceeded to lift his leg. Myrna waved a hand at him.

"Although I imagine Briscoe could follow the trail just as well, I mean the way they mark over each other's scent and all."

His smile was perfunctory. Her stomach started to ache.

"Jessup? Did I do something wrong?"

He sobered at the tremor in her voice and shook his head, his eyes now warm and his smile gentle. "Come here, Myrna."

She eagerly slid across the bench seat and into his arms, her nose buried in his shirt, breathing him in.

"I guess I'm finally realizing how lucky I am." His arms tightened around her before he leaned back. She tipped her chin up and his kiss dissolved any lingering fears. This man wasn't like Tom Hutchinson. This man listened to her story, knew about her past, and he still was here with her.

Myrna broke off their kiss.

"You know, William Tell really, *really* likes you." She toyed with a button on his shirt, making only fleeting eye contact. "In fact, even though he hasn't known you very long, he might actually ... love you."

Jessup cupped her cheek tenderly. "Really? Well, I really believe I might actually love him, too."

Myrna wasn't completely sure, but that just might have been the best moment of her life.

Fifty-Five

Myrna's final experiments were humming through the equipment behind her. Time to fit the last pieces of the elk deaths puzzle into place. And she knew exactly where to find them.

She raised her hand to knock at the door that divided her and Harley's labs. No answer.

She peered up at the mini cameras she'd repositioned that morning to point at the ceiling—just like when her rotting elk cam had somehow pointed to the sky—which allowed her to pick the lock into Harley's lab in peace. A skill her mother had taught her while breaking into those empty cabins.

The last click of the tumblers, turn of the knob, and an innocent, "Harley? Do you want to go to lunch with me?" and Myrna stepped inside the dark lab. Nothing. "Harley?" She checked for cameras. None. She hit a wall switch and overhead lights came on as the door closed behind her.

The lab's layout mirrored hers, but instead of spectrophotometers and HPLC machines, a plethora of 3D printers, drill presses, lathes, saws, shapers, millers, multimeters, oscilloscopes, power supplies, microscopes, and drones in various states of assembly and repair rested on the bench tops. She hurried to the far side of the lab where magnifying goggles lay next to mechanical bumblebees just like the ones from the greenhouse. Tiny dust-free cases held tools the width of thin wire and computer chips that looked like black specks. A nearby desk held a jumble of remote controls.

Myrna beelined to a sliding glass door refrigerator, just like the one she stored her samples in. Polycarbonate cryo boxes with clear plastic grid tops cluttered its shelves, dozens of septum vials tucked into the internal dividers. She slid open the door and pulled the box labeled: ☠DO NOT USE☠ TOXIC TO BULL ELK (4 DEAD—EcoNano—Cliff Meadow). The date written was the day before she'd arrived on the ranch.

She popped off the lid and pulled a vial. Less than a milliliter of clear liquid coated the bottom. The label showed only a number. Probably a code, its key somewhere in a lab computer spreadsheet. Nineteen vials with the same number, the same clear liquid, the same septum top. Only one was different. It contained tiny black pellets, not much larger than grains of sand. The top label read CAUTION MAGNETIZED.

Magnetized. Myrna scuttled over to the desk with the remotes and found what Harley had been messing with the first time they'd met: The screwdriver he'd "accidentally" dropped in the cage protecting her elk carcass. Except it wasn't a screwdriver. She brought it close to the vial, and the black grains plastered themselves to one side of the curved glass. Would it be sensitive enough to detect one single grain injected into an elk's hide? Knowing Harley and his engineering skills, she'd take that bet all day long.

She already knew how he'd delivered the toxin: the bumblebee drones. If they could collect blood for analysis, they could deliver poison to an animal using porous black *magnetic* pellets steeped in it. He must have released a swarm of bee drones in the elk meadow, and they stung the elk, depositing the tiny packet of death. Just like hunting from a distance with a high-powered rifle, the elk wouldn't have known what hit them. What had Jessup said that first day? The elk were used to drones.

And when she'd brought a carcass back to the compound, Harley cut the pellet from the elk before she could analyze the tissue—to hide what he'd done.

But Harley had become too complacent, and she'd discovered his deceit. He would lose his job, and she'd fulfill her commission and her promise. All she needed was the chemical composition of the poison in these vials to solve the mystery. Myrna opened the door and stepped into her lab.

Three bumblebee drones the same color as the paint on the lab walls hovered with a hushed buzz just above eye level. Harley Wakefield, controller in hand, stood a few steps behind them.

"So you figured it out," he said.

Myrna clutched the box of glass vials against her middle. "Pretty much." She lifted her chin. "Are you going to stop me?"

"Not at all. Congratulate you, more like. You're the first scientist who's gotten far enough along to break into my lab, even though they all were given the same clues." He smiled crookedly.

She ducked under the drones and hurried to the refrigerator, sliding open the door and depositing the samples inside. The drones followed and buzzed above her head. She itched for a flyswatter.

"But until you submit your report, the game hasn't been won."

Myrna whirled, fists clenched. "Poisoning animals is a *game* to you?"

"No, no. It's not pois—"

"Those tubes are labeled 'toxic to bull elk.'"

"And that is a puzzlement. Have you any theories?" he asked, eyes wide and innocent. The drones circled above his head, forming a halo. "Maybe internal metabolic changes based on environmental exposure?"

"You've been spying on me?" She hissed out a breath and glared at the tiny buzzing machines. "*Drones*."

"Watch as they disappear." He touched the controller, and the bees flew off in three different directions. One perched in the crease between the ceiling and a wall. Myrna could see it only because she knew it was there. When she tried to find the other two, she couldn't.

"Look." Harley handed her his controller. The drone gave a bird's-eye view of the top of her head. He touched a volume slider.

"Who else is watching me?" Her voice echoed out of the controller. "And listening."

"I warned you—cameras are everywhere. And I can't help you any more than I have. My advice? Run these samples and get your report written. But Myrna ..."

Harley walked to the door separating their labs and opened it. The drones whizzed through. He paused.

"Even though you've solved the elk deaths, you can't win. Now that I've gotten to know you, I'm very sorry about that."

The refrigerator door slid shut with a snap. Myrna massaged her neck, but it didn't give her much relief from the knotted muscles. Maybe she could convince Jessup to give her a backrub.

Her cheeks warmed at the visions swirling in her head and a small secret smile curved her lips. She had it bad. A pile of data that tied up her theory's loose ends pushed her smile into a grin. Hopping up onto a lab stool, she opened the laptop to continue her report.

Her phone rang. Myrna glanced at the time, eyes widening in surprise. Seven P.M. No wonder she was hungry. And where was Jessup?

BUGMAN flashed on her screen. Kent from Eleanor's lab.

"Hey. I didn't expect to hear from you—"

"We're done," Kent said, his voice eager and excited. "Before deadline and under budget, and the results are spec-tac-cu-lar. Your nano-methods of analysis ... I have no words, Dr. Lee. Revolutionary. I just wish you hadn't been such a ... uh ..."

"Yeah. Me, too. And it's Myrna." She swirled on the rotating seat. "I have some news, too. The chemical that killed those elk wasn't poison. It was—"

"Oh, it was poison, all right. The closest we came to a natural structure is similar to a neurotoxin—"

"From a rare coral. Even tiny amounts are deadly."

"You already knew?" Kent's voice held disappointment.

"I suspected but didn't have enough evidence. That's why I needed Eleanor's equipment. They're correctly configured for the analysis. And your expertise. You really came through, Kent."

"Yes, I did. But not just me. Jeannie and Noemi and Rohaan worked late last night and came in early this morning to process the data."

Myrna raised her eyebrows. "Eleanor gave you permission?"

"Better to ask forgiveness after the job's done than permission and receive a *no way in hell*, right Dr., uh, Myrna? Besides, she emailed us and said she'd be away for a few days," Kent finished. "Let me put the phone on speaker for the rest of the results. Say hi."

"Hi, everyone. And thanks. With the analyses I did today—"

"Wait," Noemi said sharply. "Let us finish before you butt in." Uncomfortable pause ... "I'm sorry. I'm just not used to—"

Contrition ate at Myrna. She had a lot to make up for.

"That's all behind us now," Rohaan said soothingly. "Let us continue without recriminations. Noemi and I handled the stone points swabs. I'm afraid there's nothing, Myrna, that had a poisonous profile. I'm sorry. If there was some concoction on the points, it's just too degraded."

Myrna's heart sank a little. Not unexpected, though.

"On the bright side, we were able to identify collagen in some of the samples. Tentatively, the amino acids profiles match to camelids, giant sloth, and mammoths. A solid publication, I believe. Now, the substance on the stone knife—"

"Let me do the stone knife," Noemi interrupted. "That black tar-like stuff on the knife was a weird, oxidized crust. It wasn't until we sampled underneath that we found poison."

Myrna jumped off the stool with a gasp. "But you said—"

"Not ancient."

She sank back down again. "How old?"

"Its radioactive isotope profile puts it a few years after the atomic bombs were dropped. Maybe even from Trinity site. The isotope level is too high. I'd say anytime between 1945 to the late 1950s."

Myrna swallowed her disappointment. "But it is poison." The cowboy had been stabbed with it.

"Probably killed the man whose blood was smeared all over the knife," Noemi continued.

It might have. If he hadn't been forced off a cliff first.

"I'll let Kent take over from here. He's practically jumping up and down to talk," Noemi said dryly.

"That's just it, Myrna. The poison on the stone knife? It's a *beetle* poison. A bug poison. I haven't been able to do much research on it yet, but it resembles a natural toxin developed in World War II by, get this, the *Nazis*," Kent said. "It's like cantharidin. From blister beetles."

"Blister beetles? You mean ... *Spanish fly*? The Nazis turned an aphrodisiac into a bioweapon?" Myrna said.

"Its structure is just a tiny bit different, and we need to do some studies before we can quantitate its toxicity, but yeah. And that beetle you gave me in the amberat? It bored its way in, so it's not from the Pleistocene. Best guess someone brought it into the area around the same time as that poison on the stone knife. 1940s to 1950s. The state has blister beetles, but I need to check genetics to see if this one has been identified and cataloged. They may be the source of the poison on the knife. Didn't New Mexico have Germans in prisoner-of-war camps?"

"That's a leap," Noemi said, voice dripping sarcasm. "Why would the Nazis develop a bioweapon here?"

"I don't know, Noemi. Maybe they didn't." Kent's reply was subdued. "I'd like to run more tests, okay? Myrna, can you get me more beetle samples?"

"Yeah. Sure." It would mean going back into the cave. "What about the DNA from the blood on the knife? Too soon, right?"

"As a matter of fact, no." Jeannie sounded smug. "Dr. Sengupta's lab is beta testing that DNA-in-a-Day Sequencer? They let me use it. I loaded the results into a couple of national databases for matches and got hits." Papers rustled importantly. "There were two different DNA samples on the stone knife. Both men are linked to Spanish colonists who settled in New Mexico around Santa Fe in the early 1700s, then spread east to Colfax, Mora, San Miguel counties. Interestingly, both samples contain a small percentage of European Jewish DNA, which solidifies their ancestry because Spain had outlawed Jews, so a lot of them came to the New World hidden in with the conquistadors. Both men are of Hispano ancestry. Have you ever heard of Hispanos?"

"I have." From Isaac Marín. He'd also said that many of the ranch families had lived in the area for generations. "You linked them to a family tree?"

"One to a family tree at the second cousin level, and the other directly to a submitted sample, so we actually have a name. Well, initials. Which one first?"

"The submitted sample."

"Okay. The initials are M, C, D, and B. His parents are part of the tree, so it was easy to figure out the last name. CDB stands for—"

"Cabeza de Baca." Myrna sank onto her lab stool, knees watery. "M for Miguel. Mike."

Mike Cabeza de Baca had been one of the murderers of the

man who'd fallen from the cliff. Of Ron Pay or Payne, Elsie Chance's husband and one of the men in the photo at the museum.

"Correct. And I did a database search and found Miguel Cabeza de Baca associated with an address in your area. Based on his birthday, he'd be over a hundred years old."

"He is."

"You've met him? Ask him how his blood got on the knife, then. The second guy is related to a family tree going back to Spain four hundred years ago. There are a dozen surnames associated with it, both Spanish and Anglo. Do you want me to send you a list?"

"Read them over the phone."

"Okay. Ready? Romero, Tafoya, Jaramillo, Baca—not Cabeza de Baca—Davis, Page, Wilkins, Gallegos ..." Jeannie's voice hollowed until it was only an echo.

Page.

Not Ron Pay or Ron Payne. Elsie's husband was Ron *Page.*

Jessup—Jessup *Page*—hadn't told her the truth about who the murdered cowboy was to him.

Myrna closed stinging eyes and dropped her head into her hand. Is that why Jessup had acted so weird that morning? Why he hadn't come to the lab to take her home? Because he knew she had everything she needed to figure out his connection to the dead man? His connection to the treasure?

Numb, she mumbled a thanks and hung up. Slipping her hand in her pocket, she pulled out the key to the four-wheeler she'd acquired the first day she'd been on the ranch. She could drive it to the little house, collect William Tell and her car. It would be easy to disappear, find someplace remote to lick her wounds.

But Jessup had promised her she could trust him. She clung to that promise. Myrna closed her hand in a fist.

No. This time, she wouldn't run.

Jessup owed her an explanation.

Fifty-Six

Myrna barged inside Jessup's home and slammed the door behind her. He stood like a statue, his face pale. William Tell guarded the closed bedroom door, the ridge of hair down his back bristled, staring at the crack underneath. Tan Turtle lay on the floor by his front paws.

She stalked toward Jessup, stepped in close, face tilted up to his. "You knew, didn't you? You knew all along who the dead cowboy was."

His mouth tightened, but he otherwise didn't respond.

Myrna turned away, fingers gripping the back of the sofa. "I got a call from my lab mates in Socorro. They confirmed the DNA on the stone knife, and things started falling into place." She twisted on the ball of her foot to face him again. "Like that man at the Second Chance Trading Post who recognized the painting. He called the cowboy Ron, and I thought he said Pay, but it was *Page*. Ron Page." Her voice choked.

"I recognized him in the cave from an old photo. But when you told me his first name, that's when I truly knew," Jessup said quietly.

Knew *what*? Why hadn't he said something to her about his

connection to the murdered cowboy? What was he hiding? Was this about the treasure? She raised a shaking hand to rub her forehead.

"The Caravaggio. It's real, isn't it?"

He hesitated. "When Ron Page disappeared, people in my family thought he'd stolen it. And that he took other ... valuables and left in the middle of the night with two close friends. Everyone, including his wife, thought he'd run away, changed his name, even murdered his friends so he could use the treasure to make a new life for himself. My grandfather—Ron Page's nephew—was the only one who never believed the story. Said the man he knew was the most honorable person he'd ever met. A war hero. He believed Ron Page had hidden what he'd taken somewhere on Donavan land. That something bad must've happened to him and the others."

Myrna took a tentative step closer to him, eyes burning with unshed tears. "I don't understand why you didn't tell me. Why didn't you trust me?"

Jessup's hands cupped her cheeks, his gaze roving her features like he was trying to memorize them. He leaned in and pressed a tender kiss to her lips. "I didn't tell you because—"

William Tell's low growl crescendoed to a series of sharp, nasty barks.

From behind Myrna, her sister's voice rose above the noise of the dog. "Because he was afraid he'd lose you."

Myrna pulled away from Jessup. Her thoughts pinballed dizzily, but an explanation for her sister's presence escaped her.

"Eleanor? What are you doing here? William Tell, *shut up*. Were you waiting for me? Did the Donavans call you about the report? It's written and ready to submit. I could have briefed you over the phone. *William Tell. Shut. U—*" Her sister's words finally penetrated. The dog backed away from Eleanor and huddled next to Myrna's foot. "Because what?"

Eleanor kicked Tan Turtle toward Myrna, who mindlessly

picked up the toy and slid it into a pocket. Her sister sauntered out of Jessup's bedroom, twiddling a rectangular plastic card. "He was afraid he'd lose you. He's fallen in love with you, and that"—she circled around Myrna to stand next to Jessup—"was never part of the plan."

She flicked a finger against his ear. He flinched but stayed focused on Myrna. Eleanor leaned toward him and held up THE LODGE card Myrna had found in the box on Jessup's dresser. "You kept my hotel room key. How sentimental. It *was* a memorable evening."

Jessup's gaze drilled into Eleanor's. "Nothing happened."

"What a strange definition of nothing. A candlelight dinner under the stars at the Donavan Lodge. Your kisses tasting like that wonderful smoky bourbon we were drinking in celebration of our brand-new partnership. And my key card slipped into your shirt pocket so we could preserve, uh, discretion."

Stricken, Myrna backed away from Jessup. William Tell huddled against her legs. "You *slept* with her?"

"No."

Eleanor snapped the card down on the breakfast bar counter. She smiled at Myrna.

"Do you know why I sent you to the Donavan Ranch for this commission? Because everything fell into place like it had been prearranged, like the gods were on my side. The box with the letters, the elk poisonings, the mammoth kill site. And *you*. Isolated, so *lonely*, like ripe fruit ready to be plucked by any attractive *older* man giving you attention. We needed your expertise because the treasure journal wasn't in the mammoth skull like the letters said it would be."

"Letters?" Myrna whispered.

"A packet of letters addressed to a woman named Elsie Chance Page. They were in that wooden box—you saw it on my desk, didn't you? It was donated to the university and stored in the basement archives, along with a whole pile of antiques. I remembered the name the first time I visited the Donavan Ranch and met Jessup Page. Such a handsome, attentive, flirtatious cowboy. I was curious. I went back down to the archives and found the letters, one of which talked about a journal detailing the contents of a priceless treasure and a map to its location tucked into a mammoth skull near the Cabeza de Baca formation on the Donavan Ranch. I knew that if anyone could find that skull, it would be the foremost expert on Pleistocene *Mammuthus columbi*." Her expression bordered on pity. "You were so easy to set up."

Myrna threw a desperate glance at Jessup. "Is this true?"

Mouth grim, he wouldn't meet her eyes.

"You see, Jessup and Bard have been searching for the treasure for years with no luck, and here I was with vital information. I joined their little team and came up with the plan to have Jessup seduce you. I knew Dillon Bard wouldn't work because you have such a daddy complex. Poor little girl. Growing up without a father the way you did." She leaned toward Myrna and said in a secret-sharing undertone, "Jessup Page was perfect for you."

And he was. Myrna crumpled inside.

"I'll tell the Donavans," she choked out. "The press. I'll tell everyone about this treasure."

Eleanor laughed. "Everyone around here already knows. And everyone thinks it's a legend or a lie."

Harley had, when Isaac talked about it a week ago—had it only been a week? But surely Charles Donavan ...

"You think Charles Donavan would help you? He was in a panic over how an insignificant die-off might affect his presidential aspirations. How do you think he'd feel about the press digging into his grandfather's role in the disappearance of three men?"

Three men had been in the cave, carrying bags. Was Charles Donavan's grandfather responsible for the deaths of all three?

Eleanor tsked. "Donavan won't take the risk. He'll ruin you instead. It won't be difficult since you're already so close to the edge of a career-ending drop off a cliff. Just like Tom Hutchinson."

No. Just like the dead cowboy, Ron Page. Except the knife stuck in Myrna's back came from her sister and the man she loved.

"And even if you do tell Donavan and he believes you, it'll be too late." Eleanor tapped her smartwatch. "Dillon will be here in a few minutes. Jessup told us about the, uh, markings left by your little dog. Bard's big dog can track those in case the remaining chalk marks aren't enough. The treasure will be long gone by morning."

And so will I, Myrna thought. She'd delete her report, all its files, pack up her things and William Tell—

"And if you think abandoning the Donavans' commission is going to hurt me, think again. You have a decision to make, Myrna. Wrap this contract up successfully and you still might have a career. Tank it, and you'll never work in science again. I can guarantee it." Eleanor's smile was smug.

"Why are you doing this to me?" Myrna asked. "What have I ever done to you to deserve this?"

"I can answer that," Jessup replied. "I chose you over her."

"You flatter yourself. I used you just like you used her," Eleanor snapped.

"I love you, Myrna," Jessup said. "I just didn't realize until too late. I'm sorry."

"Sorry enough to give up the treasure?" Myrna asked.

"I can't do that. I made a promise to my grandfather before he died. I'd find out the truth behind his uncle's disappearance and recover whatever this treasure is, just like he made a promise to his Aunt Elsie to do the same. He failed. I won't. Please understand. I needed to solve this mystery, and I know I messed up. I made a terrible mistake."

William Tell's leash was on top of the bookshelf by the front door. Numb, Myrna took it and clipped it onto his harness.

"And I was that mistake."

"No—"

"Stop." Myrna straightened and faced her half sister. "Dr.

Kelly? I'm resigning from your employment. I don't need you or your lab or anyone. I was stupid to believe I ever did."

She shifted slightly but not enough to directly face Jessup. "Mr. Page? I have one more piece of information. The second blood sample on the stone knife. Do you want to know who stabbed Ron Page in the back?"

"What good will that do?" Eleanor said. "I'm sure he's been dead and gone for—"

"Mike Cabeza de Baca."

And without a backward glance, Myrna swung open the door to march out of Jessup's life with as much dignity as she could muster. She'd cry her heart out while she packed.

William Tell rushed past her, barking madly as Finn Posse pulled the screen door and stepped inside.

Preceding him into the room was a matte black handgun he pointed at Myrna's heart.

~

So much for a dignified exit.

Myrna stumbled back, tugging hard at William Tell.

"Shut the dog up, or I will—permanently," Finn Posse ordered in a pleasant voice. The gun's barrel tilted downward as Paul, John, Ringo, and George—Myrna couldn't for the life of her remember their names—funneled in behind Posse, all armed and dressed in black.

"Even if I pick him up, he won't stop. Can I p-put him in the bathroom?" Only one little stutter, which was amazing considering her heart literally thrummed like a hummingbird's.

Finn Posse glanced at a minion—Ringo—who stepped forward and motioned to Myrna with his gun. He followed her to the bathroom. She pushed William Tell behind the door and closed it. He marched her back into the living area and shoved her at Jessup and Eleanor before closing the bedroom door behind them. Even muffled, every one of William Tell's feverish barks hit Myrna like a hammer blow.

"Ah, ah! Please separate," Posse instructed. She and Jessup shuffled away from each other. Eleanor didn't move. Posse raked a dismissive glance over Myrna's capris and knock-off Keds and Eleanor's tight jeans and ridiculous boots. "Search Mr. Page for weapons." One of the men threaded his way through furniture and aggressively patted Jessup down, shaking his head when he finished.

"You two I know. But who is this?" Posse raised a brow at Eleanor.

"Dr. Eleanor Kelly," Eleanor replied haughtily. "Professor of toxicology at the New Mexico Institute of Mining and Technology. What is the meaning of this intrusion?"

"The third member of the little treasure-hunting trio. Did you think you were the only ones looking?" Posse said. "Dillon Bard is a loquacious drunk. One might even say a jabbering fool. Unfortunately, when sober, the SEALs trained him well. He refused to give up any more information when we questioned him. Luckily, Dr. Kelly's text message to meet here tonight gave my team the information we needed—almost." Posse waggled a blood-splattered cellphone, then gestured to Myrna. "Give me your satchel."

She wrapped her hands around the shoulder straps.

He turned his head slightly toward Ringo. "Break the dog's neck."

Myrna's knees wobbled. She unslung the satchel and held it out.

Posse holstered his weapon and unzipped the backpack. He slipped in a hand to rummage around. When he drew out a package of snack cakes and tossed them to minion George, saying something in German, all the men chuckled.

He inserted his hand inside again, this time extracting a small white oval the size of a quail egg. He held it out toward Myrna. "Since it has been observed that you take your pack everywhere with you, I simply placed this device inside after you and Mr. Page were escorted from the mine. You see, we've been listening and tracking you, hoping you would take it back down in the caves and lead us to the treasure. But the information we received about the little dog turned out to be just as valuable."

"What information?" Eleanor snapped.

Finn Posse raised his eyebrows. "The dog, er, marked a trail back to the passage containing the treasure."

"Oh, that." Eleanor waved a hand. "Yes, but he also said any dog could follow it. We were going to use Bard's dog."

Jessup dropped his head and shook it.

"The large German Shepherd? I'm afraid he ran off after we ... detained his master. Instead, we will use the small dog and Dr. Lee to guide us through the mine and caves."

"You mean you lied when you told that guy to break my dog's neck?" Myrna said.

Posse smirked. "This means, Mr. Page and Dr. Kelly, we will not need you."

Jessup lifted his head, and Myrna shivered at the icy cold in his eyes.

"Then you're making a mistake," he said quietly. "Unless you've found the other booby traps."

"We found and disarmed it," Posse said dismissively.

"I said traps."

Posse frowned. "What do you know, Mr. Page?"

"How to get past the remaining traps. And I can also handle the dog. You don't need Dr. Lee. You need me."

Pain shot through Myrna's heart.

"I don't believe you," Posse said.

Jessup shrugged. "'S your hide."

Finn Posse studied him minutely. He barked a command and minion Paul rushed to Myrna, grabbed her arm, and pressed the gun's muzzle against her temple. The cold circle warmed quickly, even as her blood froze.

"Then you will lead us to the treasure, or we will kill Dr. Lee before your eyes."

Though Jessup's face turned gray, he didn't waver. "This village is full of ranch hands who will recognize the sound of a gunshot. Every one of them is armed to the teeth. You'll be pinned down so fast, it'll feel like the second coming of Butch and Sundance. And besides, if you harm one hair on Dr. Lee's or Dr. Kelly's heads, you can kiss my ass."

Finn Posse's lips twitched. "Cowboy chivalry. How quaint and completely expected." He nodded to Paul, and the man stepped away from Myrna and into the rest of the Beatles. "Then we negotiate."

"Here are my terms: I'll take you into the mines, point out the traps, and use the dog to lead us to the treasure, but only if you let Dr. Lee and Dr. Kelly go. Release them up by the Cabeza de Baca formation. That's miles away from the nearest homestead, and it's not like they're a threat anyway. Look at them," Jessup said. "Dr. Kelly knew we were going to explore the cave tonight and she's wearing skinny jeans and I don't even know what's on her feet. Dr. Lee's dressed completely in pink."

"These jeans have a slight stretch in the fabric and Ugg makes a very comfortable hiking boot," Eleanor shot back, nose in the air.

"It's not pink. It's peach and it compliments my coloring," Myrna said, mirroring her older half sister's expression. "I'm a Spring."

"You'll be long gone before those two find their way out of the forest," Jessup said.

Myrna whipped up tears and blinked moisture-filled eyes, her bottom lip trembling. "Please don't let us go in the wilderness. Leave us here. We promise not to call anyone for a whole day. Or take me, not him," she implored Posse. "Those traps can't be that hard to find."

Jessup snorted. "You missed every one of them last time because you were whining so much about being dirty."

"I take back what I said earlier. I hate you more than the outside," Myrna spat.

Posse raised his brows. "I thought you two—"

"As fun as it was, the treasure always came first," Jessup said firmly. "But I don't want to see them hurt."

Finn Posse pointed at the bulging satchel.

"Dr. Lee hates the outdoors? Then what about the contents of her backpack and her mastery at archery?"

"I filled her pack with that gear," Jessup said. "She usually only carries cake and dog food in it."

"That's not true. The flashlight's mine. And a water bottle. I refuse to drink out of a stream. You can get parasites." Myrna shuddered, adding another stick to the *please don't throw me into the wilderness* pile.

"And how good can she be if a twelve-year-old girl beat her in the archery contest?" Jessup asked.

Posse contemplated Myrna, who deliberately morphed her expression into its most innocuous. Tears burned her eyes and blurred her vision—although that wasn't as difficult as not allowing them to fall.

"Please," Myrna said. "Don't take my dog." This entreaty was real. And he wasn't really *her* dog. He'd always been so much more than that.

"That is the only nonnegotiable element, Dr. Lee. But once we have the treasure, we will leave Mr. Page and your dog in the caves. All you will need to do is find them."

Then he literally patted Myrna on the head. She dropped her gaze so no one would see the hot rage that vaporized her tears.

"Mr. Page and the dog ride with me," Posse continued. He nodded to George. "Load the two women in with you and follow us. We will release them in the wilderness as you requested, Mr. Page, and you will cooperate. They will not be harmed. You have my word. Now, get the animal."

Jaw set, Jessup, followed by John, gun at his back, disappeared into his bedroom.

"I don't understand any of this," Eleanor said in a querulous voice as she and Myrna were pushed out the front door and down the steps. "Who are you?"

Finn Posse politely opened the back of a dark late-model truck.

"Ah. If I tell you, I'm afraid we'll have to kill you. But since I promised Mr. Page you would come to no harm ..." Finn Posse smiled mockingly at Eleanor.

The men around him chuckled, their shadowed faces sinister. Hackles rose on Myrna's neck.

"This treasure disappeared from Germany after the end of World War II," Posse said. "Although we do not know its exact contents, we do know it was hidden away by Mr. Jessup Page's relative, a member of the vaunted Monuments Men. Now do you understand what it might contain? Priceless works of art from the great European masters. Sold on the black market, this treasure will raise enough money to finance political campaigns, pay off politicians, subvert social media. Even subsidize an army. *Our* army. We are part of an elite guerrilla unit, a resistance force formed at the end of the war to work behind enemy lines. Unternehmen Werwolf. Operation Werewolf. This treasure is our birthright as the descendants of the Third Reich." He winked at Myrna. "Heil Hitler."

Posse closed the truck door behind her, and the locks engaged. As the truck drove away, Myrna's hand stole to the hard outline of the knife tucked away in a special pocket of her pretty peachy-pink capris. The genesis of a plan formed in her head.

FIFTY-SEVEN

Myrna held tight to the back passenger door, glad of the seatbelt strapping her in as the truck jounced and bucked over the pot growers' patched-up logging road deep in the Donavan Ranch wilderness. Eleanor sat next to her, arms crossed, lips tight. George drove, Ringo in the passenger seat, a gun resting casually on his lap. Tall pines with heavy trunks lined the road, hovering like black-draped crones over shadowed thickets. The moon hadn't risen, and dark didn't begin to describe the nighttime blackness that enfolded the truck.

Ahead of them, the brake lights of the truck carrying Finn Posse, the other two henchmen, Jessup, and William Tell flashed with increasing rarity. The vehicle she and Eleanor rode in fell farther back, the deliberateness of the maneuver chilling. Still, Jessup had given her time and opportunity. She would use it as best she could. With studied casualness, Myrna slipped her hand into the hidden pocket and touched the mammoth fetish for courage before her fingers curled around their ultimate prize.

"Neo-Nazis. Somehow, I don't trust them not to murder us," Eleanor said under her breath.

Exactly.

But these men had already underestimated her when Finn Posse hadn't searched them for weapons. Sloppy. What had Posse said? How completely expected.

Ringo pressed a button on his phone. It beeped. No service. Myrna hadn't seen the glow of taillights for at least ten minutes.

The truck stopped. George turned off the engine. He killed the headlights. Total blackness. But Myrna had recognized her surroundings. Up the slope to her left was the pot farm and Cabeza de Baca formation. On Eleanor's side of the truck, dense forest ran down to the cliff and the mammoth jump.

George opened the driver's side door. The cab light popped on. Ringo swung open the passenger door and jumped out onto the road. These men would take them into the darkest part of the woods and murder them.

It would be useless to channel Eleanor or anyone else. Myrna needed to be the nameless feral child now. The one who could disappear into the wilderness without a trace. The one who knew how to keep herself and her sister alive.

She whispered to Eleanor, "They'll take us into the forest to kill us. But it's pretty thick and dark, so we have a chance to get away. On my signal, run as fast as you can, don't stop, and stay in the trees."

"This is ridiculous. Things like this just don't happen in real life. Let me talk to them. I'm very well-known and have money. That will make the difference."

"No, Eleanor. *Listen to me—*" But when had her sister ever listened to her?

Both doors to the truck's back seat opened. Myrna quickly slipped away from George and slid to the ground on Eleanor's side.

"You don't have to leave us here. I can give you money if you just take us to Cimarron." Eleanor spoke firmly and authoritatively with that faint edge of disdain. The same tone Myrna used when she'd spoken to her team members in Eleanor's lab. It hadn't worked for Myrna then, and it wasn't working for Eleanor now.

Ringo said something in German and swept the beam of his under-barrel light toward the trees.

"No, no. Don't you understand?" Panic now replaced Eleanor's disdain. "I have money. I can make you rich."

"Into the trees," he replied. "Go."

Eleanor pulled in an unsteady breath. "Oh, my God. They're really going to murder us. Myrna?"

Her sister reached out to her. Shock held Myrna captive for a moment before she took Eleanor's hand and gripped her fingers tightly. For the first time in forever, her sister needed her.

Myrna's skin tingled as her night vision kicked in. Calm settled into her bones. *This is who I am.* Time to embrace it.

She stepped between the two men, tugging Eleanor behind her, weaving amid trees, and pushing through thickets. The wash of the gun's under-barrel light teased out animal trails. Instead, Myrna chose to forge into the thickest and blackest holes in the undergrowth.

She pulled Eleanor beside her. "Walk faster, don't follow the light," she whispered. About ten feet behind them now, the two men spoke in low tones, their voices a muffled hum.

Myrna's brows pinched. Not their voices. The truck engine starting remotely? That meant they were still too close to the road and the stench of decaying bodies would alert searchers. But another fifty feet ...

She released her sister's hand, and Eleanor stopped. Myrna shoved her in the back. "Keep going no matter what happens."

With a flip of her thumb, Myrna opened her knife. She'd get one chance.

She slowed until her sister took the lead, then, with a cry, stumbled, her right side blocked by a tree trunk. She hit the ground with a jolt. One of the men rushed to her and grabbed her left arm, jerking her up. She reeled, pulling him so that he stood between her and the second goon. But his attention was on the fast-disappearing Eleanor.

"Hey. Halt!" He pointed his gun at her sister's back.

Myrna swung her blade in a vicious arc, driving it deep into the man's belly. Hot blood coated her fist. She yanked her knife out and slashed at his gun, knocking it from his hands and out of easy reach.

"Run!"

Eleanor bolted, Myrna behind her. Branches snapped and cracked. The men shouted. A barrage of shots slapped into wood and whizzed past. Were they following? A thump and curse. Yep. But only one light bounced through the darkness now. She sped up, leaping a fallen log, Eleanor a dark blur of movement just ahead. If they kept going in this direction, stayed under the cover of the trees, they'd parallel the cliff and end up at the lot where she and Jessup parked when they'd discovered the pot farm. That road led to the Cabeza de Baca ranch house where they could call for help, use that big blue truck to get to Jessup and William Tell. Myrna smiled grimly, for the first time seeing a way out.

Her sister darted into a treeless meadow.

Crap. Or not.

The beam of light jagged after her sister. Myrna ducked behind a tree. One of the henchmen ran straight toward an exposed Eleanor, who'd halted near the edge of the cliff. Ringo slowed to a deliberate walk, his light drilling a bright white hole at the level of Eleanor's heart. But he didn't shoot her. Instead, he grabbed her wrist and wrenched her into his body. He pressed the gun against her temple, the light under the barrel casting ghastly shadows over her features.

He yelled something in German, which Myrna guessed was along the lines of *Come out or I will shoot your sister.*

Her arrogant, condescending, brilliant, difficult to like, much less love, sister. And except for that betrayal thing with Bard and Jessup, the only relative who'd ever given her a chance.

It would be easy to slip away, to disappear, leave Eleanor to die. Like her mother had when Myrna was twelve.

Except ...

Her mother hadn't left her to die. She'd left her at a hospital, to live. And she'd written her a note. A simple three-word statement that explained nothing and everything.

It's time, Myrna.

Time for her mother to go. Time for Myrna to have a chance at a life away from the one she hadn't chosen. And, for the first and only time, her mother had used *Myrna* instead of *girl*.

Myrna had taken the opportunity and forged a path to a career she loved and made *huge* mistakes along the way. She'd shunned the nameless child she'd once been, ashamed of how different she was from the people around her. Other girls at school, members of her family, Eleanor, the people she worked with on digs and in labs.

But where did she always seem to end up? Where did the work she chose take her? *Outside.* To Pleistocene excavations in the wilds of Siberia. To the Donavan Ranch and its wilderness. And when she picked up William Tell, her visions opened up places and times away from the safety she'd craved as a child. Places and times she couldn't be without her education, ones that she understood and connected with because of her childhood. Her mother had ultimately given her the gift of standing in two worlds. Both made her into who she was.

It would be easy to fade into the wilderness, take back William Tell. "*And Jessup,*" she whispered. Leave Eleanor to her fate.

But she wasn't her mother. A buzzing started in her ears.

She took a deep breath and stepped to the forest's edge, a pastel blur against the black wall of trees.

"Let her go, and I'll come out," she called.

A light caught her clothing. She dove for cover. Wood splintered from the echoing shot.

"I will shoot her," he yelled.

"If you harm my sister," Myrna yelled back, "you'll never find me."

They were in a stand-off. But what was the endgame? If she left, he'd kill Eleanor. If she stayed, he'd kill them both. And the longer she delayed meant the closer Jessup and William Tell were to being murdered in the caves.

Eleanor screamed. "*Myrna!* Help me. *Please.*"

Myrna peeked around the tree. Ringo had pushed the gun's muzzle into the soft skin under Eleanor's jaw, but he'd moved closer. A mistake. The buzzing in Myrna's head grew louder. She ducked behind the tree, searching the undergrowth. She picked up a rock, hand tightening until it cut into her skin.

"Don't hurt her," she said. "I'll come out."

Stupid. Futile. What she was about to do made no sense. Between the rock and a bullet, she'd have zero chance. But maybe Eleanor would.

Myrna stepped out from the behind the tree. Ringo smiled and leveled the gun at her.

He still thought she was no risk to him, that he held the winning hand. *Ass.* She cocked her arm.

The humming buzz grew louder and a drone, glowing eerily blue, swooped into the clearing. Ringo swiveled, light swinging from Myrna to illuminate a swarm of black dots as they dropped out of a trapdoor. *Harley's bees.* Ringo fired wildly as the bee drones swarmed him and Eleanor. He released her, spinning, swatting. He slapped at his neck—

And stood in total stillness for a count of three, two, one, then dropped like a sack of sand to the ground.

Eleanor, who'd been swiping just as wildly at the bees moments before, toppled right on top of him.

The buzzing nano drones coalesced into black clump above

the downed bodies. Myrna took a tentative step toward her sister. In a single blink, half a dozen bees broke off from the colony and arrowed in Myrna's direction.

Harley's voice yelled, "Myrna, stop!"

She froze, but it was too late. A tiny black drone lighted on the bare skin of her forearm.

Fifty-Eight

"Stay absolutely still. It won't sting you if you don't react," Harley called. "I'm not close enough yet to deactivate."

Breath frozen, only her eyeballs moved as the drones above Eleanor swarmed toward a fast-walking Harley. But when they were maybe twenty feet away from him, they dropped like tiny black stones into the high grass. He kept coming, a controller in his hand. The five bee drones hovering around Myrna swirled in the air and zoomed toward him. They, too, nosedived to the ground.

Myrna rolled her eyes to her arm, the need to take a breath building. The little drone pivoted on her skin, its wire-thin legs tickling. It tensed suddenly, and Myrna braced, anticipating the needle sting. The drone rolled off her arm. Relief turned bones to jelly.

Harley pointed a light at the ground. The bee drone lay on top of Myrna's shoe. He bent to pick it up and placed it in a shirt pocket.

"The drugs aren't long acting because the dose is small. Come on. We need to disable that wanker before he comes to."

Myrna ran toward Eleanor and Ringo, Harley taking one stride to every two of hers. "What about George, uh, the other, er, wanker?"

"Paden, Webb, and Isaac are rendering aid. Someone stabbed him in the gut."

"Me." She held out a blood-covered hand.

Harley muttered, "Remind me not to cheese you off," and extracted a roll of silver duct tape from a fanny pack. He slid to a halt next to the lump that was Ringo and her sister.

They rolled Eleanor to one side and Ringo onto his stomach, exposing the gun. Harley picked it up and released the clip, using the under-barrel light to count leftover bullets. After racking the slide and checking the gun for obstructions, he expertly slapped the clip back in and tucked it into his waistband at his back. Myrna stared.

"Three years in His Majesty's Secret Service." At her slack jaw, he said, "Kidding."

Ringo groaned. Harley grabbed his arms and twisted them behind the man's back. "Hurry, he's reviving."

Myrna deployed the tape and wrapped it a dozen times around Ringo's wrists before moving to his twitching legs and securing his ankles. They turned him over again. He blinked at them. His gaze sharpened.

"Verdammt," he spat.

Myrna whipped out her bloody knife. Ringo's eyes popped. She cut a piece of tape and slapped it over his lips. He struggled mightily as she and Harley stood.

"This one of those Brazilians from the mine reclamation? Nasty fellow." Harley prodded the writhing man with his toe.

"I think Finn Posse, this guy, and some others murdered Bard," Myrna said.

"Bard's not dead, but he's pretty beat up. His dog—Briscoe— led us to him. Do you want to roll him off the cliff, see if he bounces?" This time Harley didn't modify his words with *kidding*.

Ringo stilled.

Eleanor moaned at the same time undergrowth cracked behind them. Harley reached for the gun but relaxed as a lone man hobbled into the clearing.

"It's Isaac," Harley said. "Check on Dr. Kelly—is she really your sister?—whilst I gather my bees before they're trampled. Isaac says there's an old logging cabin nearby."

"We don't have time—"

"Your sister will need a place to recover, and we need to retrench. Him"—Harley squatted down and stared into Ringo's wary eyes—"we leave right here. And to make sure he doesn't escape, I think we need to apply more duct tape. A lot more duct tape."

With Eleanor strung between Isaac and Harley, head lolling, feet dragging, Isaac explained Webb and Paden's whereabouts.

"Took Briscoe and the stabbed guy"—Isaac slanted a glance at Myrna's bloody hand—"to Paden's mother's house. Said they'll call once they get there and see if we need any, er, supplies. I brought a satellite phone, only thing that works up here." The forest thinned, the moon sitting above the horizon, and he notched his chin at the Donavan truck parked where the bad guy's truck had once stood. "Paden took their truck. Pendejos left the key in the console."

"Finn Posse has William Tell and"—Myrna's voice wobbled— "Jessup. They're taking them into the mine because of the treasure. They think Jessup and I found it."

"Did you?" Isaac asked. Eleanor jerked and mumbled.

"This treasure's real?" Harley readjusted his burden.

"We never saw it, but there were clues." Ghostly Clovis People and cowboys with canvas sacks and gas masks. "How did you know— I mean, why are you here?"

"Tonight's poker night at the café," Isaac said. "Me, Webb, Paden, Jessup. We invite Buzz because he's a terrible card player."

"I'm getting better."

Isaac rolled his eyes. "No, you ain't. Jessup didn't show up, but Briscoe did. That dog led us to Bard, who explained as much as he could."

"And I retrieved the drones," Harley interjected. "Just in case."

"We came after Jessup and saw them Germans driving off. Thought we'd better follow," Isaac finished.

They climbed into the truck, Eleanor listing against Myrna. Harley drove following Isaac's directions.

"Good thing this road was patched, otherwise we'd be outta luck."

"Jessup and I ran into an illegal marijuana grow up by the Cabeza de Baca formation. That's sort of how we found the treasure caves," Myrna said. "Why isn't Eleanor recovering the way that guy did? What's in those bee drones?"

"Iocaine powder," Harley said over his shoulder. "Kidding. A muscle paralytic mixed with a teensy bit of extremely powerful sedative. It would stop the breathing of anything smaller than about twenty-five pounds, but otherwise recovery's weight dependent. Since your sister probably weighs around a hundred and twenty-five pounds—"

Eleanor slurred, "A hundred and fifteen." She shook her head and stretched her jaw, before continuing much more coherently, unfortunately. "My God, Myrna. Those men were going to *kill* us. I give you one simple task to prove yourself, and you mess it up. Harley, take us back to the Donavan Ranch immediately. We need to call the police."

The two men in the front exchanged glances.

"Charley Donavan'll probably want this handled in-house, at least for now," Isaac said.

"*Attempted murder* handled in-house?" Eleanor exclaimed as Myrna blurted, "But Jessup and William Tell."

"With all the driving back and forth, it would take the sheriff hours to arrive," Harley replied. "I believe we should discuss all this at the cabin, perhaps ask Webb and Paden to bring back those extra supplies if we end up needing them."

The bouncing headlights glanced off a single dusty pane of glass.

"Here we are," Harley announced. "I don't know about you all, but I could use a snack."

Isaac opened the truck's door. "You are a bottomless pit, Buzz, that is the God's honest truth. Outhouse is out back, ladies, and pump in front. Myrna, 'jita, you may wanna wash your hands."

Myrna paced the linoleum floor of the logging cabin. It needed a good sweep and dust, but the bunk beds appeared sturdy and the furniture solid. Isaac laid wood and started a fire in an old iron stove before he brought a box inside from the back of the pickup and started a pot of cowboy coffee. His quick, "Good place if someone needs a couple of thinking days," explained the cabin's condition as did the wooden table topped by a cigar box filled with a well-used deck of cards and plastic poker chips. He laid aluminum-wrapped burritos on top of the stove to warm up. Harley lounged at the table working his way through a plastic container of homemade pastries. Eleanor sat across from him, picking forest detritus out of her hair and off her clothes, her face a storm cloud of discontent. When Isaac plunked a steaming mug of thick black coffee in front of her, she ungraciously pushed it away and muttered, "Seriously?"

"It's been more than an hour since we split from the other group," Myrna said. "After they killed us, those two men were supposed to join them at the mine. Finn Posse must know something's wrong, or he will soon."

"Do you think they'll send someone back to check?" Harley said, mouth full of cherry turnover.

"Maybe," Myrna replied. "There were two other henchmen with Posse, but I don't know how many more were going to be at the mine." She sat down heavily in a chair.

"How long will it take for 'em to get to the treasure?" Isaac asked.

"From the packrat burrow, it took close to five hours for Jessup, me, and William Tell to walk out, but we made mistakes and went down a few dead ends." Including to the opening under the Cabeza de Baca. Myrna chewed her lip. "Jessup marked the stone in places as a guide but ended up erasing the ones near the mouth of the mine. But that doesn't matter. They have William Tell."

"Why did they take the dog?" Harley slurped hot coffee.

"He scent-marked the cave all the way to the burrow. Given the right enticement, he'll lead them back there, probably shave an hour off their time."

Harley unpeeled the foil from a steaming burrito. "Enticement?"

Myrna pointed at his food. "Since I have Tan Turtle in my pocket, snacks."

"So unless they're waiting for those two goons, they'll have a pretty good head start before we get there," Isaac said.

"And when they don't show, Posse will suspect you escaped and expect you to follow them into the mines," Harley said around a bite of food.

"*Follow?* Go into the mine after them?" Eleanor crossed her arms. "That's ridiculous."

Not follow, Myrna thought. Harley was right, they'd expect that. What they wouldn't expect was someone already in the caves waiting for them. A plan began to form.

"Harley? Are your bee drones easy to use?"

"Not the ones from the field, but *these*." He stood, his hands diving into capacious pockets in his jacket and trousers, emptying out everything in them on the table. Wallet, the truck key fob, a handful of change, comb, candy bars, a pack of gum, a flash drive, scraps of paper, a golf pencil, a .22 caliber shell casing, cigarette lighter, chalk, spark plug, a small harmonica, a lockpick, a knot of cannon fuse, electrical tape, alcohol wipes, a fishing fly, packets of sugar, a multitool, a face mask covered with tiny Union Jacks, a broken flip phone, drone controller, and finally, a double-zippered shell case. Jeez. His pockets acted for him like her backpack did for her. He sat, scooched his chair closer to Myrna, and opened the case. Inside, four bumblebee drones were nestled in gray foam.

"These have very powerful headlamps. They can be recharged by the warmth of your hand. And"—he grinned, his crooked face charming—"they contain an internal reservoir filled with curare, a muscle relaxant that blocks the nicotinic acetylcholine receptor, rendering the injectee paralyzed, at least for a few minutes. But it would give the deployer the ability to either to run away or disarm an opponent."

"Do they need an app or something to work properly?" Myrna asked.

"Nothing so crude. I've developed a prototype miniature controller." Tucked into the foam was a silver circlet with raised jewels dotting the exterior. He plucked it out and placed it in his palm. "Pressing these jeweled buttons deploys the drones. Push emerald green for go. Push it twice to fly forward. Opal to turn on and off their lights. Ruby for stop. Press the ruby twice for them to return to their dock. This poisonous-looking citrine directs the bugs to land on a target and sting. Nifty, huh?" He held it up to the light, jewels glinting.

Eleanor shoved her chair back and stood. "This is ludicrous."

"You know, you haven't even said *thank you, Harley, for saving my life,* so buzz off."

Eleanor snorted, skirted Isaac, who sat cradling his cup of coffee, and grabbed a burrito. Crossing to Harley, she pushed the pile of his pocket litter to one side. "Thank you, Harley, for saving my life," and she placed the burrito at his elbow. "I have to use the facilities."

"TMI," Harley responded. Eleanor marched out the door, slamming it behind her. He turned back to Myrna. "Once you press the citrine, they'll sting the nearest moving object."

The satellite phone buzzed at the same moment the truck's heavy diesel engine revved.

Myrna jumped to her feet. She glanced at the jumbled pile on the table. "She took the key."

Harley dashed to the door and flung it open. Red from the taillights lit his face, the engine sounds fading as the truck sped down the cabin's narrow dirt driveway.

"She'll just get lost and have to be rescued again." Isaac grabbed a sugar packet from Harley's pile and poured it into his coffee. "Get the phone, 'jita."

"Isaac? Harley? Is everyone okay?" Paden's voice was edged with urgency.

"It's Myrna. Everyone's fine here, but the men from the mine reclamation are making Jessup and William Tell lead them to the treasure."

"Those guys are going to steal the treasure?"

Myrna frowned. The treasure was secondar—

"Yeah. That's what she said." He seemed to be speaking to someone else. Webb or maybe his family.

"*Paden*. William Tell and Jessup are in trouble. We need to get them back. Listen closely."

Myrna detailed her rescue plan and the supplies needed. "Bring Briscoe. He's the only one who can follow William Tell's scent marking. And hurry."

She hung up the phone and blew out a breath. "Finn Posse has already proved he's ready to kill for this treasure, but it could be our only chance."

Isaac pursed his lips. "Might work, especially with those bees on our side. Harley?"

"I think it's our best shot. So, Myrna, my dear." His grin was back. He got down on one knee. "Will you wear my ring?"

She held out her hand, and he slipped the drone control circlet over her right index finger.

FIFTY-NINE

Myrna watched, fingers knotted, as the upper half of Paden's body squirmed under the bright flashlight beam pointed down into the rocky opening under the Cabeza de Baca formation. His torso cast a hard shadow against the looming stone behind him.

"I can't— The gap's too narrow. I don't— *Ouch. Fu—*"

"*Paden.*" Isaac yanked on the rope that tethered the younger man.

Paden dislodged himself and scrambled out of the jumbled boulders. He jumped lightly onto the packed earth, rotating his arm with a grimace of pain.

"Are you okay?" Myrna asked.

"Hurt my shoulder the other day."

"And been moaning about it ever since," Isaac said as he coiled the rope.

"Hey. I might have chipped a bone." Paden massaged his upper arm. "I can't get through. Sorry, Myrna. It was a good plan, too."

When the homicidal pot farmers had dumped their garbage down the hole into the chamber below, she'd assumed the opening would be large enough for people to crawl through because she'd believed that the Clovis people and the cowboys used it for access. She chewed her lip. Paden had nowhere near the shoulder breadth of Ron Page, but the way he'd struggled ...

And they'd lost another precious hour since Paden and Briscoe arrived at the cabin, and they'd all driven up to the Cabeza de Baca formation. What if she'd been wrong to try and enter the cave system here? Had she condemned Jessup and William Tell by not heading to the mine opening instead?

Like Paden had read her mind, he said, "Maybe we should just wait for them to come back out at the mine entrance. I can call my mom and dad to meet us there. You've seen my mom with the shotgun. She wouldn't let those bastards get away."

Briscoe, who'd been lying in the dirt, chin on his paws, lifted his head. But there was no brightness in his eyes, and his ears drooped. Even being fitted with a dog-sized safety harness hadn't perked him up.

"Give me your gear," Harley said.

Paden shook his head. "If I can't get through, you can't get through. You'd get hung up for sure."

"My turn," Myrna said.

"No way. You'd be down there by yourself without a ..." In the stark white lantern light, Paden's face turned the color of beets.

"A man?" Myrna said dryly. "Really?"

"No," Isaac said. "A team. You're one of us now, Myrna. Family."

Family? Myrna stared at him. Isaac said it so casually, like it was well-established truth, not an earthquake under her feet.

"Wish that danged McJunkin had come back with you, Paden," Isaac continued. "He's skinny enough, que no."

"Mom was too scared to have that German guy in the house without someone to deal with him. That's why she wanted Webb to stay."

Isaac waved away Paden's explanation. They'd already heard it half a dozen times.

"What? Her infamous shotgun not work inside your house?" Harley smirked.

Paden clenched his fists. "Shut up, Buzz."

"Wait," Myrna said. "What do you mean, I'm one of you now? You barely know me."

"Sure we do. We know you because Jessup loves you, verdad? That's good enough for us," Isaac said.

"Hold on." Harley stopped looping the climbing rope and stared at Myrna. "You and *Jessup*?"

"Never seen him so happy." Isaac smiled at Myrna. "I remember him buying that big box of condoms a while ago, but he never did sleep with that, er, Dr. Kelly. Glad he got to open 'em for you."

Horrified, Myrna gaped at Isaac. "You know I ... we ..." She blinked. "He didn't sleep with her? But she said—"

"She's your sister, so you believed her. That's how it is with family." Isaac patted her shoulder. "And we'd do anything for our family, sometimes even when they've done wrong. Ain't that right, Paden?"

Paden, harness off and dangling from his hand, stilled, but Myrna barely noticed.

Because Jessup loves you.

He and William Tell were down in those caves. They needed her to rescue them.

"Lower me down. I won't be alone. If I can get through, Briscoe can, too. I'll have him, Harley's drones, and a bow." At Myrna's request, Paden had brought his mom's compound bow and a stash of arrows, but, dang it, he hadn't brought any headlamps or flashlights. She'd have a single Coleman lantern. "Once Posse and his men find the treasure, they won't need Jessup or William Tell anymore and ... and ..." She set her jaw. "I'm going in."

The men—her *team*—exchanged a series of speaking glances before, one by one, they nodded their support.

Harley clipped the rope onto her harness and checked her gear. "Do you want the gun?"

Myrna shook her head. "I'm fine with the bow."

"Yes." He smiled his endearing, crooked smile. "You are. Unhook when you're ready, and we'll send the dog down. Use the drones for light and recharge them with your hands, which are way too cold now." He picked one up and chaffed it between his, his expression rueful. He hesitated before leaning down to kiss her cheek. "You and Jessup. Drat."

Releasing her hand, he stepped back and grabbed the climbing rope.

Taking a deep breath, she scrambled onto the pile of boulders and sat, her feet dangling into the uneven black hole below.

"We'll wait for you at the mine entrance," Isaac said. "Ready?"

Myrna slipped into the darkness below.

She squiggled through the opening to the cave without any problem. It wasn't that tight, but again, she was the size of a prepubescent child. Or maybe Paden hadn't wanted to be part of an advance guard. Myrna worked her way through the short serpentine passage that opened abruptly over the cylindrical silo she and Jessup had discovered the last time they'd been in the caves. The men above played out the rope, lowering her until she dangled thirty feet above the trash-strewn floor, although she was close enough to the wall to push off with her feet. From the refracted light above her, she could see a man-sized niche about four feet high chipped out of the stone. Curious, she positioned her shoes just above the opening and called up to the men.

"Let out the rope until I tell you to stop." Using her feet and hands against the rocks, she controlled her descent until her toes rested on the niche's lip. "Stop."

A few feet in, mud bricks from a collapsed wall lay tumbled on the floor, along with rocks and more camp trash. But the light from above didn't penetrate the pitch-black depths. Myrna pulled out the drone case and picked one up. It revived in her hand, the legs tickling as it stood. She pressed the raised jewel on her ring and released it. Its light was small, but powerfully bright, the hum of its wings barely audible. It illuminated the back of the niche, spotlighting a lump of rocks surrounded and packed in by years of detritus. A domed, whitish structure sat on top. Arrested, she stared.

Was it bone?

Dang it. She didn't have time for this. Every minute that passed brought Jessup and William Tell and the bad guys closer to the treasure. She slid her finger to the drone retrieval jewel on her ring, but hesitated.

What if ...?

She pulled herself inside and tugged on the rope. It slackened enough for her to move closer, tiptoeing over the scattered bricks. The drone hummed in front of her. It spun, its piercing white blinding her for a second before it landed on the domed object, its thin black legs dancing before it settled. A soft click and the narrow beam changed, creating a bright bubble of light that illuminated the air above and below.

Myrna caught her breath. A single cyclopean cavity smiled back at her from the top of the piled rocks.

Not rocks. *An altar.*

She hurried to the back of the niche and brushed away debris.

Her hand stilled and her breath left her in a rush.

The baby mammoth skull. *The bonehead.*

Tell her I hid it where those boneheads will never find it. The cowboy had whispered those words before he died. Letters Eleanor had obtained confirmed where his journal was hidden.

The brightness dimmed. Myrna scooped up the bee drone and cradled it in her hands. Seconds ticked by, excitement winding her higher, until light escaped through her fingers once again. She held out her hand and the drone climbed onto the skull and into the sinus cavity. It came to rest on a bundle of crumbling oil cloth.

Myrna slipped a shaking hand inside and gently extracted a wrapped rectangular package. She untied the leather thong, carefully peeled the cloth away, and revealed a leather-bound book. Stamped on front and picked out in gold was a flaming sword topped by a rainbow.

She opened the age-stiffened pages and read out loud.

"*If you've found my journal, I must be dead. Please tell my wife I love her and to deal with the trove of art responsibly. It isn't mine or yours. It's the world's.* Signed Ronald J. Page, 05 JAN 56."

Breath coming fast, Myrna paged through the diary, scanning entries. Near the final entry, she read an astonishing list of the contents in a room somewhere deep in the caves with the annotation *see map.* She flipped and found a detailed map. Through the mine, the tunnels, past the packrat burrow ...

The blood drained from her face.

A final booby trap, so diabolical it would kill anyone who tried to access the treasure without the knowledge contained in her hand. Now she understood the gas masks the men had worn around their necks when she and Jessup had seen their vision in the packrat burrow.

She had to get to Jessup and William Tell before they entered the treasure room, or—

"Myrna?" Harley called. "Everything all right?"

"You're not going to believe—"

The drone lifted and flew past Myrna to light on the wall behind the mammoth skull. Below it, almost completely hidden by detritus, was a metal box. Myrna tucked the book into her waistband, scrubbed the lid free of debris, and bared a stenciled US ARMY. She unlatched the lid.

The goggle eyes of an olive-green gas mask stared back at her.

"Thank you, Ronald J. Page," she whispered. Extracting it, she strapped it over her face. Too big. She tightened the straps. Almost perfect. She hung it around her neck.

"Myrna?" Harley again, but this time, like it heard his master's voice, the drone flew toward the sound. Myrna lurched after it, scattering trash, ready to snatch it from the air. She stumbled and kicked a rock.

Only it wasn't a rock. It rolled in a wavering path to the niche's edge, the sound hollow and metallic, to poise on the lip's edge, wobble ...

Myrna dove and grabbed it, fingers closing on the cold, ridged pineapple-shaped grenade. As the bee drone hovered above her, she smiled a slow, satisfied smile.

"Guys?" she called. "Don't go to the mine entrance when you leave. Head to the elk die-off meadow and the arroyo with the mammoth bones."

"Why there?" Paden asked.

In the drone's light, she cleared camp trash from the niche floor and counted half a dozen more hand grenades mixed in with the rocks and bricks. Her smile widened.

"Because I have an idea."

~

Briscoe, whimpering all the way, touched down on the dirt floor and cowered as Myrna unhooked the rope from his harness. She clipped on his leash.

"Set, Myrna?" Harley called.

"Set." She cleared her tight throat.

"We'll be waiting for you," Isaac said. "Bring back Jessup and William Tell safe."

And the light from above faded.

She slipped the bow over her shoulder, five arrows in a makeshift quiver strapped on her back. Her team had lowered down the Coleman charged with a new fuel canister. She'd use it until she got close to the cave behind the mammoth jump site, then switch to the drones and pray she'd arrive before Finn Posse.

Myrna stared at the German dog commands Paden had written on her arm in black ink. "Okay, Briscoe. *Finden.*"

Briscoe sat, back hunched and head down.

Myrna dropped to her knees beside him and wrapped her arms around his neck in a tight hug. She buried her face in his fur, but only allowed a few tears to eke out. If she let her fear win, she'd never stop crying.

Myrna lifted her head and wiped her eyes. "I know how you feel, buddy. But I need you now. I need to you help me find William Tell and Jessup."

She slid her hand into her jacket pocket and pulled out a smushed burrito. If Briscoe was anything like William Tell, snacks were a powerful motivator.

The dog's ears perked, nose sniffing. She peeled back a corner of the foil and pulled off a piece. The sniffing intensified. He bumped her, leaving wet nose slime on her jacket sleeve. Blech. She threw the burrito chunk toward the passage that led out of the rock silo. Briscoe rose and Myrna scrambled to her feet. He padded to the burrito then looked at her.

That's right. Paden had told her the dog needed permission to eat.

"Uh. *Essen.*"

Briscoe vacuumed the food. He sat, staring at her, alert.

Myrna chewed her lip. There wasn't enough food to take them very far and what she really needed was Briscoe to follow William Tell's scent mark.

Tan Turtle.

She put away the burrito, thrust her hand into her pocket, and pulled out William Tell's favorite toy, fabric stiff with dried drool. She shoved the toy under Briscoe's nose. A low growl rumbled in his throat. "*Finden,*" she said, and pointed down the passageway.

The shepherd darted forward, almost yanking the leash off her wrist. Myrna dug in her heels and grabbed the Coleman lantern. Stopping at the silo's opening, the faded pictograms of a dozen hands arced over his head, Briscoe sniffed the rock, lifted his leg, and peed copiously before starting down the passageway, pulling Myrna behind him.

In a little under an hour, she found the first of Jessup's chalk circles.

Standing in the bubble of light from the bee drone on her shoulder, Myrna studied the bottom of the collapsed backfill that closed off the arch of the large cavern. Just outside the tons of dirt, sand, and rock was the mammoth arroyo. She picked up the second to last of the grenades and, feet digging into the slope, powered two-thirds of the way up to snuggle it in a dirt nest she'd scooped in the earthen blockage.

Briscoe's whines echoed from farther down the tunnel near the packrat nest, setting her teeth on edge. She'd left the bow, the arrows, and the other bee drones with him, lights on low, and told him to *bleib*—stay. He had, but his body shook, his fear palpable. Poor guy, but she wished he'd shut up. Who knew how far sound traveled in the tunnels, and if Posse heard the dog ...

The bad guys had to be close. Unless Jessup had taken a couple of wrong turns after she'd deliberately converted one of his circle marks into a happy face using chalk she'd taken from Harley's pockets. Hopefully, that would be enough to clue Jessup to her presence in the cave system.

If it wasn't, the explosion would. Myrna unscrewed the top on the lantern's fuel tank, wrinkling her nose at the rotten egg scent, and doused the five grenades nestled in the dirt with what was left. She hopped down the slope, going over her plan in her head. The grenades the pot farmers threw down the packrat burrow took about five seconds to explode. She'd pull the pin on the single grenade she'd held back, toss it into her grenade nest and book down the passageway to duck and cover behind a bend. If she set it up correctly, the grenades would blow an opening in the blockage, but not collapse the cave's ceiling.

After that, her plans were a bit fuzzier. She had the drones and her bow. And Harley, Isaac, and Paden outside by the arroyo. But if Finn Posse had sent his henchmen into the forest to investigate why George and Ringo had gone missing ...

Myrna picked up the grenade, stomach jumping. Her finger hooked into the pin.

It was now or never.

Briscoe's whines changed to sharp barks. She frowned. "*Shut up*, Briscoe. Uh, *stille*." What made him start up *now*—

An echoing *gruff* from behind her made her breath catch. She whirled, eyes fixed on the rising glow of light coming from the tunnel at the back of the cavern.

A hard, furry body slammed into the backs of her knees, sprawling her to the dirt with an *oof*. The grenade flew from her hand, but the bee drone clung to her shoulder. Briscoe slid to a stop below the shelf to the tunnel, barking furiously.

William Tell, dancing on the very edge of the ledge, met each of Briscoe's barks with his own. Behind him, Jessup, Finn Posse, and a single minion materialized out the tunnel's mouth.

Where was Posse's other goon?

"A welcoming party. How kind," Posse said. "Briscoe, stille. Sitz."

The stupid dog stopped barking and sat. William Tell didn't. *Good boy*.

"Get her," Posse ordered his henchman.

Myrna scrambled to her feet and bolted down the rock-hewn passageway, the bee drone giving off just enough light that she didn't go crashing into the walls. She had to hide Ron Page's journal. She'd rather die than let Finn Posse get his slimy Neo-Nazi Werewolf hands on it.

Okay, that was a lie. She'd rather not die, but the journal would lead him right to the treasure and avoid death by booby trap, and there'd be no reason for him to keep Jessup, William Tell, or her alive.

Myrna skipped around a corner, spotting the three drones she'd left with Briscoe glowing dully through the amberat of the packrat nest. Slithering to a stop, she grabbed the journal from atop the quiver of arrows and shoved it into a shallow crevice, eyes on the tunnel behind her. She pressed the ruby on the ring twice and the bee drones buzzed toward her, lighting on her fluffy hair and burrowing under, sending a shiver along her skin as they crept deeper. The heat of her scalp would charge them up. The little bee on her shoulder scampered up her neck to rest behind an ear even as the passageway around her brightened and a barreling figure emerged. She nocked an arrow, swung the bow up—

The henchman's ram to her shoulder skewed the arrow into the ceiling, shattering its tip. With one hand, he yanked the bow away and flung it behind him. With the other hand he twisted her wrist behind her back, jerking it up. She yelped at the pain.

"*Stille*," he growled in her ear. "Or I will break your arm."

A snarling William Tell leaped from the darkness and latched onto the man's calf. The man's hold loosened. His flashlight fell to the floor, dimming the air around them. Myrna jabbed him in the abdomen with a sharp elbow, stamped on his foot, and slung back her head, hoping the satisfying crunch was from the man's nose and not one of the bee drones. She wrenched free. William Tell's leash snapped and snaked as he continued to chomp on the bad guy. She grabbed it, yanked the dog away from the doubled-over figure, bolted down the tunnel—

In the wrong direction.

Myrna slid to an arm-whirling stop. In front of her, Jessup, bruises covering one side of his face, held a docile Briscoe's leash. Finn Posse stood behind him, pressing a gun barrel to his head.

"Are you finished, Dr. Lee? Because I'm getting very tired of both you and your dog." He shoved Jessup toward her. She grabbed him as he staggered.

"Oh, Jessup. What have they done to you?"

He straightened with difficulty, one arm wrapping his ribs. She gently touched a swollen cheek. The faint light from the burrowed drones caught in the crystal depths of his only open eye, the other swollen shut.

"Seems I don't take direction well, Meerkat," he rasped. "Your hair's glowing."

She pressed a finger against his lips.

"Touching," Posse sneered. "Santiago."

"Ja." Finn's henchman walked out of the darkness, wiping a bloody nose with the back of his hand, the gas mask she'd taken from the niche in his other. He skirted Myrna and Jessup, sending her a murderous look.

"What is this, Dr. Lee?" Posse asked. "Why might someone need a gas mask?"

She curled her arm around Jessup's waist and shifted to face Posse and Santiago. Jessup listed against her, but it was controlled, his muscles coiled and tense. He wasn't as hurt as he was making out to be.

"I—I came into the cave system through the Cabeza de Baca formation. That's where I found that mask with a note inside. There's another booby trap. It said to put the mask on before you open the door."

"The door to the treasure room?" Posse asked. "Where's the note?"

"I didn't bring it," she said, eyes innocently wide.

"Such a little liar," he said with a smile, gun pointed at her chest. "And where did you find this?" He pulled the grenade from his pocket and tossed it playfully in the air. Both dogs alerted, their heads bobbing up and down as they tracked it, Briscoe still, William Tell's butt wagging. "Ah. They want to play fetch. I pull the pin, toss the grenade, they chase. Boom."

Santiago chuckled. Myrna wanted desperately to kick him in the nuts.

"Search her," Posse ordered. "A mistake I won't make again."

Santiago gripped her upper arm hard enough to bruise and dragged her away from Jessup. Hands rough, he frisked her thoroughly. He grinned into her eyes when found her knife and red jasper mammoth fetish. Fishing into the secret pocket, he yanked them out to hold up to Posse.

"Hey! My mother gave me that knife. And that fetish was expensive."

Santiago shoved Myrna into Jessup and pocketed the knife and fetish with a smirk.

Posse's expression hardened. "Although I wish to understand how you escaped my men, Dr. Lee, we don't have time for conversation. Move."

Body shaking in fear, anger, and bone-deep resolve, she looped her arm around Jessup's waist again. He slung his arm over her shoulder and they carefully rotated toward the treasure tunnel; she pulled William Tell's leash while Jessup tugged at Briscoe's. The dogs eyed each other suspiciously but plodded forward. They headed down the tunnel brightly lit from the bad guys' halogen lanterns, Posse and Santiago trailing out of reach behind them.

As they limped by the amberat, Myrna's glance flickered to the crevice that held the journal. The bow, its string snapped, lay a dozen feet farther, broken arrows scattered around it. They hobbled past the blocked entrance to the original blown-up packrat burrow and into an unknown area of the cave.

"Any more traps here, Page?" called Posse.

"No." His head listed toward Myrna, his voice barely audible. "Posse might not want to know how you got away, but I do, even though I knew you would."

She stared into his eye, hers wide. "You did?"

"Never doubted it. I knew you had a better chance than me. And when I saw that chalk happy face ... I wish you hadn't come back for us, hadn't put yourself in more danger. But I'm glad you did."

He squeezed her shoulders, and the warmth of hope replaced some of her fear. They could get out of this. Together.

"Harley and Isaac and Paden. I mean, they helped. A lot. They're waiting for us at the mammoth dig, right outside that big cavern back there."

"Posse sent someone after you when his men didn't show."

Great. With any luck, her team could take care of him. She adjusted her arm to pull Jessup closer. "You must do exactly as I say. Promise?"

He bobbled his head, good eye slanted to her.

She opened her mouth to tell him about the drones and the gas masks—

"No more talking, or I'll shoot you in the back," Posse said pleasantly.

Myrna compressed her lips. He would, too. They picked their way along a sandy path littered with rocks for another twenty minutes, Finn Posse and Santiago muttering in German.

The passage ended at an arched opening, blackness beyond.

"Halt. Separate. Dr. Lee on the right, Page to the left. Hold the dogs." Posse nodded to Santiago, who crept forward to check the archway. He flashed his light through.

"Large room. Some stacked boxes ... and a door in the far wall. The treasure." The man grinned and turned to step inside—

"Wait! Dr. Lee and her dog will enter first, just to make sure Mr. Page didn't lie about the traps."

Jessup straightened. "I'll go."

"You'll stay where you are. Dr. Lee? Now." Posse waggled his gun.

"I need light," she said. Santiago quickly converted his flashlight to a lantern. She grabbed the handle with a sweaty palm. With once last glance at Jessup and throat dry as the sand at her feet, Myrna and William Tell stepped through the arch ...

And into heaven. Well, heaven for a paleontologist who studied the North American Pleistocene epoch. Because painted— actual *pictographs*—on the walls all around, glowing under the brilliant white light of her lantern, were the most beautiful images of Pleistocene megafauna since the discovery of Lascaux, Altamira, and Chauvet.

Myrna's knees buckled, and she sat hard on the sandy floor. Scarcely able to gasp in air, her head swiveled to take in the beauty —iron and manganese oxides, charcoal, red and violet hematite, yellow goethite, chromium green. Mammoths, trunks raised, bison with huge, curving horns, dappled horses, camelops, short-faced bears, big cats.

Then William Tell climbed into her lap, and her vision narrowed and exploded. Her arms tightened around the dog, and she saw *them*. People in fur and masks, using thin hollow bone to blow pigment along cutouts in hide stencils tacked to the wall, color-coated fingers tracing flickering projections of carved fetishes perched in front of tallow lamps, bristle brushes laying in three-dimensional details of an array of painted animal outlines.

A distant voice called her name, warm arms embraced her— and her vision changed. The cowboys sat on tripod folding chairs, hands glove-encased, gas masks covering their heads. They poured glittering green powder into short olive-green cylinders, then screwed the cylinders—no, they were *air filters*—onto gas masks draped across their knees. With cautious hands, they loaded the rigged masks into metal boxes next to the wooden door. One man screwed the metal lid on a mason jar half-filled with green dust and snuggled it into a canvas bag.

Sparkling green powder. Blister beetles. Deadly cantharidin-like toxin developed by the Nazis in World War II. The poisonous substance Kent, just a few hours ago, told her was smeared on the knife used to stab Ron Page. And Page and his friends had used it to taint the gas masks. The final booby trap.

William Tell jumped off her lap. Myrna fell back to the present with a jolt. The dog sat before her carefully scratching the inside of his left bat ear, his button-black eyes never leaving Briscoe. The arms holding her tightened.

"You okay?" Jessup asked.

"Oh, yes."

"You scared me, Meerkat. I thought, we all thought, you'd lied about the gas masks and been poisoned by something in the air. But it's the paintings on the walls, isn't it?"

"They're ... overwhelming. No matter what's behind that door, these images are the real treasure. They'll change our understanding of Paleolithic culture in the Americas." She turned her head to stare into his unswollen eye. "Did you see what the cowboys did?"

"It's the masks that are toxic, not the treasure room."

"Yes. I found Ronald J. Page's journal tucked inside the baby mammoth skull under the Cabeza de Baca. He wrote about the gas mask booby trap and included a list of stolen art from the war worth hundreds of millions of dollars on the black market. Enough money for Finn Posse to start his own country or buy off hundreds of politicians." Myrna paused. "Breathing in that green powder will kill you."

"Then we have to make sure Posse and Santiago put on the poisoned masks."

Jessup helped Myrna stand. "She's fine. See? I'm okay. Dogs are fine." Briscoe hackled and growled at William Tell as if to acknowledge Jessup's statement. William Tell bristled and growled right back.

Posse entered the cave painting room, gun steady, Myrna's untainted mask dangling from his fingers. His eyebrows arched as he studied the walls. Beside him, Santiago's gaze never wavered from the door to the treasure room.

"I can see how you would be overcome, Dr. Lee. And it certainly appears what you said was true. We don't need the masks until we enter the treasure room. But we only have one."

Myrna pointed to the stack of metal boxes near the door. "I found my mask in a case like those."

Santiago hurried across the room and unlatched the top box. He pulled out a mask, olive-green filter in place. He unlatched two more boxes, pulling out masks with black respiration filters. Myrna exchanged a pregnant glance with Jessup. During the vision, she hadn't seen any black filters being loaded with toxin. Briscoe growled at William Tell again.

"Standartenführer, we don't need them anymore if we have these." Santiago held up the masks, his eyes ablaze with murderous avarice.

Finn Posse sauntered forward, his attention on Myrna. Briscoe took a step toward William Tell, teeth bared.

"How could a wooden door maintain a toxic atmosphere in that room such that masks are needed? Perhaps canisters of gas are opened when the door is breeched? Perhaps toxic chemicals are triggered by an increase in expired carbon dioxide or the moisture in our breath? But if toxic air was the final trap to protect the treasure, why would they leave masks?" Posse frowned and held up his gas mask. "Perhaps it's not the air that's toxic?"

William Tell yanked hard on the leash, tired of Briscoe's disrespect, thankfully jerking Myrna's gaze away from Finn Posse. Had her expression given her away?

William Tell released a series of short sharp barks. Briscoe lunged to end of his leash.

"The rubber would surely degrade over time, as would the filter." Posse lifted his voice to be heard over the snarling, barking dogs.

"Die hunde. The dogs. Let's use them as our canaries. They can test the air, and she can test the masks," Santiago said.

"I'll go," Jessup said, holding tight to a lunging Briscoe. "I can handle Briscoe, but not both dogs at the same time. They'll fight."

Posse studied Jessup, as if weighing his words for a hidden meaning. "Give him a mask."

Santiago handed Jessup a black canister mask. Myrna bit her lip, insides twisting. Jessup caught her gaze and held it as he slipped the mask over his head, positioned it on his face, and tightened the straps to seal it. He breathed deeply, chest rising and falling three times, five times, ten times. He pulled the mask off.

Myrna closed her eyes in relief. No poison.

"This mask seems fine," Jessup said. "Rubber's intact. Filter's good. But if toxic gas is released when I open the door, it could well seep into this room and the tunnels. We'll all need to wear a mask."

Posse nodded to Santiago again. Santiago extended the olive canister mask to Myrna.

Myrna shook her head and turned to Posse. "Can I have that one instead? I've already adjusted it."

"So you know it works properly." Posse smiled. "Then I'll use it." Santiago tossed Myrna the poisoned mask.

The men slipped their masks over their heads, adjusting the fit. Myrna fiddled with the straps, mind working frantically, when Jessup, the little round goggles hiding his eyes, grabbed the lantern and shoved against the door. It swung open, and Jessup stepped inside.

"Your mask, Dr. Lee," Finn Posse said from behind his. He turned the gun on her. "Put it on."

She gestured to the open door. "But everything seems okay."

"Now. Or I will shoot the dog."

"You know, that threat's getting pretty old," Myrna muttered and lifted the mask. Hands trembling, holding her breath, she fit it over her head—

Jessup leaned out of the doorway, mask pulled up, his face stamped with wonder. "Dear God, you won't believe ..." He disappeared back inside.

Posse and Santiago ran into the room.

Myrna dropped the toxic gas mask and pressed the green jewel on her finger. The drones untangled themselves from her hair and took off. She pressed green again, and they flew in formation into the treasure room.

"Jessup, *freeze!*" she screamed. Praying he'd remembered to do exactly what she told him, she pressed the citrine jewel—the signal for the bees to sting anything that moved.

William Tell yanked the leash off her wrist and dashed into the treasure room. The sounds of a vicious dog fight ensued for less than a count of three, followed by two high yelps. Briscoe darted from the room, tail tucked, eyes rolling white, and collapsed at Myrna's feet. A bee drone climbed out of his coat and buzzed up to the ceiling to fly in a lazy circle. Santiago followed Briscoe. He staggered, ripped off his mask, and fell hard, dirt puffing up around him. His drone flew to join its sister above. The last two drones buzzed out of the treasure room and spun in a halo with the others above Myrna's head.

Jessup. William Tell. Myrna sobbed and dashed through the threshold.

William Tell lay still by a vertical stack of oil paintings. She dropped to her knees and pressed her ear to his barrel chest, able to detect his heartbeat and feel the shallow rise of his ribs. Tears burned her nose, and her whole body went limp. *Alive.*

Which meant the dose wouldn't last very long on grown men.

Jessup, mask discarded, knelt over a paralyzed Finn Posse and pulled off the man's gas mask. He tugged the gun from Posse's hand and tucked it into his waistband. "What the hell just happened?"

"Harley's drones inject a paralytic, but the drug wears off fast. We need to go—" Her gaze darted around a small rock-hewn room stuffed with paintings, objects d'art, statuettes, a Fabergé egg. "Is that a basket of—of *amber*? Look! The Caravaggio."

Finn Posse's eyes pinned her from a slack face. He was listening to their every word.

Myrna shook herself. "You'll have to carry Briscoe. I'll take William Tell."

"But—"

The visions.

"I know." They'd be disorienting, but it was a chance she had to take.

Jessup nodded and ran to Santiago to disarm him.

Myrna slid hands under William Tell, immediately experiencing the mental buzz.

Then she remembered. She scuttled to Finn Posse, rifled through his jacket pockets, and pulled out the grenade. His gaze cut into her like an obsidian knife. His finger twitched.

Pocketing the grenade, Myrna scooped up William Tell. Rock enveloped her. *The room hadn't been cut during Paleolithic times.*

She pivoted to where she last remembered the door and bolted, banging her shoulder, the pain bursting her out of the vision long enough to see Jessup, Briscoe slung around his neck. He faded to a telescoping specter in a room filled with Clovis People dressed in skins and woven cloth, but she could still see him, sort of. The effect of the curare on William Tell was messing up the vision.

"Go. I'll follow," she yelled, and pressed the opal jewel to light up the drones, then the green emerald twice. They flew past her and down the tunnel, like strobing lightning bugs.

Her trip was psychedelic. The light bent and twisted, rock walls bulged and smoothed. She dodged Paleoindians, their silhouettes throbbing, some of whom reached out as if feeling her pass. A flickering Jessup pounded ahead, hunched with the weight of Briscoe, once going down hard on his knee, something tumbling from his body and skidding away. He splayed a hand in the dirt, pushing up and grinding forward. She darted around the old shawoman who blew glittering green dust at her face. William Tell hung limp and flaccid in her arms.

And frickin' heavy.

"No more pastries for you," she grumbled, breathing hard. "Jessup! Stop at the amberat!"

It had to be close.

Two more long stretches and bends, and Jessup halted. Myrna pressed the ruby and the bee drones stopped in midair. Skidding to a stop beside Jessup's wavering form, she laid William Tell gently on the ground. The world popped back to normal and Jessup's face and the cave around her sharpened into focus. She dipped her hand into the amberat crevice to retrieve Ron Page's journal, tucked it into her waist band, then grabbed Jessup's arm and held out the grenade.

His good eye widened. "How the *he—*"

"I'm going to blow up that dirt wall in the big cave so we can escape," she said.

"Briscoe." He adjusted the dog across his shoulders. "He's waking up."

"That means Posse and Santiago already have."

"Myrna. When I fell, I dropped one of the guns."

"Maybe they won't find it." But she didn't believe that for a minute and stared into his dear, battered, exhausted face. The clock was ticking, but there was always time for a kiss. She placed a grubby hand against his cheek and pressed her mouth to his. Breaking away, she pocketed her grenade. "Follow me."

She scooped up William Tell, staggered back into the past, and took off at a run. The drones lifted off the amberat and buzzed ahead. Jessup ran next to her.

At the bend before the cavern, they both slowed, Myrna's heartbeat hard and fast. She laid William Tell down in a protected fold of rock and her world reappeared. Jessup held hard to Briscoe, but the dog struggled mightily.

"Get him on his feet, but you both need to stay here," Myrna said. Jessup looked like he might argue. "I'll be right back, I promise." She pressed the green gem, and the drones buzzed with her into the cavern, their light dimming by the second.

Myrna pulled the grenade from her pocket. The drones barely lit up the depression in the dirt on the slope above her. She'd have five seconds. She blew out a steadying breath and pulled the pin.

One. Then she pitched the grenade just like her mother taught her to throw a rock.

The grenade sailed up and landed with a metallic clang in the nest she'd filled with the other grenades she'd doused with fuel. *Two.* She pivoted and ran toward the tunnel opening—*three*—sprinting through and around the bend with plenty of time. *Fou—*

The concussion knocked Myrna forward. Jessup grabbed her and pushed her body behind his. Sound and pelting rocks and dirt clouded the air. Briscoe cowered next to them; William Tell, still prostrate, was tucked safely in the rock fold. Darkness enveloped the tunnel.

The echoing sound died only to be replaced with angry German voices. Myrna lifted her head. A harsh white glow built down the tunnel to the treasure room.

She grabbed Jessup's arms. "They're coming."

He pulled her to her feet. She once again scooped up William Tell. Jessup grabbed Briscoe's leash. They ran into the cavern's roiling dust.

Jessup grabbed William Tell from Myrna's arms and staggered. "Guide me," he said, coughing. "I can't see an opening." Not if what he saw was during Ron Page's time.

Weak sunlight glowed from the top of the dirt wall, but there was no time to feel triumph or relief.

She latched on to Briscoe's leash, its loop slung around Jessup's wrist, and climbed the smoking dirt and rocks, thighs burning, stumbling, pushing, up and up. Briscoe bounded past her, darted through the gap, yanking Jessup to his knees. Myrna pulled the leash from Jessup and released it to slither out the opening and disappear.

She slipped outside on her stomach and turned. "William Tell." Jessup thrust him under the arched rock. Myrna rolled him down the soft loose sand and dirt. Jessup ducked his head and shoulders through, elbow-crawling out when Myrna heard Finn Posse's shout.

With strength she didn't know she had left, Myrna yanked Jessup into the sunlight. A shot rang out inside the cave.

Of course they found the stupid gun.

She tumbled back, the world spinning, landing on a soft sand at the bottom.

Myrna sat up, orienting herself. "*Aw.* It filled up the mammoth dig."

And where were Isaac, Paden, and Harley? And Briscoe?

Jessup rolled to a stop beside her, jumped to his feet, and pulled her up. He grabbed William Tell.

"Bad guys right behind us," he said.

Myrna latched her arm through his, and a vision swamped her. The gentle morning light turned freezing and dark, a leaden sky spitting snow. She hurriedly led a stumbling Jessup along the cliff toward the mammoth rub and the elk die-off meadow, only to be stopped a posse of mounted men, horses steaming in the cold, rifles shouldered, fingers on the triggers. She staggered to a halt, grabbing at Jessup.

"It's them," Myrna hissed. "The men who killed Ron Page. See? The middle one looks like Charles Donavan. *Our* Charles Donavan, but it's not. It's the *first* Charles Donavan. His grandfather. And the guy behind him—"

A wide-brimmed cowboy hat shadowed the second man's features. He lowered his rifle, eyes hard on the copse of pines that lined the meadow behind Myrna and Jessup.

"Mike Cabeza de Baca." Jessup's arms tensed.

"Look." Myrna pointed to an area near the cliff. "Scattered clothes. They've already searched Ron and carried the body off. This is right after my second vision."

"Can they see us?" Jessup asked, voice low.

"It wouldn't matter if they could."

Jessup set his jaw, his eyes sheened with emotion. "Then I want to stay. I need to know."

Myrna squeezed his arm, throat tight. She understood. He'd

searched for so long to find out the fate of his great-uncle, as had his grandfather before him. This wasn't about her and Jessup's budding relationship. This wasn't about the treasure. This was about family.

But Finn Posse and Santiago could show up any second. And they had a gun.

In the stillness, the hard crack of a branch echoed off the cliffs.

"Someone's in those trees," Mike Cabeza de Baca said. "He might've seen what we did.

"It's probably that damn Indian Page pals around with," Donavan said. "You two, go. But I want him alive. I want him to lead us to the treasure."

Two men slid their rifles into saddle scabbards and spurred their horses toward the trees.

"We need a better place to hide the body," Donavan said.

"On it, Major." The young Mike Cabeza de Baca swung his horse toward the cliff.

Donavan turned to the one man left, opened his mouth, but with a sudden hard twist, William Tell squirmed out of Jessup's arms, jumping clumsily to the ground to wobble and sit. Cowboys and cold evaporated into morning light that cut the air in half over the cliff with a sharp shadow's edge. Myrna dropped to her knees and hugged the little dog, blinking back a rush of tears. He was okay.

More brush crashed, but in real time. William Tell alerted. He stood, back ridged, his growl low and mean. *"Finn Posse and Santiago,"* she whispered.

Her tears dried in a surge of adrenaline. She latched onto the dog's leash to tug him behind the rubbing rock. "We can hide back there."

Jessup shook his head, his narrow-eyed gaze never leaving the four figures who emerged from the between the trees. Unlike the cowboys from their earlier vision, the guns now pointed at Myrna and Jessup were flat-black modern, except for the shotgun carried by Trini Cabeza de Baca. Those two deadly black bores had a time-less quality that made Myrna want to throw up. Jessup slipped his palm over the gun in his waistband.

The Cabeza de Bacas picked their way through the tall yellow grass, the present-day, old-as-dust Mike Cabeza de Baca using his grandson's shoulder to steady himself.

"Arthur, Trini," Jessup called in greeting. "You mixed up with this, too, Paden?"

Paden's face reddened. He looked away from Jessup and dropped his chin.

"Family, Jessup," Trini called back. "You understand. You've been after the treasure for years because your great-uncle asked you to find it. But we really need it, or we'll lose our ranch. And you owe us for reporting the poaching. They'll take our landowner tags, and we'll have nothing. I also hear you chased away those men who ran that cannabis grow, so we've lost the money they pay us for access. We're desperate, and you keep getting in our way."

"This isn't the place to talk," Jessup said. "We've got men chasing us who'll kill for that treasure."

Mike lifted a handgun and held it unsteadily. "Then they're a lot like me. I killed Ron Page. You know that? And that damned Indian friend of his. He led us into that booby trap, and I made sure he died under those rocks."

Myrna wrapped William Tell's leash around her hand. The dog's growls at Paden were taking on *Exorcist* vibes. "Paden? Where are Isaac and Harley? And Webb? You didn't—"

"No! I—I *wouldn't*. At the Cabeza de Baca formation. I stranded them after you went into the hole. Webb ..." Paden slid his eyes to his mother.

"We locked him and the German—"

"Brazilian," Myrna corrected.

Trini frowned. "—in the meat-hanging room at the barn. Jessup? You need to lead us to the treasure."

"Drop your guns. Now!" A booming voice soared across the

meadow. Myrna and Jessup twisted to find it, and, in dramatic Western hero fashion, a dozen people on horseback appeared out of the dazzling sunlight. Charles Donavan, Webb McJunkin alongside, staff Myrna recognized from the archery contest, women, men, everyone in chaps, dusters, and cowboy hats. Donavan's hat was even white. And walking in front of them, fingers laced on their heads, were Santiago and a scowling Finn Posse. Away from kicking hooves stood Briscoe. William Tell plunged toward him, barking furiously, yanking hard on Myrna's arm.

Myrna swiveled her head from side to side, neck hair prickling. She, William Tell, and Jessup were sandwiched between *way* too many deadly weapons. She let the leash go, and William Tell galloped toward a suddenly cowering Briscoe. She seized Jessup's sleeve to drag him out of danger—

A shotgun racked. Paden begged, "Please, no, Mom. It's not worth it."

"*Shut up*, Paden. None of this would be necessary if you'd just taken that damn dog from the trading post or gone down into the cave with her."

"But my shoulder hurt."

Myrna's astonishment choked her until she burst out, "That was *you*? Did you trash my house and take William Tell's dog toy, too? I thought you were his *friend*. *My* friend. You *lured* him to you with it, you tried to—" Myrna jabbed a finger at him. "Is that why your shoulder hurts? Because I nailed you with that can of SPAM? *Good*."

Paden swallowed, eyes darting everywhere but Jessup and Myrna. "I ... I had to— Because, because ... *Family*."

Jessup pulled Myrna behind him. "Trini, you're like a broken record. You gonna shoot us all?"

One of the women with the posse placed her hand on the gun butt at her hip and asked, "Mr. Donavan?"

Charles Donavan shook his head. He leaned his arms on the saddle horn. "Arthur? What the hell's goin' on here?"

"Don't talk to him, Donavan. You talk to me!" Mike Cabeza de Baca let go of his grandson and strode unsteadily toward Jessup and Myrna, waving his gun. "It's my land, and you owe me that treasure. Your granddaddy made us do some low-down, vile—"

Shots rang out from the clifftop and bullets sang past Myrna to slap into the ground. She glanced up. The sun backlit two men with guns. Donavan's ranch hands drew their weapons, but their frightened, heaving horses threw off their aim. Jessup yanked Myrna into a run when Mike grunted and dropped. Jessup let Myrna go and dove back to get the old man, converging with Arthur. Paden dragged his mom into the trees for shelter.

Bullets flying, Myrna crouched as riders tumbled from rearing animals, the horses bolting past her, wild-eyed and out of control. Except one.

Webb McJunkin kicked his horse toward her, bending low and holding out something in his hand. She narrowed her eyes and extended her arm as he slapped her bow and a single arrow into her open palm. In one smooth move, she knelt, nocked the arrow, and shot at the backlit silhouette atop the cliff. Knees controlling his plunging horse, Charles Donavan raised his arm and shot the second figure.

Her arrow flew true, as did the bullet. Both men on the cliffs dropped out of sight. The shooting stopped.

"Who the hell was that?" Donavan's eyes were wide behind his Roosevelt glasses, gun barrel smoking and still pointed upward.

"More of Finn Posse's henchmen." Myrna whirled in a circle but couldn't find Posse. "He's escaped!"

"He won't get far. Security cameras everywhere." Charles Donavan tipped back his hat to wipe his brow. An unsteady hand holstered his gun, and he patted the neck of his trembling horse. "*Damn*. That was—"

"Hey!" Two more silhouettes stood at the cliff's edge, waving their arms.

Donavan and the ranch hands pulled their guns.

"No! It's Harley and Isaac," Myrna said. A woman appeared next to them. "*Eleanor?*"

"Charley." It was Jessup. "Call in a helicopter. Better get the sheriff, too."

Charles Donavan dismounted, and he and Myrna ran to Jessup, joining the group kneeling and standing around the body of Mike Cabeza de Baca.

"Is he...?" Myrna asked.

"Not yet," Arthur replied, tears standing in his eyes, holding his grandfather's hand. "Grampo? Answer Jessup's question. Do him the kindness you didn't give his great-uncle."

"Where's Ron Page buried, Mike?" Jessup asked. "I need to take him home to rest beside the woman he loved."

Mike's eyes stayed closed, but his lips curved in a smile. "Ah, that Elsie of Ron's. Something of a mystery, that woman. My biggest regret was hurtin' her." He drew in a labored breath. "Ron didn't have the journal. Didn't have nothin'. We buried him by the cliff, but that friend of his was watching. So the major asked me to hide the body. What better place than the cemetery behind my home. I buried that shot-up silver dollar I took away from you by his gravestone. Seemed right."

William Tell squiggled in between Myrna and Jessup, pressing tightly against the two of them. He snuffled Mike's ear and placed a paw on his shoulder.

The air shivered over Mike Cabeza de Baca. His age melted away. Eyes opened in a young man's face, his sharp clear gaze catching and holding Jessup's. He took another breath, deep and calm and even.

"Ron? You tell Elsie I'm sorry."

Sixty

Three days.

Three days of interviews, interrogations, and grilling by everyone from local law enforcement to the FBI and CIA to Interpol. Myrna and everybody involved were isolated from each other, all methods of communication confiscated and secured inside the Donavan Ranch compound. Security guards practically followed her into the bathroom. William Tell was hoarse from barking and drained from peeing on their shoes.

She'd come under increased scrutiny since she'd actually shot and hit someone with her arrow. Myrna was pretty sure Charles Donavan's political clout and buckets full of money saved her from being jailed until a determination of self-defense was rendered. As it was, Myrna was duly warned by about eighteen official agencies to stay in the country and available for further questioning, which she duly agreed to.

What happened to the treasure, she had no idea. It was probably being studied by Top Men.

At least no one had died—except Mike Cabeza de Baca. And that turned out to be because of a heart attack, not a hail of bullets.

And Dillon Bard was in a hospital in Albuquerque, recovering from the working over he'd gotten from Finn Posse's minions.

And they hadn't found Finn Posse.

And she hadn't caught a single glimpse of Jessup. She didn't even know where he was.

Sitting on her front porch stoop with a cup of coffee in hand and mooning over Jessup's empty house did her no good. She still had one last experiment to analyze—Harley's TOXIC TO BULL ELK vials. Did her original commission even matter anymore?

With a pathetic sigh, she leashed up William Tell and drove to the ranch compound and her lab. The door still opened with her code, and she flipped the lights on and shrugged on her lab coat. William Tell wandered into the fenced area and flopped down on a blanket, Tan Turtle between his paws.

Myrna checked the instrumentation and downloaded the analysis. Once the results were added to her report, she'd send it to Charles Donavan, and ... What? Leave? To where? She'd quit her job after her sister's betrayal. Her heart contracted at the thought of leaving all the friends she'd made in the lab.

There was still the mammoth dig, the baby mammoth skull altar, the Paleolithic gallery ... If Charles Donavan wanted her around. That was a big *if*, since she'd been part of crashing his potential presidential campaign.

But *if* she did end up staying, she wouldn't throw herself back at Jessup. Nope. She'd be firm about that. Yep. Firm. He had trust to rebuild with her. Big trust.

If she got to stay.

Daydreaming of a future in a place where she belonged, Myrna concentrated on finishing her report. An hour later, a huge grin on her face and the room filled with William Tell's snores, Myrna hit save.

Her file disappeared. *No, no, no.* She typed frantically into the *search* function, hit enter ... The computer screen flashed. *All* her files disappeared.

William Tell jerked to his feet. He faced the lab's front door and growled.

Myrna looked up. Dame Sylvia stood in the threshold, a smirk on her face. She ambled in, shutting the door firmly behind her, a package of chocolate snack cakes in her hand. She waggled the cakes before she tossed them on the nearest lab bench. Like two delicious dark round eyes, the tops of the cakes stared at Myrna.

Unblinking, she stared back, as the proverbial other shoe dropped on her head. *Sylvia Donavan.* She should have known.

What had Harley said to her after she'd broken into his lab?

Even though you've solved the elk deaths, you can't win. Now that I've gotten to know you, I'm very sorry about that.

Jaw tight at the injustice that seemed to be using her as a punching bag, she said, "No eating in the lab."

"I can top that. No eating *those* on my ranch." Dame Sylvia smiled. "Since tomorrow is your official last day, I came to check the progress of your work."

Myrna smiled right back. "I'm finished. Under budget and ahead of schedule."

"Wonderful! Then I can expect your report ..." The Dame tipped her head, her expression morphing to phony concern. "Why, Dr. Lee. Is everything all right? You look like you've lost something very, very important."

"Funny you should say that. I did lose something. But not my snack cakes. I always keep extra. Is that the excuse you'll use to fire me?"

"Not an excuse. Didn't you read the contract you signed your first day? Highly processed foods are banned on Donavan land because most people don't know what's good for them. You broke my rules, and your commission and *you* are terminated. *Immediately.*"

"Huh. Is that why all my data magically disappeared from my computers? No matter. I'm sure it's backed up on the Donavan servers. Or did lightning strike again?"

Dame Sylvia shrugged.

Myrna stood and, mimicking the Dame's nonchalance, ambled out from behind her desk and computer, hands buried in her empty pockets to hide her shaking fists. No mammoth fetish to soothe and comfort her. Stupid Santiago had taken it and her knife.

She shrugged right back. "Luckily I made sure I gave a flash drive with most of the report to my lab in Socorro. It should be pretty easy to reassemble."

Dame Sylvia's laugh was real and chilling. "And what if I told you all that information—raw data, polished figures, tentative conclusions—had been intercepted by Dr. Kelly." She held up Myrna's flash drive.

"I need to warn you," Myrna said. "Dr. Kelly's not trustworthy. She'd sell her own sister— Oh. That's *right*. She did. She'll have no trouble negotiating with your husband for the data. Something I bet *he'd* be interested in since you're the one killing off his trophy elk. You and Harley Wakefield."

"Accidental deaths. It was never about harming animals. It was about saving them from bloodthirsty redneck hunters who pay outrageous sums to *murder* for trophies. It was about getting guns off this ranch." Dame Sylvia circled around a lab bench. "I wanted a safe method of birth control for the male elks. Decrease the population over time until the head counts no longer sustained hunting for sport."

"But instead of being up front, you went behind your husband's back."

"How could we have known an illegal marijuana farm would change our drug into a *poison*? It'll work next time. We'll clean up the contamination, inoculate more elk— Don't shake your head at me."

"You can't keep experimenting on live animals, hoping for the best. It's cruel. And even if I don't have the data or my report, I'm still telling your husband what I found."

"I don't think so. Because if you even get close to Charles, I'll make sure Jessup Page not only loses his job but is linked to Finn Posse and his Neo-Nazi Werewolf group." Dame Sylvia smiled. "My husband isn't the only one with connections in the government, you know."

"But that's a complete lie!"

"Maybe, but he'll be tangled up with federal agencies for years. Or hadn't you noticed that's how they operate now? Guilty until you can prove you're innocent? It will drain Jessup Page of all his savings, he'll have to sell that trading post and his family's land. Oh. Didn't you know he inherited that place? He'll be ruined and blame you." Dame Sylvia tapped the flash drive against the benchtop. "Unless you tell no one what you found on the ranch and disappear."

Myrna's breath stuttered. *Disappear?* But—but she was part of a team, had made friends, was considered *family*. She'd found a place—a *home*—and someone to love.

Then the reality of her situation came crashing down on her. The Clovis points she'd tested were negative for ancient poison—she'd lose her grant and the rest of her scientific reputation. The mammoth jump and kill site she'd hoped to excavate was now covered with dirt from the cave wall collapse, and this time she didn't have a bunch of Girl Scouts to help her dig it out. Her sister had betrayed her, she had no job, and soon, no career, very little money.

A pit opened up in her stomach. She was alone again. Like she'd been in that Idaho hospital when her mother left her, at boarding school, after Tom Hutchinson stepped off that cliff. After Jessup's betrayal. He hadn't even tried to see her or contact her or—

Her eyes blurred with sudden tears. Everything she'd wanted —*no*. Everything she really, truly needed, gone.

She had nothing.

William Tell's metal cage scraped against the linoleum floor.

Myrna dropped her gaze to the tan and black dog, who stared up at her with perked ears and shining eyes, Tan Turtle in his mouth. He waggled his butt.

And her heart filled up.

She wasn't alone. She had William Tell. She could take care of herself. She was the woman who could thrive in a sterile lab environment *and* the girl who'd been raised wild. And she was okay with that.

Maybe she'd try to get hired on a dig far, far away. Maybe she'd melt into the wilderness, try for real to find her mom. Maybe—

"I'll sweeten the pot," Dame Sylvia interrupted her thoughts, an edge to her voice. "I'll pay you the money for this commission and buy you a one-way plane ticket to anywhere in the world."

Myrna wiped her eyes, peeled off her lab coat, and hooked William Tell's leash to his harness.

"I'll accept your offer if you won't harm Jessup. You won't ever see me again."

"I'll leave Jessup Page alone if you don't approach my husband personally or by any secondary means."

"Understood. I need to get my stuff."

"Already packed and in your car."

Myrna kept her back to Dame Sylvia because all the blinking in the world didn't stop the tears. This was it. The end. She marched to the door, grabbed the handle—

Harley's lab door opened.

"I am *so* sorry, Myrna. I forgot to retrieve that little spy drone from your lab the last time we talked." His voice echoed out of the controller he held in his hands.

Charles Donavan stepped out from behind him. The subzero freeze of his eyes pinned his wife in place as if she'd been turned to ice.

Sixty-One

The truck bumped and bounced over ruts in the dirt road, its driver, Charles Donavan, silent. The waves of anger coursing off his body after the confrontation with his wife had diminished—at least a little bit. Myrna braced herself on the passenger side, glad for her seatbelt because Donavan was going way too fast up the forest road, one she easily recognized.

He was taking her back to the elk die-off meadow—or the shoot-out meadow—where that final confrontation occurred between the Cabeza de Bacas, the Donavan crew, and Finn Posse's henchmen. Where Mike Cabeza de Baca had passed away. Myrna refused to break the silence. Charles Donavan deserved to fume. She just wasn't sure whether he'd take out some of his anger on her.

The meadow came into view, tall grasses browning with fall, crushed and blown out where the helicopter had landed to pick up the wounded. The red-gold cliff wall bordering the meadow loomed bright in the afternoon sun.

Charles Donavan hit the brakes, and the truck slithered to a stop. He could've driven closer to the cliff. The Feds had smoothed a road to the cave opening while they investigated and extracted the priceless artwork from the lost Nazi treasure. Instead, Donavan sat, fingers tight on the steering wheel, staring straight ahead.

"Dr. Lee? Myrna. If you could give me a minute, I'll, ah, meet you up there, by the cliff."

She nodded and slid out of the truck. Shoes crunching on tiny rocks, she opened the back and let William Tell jump from the seat to the floorboards to the running board to the ground. He buried his nose in the earth and snuffled up the road, pulling Myrna along behind him.

She stopped next to the cliff, the heat radiating from the stones behind her cutting the edge off a cool, breezy day. The denuded ground ran along the cliffside crisscrossed with tire tracks. The mammoth dig arroyo, backfilled with the sand from the exploded and collapsed wall, had been flattened as a staging area for the artwork to be photographed, cataloged, and repackaged before it had been swept off for authentication and study, and hopefully for return to the rightful families. All done and gone like it had never been there in the first place.

But treasures had been left on the cave walls and ceilings: Paleolithic pictographs in the antechamber outside the treasure room. What would happen to those?

The truck door slammed. Charles Donavan dropped to the ground before tugging off his glasses, wiping the lenses with a handkerchief, pressing the cloth over tightly closed eyes. All the money in the world couldn't heal the hurt of his wife's duplicity. But that didn't mean he could stop loving her.

She understood how he felt.

Myrna sighed and squatted next to a lounging William Tell. Elk tracks pressed crescents into the dirt over the tire tracks. She traced one with her finger. Yep. Love was hard to stop when it had burrowed deep inside her soul. Whether it was for a mother, a half sister ... a lover.

William Tell snuffled the tracks she'd traced before lifting his head and watching Charles Donavan stride up the slope. Myrna stood and faced him.

His eyes were red, and he turned away to draw in a cleansing breath, his shoulders relaxing as he viewed the valley that stretched from the elk meadow through stands of mature trees to the open space beyond.

"I'll have a cleanup crew at the Cabeza formation by week's end to wipe away the damage of that illegal pot grow," he said finally. "It was that contamination that caused the die-off?"

He must've been listening closely in Harley's lab.

"Indirectly," Myrna said. "I'm afraid I don't have all the data anymore"—Donavan's jaw bunched—"but I can recreate some of the report for you."

He nodded and toed a rock with his boot. "The other die-offs we've had on the ranch?"

"If the birth control experiments have been going on for the past few years, it's possible other illegal grows on the ranch had an effect. But die-offs happen for a lot of reasons, not all of them human-caused." She hesitated. "The Cabeza de Baca family?"

Donavan shot her a quick glance. "Can't have them living here anymore, not after their disloyalty. I bought their ranch at a fair price. They'll be allowed back on that property to move out so long as they're supervised."

Myrna swallowed. "Paden?"

"Is no longer in my employ, although he apparently was also employed by my wife to muddle up the results of the other die-off lab crews I've hired. He was also the one who messed with your cameras on the cage experiment and cut that chunk out of your elk from the Girl Scout camp before it was buried. Even emailed a trading post in Albuquerque about some jewelry using an official Donavan email. In the end, that young man chose his side."

"He chose his family," she said in a small voice.

"His family." Donavan's mustache bristled. "Paden's mother threatened to go to the press about Ronald Page's murder, tell everyone that my grandfather ordered it, that it was all about money. I shut that down real quick. Told her that she opens her trap, I'll get the district attorney to press charges against her and Arthur and Paden as accessories after the fact to the murder of Ron Page and the man in the mine under those rocks. They knew what Mike did and didn't report it. There's no statute of limitations on accessory to murder."

"Everyone's dead now. There are no witnesses."

"Ron Page's body was found just where Mike said he'd be. Jessup oversaw his disinterment. According to the autopsy report, there's evidence of the stabbing and poison, as well as trauma from a fall. That man suffered. Even if it never goes to trial, their defense would pauper them. They'd have nothing."

He looked directly at Myrna, the ruthlessness of a man who ran empires barely leashed. A perfect match for his wife. She shivered.

"What about the man I stabbed and the one I shot with my arrow?"

He waved a dismissive hand but his eyes gleamed. "And the man I winged. Press doesn't know what to do with that story. Am I a reckless cowboy with a gun, or a hero? I'll get days of free radio, TV, and cable airtime. As for the two men you took out? Self-defense. They'll all make a full recovery. They found the third man hiding in that old logger's cabin, so all four of those bastards are in custody. Except Posse. He's disappeared. He lied to me about the gold in my mine so he could search for the treasure. He knew his days were numbered when I hired an expert to come in for a second opinion. That's why he and his men beat up Bard and kidnapped you and Jessup when they did." He cleared his throat. "Dillon Bard will be back in my employ after he's finished his rehab—both physical and for his drinking problem. I'm getting sick of his dog moping around the lodge."

"What about Harley? And ... your wife?"

"Buzz? He'll stay. He came to me and confessed everything

because he was worried about what my wife could do to you. That young man has quite the crush." For the first time, Charles Donavan's face cracked a smile, but it quickly faded. He rubbed a hand against his brow. "And my wife. I knew how passionate she is about all this hunting stuff. I wish I hadn't been so dismissive and patronizing when she first brought it up years ago. We're such a great team, better together. She's pregnant, you know." His face reddened. "I'd appreciate if you said nothing about that. But we've gotten a little off topic. Look, I brought you out here because I have a proposition for you."

Myrna's heart rate ticked up. "The mammoth bones?"

"Yes, well, that and a few other things. But first." Donavan cleared his throat. "You realize that once this treasure is assessed there'll be a finder's reward of ten percent to be split between you and Jessup Page."

"I'll have money?" William Tell jumped to his feet, alert to the excitement in her voice.

He chuckled. "Probably not for another year or so. I spoke to Jessup. He confessed that he, Bard, and your sister used you as a pawn to help them find this treasure. I'm not happy with any of them about that, and one word from you and I won't keep Bard or Page on my payroll. I can also make sure Dr. Kelly loses her position at Tech. Your choice."

Myrna blinked at his offer. She completely believed he had that kind of power, and it would serve Eleanor right. Myrna opened her mouth to say yes and closed it again, pressing her lips tight.

"I can't. She's a really good scientist and the people in her lab would lose their jobs and ... she's my sister. *My* family."

He nodded, his mustache lifting from his smile. "She's a good scientist because she hires good people—like you. That's why I'd like to offer you a job as my museum curator. It comes with a solid salary, a place to live—same little house you're in now—and a few special projects. The mammoth bones." He nodded at the filled-in arroyo in the distance. "Those caves paintings, the elk birth control project—if you can do it safely. You could continue with your Pleistocene poisons work, too. And it turns out the list of art in the treasure caves doesn't quite match the one in Ronald Page's journal, only the Feds don't know that because I didn't turn the journal over to them. In fact, they only suspect the journal exists since you never told them you found it, either. Why's that?"

Myrna blinked innocent, wide eyes. "They never asked."

Donavan chuckled. "As part of your job description, I'd like you to put together a team to investigate and find the artwork that should have been in that treasure room but wasn't. I'll hire anyone you like, but I've already offered one man a job on your team. He'll only agree if you don't want him fired for his part in your sister's scheme."

Her brain congealed at his implication, but all she could think to say was, "You kept the journal?"

"Didn't belong to me. I turned it over to Ronald Page's nearest relative. Your new partner, if you approve." And Charles Donavan turned toward the cave opening and waved.

Jessup Page stepped out of the shadows.

Myrna froze. Charles Donavan reached out to pat her arm and smile. Without another word, he turned and headed back down to his truck. William Tell saw Jessup and ran to the end of his leash, yapping happily and yanking Myrna's arm. Feet stuck to the earth, she hardly felt the tug. Her eyes drank him in, seeing the same longing she felt reflected in his face. Jessup strode toward her like he'd sweep her into an embrace, but instead halted a few feet away. He slid his hands into his back pockets, body tense, shifting his feet. The swelling had gone down, but bruises still colored his face. His blue eyes were as clear as a spring. It felt like she could see into his soul. Heart thumping, she took a tentative step in his direction, then another, William Tell frisking and releasing adorable yips.

Myrna stopped short, but close enough that the dog could climb Jessup's camo-clad leg, butt waggling ecstatically. Jessup dropped to his haunches and rubbed his neck and head, William Tell whining and panting.

"Looks like this guy's forgiven me." He stood slowly, his questioning eyes never leaving hers. "Can you?"

"I—I'm not sure. What you did ... And my sister ..." She looked away, into the valley, blinking at the prickle behind her eyes.

"I'm sorry, Myrna," he said gruffly. "I can't take what I did back. And I don't want to because whatever we did—I did—brought you here. To me."

She peeped at him, and heat flashed up her neck. His gaze touched her face and his lips curved into his small, smirky smile, but his eyes were grave. "I promise I'll work hard to win your trust again if you'll stay on the ranch. Please, Dr. Lee. Take Charles Donavan's offer. We can start over, or we can be friends or just colleagues. Your decision." He dug into a pocket. "I meant to get it back to you sooner, but ..."

Jessup handed Myrna her knife and mammoth fetish.

She turned them over in her hand before she clutched them tightly. They were warm from his body heat. "You took them from Santiago?"

"When I grabbed his gun in the cave. I knew the fetish was your new worry stone and that the knife was special to you," he said.

"I thought I'd lost it forever. It's the only gift my mother ever —" She choked on a sudden lump in her throat. She slipped them into her secret pocket, and the knots in her chest loosened.

"I'd like to hear its story one day," he said.

She licked her lips, so tempted to throw herself in his arms. Instead, she asked, "Have you spoken to Eleanor since ..."

"I apologized to her, too. I wasn't as interested in what she offered as I was in her information on the treasure." He shifted. "I never slept with her."

William Tell sat on Jessup's boot.

"If I stay, Charles Donavan said I could hire anyone I want. I'm thinking I'll ask my team in Eleanor's lab if they'd like to work for me. With me." She was done trying to be Eleanor or anyone else. "Donavan's interested in pursuing the elk birth control project if we can do it safely. And I'd like to investigate those green bugs and the toxin used to murder your great-uncle, maybe find its origin. Donavan's given me permission to start an official dig of the mammoth jump, as well as study the paintings in the caves outside the treasure room. Then there's the Donavan Ranch museum."

"Sounds like you might take the job."

Myrna shrugged. "I guess."

"He told you about the missing artwork from Ron Page's list?" His hand slipped out of his pocket holding the tattered journal. "You kept it a secret."

She shrugged again.

"I'd like to be part of your team, if you'll have me," Jessup said. "As would Webb, and Isaac, and ... Paden."

She blinked at him. "Charles Donavan said Paden was fired and off the ranch."

"Donavan's a hard man. But he's also a forgiving one. I'm hoping I can change his mind." He moved William Tell off his foot and stepped in close to Myrna. He took her hand in his. "I'm hoping I can change yours, too. Someday. In the meantime, I have work to do back at the ranch. Hunts to arrange and a new manager to hire, if ..."

He squeezed her hand, let her go, and retreated. Myrna mourned the loss of his nearness, but he was right about them starting over. No matter how much she loved Jessup, wounds needed to heal.

"My truck's behind those trees if you want a ride back. Otherwise, Donavan will take you."

When she didn't answer, he dropped his chin in a single nod. "I'll get going, then." He turned—

"Wait." She and William Tell hurried to his side. "I think I've figured something out about how William Tell's visions work through me and you. It has to do with what's most important to me—to study mammoths and the Pleistocene." Which also explained what she'd seen in the trading post. Her vision in the bullpen had become something essential to her because *he'd* become essential to her. "For you, the most important thing was your promise to your family. To find your great-uncle, to solve the mystery of his disappearance and death. You've done that, so now, maybe, if we both hold him, you can see what I see."

Jessup closed his eyes and breathed deep. When he opened them, his smile struck her in the heart like an arrow.

"And that would be a gift, Meerkat, because it's a big part of who you are."

She couldn't speak for a moment, caught in his gaze. She shook herself.

"Ready?" Myrna reached down, slipped her arms under William Tell's belly, and lifted him to her chest. Jessup pressed his body against her back, his arms sliding around both her and the little dog, to hold them warm and steady as the earth shifted and the air shimmered.

Cold settled on their skin, a chill deep and clean. The sky turned from blue to a silvery gray, an icy white sun veiled by clouds. The trees in their world faded, replaced by a smooth blanket of fresh crystalline snow that had fallen and melted thousands of years in the past.

Jessup's arms tightened around her as their gazes found a large group of mammoths in the valley below. The matriarch in her thick winter coat plowed the snow as she patrolled, always alert, swinging her enormous, curving tusks, ambered yellow with age, one broken in a lifetime of defending her family of sisters, daughters, granddaughters. Shaggy mothers with bulbous heads and humped shoulders shepherded juveniles as they cleared furrows of white to pull up the still-green grasses. And the babies flapped small ears and dashed around the legs of the adults, swinging tiny trunks like living golf clubs into the plowed-up piles of white, knocking snow clumps high in the sky, only to squeal and run when they fell back to earth. Vibrations shuddered and wrapped around them as the herd members trumpeted and rumbled to each other. A youngster fell in the snow. She picked herself up and ran to her mother, their trunks twining for a moment of comfort, before she dashed off into the game again.

William Tell in their embrace, Myrna stood in silence, heart full, absorbed in the ancient scene until the matriarch, tusks gleaming in the silvery winter light, turned her shaggy body and lumbered toward a distant ridge, her herd falling in line after her.

They cradled the dog, arms entwined, and watched until the mammoths disappeared from sight.

The End

ALSO BY CAROL POTENZA

Nicky Matthews Mysteries

Hearts of the Missing

The Third Warrior

Spirit Daughters

Sacred Ghosts

De-Extinct Zoo Mystery Series

Unmasked

Signs

Coming 2024: Ambushed

Lies Mystery Series

Sting of Lies

Non-Fiction

Demystifying the Beats: How to Write a Killer Book

If you enjoyed this book...

Word of mouth and reviews help other readers find my books in a world where millions of books are published each year. If you enjoyed this story or any other of my books and have a few minutes, please recommend it to family and friends, give it as a gift, request it at your local library, or leave a quick review on my website, at Amazon, Barnes and Noble, Kobo, Google, Apple, Book2Read ...

Short or long, your words can make all the difference.

Thank you.

Acknowledgments

Writing a book is a team effort and I'm so glad I don't have to do it alone. I want to thank my critique partners, my editor, my proof-reader, and my cover artists. I can't tell you how much you all made this story better.

ABOUT THE AUTHOR

Carol Potenza lives in southern New Mexico with her husband, Leos, and an extremely grumpy chihuahua, Hermès. She loves her adopted state, its beauty, and its strong multicultural history shaped by diverse peoples and cultures. Carol has a Ph.D. in biomedical sciences from UC San Diego and worked in a plant genetic engineering laboratory at New Mexico State University for years before she moved to full time teaching—Molecular Biology and Biochemistry. She has since retired and writes full-time.

Please visit Carol at her website: carolpotenza.com

www.ingramcontent.com/pod-product-compliance
Lightning Source LLC
Chambersburg PA
CBHW031510010826
48973CB00012B/158